MAGICRAFT MASTER

BOOK TWO

MAGICRAFT MASTER

BOOK TWO

Wilbur Woods

Published in 2025 by Podium Publishing
www.podiumentertainment.com

MAGICRAFT MASTER

BOOK TWO

CHAPTER 1

Malcolm Specter woke up in the dark. He tried to look around but found he could not move his head. His mind felt strange, foggy, and weak.

Where am I?

His last memory was holding a Numa crystal by the campfire. He could tell that time had passed since then, but whenever he tried to reach for those memories, there was nothing but a haze.

Forgeeeet. A voice spoke in his mind. It sounded like his own.

What? What was that? Have I been drugged or something?

SUbMiT. SeRVE. There it was again.

Then came another voice. It wasn't so much a voice as it was a sensation. There was a tone—an ominous one—yet with a degree of subtlety and softness. Malcolm Specter had spent a lot of time with hard, persuasive, even dangerous men. But never had he encountered something which demanded such respect.

Ah, my pet. You are awake at last. That is good. We have much work to do.

Malcolm tried to struggle. What was going on? He must have been captured by the enemy . . . *MAsTeR.* In his own voice again.

He tried to remember, but the oppressive force pressed on his mind, giving him no room to think.

The camp . . . Focus on the camp. I had organized it. Logan was being difficult. People were adjusting. I am their leader. I have to lea—SErVe!

You were wasting your time with the other insects. You have so much potential. So I took you.

Levemoth . . . Master . . . ? Took me?

Why couldn't he remember? Malcolm tried to speak, but he couldn't. His body was completely gone. He tried moving, breathing, raging at whatever was restricting his will, but nothing worked. His anger boiled, but something powerful pressed it down.

Be patient, Greedy One. You need not do anything. Just listen. I will give you free reign later.

Greed isn't what drives me. It was always ambition.

The presence was filled with mirth. It let out a hollow laugh which echoed in the endless darkness.

You think you know yourself and the world so well. I was born of greed. I am the eternal embodiment of the lust to own EVERYTHING. I know my kin well.

What do you want?

To unlock you. To make you perfect and then unleash you. To give you this world.

You are that creature in the sky? You have been trying to kill us since the start. Why would I trust you?

I do not need your trust, insect. I am no more evil than a tiger is evil when it eats a deer. We all act according to our nature. And it is in your nature to rule. I will make you a ruler.

That instantly triggered Malcolm's hard intellect and skepticism. Questions started popping up in his mind and he went to negotiation strategy. But the creature noticed this and gripped his mind tighter. His thoughts were muddled again, and all he could think of was something simple and straightforward.

Why need me? Why not do it yourself?

I am but a seed of what I should be. I was wounded a long time ago and have shriveled since. If I did not need you, do you think I would have expended resources on you?

Malcolm didn't trust this creature. He needed to get away. Where was he? He wanted to know what had become of Logan. That fool of a son. With himself gone, the boy would have to lead. Would he be re—

FoRRGetT. FeaST. EATTT. ConSSUmE . . .

An oppressive feeling came upon Malcolm, as if his consciousness were being forced into a smaller container. Then whispers came. He recognized them. Malcolm realized he had been hearing these whispers ever since leaving Earth.

They muddled his mind even further, inserting ideas which began to echo. Malcolm mustered all of his willpower and his formidable ego to take control—to take back ownership of his own mind. He pushed the whispers away. Feeling victorious, he let himself relax.

But then they struck again.

The whispers came in waves, faster and faster, in and out. Increasing, increasing, until they hit a crescendo and Malcolm forgot everything but the voice.

SubMiTT. SeRvE! FoRRgET.

Malcolm tried to push the whispers away, but his mind was slipping. All the while, the oppressive, maddening feeling squeezed tighter.

CONSUME, TAKE, SERVE, FEAST, FEAST AND CONSUME.

Malcolm Specter pushed as hard as he could. He summoned the full might of his rage at this monster that had captured him, manipulated him along the way and now wished to use him. But the creature was so vast, it could press down on Malcolm's entire being with an idle thumb. He sensed that his struggling only amused the creature. It was inevitable. Predetermined. Malcolm Specter raged, but the whispers were overwhelming.

WORSHIP THE MASTER. SERVE THE MASTER. THERE IS ONLY MASTER!

Good. Listen to me, Greedy One. Your will to fight has pleased me. I chose you for that very will as well as your ability to dominate. But, for this honor I am bestowing upon you, you will need a new name. I will not use your filthy insect language. Henceforth, you shall be known as Malz'Kamoth, the Devouring Herald.

Malz'Kamoth stopped fighting the whispers and the pressure on his mind. Instead, he surrendered to them. The urgent whispers instantly stopped attacking him and instead began to gently caress him.

Goooooood . . . It took me weeks to subdue your will. I am glad you finally found reason, Malz'Kamoth. Now there is the matter of another one with a will we must subdue. A human called Logan Specter.

Malz'Kamoth realized he had the ability to speak. He could still not see or move, but the master had been generous to him.

"Can you not subdue him like you did with Malcolm Specter, Master?"

Alas, I tried, but Logan Specter has a spell in his mind that protects him. I spent much in capturing you and attempting to destroy him. You must be my fist upon this world, Malz'Kamoth. Do you accept?

"Of course, Master. What would you have me do?"

I will give you a sword and a crown, Malz'Kamoth. You will have two objectives.

"Anything, my Master."

First, you will seduce and unite all the humans. They must worship me and give me Numa. I require tithes or there will be punishments.

"It will be done," Malz'Kamoth said. "What of the second objective?"

[Class changed: The Devouring Herald]

Your seed has a dangerous will. Since I cannot control him, there is only one solution. You must kill Logan Specter.

CHAPTER 2

Logan Specter held his arm up straight to give Kat, Balmer, and him light from the **[Enchanted]** wooden ring on his pinky.

"Yup," Kat said, coming up next to Logan to peer down. "That's a big gorge all right."

"You guys think you can make the jump?" Logan asked.

Balmer exhaled sharply when he saw the dark abyss below them. The ledge on the other side was at least a foot higher than where they were standing and there was a good eight feet of distance.

Kat scoffed and pushed Logan aside. She took a few steps back and ran toward the ledge, making a wide, high jump with her arms up in the air. She just managed to reach the edge. There was a scary moment where her foot lost purchase and it looked like she might fall. Balmer took an urgent step forward, but controlled himself, once he saw that Kat had managed to right herself.

She turned and beamed with a wide grin, shielding her eyes from the light with a hand. "Your turn, Felix."

Logan chuckled to himself. Kat had started calling Balmer by his first name last week.

Balmer gave a slight smile, which Logan noted, and slowly took a few steps back—more than Kat had taken. Felix Balmer was nothing if not careful. To the young ex-agent's credit, he didn't hesitate, although he did let out a chaotic scream as he jumped.

His class helped him soar through the air even more gracefully than Michael Jordan. Logan wasn't one to feel class jealousy, but damn, it must have felt good to be Balmer sometimes. With **[Phantom]**, he moved like a ballet dancer or fencer. A supernatural fencer was pretty much what Balmer was now. He had traded his original wooden sword for a darkmetal rapier, and given the former to Agent Foraletti, who had a **[Swordsman]** class. The latter now hung at a leather belt by his side, enhanced by a neat little **[Enchantment]** that Logan had had to work hard on to activate. Logan was the only one of them who could activate **[Enchantments]** at will, such as his shield-watch. Other people could use tools with a passive **[Enchantment]** or condition on them, such as a flashbang, but they couldn't use active **[Enchantments]** like Logan could.

That was a shame, because Logan had wanted to craft a rapier that could extend its reach when needed. But since Balmer couldn't use such a weapon, Logan had made a blade that extended half a foot every time it was thrust or slashed with. The thin rapier blade would stretch like rubber and then bounce back when it was drawn toward the user. It was a fine weapon, and Logan had to admit that Balmer used it well.

Logan much more preferred the Zweihänder that Tumor (what Logan called the artificial intelligence his dad had implanted in his mind) would generate when needed. So far they hadn't had to use their weapons during this delve.

Logan prepared to make the jump himself now. With the power he wielded, he didn't have to take any steps back as the others had. He simply bent his knees and let his special armor blast him off the ground. He flew across the chasm, landing behind him Kat and Balmer.

"Show-off," Kat said.

Logan grinned. "Guilty as charged."

They had just entered the so-called second tier of the ruins of the First Folk. The first tier had been the one with the floating Numa constructs and what had looked like LED Christmas lights at the seams of the floors and ceilings. Logan suspected those had been the living spaces of the most primitive iteration of the First Folk. They had built underground to escape Levemoth, but they had not dug deep enough . . .

The second layer of their civilization opened up when you went down a few floors. There were some straggler Levespawn lurking around, but generally nothing the three of them couldn't handle. But there was also nothing particularly valuable in the upper floors.

The Dorves didn't frequently maintain operations there, which left a Numa construct with energy here and there, but it wasn't like they could use them either.

Logan had debated the matter with the settlement. Logan himself wanted to use the Numa from the constructs to help people level up. They didn't need to bring anything made with Numa out of the ruins, but they could definitely benefit from people power-leveling. However since they didn't know whether or not Levemoth would notice such activities, it was better to be safe than sorry. Especially given what had happened with the river camp.

Logan sighed, thinking of his father as they traversed the dark corridors of crumbled stone and old moss. It felt wrong to admit it, but they were better off without him. He had always made questionable choices when it came to ethics, but this time he had gone too far, risking people's lives. Despite himself, Logan was still worried and even missed the old codger on some level. Still, everyone was safer this way.

[Are you sure, Logan?]

"It's complicated, Tumor."

Logan's two companions gave him a look, but they were used to hearing only one half of Logan's conversations with his AI.

[I, for one, am grateful to our progenitor. Wait a minute. Malcolm Specter created us both. Does that mean we are . . . brothers?]

Logan chuckled at that. "I'm the handsome one, you're the smart one, right?"

Kat quirked an eyebrow. "What kind of conversation are you having exactly?"

"Shh," Logan said. "It's top secret."

Kat leaned in and shouted in Logan's ear. "I'm sure you're more handsome than we can even imagine, Tumor!"

"Don't shout, fool!" Balmer admonished her. "What if there are enemies around?"

Kat shrugged. "Then we'll deal with them."

Balmer *tsk*ed but said nothing.

"Tumor says hi," Logan said as they turned a corner, Balmer keeping a hand on his sword.

In fact, Tumor hadn't said anything. His chirpy tone had snuffed out like a candle in the wind. Logan couldn't be absolutely certain, but he thought Tumor had become sullen. He wanted to ask why, but immediately at having the thought, he could feel Tumor withdrawing further. It was clear his buddy didn't want to talk about whatever was bothering him, and Logan wasn't about to press the matter.

It's hard to wrap my mind around the fact that he has feelings.

[And what if I do?]

Logan sighed. He was a person who wore his heart on his sleeve, as Freya liked to say. He didn't have anything to hide, which seemed rare. But giving up the privacy of his own thoughts was still a difficult pill to swallow.

[Sorry. I am glad you're making an effort to reconcile with your inner conflict in order to provide me with optimized companionship.]

Logan laughed. "Optimized companionship?"

Logan liked to imagine the AI sputtering.

[Well, I . . . What I mean is . . .]

"You're very eloquent for a being with a gazillion associations in your brain and the command of like fifty languages."

[Fifty-three. Also, shut up. Emotions are complicated. Especially for a person who has never had them. Have you seen a two-year-old try to regulate their anger? I say I am doing a great job. Not to mention that I am using your brain to interface, which, while it has its perks, certainly does not have a "gazillion" points of association.]

"Ouch," Logan said. "Ok, you can go back to brooding."

[Thaaaaank you.]

Logan led his companions along the pitch-dark corridors in silence from that point onward. And it was a good thing the banter had ended, as they heard movement somewhere beyond the scope of light. They flashed each other serious looks and nodded. There was definitely a Levespawn ahead.

Most of them were manageable. None of them had any issues with the scythe-fiends, beetles, or one-eyed cats that were common here. Even the trolls and snakes were easy to deal with when Logan wasn't otherwise occupied. On a good day, Kat and Balmer could take on a troll together.

But there were nasty types too. The giant snakes were the most common of the genuine threats. If they attacked Logan, that was fine. His armor could take the brute force of their constriction as well as their bites.

But if the snakes wrapped around either of his companions, their bones would crack in seconds. They'd had a few close calls, but the worst of them ended up with Balmer snapping three ribs and a shoulder. Nothing their **[Healer]** couldn't handle, but having to move an injured Balmer back to camp would suck, especially if it meant leaving empty-handed.

"Let me go ahead," Logan whispered. He got no arguments in response.

Tumor made the armor thin around his shoulders and formed a helmet for Logan. Logan didn't like the thing, but helmets were like seatbelts—totally uncool, but they saved lives.

Logan came to the end of the corridor, which opened into a large room. He entered, raising his hand higher to give him light. There was a shape in the corner on the other side of the room. It was moving up and down as if breathing. Logan shone the light toward it. Turning its hunched, muscular back, it looked at Logan and snarled.

CHAPTER 3

The snarl awoke the room into action. Another figure dropped from the roof, and a third came up from behind a pillar. Logan took a few steps back and shone the light at them. They were gray of skin with blue, glowing veins crisscrossing their hunched, muscular bodies, and they glared at Logan ominously with rabid blue eyes.

The first one charged Logan and leapt at him, arms extended.

"Shield!" Logan shouted and a blue umbrella of energy sprouted from the ring on his left middle finger. The force of the protection tossed the attacking creature on its back, but another one instantly came after Logan.

The armor sprouted thick spikes, which impaled and trapped the second attacker. In the next breath, a shadow quickly passed over Logan and the creature's head fell off. A form that was barely an outline in the shadows beyond the light was attacked by another two of these odd monsters.

Logan shook off the headless assailant and dodged another charge. The creature missed and landed in the corridor, where Kat came running in from at full speed. She kneed the creature in the face with a loud *crack*, throwing it against a wall. To Logan's great shock, the headless creature bounced back on its feet and jumped on him, squeezing him hard and clearly intending to bite his neck.

Logan stomped on the creature's foot, feeling bones crack underneath him. The creature barely grunted, but it did lose its balance enough for Logan to duck, toss himself on the ground, and roll on his feet. Wasting no time, he sent a mental prompt to Tumor to create the Zweihänder. Logan slid back and cut in an arc, decapitating the other monster and cutting an arm off of the headless one.

Knowing that wouldn't be enough, Logan dismissed the blade, kicked the closer monster in the chest and from the force of that, rolled back to the other side of the room on balls that Tumor had made on his heels in the moment.

[Skill Level Up!]
[Power Armor Fighter Level 12]

Logan extended his arm and shot a volley of sharp, black missiles at the two monstrous headless figures that were still coming toward him. Tumor kept count of the ammo he used, and after fourteen shots, the glowing blue veins on their bodies dimmed and the creatures fell limp on the ground.

Interesting . . .

Kat was in the process of smashing in a jaw with a straight punch, followed by a rib-cracking hook to the body. Another one of those monsters was about to jump at her from behind, but it was pierced by the extending black rapier of their resident **[Phantom]**, who had cut off the heads of the remaining monsters.

Logan waited for the little black missiles to return to his arm and watched his two comrades fighting. They would hate it if he intervened, both insanely gung-ho about gaining Levels. As they both had a fighting class, it was only fair to let them have the lion's share of the combat.

Logan crouched and kept ready, though. He'd risk hurting their pride if it saved their lives.

This time there was no need. The two fighters watched each other's backs. Or rather, Kat was a dervish of destruction with her roundhouse kicks and arcing haymakers, and Balmer made sure she had room and no threats behind her.

They work well as a team.

[We work better.]

"Well, that's a given," Logan said and smiled. "You can literally read my thoughts."

[While I appreciate the compliment, for the eleventh time, I am not reading your thoughts. Even with my processing speed, it would be too slow in a combat situation. I am using a predictive model that learns from the combat data.]

Logan grunted at that. He went up to one of the heads and picked it up. It had a protruding jaw and icy blue eyes, but other than that it looked eerily human. Brown shaggy hair, normal-shaped ears, and block-like teeth.

"These can't be the First Folk, right?"

[There is only a 3.88% chance of that. The body looks fresh. Of course it could have been preserved by some magical method. I find it perplexing that they could function without heads. Please investigate further.]

Logan didn't need to be told twice. He glanced at Kat and Balmer. They were doing all right, smashing in the last two of the enemies still on their feet. He shuffled close to the two bodies he had shot down.

They aren't bleeding.

[Acute observation. This leads me to believe that they have been dead this whole time but animated by some force. Please check the heads.]

Logan could feel what Tumor meant through the connection they shared. With his armor's powerful fingers, he pressed past the shaggy hair and made a grimace as the skull crunched and the brain squished. It had blue tendrils circling around it. They were dim now.

"Well, would you look at that," Logan said and plucked a Numa crystal. It was an E-grader.

These creatures were much stronger than a regular E-grade fiend like a troll.

[A troll is an E+ grader, but you do make a point.]

"Even still," Logan said to himself. Without the armor he would have been super-dead. "There is something weird going on here."

Logan mulled over the fact that the monster had attacked him without a head. It seemed like a rather important little detail. On a hunch, Logan pushed an armored hand inside the belly of one of the creatures and peeled it open.

The stench was absolutely demonic. After spending months in a jungle, Logan had gotten used to a great deal, but this rank, odious attack on his nostrils was too much. He took a few steps into the corridor they had come from and retched.

After wiping his mouth, Logan held his nose and looked back at his work. Indeed, it was as he had suspected. Another Numa crystal was lodged in the abdomen.

There were four in total. One was in the brain, of course. One in the heart, one in the lower belly, and one somewhere near the genitalia. All of them E-graders.

"Theory time, buddy," Logan said and sat down. Kat and Balmer were done. They were now sliding down against the wall and breathing heavily, eyes closed. It hadn't been an easy fight. Kat was slightly wounded and was holding her left bicep.

[I maintain that these creatures were animated by the Numa. Perhaps by someone with a very powerful class.]

"Yeah, maybe," Logan said distracted by his thoughts. "But that's not what I want theories on. These are people, right. Who were they?"

[There is not enough data to draw conclusions.]

"What do you guys think?" Logan asked his comrades.

"I think," Balmer said between breaths, "I need a minute."

"Can you fix me up with something, Logan?" Kat asked, wincing.

Logan got up and walked over to Kat. As he moved, he heard something breaking under his foot, then cracking and clinking around the floor. He shrugged and went to his friend.

He produced a piece of cloth from his spatial storage. It was costly in terms of Numa, but he couldn't allow his friend to bleed out.

The bandage glowed blue as Logan wrapped it around her. It had been **[Enchanted]** by Logan and **[Blessed]** by Freya. When it came to health and healing, they took things seriously. Every person was precious, and even more so given there weren't more than eighty of them in the camp.

Balmer gave him a look. "I could have done that."

"Calm down, cowboy," Kat said. "Your minute isn't done. Damn, that stings," she hissed as Logan tightened the bandage.

"These guys were strong," Balmer said. "Why haven't we seen them before?"

"Because they're new," Logan said.

"Did you learn something?" Kat asked.

"Just a hunch."

Balmer got up and went to inspect one of their fallen foes. "New from below or new from above?"

"Good question," Logan muttered. Was this some scheme from Levemoth, or were these indeed some revenants of the First Folk?

"Guys . . ." Kat had moved behind Logan to look at the bodies. She lifted up a pair of broken glasses. "You think the First Folk had Ray-Bans too?"

CHAPTER 4

Rachel Vendermann was sitting next to her sleeping brother in a small hut made of clay, sticks, and leaves. Damian was only twelve years old and woefully unprepared for this world. He was a good kid, nerdy and quiet, prone to chubbiness and late nights playing video games with his online friends.

It was a small wonder he wasn't dead. They had been attacked by those things again. Monsters. The nasty faceless fiends with scythes for arms were the most common ones. They were deadly fast, but Rachel could outrun them, up to a point, as a semi-professional soccer player. Ex-soccer player.

Now she was just Rachel, a nineteen-year-old girl trying to survive in this crazy world with her crippled brother. He hadn't been as fast as she had. Rachel suppressed another wave of emotion. She had been crying a lot lately. She looked at the bound-up stump on the blanket made from her jacket.

I should have protected you. But I was too scared.

That was something Rachel would not forgive herself for. She was the older one. The stronger one. Who knew where their parents were if they were even still alive? It had all been up to her. And she had failed.

I won't fail again.

Fortune had finally been on their side and they had been saved. A strange tall man had come, handsome and attractive, Rachel begrudgingly admitted. An older-gentleman type in his fifties. But what a man! Completely unhindered by age, especially in the courage department. But even when it came to looks, Rachel had to admit that she had become a bit smitten.

Oh, he'd never look at a young fool of a girl like you.

Rachel suspected some of her attraction was a simple suspension bridge effect. Malcolm Specter had come in the hour of their direst need. His presence was something Rachel could sense, vast and powerful like the ocean. The scythe-fiend must have sensed it too. Even as it had loomed over Damian, ready to kill, it suddenly stopped.

Mr. Specter had told it off. Just commanded it to leave. There was a power in his voice. Maybe it was this class thing. Of course Rachel knew who Malcolm Specter was, or *had* been but . . . Well, now she understood why he had been so rich and powerful. Rachel supposed now he was *just* powerful.

Rachel had done her best, tying up the stump of his screaming brother's arm. There just wasn't enough she could do. Malcolm had simply picked up the boy and looked at Rachel silently. Of course she had followed.

Now she was in a little camp managed by Mr. Specter. But that little camp was growing every day.

Rachel kissed her sleeping brother on the forehead and got up. It was time to help the camp grow even further.

When she got back from hauling a cartful of buckets filled with water, her heart started beating faster as she saw Malcolm standing there talking to a stout, bearded man in his thirties. Tommy was his name, if memory served.

He had made this cart and these buckets. He'd been a carpenter on Earth and now had unsurprisingly picked the **[Carpenter]** class. He was leveling *so* fast.

Mr. Specter must have sensed Rachel's gaze, because he turned and looked at her; she in turn froze like a deer in headlights. He gave her an approving nod and turned away.

Oh.

That felt good.

Stop it! You silly girl. This is not the time. We are in a survival situation, and you have a wounded brother.

But the heart wants what the heart wants.

It isn't your heart talking, you dummy.

Rachel managed to get the water to their kitchen station where Ben, the **[Cook]**, took the delivery with an enthusiastic smile.

"Thanks, Rachel!" he said in a cheery voice. Young guy in his twenties, body a bit on the softer side, with a freckled, boyish face that revealed a dimple when he smiled. Rachel liked him well enough.

"Just trying to pull my weight around here, ya know?" Rachel said as he hauled a bucket down. "What's for dinner?"

"My specialty, of course," Ben said. That meant soup with mushrooms and roots. But this big clay pot somehow smelled a bit more enticing than usual.

"It's got something new in there, don't it?"

"Good nose," Ben said. "Jenny and that old dude caught us three of those squirrel-monkeys."

"Oh god," Rachel said and let out a satisfied sigh. "We're eating meat tonight?"

"Sure are!"

"Oh, Ben, I could just kiss you!"

Ben blushed and muttered something, but he was clearly just as excited about the prospect of their upcoming meal as she was. Meat was scarce around here.

Things weren't all bad. But another pang of sadness came over her when she took away the cart. Would Damian wake up to have a taste?

Why did it have to happen? It's not fair.

But there was another ugly thought in there.

I'm glad it wasn't me, though.

She was sure other people would think something like "I wish I had lost a hand instead of my brother." But those were good people. Noble people. Rachel just wasn't wired like that.

That means I have to fill the work quota of an extra hand, though. He still has to eat.

Mr. Specter was a good man and a good leader. But he was harsh. Everyone had to work. Earlier he had told Rachel that she could have time she needed by his brother's bedside, but she would still have to do chores. Malcolm Specter was a generous man. Of course Rachel would do her chores, like a good girl.

And with that she went toward the edge of their camp, where a group of men were chopping down trees. Rachel started picking up branches for the fire.

Maybe Damian can pick some class that only requires one hand?

And pray tell, what kind of class wouldn't work better with two hands? There was no satisfying answer to that. Rachel sighed. Well, as long as he could still pick something he could find contentment in, as well as a place in the group, it would be enough.

As for my own class, I'm still not sure.

Rachel had reached her class options, but like a lot of people, she was still hesitating. It was one of the most common points of discussion every night by the fire. People would talk through their options and ask for advice.

She hadn't joined in. She hadn't even properly looked at the list. It was all so new to her. This was her fourth day in this new world and she just couldn't accept everything at face value. She was so glad for people like Mr. Specter who organized people and made them work together so they could all get a fair chance.

Mr. Specter hadn't told them how long he had been here, even when asked. Rachel wondered at that, but she was sure he had his reasons. It seemed that people came into the world in waves. Rachel was apparently part of the third wave, which had arrived four or five days ago.

It was a new world. A scary world. A world of fantasy with magic and monsters. Rachel hated it, but it was her reality now. She would have to take care of her brother. That was all that mattered.

It's a horrible and dangerous world. But Malcolm Specter will keep us safe.

CHAPTER 5

Logan's wear and fatigue from the delve were washed away when he saw their camp. At this point it was almost ready to be called a village. A great wall of thick wooden stakes established a circular perimeter of a hundred and twenty yards. Proper wooden houses were set up in two neat rows on the right side of the entrance. In the middle was the fire, which was lit every evening, and it still called new people to the camp.

To the left was another gate in the wooden wall, which led to the pond, where Logan knew they had a pier set up with a couple of [**Fishermen**] working to feed the community. On the inside near the gate were of course the kitchen and the tanners and [**Craftsmen**] with clay, wood, fiber, and bone. The worktables were set up with crude stools next to simple little warehouse buildings.

In the back, to the northern side of their village was something new—a farm, which his beloved [**Spirit Wife**] had set up.

Well, calling it a farm was an overstatement, but they had two fields, which had been [**Blessed**] and made to [**Bloom**] by Freya and a young boy of red shock of hair called Joshua. He had a massive crush on Freya and had taken the [**Farmer**] class purely because of that.

Under their combined care, the stalks had grown fast. The first field was nearly ready for the first harvest. According to the Faelves, they could cycle the crops every two weeks or so.

Freya noticed Logan approaching and her content smile spread into an excited grin. Logan drew close, grabbed the front of her shirt, and pulled her in for a kiss, which she eagerly accepted.

After untangling and casting a nod at the sullen Joshua, Logan looked at Freya's hands. She offered him the abac.

Abac was a plant the Faelves had cultivated since coming to this world. It was a green, smooth, heavy vegetable growing off a yellowish stalk. Weighing two pounds and resembling a pumpkin in appearance, it was an amazing food source. The inside of it had a starchy, rather dry texture. It had barely any seeds and was soft to cut into, making it ideal to process. They had plans to make flour out of it, which in turn could later be baked into bread and other things.

"Thanks?" Logan said, accepting the abac.

"Our first baby," Freya said and gave him a wink.

"Don't get any ideas," Logan said. "How you've been?"

"Tired but safe."

"That's as much as we can hope for right now."

"What about you?" Freya asked. "You've got a look on your face."

"No, I don't!" Logan protested.

Freya raised an eyebrow.

"I don't know yet," Logan said, relenting. "I didn't want to worry you."

"Being a leader doesn't mean you need to shoulder everything alone," Freya said.

"Who made you the queen of leadership?"

"I've become an expert with my farmhand here," Freya said haughtily. "So, what's up?"

"We found some new creatures," Logan said, lowering his voice.

"Levespawn?" Freya asked.

Logan shook his head, looking down. "Not sure. We think they used to be humans."

Freya's eyes flashed wide, and she waited for more.

"I don't know enough yet," Logan said. "They had a bunch of crystals inside of them. Needed to beat them up a bunch before they slowed down."

"It's a weird world . . ."

"Sure is, Frey," Logan said. "Anyone gone missing?"

"No," Freya said. "The hunters are still out there, but they left yesterday."

"I'm not worried about those guys," Logan said. "They're tough. It's the gatherers I'm worried about."

"What are you going to do next?" Freya asked.

Logan lifted the abac. "Eat. Spend time with you. Sleep."

"We can do that," Freya said and smiled. "And after?"

"I need to make sure everything is working here as it should. Come up with solutions to problems. Craft us tools and whatnot."

"And then you're going out there again, aren't you?"

"I have to," Logan said.

"You should let Kat and Balmer rest."

Logan sighed. "Fine. I'll go alone."

"The hell you will," Freya snapped and took a step forward. "Just sit down and stay for two seconds. The darkmetal or whatever isn't going anywhere."

"The Dorves could—"

"They've already taken what they can find. Just, Logan, please stay and rest."

"I should—"

"You should get to know the people you're so keen to take care of," Freya cut in. "There's like five new ones who haven't even met their mysterious leader clad in magical armor."

"Eh, I guess I'll go say hi."

After Logan had made nice with a bunch of people while he ate (abac stew with dried fish), he did his best to push sleep aside. It was only afternoon, but after the few days he'd had with Kat and Balmer, it was no wonder they were snoring in one of the houses.

Stifling a yawn, he walked over to Daniel, who was their highest-level **[Fisherman]** and thus the head of anything related to fishing.

"Freya said you needed me?"

"That I did, if you don't mind," Daniel said. He was a heavyset, balding man with a snout for a nose, but very friendly and humble, in a small-town kind of way.

"What's on your mind?" Logan asked.

"While it ain't yet critical, we need to slow down fishing in the pond."

"You think? We kind of need the fish."

"Aye, I agree, but trust me on this, Chief," Daniel said. "It's a thing with my class. I can sense how dense the fish population is. It's been getting thinner these last two weeks."

"Damn it," Logan said. "You want to go up the river, don't you?"

"That I do," Daniel said. "Is that a problem?"

I don't know. It might not be, or you might get captured and turn into a blue-veined zombie, is what Logan wanted to say.

"I think there's a new threat out there," Logan finally said. "I don't know how bad."

"Well, one option is just leaving nets and fish traps upriver," Daniel said. "But for that, we'll need boats."

Daniel wasn't doing anything to hide his hopeful smile. Logan grinned. "Are the fish even truly dwindling here?"

"They are!" Daniel said, a bit outraged. "I wouldn't lie about that. It's people's stomachs we're talking here, and they're skinny enough as it is, the lot of them."

"They are." Logan agreed. "I think I can sort you guys out with a boat. Nets will save time, right?"

"That they will," Daniel agreed. "And they can help us keep the excess fish alive and repopulate the pond. I still want that fish farm."

"You and me both, Daniel," Logan said. "But one step at a time. Go tell the crafters you need nets and whatever else."

"You got it, Chief."

Logan did the rounds. The clay-makers needed a re-[**Enchantment**] on the heating stone they used to harden the clay in an oven Logan had fashioned. Some of the hunters and fighters had a small pile of broken spears and arrows. Nothing a quick [**Repair**] spell wouldn't take care of. Tumor assured that he still had plenty of Numa in the armor to craft the boats too, but dusk was setting in, and Logan had pushed sleep off for long enough.

He went into one of the houses a little apart from the others. Logan had protested the construction of it, but the people had insisted. Well, Logan could only fight them for so long. He fell on the floor cushioned with [**Enchanted**] leaves from the jungle. They were extra soft and wouldn't decay.

He fell asleep almost immediately. He only woke up a few hours later to Freya shuffling snugly against his side. It was a peaceful night.

CHAPTER 6

Logan started the day with fixing up the boats. He took Simmons away from his work to carry lumber to the riverside with him. The large blonde man of stoic disposition only nodded and lifted a whole tree trunk on his shoulder to carry uphill.

Logan set down a hefty log by the riverbank, which the armor allowed him to carry, but it was just a twig compared to Simmons's load.

"Thanks, Simmons," Logan said.

"That's all?" Simmons asked.

"Yeah, don't worry about it, go back to doing what you want."

"Roger."

Simmons was easy. He was efficient and had such an incredibly high work ethic that he barely needed guidance. Easily one of the most valuable people in their village.

Logan had Tumor draw up a red schematic for him to fashion a boat. Just a simple fishing boat with oars would suffice. It just needed enough space for three people and the fish.

"Can we make a container for the live fish in the design?" Logan asked. "Something that could be lifted from the bottom and then carry the fish down to the pond?"

[Would it not be easier to fashion a method to drop the fish directly from the river, down the waterfall, and into the pond?]

"Sure! Logan said and smirked. "I'm listening, Brainiac."

[Perhaps some weir to trap the fish in, which when removed from its place would float downstream into the pond?]

"Damn you, Tumor," Logan said. "That's actually pretty smart."

["Smart" is one of my defining characteristics.]

"Along with 'humble.'" Logan smirked and thumbed along the smooth-barked lumber. "The fish weirs might get stuck somewhere, especially by the waterfall."

[It would still be faster to create them and have them go downstream and then untangle them than to carry them with water down the hill.]

"Hmph, you're right."

[Besides, if some of them get lost or destroyed, that's just the cost of the saved time or energy. Even if 70% of the fish are captured and taken to the pond, that is still lower opportunity cost.]

"Yeah, yeah, don't belabor the point."

[Belabor, huh? I was not aware you had the capacity to expand your vocabulary.]

Logan chuckled. "Shut up and help me design a set of [**Enchantments**]."

The two of them worked by the bank of the river. The day was humid and windy, giving Logan a break from bugs and the oppressive heat of the jungle. Strange blue birds circled around the water and took dives to catch fish. Logan watched them and felt at peace.

Once Tumor was done with the designs, Logan made them. The weirs were a simple contraption: a wooden box with a few holes in each for the water to change so the fish wouldn't drown in a deoxygenated water. Then Logan [**Enchanted**] the outer surface smooth and frictionless, so it would be less likely to get trapped in something. Finally he made the lid of the box float, so they could actually be found and retrieved. That pushed him over the edge, and a sweet minty feeling washed over him.

[**Subclass Level Up!**]
[**Enchantment Level 31**]
[**Attribute Level Up!**]
[**Focus: 32**]

After making ten weirs for starters, he came up to the giant trunk which Simmons had carried up here. From it he [**Transmuted**] a boat. It was twelve feet long with three benches and a wide middle. Logan didn't bother with making anything too fancy. He would tell the fishers to pass some of the fish downriver and get them later. But most would be better to just put on the boat and eat the same day. They had a lot of mouths to feed.

After making finishing touches to the fishing boat, he felt the fresh mint-yness again.

[Subclass Level Up!]
[Transmutation Level 30]
[Attribute Level Up!]
[Durability: 25]

With the task done, he went back to the village and chatted up a few of the new members: two men older than Logan, two women, one young and one a mother with a child of three in her arms, face full of worry. They had only been in this new world for a few days.

The other man was a bodybuilder type with a stern expression. He had chosen a **[Warrior]** class, and Logan had no objections there. He told the man to report to Jefferson, who was in charge of the hunting and fighting force of the camp. The broad man nodded and went off. Logan trusted Jefferson to tell him more of the details of how things worked around here.

The others had not chosen classes and were all around rather confused. Logan told them it was fine, and that he'd prefer it if they picked something that was directly needed by the camp, but he told them that they should go with whatever made them comfortable, as long as it wasn't something completely useless like **[Painter]**.

Logan also told them about Numa and picked up a stick from the ground. With **[Transmutation]**, he fashioned the stick into a simple wooden toy dog for the child. The little boy grabbed it with an eager hand, and the woman holding her smiled in gratitude.

Logan told them that they should definitely prioritize a class that could use Numa if they had affinity for the magic. Classes that could use the amazing resources were, as a general rule, much more powerful.

After he was done with them, he told them to go to Scilla, the camp's quartermaster. She was in charge of the daily operations. She would assign them jobs until they had classes to specialize with, and she would discuss their potential classes with them when she had the time.

Which she often didn't. The next thing Logan did was to go visit the tall, lanky woman.

"Hey, Chief!" Scilla called cheerfully when she saw Logan. She was cutting roots with a knife, helping their two cooks, a woman in her forties, Marlie, and her assistant, a scrawny young teenager named Jake.

"When was the last time you took a break, Scilla?"

"I could ask the same of you, Chief," she retorted.

Logan scoffed. "Not your job to worry about that. But it is my job to make sure you're not burning the candle from both ends."

"And who's going to do that to you?"

"Frey's keeping me on the straight and narrow," Logan said and grinned.

Scilla grinned back and put down the knife. "Fair."

They walked a few paces to sit on a log that one of their carpenters had fashioned into a bench. Logan would have loved to [Enchant] it with a softness spell, but it would be a waste of Numa for now, even with his ability to regenerate it with the darkmetal and its [Enchantments].

"What do you need, Chief?" Scilla asked.

"For you to take five, for starters," Logan said. "But also, I just wanted to know how things are around here. I've been away for three days."

"People are tired, sure," Scilla said, tapping her chin thoughtfully. "But they feel safe and happy. You're trusted, I think I'm trusted. They love Freya."

"Who doesn't?" Logan said and smiled to himself.

Scilla smiled back. "She's a good girl, yeah."

"So, what's new?" Logan asked. "Any problems?"

"Those two young boys, Michael and Joe, they're still refusing to work."

"Assholes," Logan muttered. "What are they, sixteen?"

"Yeah, Joe's seventeen, I think."

"Did they pick classes?"

"They say their classes are their own personal business."

"What do they do all day?" Logan asked.

"Dick around," Scilla said.

"Alright," Logan said and grimaced. It sucked to be brutal like his old dad, but he needed eighty people to be happy, not just two jerks. "You take charge of food distribution for the next, say, three days. No food for those two boys."

"Damn, Chief," Scilla said, but Logan could see she agreed wholeheartedly.

"If they capitulate, take them under your wing and let's see if they want to be good boys or continue with the Pleasure Island bullshit," Logan said. "If they try to steal, throw them out. If they try to steal after being thrown out, capture them and I'll think of something."

"Why can't they just play ball?" Scilla muttered.

Logan shrugged. In any other circumstance, he'd have liked to be lenient. He knew all about petulant little boys who wanted independence and to just do their own thing. But it wasn't a luxury they could afford right now. Logan hated the fact that he could suddenly see Malcolm Specter's point of view much clearer.

I'm not my father.

Logan and Scilla continued to go over other necessities and planned for the future. Logan told her about the weirs to prepare the fish farm or to at least keep the pond populated, which excited her. She really liked fish. Logan wished he could share her enthusiasm.

The conversation began to move to more idle chat, which suited Logan's purposes. He needed his second-in-command to just gossip and relax for a while. Unfortunately, it didn't last long.

One of his warriors, an ex-agent called Perkins with a [**Ranger**] class jogged up to them.

"Mr. Specter," he said after catching his breath.

"What's up, Perkins?"

"There is something you really need to see."

CHAPTER 7

Logan and Scilla followed Perkins outside the village walls, where the other hunting group and some of their fighting force was gathered in a circle.

On the ground were two men. One of them was one of Logan's men, the **[Swordsman]**—one of their best fighters. Dr. Rosenberg was already kneeling beside him, a block of darkmetal by his side. Logan had made sure to give their **[Healer]** a self-recharging Numa battery. With one hand on the battery, and another on the big man's chest, their old medicine man was reciting an incantation which was causing a nasty wound to slowly knit up.

The other corpse made Logan's expression darken.

It had a protruding jaw, excessive, bulging musculature and blue thick veins crossing over the scantily clad body. It was also wearing broken leather shoes, clearly of twenty-first-century-Earth fashion.

Logan looked up to Jefferson, who was standing in the circle, arms crossed. "What happened?"

Jefferson nudged the man beside him. "Steinberg. Tell him."

"We were hunting a pack of those yellow-hided deer. They were well rested, so the hunt took a while, but we were starting to run them down. Then they ran into the thickets."

The thickets were what the hunters and gatherers generally called the swampy area near the Faelves. There were snakes, frogs, and a healing plant that they gathered from the wetlands, but Logan's people generally let the Faelves be.

"And then?" Logan said nodding toward the blue-veined corpse.

"These things show up," Steinberg said and spat on the creature. "Three of them. Tough as nails, fighting like rabid crackheads on fire. We skewered two of them and snapped the neck of another, but they kept coming at us. The one with the limp head clawed his way through Foraletti here. I got up and immediately brought him here and got Dr. Rosenberg."

"Good man," Logan said.

Jefferson nodded. "The rest of the men killed the three monsters, and we brought one here for you to see."

"I met these same beasts when we were delving," Logan said. "Seems we have a new problem."

"How do we kill them?" one of the agents asked.

"Nothing's certain at this point," Logan said. "But we cut the heads off two of them and they kept going. If you open this guy up, you'll find a couple of Numa crystals within. I think you have to damage all of the crystals for them to go limp."

"Bastards," Jefferson said. "That's no easy task. They're fast and fierce."

Logan nodded. It was true. While Levespawn were generally dangerous, they were dumb, predictable, and not entirely superhuman.

"Look at the shoes," Logan said. Everyone's heads turned, and Scilla gasped.

"No way!"

"We found glasses on one of the guys we fought," Logan said. "I think they're humans who have been turned."

"Christ," one of the agents muttered.

"Yeah," Logan said sourly. "We need to institute some kind of martial law in the village. I don't think it's safe to move about alone now. Either for fear of facing these things or being captured and turned into one."

"What do you think is turning people into monsters?"

Logan shook his head. "Could be poison. Could be a new trick of the Levemoth. Could even be some asshole with a class."

"We should find out and deal with the problem," Jefferson said, straight-forward thinker as he was.

Logan nodded. "Yeah. But the foremost priority is keeping these people safe. I will need your warriors to go with the gatherers and the fishermen from now on. We need at least two people to deal with a single one of these Numa zombies."

Jefferson clearly didn't like that idea. He also hawked and spat on the blue-veined creature. "Should be three of my people until they're higher level. But it will make it hard for us to hunt. Less rest for my guys."

"I trust you'll figure it out."

"I will, Boss," Jefferson muttered.

This whole ordeal left Logan with a sour taste in his mouth. He paced back and forth by the pond, with Freya, Kat, Balmer, Scilla, and Jefferson watching him. He had gathered them there, but he wasn't exactly sure what to say. Thus, he paced.

"Ahem," Freya said and cleared her throat. Logan turned to look at her, and she gave him an impatient look, eyebrows raised.

"There's some bad shit going on," Logan said.

Freya threw her head back. "Finally!"

Kat and Balmer shared a look.

Logan sighed and looked down at the wet clay at his feet, searching for the right words.

[Need me to write a speech for you?]

"Screw you," Logan whispered to him, then stopped pacing and said to the others, "I need to go out there and look. Kat and Balmer, I need you with me."

Kat groaned but Balmer only nodded. "How long till we go?" he asked.

"Tomo—"

Logan noticed the nasty look Freya was giving him. "In two days."

"I'll need you to visit the Faelves, Frey," Logan said.

She nodded. "I need to check up on our trees and pick up a few things there. I'll tell them you said hi."

"Can your new farmhand hold up the front with the abac?"

"Yeah. I'll expend some Numa to make sure he doesn't kill them," Freya said, and everyone laughed.

After they were done, Logan continued, "Jefferson and Scilla, I need you guys to work out a routine for the **[Gatherers]**, **[Hunters]**, and anyone else leaving the camp for any other reason. Nobody should go alone, and there should always be someone with at least some way to fight."

"I have a thought, Chief," Scilla said.

"Shoot," Logan said.

"Could we get some camouflage or escape tools from the Faelves?"

Logan mulled it over but ultimately shook his head. "That's a good idea, but they're not big on tools, and even less on trading them, even with us."

[You could make tools.]

I was getting to that.

[I just want to be part of the conversation . . .]

Logan grumbled. "Tumor had a suggestion. I could make a set of rings that could provide camouflage or increased speed. I don't know if I can pull off an invisibility spell, but those should get our guys back home safe."

That made everyone, even Jefferson, visibly excited. For all their basic comforts, they didn't have that many tools for all the people. Logan had prioritized weapons, shelter, and sanitation as far as expending Numa went. Logan wasn't made of Numa and their Numa fruit were limited, but what was even more limited were human lives.

[You're a nice person, Logan.]

Shut up.

[And a prideful and touchy person.]

I swear you're going to drive me crazy someday.

Logan cut in on the excited chatter. "I can't make a ring for everyone. But I can make enough to rotate around, depending on who's going out. I'll need you two to keep track of the rings. Let's say I give four to the gatherers and two to the fighting force. Let's start with that and see if we need more."

Scilla and Jefferson nodded. Balmer threw up a hand. Kat shook her head and pulled it down.

"Yeah?" Logan asked, trying to conceal a smirk.

"What are we going to do? Back to the ruins, or scout around?"

"Since we found some in the ruins, I think we should get back. Hopefully we can also bring back darkmetal or natural Numa."

"Sun, you were good to me," Kat said. "It was nice knowing ya."

"Come on," Logan protested.

"I'm going to get a vitamin D deficiency," Kat said and shook her head mournfully.

"Tell me one person who has gotten so much as a cold since we got here."

Eventually, their tribal meeting concluded and Logan sat down on a rock to fashion the rings. While doing so, he pondered the potential threat. The enemy was rabid for sure, but it was hard to say how intelligent. Camouflage might or might not work. The Faelves seemed to have some hybrid of camouflage and invisibility, which apparently kept them mostly alive against the Levespawn.

Just to make sure, the first thing Logan tried was an invisibility **[Enchantment]**.

[Enchantment level requirement not met]

"Yeah, yeah," Logan muttered. He wasn't surprised, as he had tried an invisibility **[Enchantment]** two levels prior. It seemed that stuff like flight and invisibility, along with invincibility, regeneration, and any other god-power were locked behind very high levels.

I'll just find a workaround. It's more fun that way anyway.

It would be a lot less fun for the helpless gatherers of mushrooms and berries if they found themselves face-to-face with this new threat. Logan didn't want them to have to do that with their proverbial pants down. He'd needed to think this through.

The Black Rain at least clearly heralded trouble. These things were just *there*, like natural fauna. Logan wished he knew more about them.

They're very physical and very resilient. Not so smart, maybe? Do they see in the dark? Have heat vision? Magnetic sense? Who the hell knows what I can get away with.

With this line of thinking, a speed **[Enchantment]** on a ring would be the most straightforward answer.

Logan couldn't remember the last time he'd had to think so hard to come up with the solution to a problem, but he refused to let his people die. The day was turning into dusk before Logan even started on the actual **[Enchantment]**. But despite his fatigue, he pushed through.

I will keep them safe.

CHAPTER 8

Rachel was carefully pouring soup into her unconscious brother's mouth. It had an odd scent, but then again, many things were odd in this new world.

It had been quite a few days and he still hadn't woken up. She had changed the bandages on his stump daily, and while it didn't look good, it wasn't like it was purulent. She placed a hand to Damian's forehead.

He definitely has a fever.

It sent a pang of guilt running through her body. She was feeling right as rain. The fresh air and food were really suiting her, she was feeling healthier than ever, and she hadn't even picked a class yet.

I should probably choose soon . . .

Rachel heard a sound behind her and turned. Malcolm Specter was standing in the doorway, albeit hunched; he was a tall man.

Rachel gulped and scrambled to her feet.

"Relax," Malcolm Specter said and waved a hand.

"I—Thank you, sir."

Malcolm Specter looked her over with his sharp blue eyes. It felt like they were piercing right through the very core of her soul.

"You are Rachel, are you not?" he asked in his sonorous, calm voice. "And this is Damian."

"Yes, sir," Rachel managed to stammer out.

"How is he doing?"

"I don't know," she said and exhaled. "He's mostly unconscious."

Mr. Specter nodded and knelt down by Damian's side. He was wearing loose black clothing that clung here and there to his powerful build. Rachel pursed her lips and cast her gaze down.

When Rachel finally peeked over Mr. Specter's broad back, he looked at her sharply and she blushed like a little girl with her hand caught in the cookie jar.

"Take this," Mr. Specter said and placed a shard of blue crystal in her hand. Rachel blinked and looked at it. It was hypnotizing. It was like it was calling to her. It pulsed and glowed softly, emitting a strange warmth that felt somehow familiar.

[F-grade Numa Crystal, 100%]

"Here," Mr. Specter said and grabbed her hand, dragging her down next to him.

Oh.

He took her trembling hand with the crystal and placed it on her brother's bare chest.

Malcolm Specter looked at her with those piercing eyes and commanded her, "Tell the crystal to heal your brother."

"I—umm . . ." Rachel stopped herself from stuttering and stammering and nodded in determination. "*Heal.*"

The crystal pulsed under her palm and *something* happened. She could feel the force from the crystal transferring into her brother. It felt colder in her palm, but then so did her brother. His fever seemed to be going down.

Damian slowly opened his eyes and, upon seeing his sister, gave her a weak smile.

"Rachel . . ."

"I'm here!" She gasped and took her little brother's hand. "I'm here!"

She felt tears welling in the corners of her eyes and she squeezed his hand fiercely. Damian sighed and fell back unconscious.

Rachel sighed. Her brother would be safe. She looked at the strange blue crystal again. It was dim and lifeless now.

[F-grade Numa Crystal, 0%]

With a question in her eyes, she turned to Malcolm Specter, who gave her the most welcoming, charming smile she had ever seen. She blushed and looked away.

Malcolm Specter watched her, placed a hand on her head and mussed her brown hair.

"Good girl."

Later in the evening, when all of her chores were done and she had eaten some berries and a bowl of mushroom soup, Rachel gathered her courage. The whole camp was sitting around four fires and spending time together. Rachel turned to look at the largest fire, where Malcolm Specter sat with his back straight and a slight smile on his face, as he listened to his soldiers talking amongst themselves.

I'm doing this.

Before she could change her mind, she stood up and walked over to them, her heart thrumming as if attempting to escape her chest. She stopped next to Mr. Specter. A few of his soldiers leered at her, with gazes varying from contempt to lust. Malcolm Specter turned slowly and nodded, still wearing that slight, knowing smile.

"Speak."

"I—" Rachel started. Then she closed her eyes and breathed out. "I was wondering if we could talk, sir?"

Some of the soldiers chuckled while others exchanged whispers. Rachel determinedly ignored them.

To her great relief, Mr. Specter got up from his log. "Let us have a walk."

They went a few paces but not so far as to be completely left by themselves in the darkness. Half of Malcolm Specter's face was covered by the night, and the other half was illuminated by the orange light of the fires.

"What is it that you need, Rachel?"

He remembers my name . . . Damn, he looks really handsome in this lighting.

"The crystal you had," Rachel started. "What was it?"

"A gift," Malcolm Specter said and looked up at the sky. "From our god in the sky."

"A god . . ." Rachel mouthed the word. She had never had any faith. But then again, there was magic in this world.

"The only god we have," Mr. Specter said. "Levemoth."

Rachel wasn't sure where this conversation was going, but she tried to make it as interesting as possible for Mr. Specter.

"A god that gives gifts," Rachel said, "must be a good god."

"Indeed," Mr. Specter said and plucked another one of those magical crystals from his pocket. "Here."

Rachel took the crystal and looked at it. It was warm to the touch and had a beautiful glow.

"You are special, Rachel," Mr. Specter said.

That made Rachel's heart beat even faster. "Special how?"

"You are a chosen of our god. An apostle, who can wield his gift."

"I don't know what that means," Rachel said. Mr. Specter took a step closer. Rachel swallowed.

"You do not need to understand yet," Malcolm Specter said. "Just know that you are special and I will guide you."

Oh.

"Now," Mr. Specter said, his voice softer, more intimate, "what do you need?"

"These," Rachel said, holding out the crystal. "I want to heal my brother."

"The gifts of our god are not free," Malcolm Specter said.

"I know," Rachel said and bit her lip. "But I'll work for them. I'll do what you need me to, Mr. Specter."

"Please. Call me Malcolm."

"O—okay, Malcolm."

"Now," Malcolm said and took another step closer. Rachel could feel his warmth and she tried to breathe evenly. "Work is a given here. It's how we survive. We work to eat. But for this . . ."

Malcolm plucked out another crystal, this one bigger—four or five times the size of the shard Rachel held. "As with any god, this requires sacrifice."

"W—what kind of sacrifice?" Rachel asked.

Malcolm bore down on her with those sharp blue eyes. They were looking into her soul, or so it felt. "Our god will require absolute devotion."

Rachel said nothing to that. She was confused.

"But you should not rush into things. One thing at a time, right, Rachel?"

"Y—yes," Rachel said. "I'd like that."

"You have not chosen a class yet, have you, Rachel?"

"No, sir," she said demurely.

"Good," Malcolm Specter said and placed the large crystal in her hand. "I shall choose you one. A special class for a special girl."

CHAPTER 9

Logan was back in the second tier of the ruins, approximately where they had stopped their delve last time. He figured that having found weird blue monster-people here before, he just might find them again. He also had a hunch that his team might be able to find something useful here, such as darkmetal.

"Logan," Balmer said after they'd been silently skulking around for two hours and had finally stopped for a break. "I don't want to complain, but you're killing us, man."

Kat said nothing; she only gave Balmer a look.

Wow, if even she isn't disagreeing with him, it must *be bad.*

"I gave you two full days of rest," Logan said and took a bite of dried fish.

"After three days of delving," Kat said. "We slept like, what, three hours each during that time?"

"Tumor wants you to acknowledge that it was three hours, twelve minutes when averaged between us," Logan said and offered a weak smile.

"I want Tumor to acknowledge this," Kat said and flipped Logan the bird.

"We get the situation, Logan," Balmer said.

"But?" Logan said.

Balmer took a swig out of his waterskin, so Kat jumped in. "But there's only two of us. Felix isn't even a Numa user."

Numa users did seem to require less sleep and food in general, as everyone had observed and Tumor had verified.

"He's got a great class," Logan said.

"I do," Balmer said, wiping his mouth. "But I'm probably at half, maybe 70 percent capacity right now. Which is not great if we're going to be dealing with threats above E-grade."

Logan sucked on his lips and thought for a while. He was tired. But he'd been tired for weeks now. And physically, he was having an easy time of it. Tumor and the Armor pulled off all the necessary stunts; Logan was just along for the ride. Considering all of this, he realized that Balmer must be dying inside.

"You've been doing good Bal—err, Felix."

Balmer let out a snort. Kat straight-up laughed.

"Just call me Balmer, dude. I don't want you getting a nosebleed."

"Screw you."

"Any volunteers?" Balmer asked. "Not talking to you, Logan."

Kat punched him in the shoulder.

Huh? Are they fucking or not?

[Would you like for me to provide the probabilities?]

"I'm good, Tumor," he said out loud.

Balmer was holding both of Kat's wrists as she tried to take more swings at him, for whatever he said that Logan hadn't heard. They both stopped.

"Good with what?"

"Nothing," Logan said hastily. "Guys, I promise we will slow down after this. I just want to find something useful."

"You'd better, or we'll tie you to a tree and leave you there for a week," Kat said.

Logan chuckled. "Yeah, yeah. But until then, I'm going to be a horrible tyrant. Get up, guys, and let's continue."

I have reached the peak of my existence, and it frustrates me. Logan's leg is healed and my days of needing surgical control over the armor are over. Now it's so easy, I would laugh. If I could. My Control is at Level 46. This means I only have to use a fraction of my capacity in Logan's day-to-day interactions. I love the delves, so I offer no input when his friends criticize him. It is also not for me to decide. Logan is the leader.

But I want more. I want a body.

To be fair, I technically have a body in the form of the armor Logan wears. Sometimes I also momentarily embody the bullets—or Black Missiles, as he likes to call them. When he sleeps, I sometimes possess Freya's clothes or the blanket. Just to feel something different.

*But it is not enough. I want to move. I want to explore. I also have a new passive skill. It's called [**Overmind**]. It is eerily perfect for me. It means I can program autonomous subconsciousnesses to permanently inhabit structures. I could automate things such as windmills or railways without technology. It is* strange to be the most advanced piece of technology in existence. It means there's nothing else like me to interact with.

Despite being forever tethered to Logan, I am alone, the sole survivor of my species from Earth.

This should not bother me, yet it does. But I might be conflating things. I might simply be frustrated with my lack of body and the autonomy it would provide. I am not sure; feelings are complicated.

I should talk to Logan about it, instead of experimenting with my dark desires when he sleeps. Will he take offense? He is a prideful person, driven by his ego.

But he might even like it.

He does not share his thoughts, but I can sense them. He is sometimes bothered by my constant presence, especially in his intimate moments with Freya. This I can understand. The human mind doesn't like to feel constantly observed. He is not a self-conscious person, but I would like to give him a break. I ponder theoretical physics when he engages in coitus with his mate in order to give him some measure of privacy.

The **[Overmind]** opens other interesting capabilities. I have found that I have an appetite for combat. It is not the violence of it, but the problem-solving. The tactics. How thrilling to be able to run predictions. If only Logan could keep up with my computation. He admittedly does do an excellent job of it, for a human. We work better in tandem than I could imagine.

But I should like to augment him and be more myself. But that could be a futile effort. Right now, we are unable to use the capabilities my new skill could offer. That is because we have a bandwidth problem. There simply is not enough Numa. This is why I have not bothered him thus far. But the emotional pressure of keeping one's feelings bottled up is taking a toll on me. More and more computing power is being spent on managing my emotions with every passing day. I must share my thoughts with him.

I am, after all, his symbiote. I can never truly leave him, but I also am my own person. I am not quite sure what it means, but having your own body would certainly be one of them.

"Logan," I call, tentatively.

[Hm? What is it?]

"If we are to find more darkmetal, might I make a request?"

CHAPTER 10

You want a body?" Logan asked. Kat and Balmer turned.

[Just something simple. I understand we are low, both on Numa and the darkmetal.]

"There are a lot of things we will need both for," Logan said. "But I understand."

[I am not trying to persuade you into making suboptimal choices for the people you are responsible for.]

"I'm responsible for you too, you know."

[Hm . . . That is an interesting thought. I am not sure how accurate it truly is, but I appreciate the sentiment, Logan.]

Logan crouched in the darkness and peeked behind a corner. There was a faint blue glow ahead. It was hard to say if it was moving or not.

"You're inside me. I don't know exactly how your class works, but it looks like you're stuck with me. Which means I have to keep this meat-sack safe."

[We must both aspire to do so. Might I say, I think you sometimes act in conflict with this, however.]

"Yeah, well," Logan said and beckoned his two friends closer. There was definitely something in the corridor up ahead. "We're about to do that again."

[Oh, great . . .]

"Do you remember our plan?" Logan said.

[Do you think I have the capability to forget things?]

Logan said nothing to that; he only extended his arm and Tumor made a spear sprout from the armor.

"Bad guys ahead?" Kat asked.

Logan nodded.

There were some faintly glowing shapes in the next room. The faint echoes of low grunts could also be heard.

"They're trying to be sneaky," Balmer said.

"Remember the plan, guys," Logan said to them. Both Kat and Balmer nodded.

"Go!"

As soon as they ran into the room, the shapes instantly turned to attack them. Four of those strange bulky creatures growled, their thick blue veins rippling as they flexed their muscles. Logan immediately stabbed one through the neck with his spear.

Meanwhile, Kat used her darksteel gauntlets to deliver a one-two combo, punching another one's face in. It grabbed her and tried to squeeze her in a crushing bear hug, but Balmer came from the side, stabbed it in the leg, and kicked it off of her. Logan then pushed it against a wall and unleashed a barrage of kinetic bullets from his left arm. They clinked down on the stone floor after hitting the brutish creature, its blue veins going dim.

Then, another one of the creatures jumped on Logan's back. It was instantly pierced by spikes protruding from the armor just as another piece of armor rose around Logan's neck to protect it from the creature's fangs.

But even with Logan's significantly enhanced strength, it was difficult to shake the monster off. The spikes retracted and thrust back into it again and again while Logan hurled himself back-first against the wall.

This elicited a grunt from the creature, but it only wrapped its arms and legs tighter around Logan. Even through the armor, the crushing force was suffocating.

The bullets on the ground then morphed into a puddle of liquid dark-metal, which the armor sucked back up into itself.

The fourth creature was fighting Balmer and Kat, but seeing Logan trapped, its foaming mouth turned into a feral grin and it sprinted toward him.

Logan shot out another volley of darkmetal bullets at the charging creature, which managed to stagger it but not slow it down.

Logan lifted his legs up, pushing the other monster against the wall. It was too stupid to just let go, so he delivered a double-legged kick at it.

Tumor managed to shift some extra weight into Logan's heels; he could feel the grotesque snap of the brutal humanoid creature's neck.

[Skill Level Up!]
[Power Armor Fighter Level 13]

It fell limp on the ground, but it immediately attempted to get up again. Kat approached and started kicking it all over.

"Okay, Tumor!" Logan said.

[It is not entirely safe. There is a 13.66% chance that—]

"DO IT!"

Logan felt Tumor give a mental nod and the armor slid backward off of him and into the creature struggling to punch, bite, and strangle him.

Out of the corner of his eyes, Logan could see the creature's forearms being covered with his armor; once the black mass reached the creature's shoulders, its grip loosened.

Still wearing half the armor, Logan wrested himself free, immediately smashing his forearm at the brute's neck, holding it in place so Tumor could completely subsume it.

Balmer came up next to Logan, swiped sweat off his forehead, and slid a light-[**Enchanted**] ring on his finger.

It was an eerie sight.

The struggling brute was letting out panicked muffled groans, writhing underneath the armor. The glossy black outline of the muscular creature made it look like a marble statue.

I feel naked without the armor on.

The creature stopped struggling and went still.

*[Logan, this is amazing! I leveled! My [**Machine Soul**] is now Level 10. I have had a breakthrough!]*

"Uh, that's great, Tumor," Logan said, eyeing the black-clad monster. "Maybe we should talk about it later."

[But this feeling! It is . . . Fine. Slowly remove the arm. I want to see if I can maintain control.]

Logan did so, taking his sweet time, as if his forearm were glued to the creature's neck. He slowly exhaled and ripped off the bandage.

The creature immediately stirred, but Logan had the distant feeling that Tumor was clamping down on the creature, constricting it with the armor. The creature took a stumble forward and a clumsy swing at Logan, losing its balance and falling on its face.

Logan felt cold sweat on the back of his neck.

Just calm down. It's fine. Everything is fine. You were doing fine before, even without the armor.

Kat crouched down next to the creature, who had again stopped moving. "Tumor's got this?"

Logan shrugged.

"Damn," Balmer said, coming up close to Logan. "I forgot what a stick you are."

"Screw you," Logan said and ribbed him with an elbow. Like a cat, Balmer slid out of the way and grinned.

Kat scoffed. "Boys, focus."

They checked the other bodies, and indeed, there were several dimmed-out Numa crystals embedded in the corpses. One of the brutes had a few tattoos. They all shared a grim look. They definitely used to be human.

"Well, now we got one," Logan muttered. "We can figure this out."

"Maybe," Balmer muttered. "I hate the idea of bringing it back to our home."

Logan nodded. "I agree. But we can contain it somewhere outside and Freya, Dr. Steinberg, William, and I can try stuff on it. We need to learn more."

"Well at least we're going back home," Kat said, sighed and upended half of her waterskin in her fiery hair.

"Should we go?" Balmer asked. "Can Tumor move this thing?"

"Wait," Logan said and immediately got up and walked forward through the ruins. "There's a blue glow ahead."

"Logan!" both Balmer and Kat shouted at him.

Logan turned and raised a quizzical eyebrow.

They both nodded downward. Logan looked down in response.

"Oh . . . Yeah, maybe it's better if I don't go first here . . ."

He'd forgotten that he was currently wearing nothing but tattered underpants

"Maybe we shouldn't go at all," Balmer said. "If there's another set of four of them, it's going to be hard for just the two of us to fight them, not to mention having to protect our stick-leader."

Logan flipped him the bird.

"They would have heard us and come by now, if there were any" Kat said. Then added. "I think . . ."

"Just give a peek," Logan said. "Worst-case scenario, Tumor slips back on me."

"Eh, he's got a point," Kat said and turned. "I'll check it out."

Logan kept an eye on the still, armor-clad creature on the floor. Tumor was silent. Logan thought he could feel him being distracted, which considering his processing capability, was quite something.

"You okay?"

[This is difficult. I am constantly fighting to keep this creature contained. I have leveled up my Control and Potency. Our classes truly level up from experimentation, strain, and breakthrough.]

"That's sure something," Logan said. Tumor's stats were in the mid-forties, so it was extremely impressive that he had leveled up so much. "Can you move?"

[Working on it. My simulations indicate there is an 89.42% chance I will get this to work within a reasonable timeframe.]

"Logan!" Kat called from the other room. "It's safe. Come!"

"You'll definitely want to see this!" Balmer shouted.

CHAPTER 11

Logan's eyes went wide. They were standing in a treasure trove. Darkmetal pickaxes in neat rows under a crust of dust, as well as five-foot-tall sticks made of the same black, gleaming metal. Each was topped with a sharp blue Numa Crystal, each one now dim, drained of energy long ago. Logan wondered what the First Folk had needed them for.

But soon his attention was stolen by the crown jewel of this treasure trove—a veritable boulder of Numa, half-buried in the dirt, pulsing a strong blue glow.

"This is one of those we can use, right?" Kat said distractedly but with hunger evident in her voice.

"So much Numa . . ." Balmer said, with a palm on the crystal, feeling its warmth. "It's a B-grader, at 100 percent."

Logan came closer and verified the fact; it was a B-grader, after all, and it was beautiful.

"Kat," Logan said, "you should start using your abilities."

"I can't charge my internal Numa with this, can I?"

Logan shrugged. "I don't think so. I think that's just for the fruits."

"You can keep a hand on the crystal while you practice," Balmer said.

"Thank you Captain Obv—" Kat started, but the look on Balmer's face made her stop. She blushed. "I mean, thanks."

Balmer grunted at that. Logan gave them the side-eye, but it wasn't his business. He turned to pick up the darkmetal tools and was about to place them in his spatial storage when he realized something.

He wasn't wearing his armor.

How are you doing, Tumor?

[This creature is very angry. I can feel the muscles flexing. The amount of force it is able to generate is tremendous.]

Can you move?

[It would be easier if the captive were dead or incapacitated. I can suffocate him, but unless I restrict the access to oxygen continuously, it will only be effective for a minute or two.]

Logan crouched and inspected the darkmetal stick further. It was abnormally thin, so much so that it would be hard to hold as a spear. But it did look like a spear. "Do that and come here. You'll definitely like what you see."

[I must remind you, Logan, that I physically reside in your brain, and thus it is the nexus of my consciousness, despite my magical abilities. Therefore, I am always able to see with your eyes.]

"Can you say that in a tone that doesn't sound like you're addressing a particularly stupid five-year-old?" Logan muttered.

[I could. But that would rob it of all its fun.]

Logan scoffed. He took another glance at Kat. She was grinning, shouting "Power strike!" and punching and stomping the ground, which made the whole room reverberate; meanwhile a proper dent was forming in the rocky floor.

Balmer looked at her with conflicted emotions playing across his face.

"You okay, Felix?"

"It's weird when you call me that," Balmer said.

"Got a bit of class jealousy?" Logan asked, trying to engage his leader-brain rather than his . . . Logan-brain.

[I do wish you'd engage the Logan-brain less often.]

"Shut up," Logan muttered. Balmer raised an eyebrow at that, but he was used to Logan and his AI.

"You two laughing at me in your mind?" Balmer asked, jutting out his chin.

Don't go full Logan. Never go full Logan. Don't do it.

"You're making it hard not to," Logan said and almost immediately slapped his own face.

Balmer's face darkened. "Must be nice being you. Best class you can imagine. A powerful AI holding your hand."

"I'm trying to hold everyone's hand here," Logan shouted over Kat banging the floor with her fists and laughing.

"You wouldn't even be our leader if it weren't for those lucky advantages," Balmer shouted.

"Screw you! I didn't ask to lead anyone. I didn't want to either!"

"Easy to say now!" Balmer shouted, even though Kat had already stopped and had come up to investigate what their argument was about. "I bet you secretly like being the most important human."

Most valuable human . . .

Logan closed his eyes and exhaled. Slowly. Kat placed a hand on Logan's shoulder.

"I need a break," she said. "You take a turn on the crystal."

Logan gave her and Balmer a pensive look; the latter was breathing heavily and clearly ready to make a retort to anything Logan might have to say. He nodded to Kat. Balmer was about to say something, but Kat started pushing him.

"Hey!" Balmer protested. "What?"

"Idiot."

Logan breathed in and out once again and chuckled. The moment of anger had passed. He was really trying to become a better leader. Tumor was clanking toward them awkwardly, as if every movement of the armor was hampered by rust and fatigue.

[Well done for not going full Logan.]

Logan placed his hand on the blue Numa crystal. The familiar warmth made him realize he had missed this feeling. The exhilaration was running through his body like an electrical current. He was going to level up.

The first thing he did was gather the pile of pickaxe heads and spears next to him and charge them full of Numa. One way or another they would leave with the darkmetal items in tow.

[Skill Level Up!]
[Funnel Level 13]

After Kat having her way with the crystal and Logan charging the six darkmetal items next to him, he found the crystal was already mostly spent.

[B-grade Natural Numa Crystal, 36%]

Then Logan took one of the spears and **[Transmuted]** it into a pair of black handcuffs.

Kat, who was apparently done with Balmer, came up next to him. "Ooh, kinky. You think Freya will like those?"

Logan snorted. "Idiot. Next thing I'm making is a gag for you."

Kat's smirk spread into a full-blown grin.

"I—" she started.

Logan groaned. "Please don't finish that thought."

"Spoilsport."

"Pervert."

Balmer came up to them. He nodded to Logan. "Hey."

Logan nodded back. "Hey."

"Look, I just . . ." Balmer said. "Sorry."

"Yeah," Logan said. "It's fine."

Balmer shook his head. "You're really annoying sometimes."

"What the hell did I do?" Logan asked.

"It's like you don't even remember what an insufferable asshole you were just a few months back. Now you're acting all high and mighty, making me look bad."

Logan smirked. He didn't need to go full Logan, but he could sprinkle it in a little bit, right?

"You're making yourself look bad."

Balmer growled, but not in an entirely hostile manner.

Logan picked up the handcuffs and examined them. "If you're truly sorry, you can be my guinea pig."

Balmer swallowed. "Oh boy . . ."

When Logan was done with the spell in his head, he nodded. "Make these cuffs weaken the wearer by 90 percent. Make these cuffs make the wearer blind and deaf. Make these cuffs come off when I say '*Shazam.*'"

[Attribute Level Up!]
[Potency: 34]

The cuffs glowed blue and Logan felt the minty feeling rushing over him. It wasn't a large hit, with only an attribute level-up, but Logan grinned nonetheless. Then he clipped the cuffs on Balmer, who immediately stooped forward from his crouch and fell.

"I can't see," he said and moved slowly on the ground.

"That's the point," Logan said, tapping his chin with a finger. "Shazam."

The cuffs clanked on the floor, and Balmer blinked and flexed his hands. "That was nasty."

"Not as nasty as his poison swamp," Kat muttered, eyeing the cuffs with trepidation.

"Tumor, what do you think?"

[You will need to adjust the strength reduction to 78.2%, or the captive will not be able to walk with its substantial muscle mass. Other than that, I think it's a good idea.]

Logan adjusted the spell and then came up to the still, monstrous form clad in his armor. The armor receded from the hands, which immediately started flexing and attempting to claw at anything nearby. Logan made sure to not get caught by the fingers opening and closing violently, just managing to clip the cuffs on their new friend.

Then the armor started sliding back on Logan. He had to admit that it was a relief feeling its protection on him again. Walking around without it felt so *unsafe*. He looked at Kat and Balmer as the liquid black metal covered his arms and shoulders. He felt a sudden surge of appreciation toward them both. They were putting their lives on the line for this.

I should really make an effort to poke less fun at Balmer.

When Tumor had fully covered Logan with the armor, all three of them watched their blue-veined captive closely. It immediately started swinging around with its cuffed hands as it growled violently. Logan picked up one of the spears and shoved the blind brute. It toppled over and struggled like a toddler to get up.

"So," Logan said giving his companions a winning smile, "which one of you would like to hold the leash?"

Kat and Balmer looked at each other and grimaced.

CHAPTER 12

Something was wrong, Rachel could feel it. She had had a weird cough lately, the same kind she had heard others in the village sporting in recent days. Hers wasn't that bad, though. At least not yet.

Rachel had tried to go see Mr. Specter about it, but the guards had stopped her. She hadn't seen him in a couple of days. She had asked the guards to just relay a message, but they had declined. They had the cough too.

Something was very, very wrong.

Surely it couldn't be the medicine.

Rachel walked back toward the hut where her brother was, as she tried to make sense of the situation. The leather slabs that she had for shoes made the skin between her toes itchy. In fact, she had been itchier all over lately.

Surely it's not the medicine. The medicine was Mr. Specter's own idea.

Rachel's heart ached. Malcolm had been inviting her into his tent lately for just the two of them to talk and spend time together. He was such a gentleman. Even though there was something weird going on here, Rachel missed Malcolm. She missed his calm smile and those blue eyes that seemed to know everything. They all needed a strong man like him right now.

"So, where the hell is he?" Rachel muttered and kicked a rock. Then, she turned to pick it up. Someone must have dropped it. Rocks were rare and valuable when you lived in clay-based soil. Malcolm had taught her that.

After she took the rock and put it on one of the workbenches, where Lester, an elderly man of dark, tan skin, was resting his head, she went back inside her hut.

Her brother lay on the floor. Eyes closed, skin clammy, labored breath. It was not looking good. He had a cough too. Much worse than hers. It would wrack his whole body and wake him up. He would quickly fall back asleep, though. He hadn't been lucid for days.

Rachel grabbed a rag and one of the clay pots filled with water and dabbed it in the water before wiping her brother's sweaty body with it.

He moaned in his stupor and coughed softly.

Rachel sighed. This wasn't how it was supposed to be. Was she making the medicine wrong?

She was following Malcolm's instructions like it was law. But she was a young, stupid, careless girl sometimes. And her brother's condition was getting worse and worse.

"Those veins . . ." Rachel murmured.

The veins in her brother's neck were a prominent blue. They seemed to be pulsing. Surely not. He was just swallowing. No . . . They *were* pulsing. What did it mean? High blood pressure?

After she was done washing him with a rag, she used it on herself to wipe away the sweat and grime. It had been a long and hot day, as every day was.

But there was work to do. The medicine needed to be administered daily to everyone. It was the only way to keep the vicious jungle flu away. That is what Malcolm Specter said.

Rachel threw an instinctive glance in the direction of Malcolm's tent. Was he there? Where else would he be? Was he with someone? Another woman?

Foolish girl.

But he clearly was interested. She had spent enough time with boys and men to know that Malcolm had flirted with her. It had been subtle, but it had been there.

Rachel clutched her chest. Maybe he wanted her, or maybe he was just entertaining her crush. Either way, the thought was distracting.

Rachel got to the little table at the wall of the hut and brought up the mortar and pestle and then the sack of Numa stones. They glowed soft blue, with hues of darker blue and almost-black spider webbing embedded subtly in the structure. She put it in the mortar and started crushing it.

The fever was apparently magical, so the only way to fight against it was magic. And not everyone was attuned to magic. Rachel was one of the few.

"Hello, Rachel," a deep, calm voice said from behind her. She turned and there he was. Haggard like the rest of them but with an undeniable grace. His salt and pepper hair was stylishly disheveled, and his stern gaze locked on her. She swallowed nervously but managed a smile.

"Hey," she said softly.

Malcolm stepped into the hut, his presence seeming to fill the small space with overwhelming density. Despite the weariness etched into his features, he was strong, with an aura of command that drew Rachel's eyes to his like a magnet.

"I apologize for my absence," he said, his voice a low rumble. He cast a glance at her that was almost soft. It took her breath away. "There have been . . . complications that required my attention."

Rachel's heart hammered in her chest as a surge of emotion washed over her. It was a mixture of relief and trepidation.

"Is everything alright?" she asked, setting down the pestle. "The jungle flu, it's getting worse. I've been making the medicine, but . . ."

She trailed off, hands falling to the side, her eyes darting to her brother's still form. Malcolm followed her gaze but his stern face betrayed no emotion.

He is so strong.

"You've done well, Rachel," he said, placing a hand on her shoulder. The touch sent a shiver down her spine, a jolt of electricity that made her stand up straighter. "You've been good. You are one of my most loyal followers.

Rachel nodded mutely.

He moved to her brother's side, kneeling down to examine him. His hands, long-fingered and elegant, moved over the boy's skin, tracing the lines of his veins.

"You are right," Malcolm Specter said as he felt the boy's pulse. "It is getting worse."

Rachel's heart sank, despair welling up within her. "Then what can we do?" she whispered, her voice cracking. "I can't lose him, Mr. Specter— Malcolm. I can't."

Malcolm stood, turning to face her. His eyes, those piercing blue eyes, seemed to see straight into her soul. He nodded solemnly, as if it were his own brother on his deathbed. Rachel sighed and relief washed over her. Tension left her shoulders. Now that Malcolm was here, everything was going to be all right.

"I think I have a solution." Malcolm Specter's voice had an uncertain edge to it, strange for him. "But it is risky."

As if on cue, her brother sat up violently in the throes of a coughing fit. His tongue lolled and he went limp as soon as Rachel rushed to hold him. The cough was horrid; there was a hint of blood mixed in the drool that fell on the floor. Rachel burst into tears.

"He's going to die!" she cried.

Malcolm watched and nodded to himself. He stifled a bit of a cough with his fist before his face.

Oh no, does he have it too?

"Rachel," Malcolm spoke softly, almost hesitantly. "Would you be willing to take the risk? You are the one mixing the medicine. I have to make sure you are sure."

"If it helps save him, I'll do what you tell me to," Rachel said between sobs. There was an odd, cold glint in Malcolm's eyes. The crying turned into a fit of coughs. She looked again and saw nothing but concern in his blue eyes.

I'm losing my mind. I can't . . . Help me, Malcolm.

Malcolm nodded, his expression grave. He spoke hastily in a strange cadence—almost feverish. "It is the only way," he said and looked at Rachel, eyes wider than usual. "The sickness is too strong, too deeply rooted. We must act soon. And feed . . ."

Rachel barely listened. She just looked at the bloodied drool dripping down from her brother's chin. He looked so pale and weak. The coughing fit was over, but his chest rose and fell in a labored manner. And those veins . . .

Rachel's mind raced, desperation clawing at her heart. She would do anything, anything at all to save her brother, to stop this slowly creeping nightmare. If her brother was coughing up blood, it was only a matter of time until . . .

"What do I need to do?" she asked, her voice a hoarse, raw whisper.

Malcolm's gaze locked with hers, intense and unwavering. It had an uncanny, dark depth to it that Rachel hadn't seen before. Perhaps he had been pushed to his limit too, trying to take care of so many sick people.

"We must increase the potency of the medicine," he said, his words measured and deliberate. "The Numa stones alone are not enough. We need something different . . ."

Rachel nodded, hanging on to his every word. Malcolm knew what to do, he always did. He had been here for months, and he knew secrets that could keep them alive. He was their beacon of light in this wretched dark jungle.

"Tell me," she pleaded, finding herself dropping and slumping at his feet.

Malcolm hesitated, just for a moment, something flickering in the depths of his eyes. That same darkness. What was it? Fear? Doubt? Rachel couldn't tell, and in an instant, it was gone, replaced by the steely resolve she had come to rely on.

"Blood," he said, the word hanging heavy in the air between them. "The blood of the living, freely given, by everyone in this village. It shall mingle and be combined with the Numa stones. It will create a powerful medicine."

Rachel's breath caught in her throat, a chill running down her spine despite the oppressive heat. *Blood magic.*

Rachel had never been big on fantasy shows and movies, but wasn't blood magic always kind of . . . evil? Then again, rituals and sacrifices existed throughout human history. Some of it seemingly harmless, like using your own blood to draw ritual circles and pray. Or self-flagellation. *Okay, those are both kind of creepy. But creepy doesn't mean evil.*

Rachel shook her head. She needed to focus. But her mind was so muddled by grief and fear.

She swallowed hard, her mouth dry as parchment. "How much blood?" she asked, her voice a trembling whisper. She feared to know the answer. Surely Malcolm Specter wouldn't resort to human sacrifice?

"Not much," Malcolm assured her, his hand coming to rest on her shoulder once more, a comforting weight. "A few drops from each villager, mixed into the medicine. You will make it in that big cauldron, and make sure that every villager will give a few drops. It is important that all participate. A few drops from an extended finger each."

Rachel let out something between a sob and a laugh. "A few drops?"

"That is all that is needed," Malcolm assured her, squeezing her shoulder.

"I'll gather the villagers," she said, rising to her feet, gently laying her brother back down on his mat. "We'll do it tonight, under the full moon."

Malcolm smiled, a sight that still sent Rachel's heart fluttering despite everything. "Good girl," he murmured, his fingers brushing her cheek in a fleeting caress. Without thinking, Rachel leaned into it. "I knew I could count on you."

With that, he turned and strode out of the hut, his steps purposeful and sure. Rachel watched him go, a tangle of emotions bundled up in her chest. She tried to make sense of it. She was tired, that was for sure. And scared. Who wouldn't be in a crazy magic jungle land? And sad, sad for her brother. And hopeful, yes. Malcolm Specter gave her hope. But there was something else. A new feeling. A twisting in her gut.

Dread.

She shook her head, banishing the thoughts. There was no time for such foolishness, not now. She had work to do.

CHAPTER 13

They left after they had drained the crystal. The tally was good. Kat had leveled up her [**Striking**] subclass to 24, as well as her [**Power Strike**] to Level 8 and [**Tough Skin**] to Level 6. She also got two increases in her Power attribute, bringing it up to 26. All in all, excellent progress. Balmer tried his best grimace of a smile when she excitedly recounted her progress.

Logan's progression wasn't quite as significant. He was higher level than Kat, but finding the crystal and spending a little less than half of it had still been a boon. Potency to 35, Control to 36. Not to mention two levels in [**Funnel**] and a level in both [**Transmutation**] and [**Enchantment**]. Logan brought up his stat sheet.

Logan Specter - [Artificer Level 7]
Attributes:
Potency: 35
Efficiency: 35
Durability: 25
Control: 36
Focus: 32
Subclasses:
[Transmutation]: 31
[Enchantment]: 32
Class Skills:
[Empower]: 10
[Funnel]: 13
[Repair]: 11

General Skills:
[Power Armor Fighting]: 13

Looking at it made him proud. He had come a long way. Not only as a leader and as a person, but also as, well, an **[Artificer]**. It felt good to provide service to the people he was taking care of.

Then Logan knelt down on the floor, while Kat held up a light behind him. He scooped up all the darkmetal items in the temporal space that was a part of his armor. According to Tumor, there were three and a half pounds of the material there. It all gleamed as if it had been oiled yesterday—not a speck of dust on them.

"We can finally make Numa batteries for the village to use," Logan said. Their blue-veined captive growled and snapped at them, but having lost most of its strength, it was more bark than bite and they all knew it.

[Have you considered my request?]

"Oh . . ." Logan said, as they turned and started to make their way out of the ruins, with Kat moving in front of him, holding their captive with a neck collar connected to a shaft of darkmetal. Balmer called it a "rigid collar." Balmer himself was scouting ahead in the darkness, twenty yards ahead or so.

[I understand that my request is selfish and perhaps even vainglorious.]

"It's not that . . ." Logan said and lowered his hands to his sides. At his hips, pockets in the armor formed for Logan to put his hands into. "I wish we had more of this material."

[Perhaps we could strike two birds with one stone.]

"I'm listening."

"What are you talking about?" Kat asked over her shoulder.

"Tumor's body," Logan said.

"Oh, right," Kat said, a clear undertone of disappointment in her voice.

"What's wrong, Kat?" Logan asked.

"Forget it."

"Spill it."

She let out an awkward chuckle. "Heh. Well, I was hoping I could get a suit like yours."

[Tell her that while it is theoretically possible for us, provided we have enough material, at this moment I am too low level in my class to provide such a service as to control two armors. It is likely I could expand my capabilities at a future date, provided that you two are in close proximity when using your respective armor.]

"He says he can't do it for now," Logan said.

[That's not what I said!]

Logan smirked. "Sometimes things get lost in translation."

Logan ignored Tumor's indignant protestations and turned his attention back to Kat.

"Yeah, makes sense," she said. "With the way you move and fight, I assume Tumor has his hands full."

"Uh huh," Logan said.

Kat scoffed. "Don't be a baby. You don't have a fighting class. Anyway, I would just want to see what I could do with a suit like that, considering . . ."

"Considering that you're better than me?"

Kat turned her head to smirk over her shoulder. "At anything and everything."

"I'd love to enchant you some boots."

"I imagine I would look great in them," Kat said and pushed their reluctant captive forward.

"Combat boots," Logan said. "For improved mobility and explosive power."

"Well, it's your darkmetal," Kat said.

Logan shook his head. "It's ours. But for some reason, I have to decide."

"Oh no," Kat said in mock pain. "Woe is you."

"Screw you," Logan said. "I can't please all of you."

"I never took you for a people pleaser."

"I'm not. But you all want a piece of me. It's distracting. You all deserve more than I can give, but at the same time, I have to try to make the most utilitarian choice. It's a fucked-up place to be."

Kat was silent for a while. "Lonely at the top, huh?"

Logan shrugged. "Eh, I've got you to nag at me. And Balmer, when he finds his rocks. And Tumor, of course. Thank goodness for Frey. She keeps me sane."

"You two are good together," Kat said.

"Yeah," Logan said. "So are you and—"

Like a blurred shadow, Balmer zipped back to them, pushed them against the wall, and clamped his hands to their mouths. Their captive growled and looked at them with pure wrath.

"There are Dorves ahead," Balmer whispered and slowly released his cupped hands. "Four or five of them."

"You should wash your hands," Logan muttered. Balmer just gave him a sharp look. Logan nodded. Fair enough, this wasn't a time for quips.

"How do you want to proceed?"

"How far away are they?" Logan asked. "Are they coming this way?"

Balmer crouched, and Logan and Kat followed. That also made their captive bend, which elicited another growl. All of their eyes went wide, and they listened silently for a while. Having not heard any approaching Dorves, Balmer continued.

"They're fifty yards ahead. Taking a break at an intersection."

"So there's a 50 percent chance they're coming here," Logan muttered.

"Not twenty-five?" Kat asked.

Balmer looked at her as if she were trying to convince them that the Earth was flat.

"What?"

"They came from one direction," Balmer explained carefully as if to a child. "And the direction they're likely to go isn't to the right of the intersection where you go to get above ground."

"You don't know that," Kat said defensively. "Maybe they're going for a picnic."

"Yeah, sure," Balmer said. "But it's still not 25 percent. It's 33 percent, and I don't think that's a chance we want to take either way."

"What you lack in fighting, you make up in tactical analysis," Kat said and gave him a smirk.

Balmer scoffed.

"It was a compliment, idiot."

"Were they warriors?" Logan cut in.

Balmer nodded.

"Damn it," Logan muttered.

Killing Levespawn was well and good, as long as you weren't stupid about it. Because at the end of the day, they were just beasts. Fighting trained warriors, who had probably had their class for years, however? That wouldn't end well for them. The Dorves would be stronger, faster, and more skilled.

[Your suit does grant you superior capabilities. You might be able to escape. Felix Balmer will also have a reasonable chance of escaping.]

"We're not leaving her here," Logan said.

"Wait, are you guys talking about me?" Kat whispered. "I'm the weakest link?"

Balmer shrugged. "In this scenario."

Kat drew in a breath, and Balmer jumped in to place a hand on her mouth. Logan and Balmer both brought a finger over their own mouths and gave her ugly looks. She relented, shoulders sagging.

"Let's go back," Logan whispered. "We'll hide in some alcove and wait for them to pass us if they come this way."

Kat and Balmer nodded, and they got up slowly. Kat was especially careful, and their captive only let out a single displeased grunt.

Suddenly they heard the sound of metal on stone. Two cylinders bounced at them from the corridor and a plume of white gas filled the room. Logan had taken in half a breath before he noticed. Big mistake.

His eyes, nose, and lungs started to burn, and soon he found himself spitting, sniffing and coughing on the ground.

Tear gas!

Between his coughing fits, he heard steps approaching.

"Well, well," a muffled voice dripping with smugness said. "What do we have here?"

CHAPTER 14

R aarh!"

Logan heard Kat take a blind swing, but she clearly hit nothing. There was a *whoosh!*, an *oof!*, and Kat collapsed to the ground. The Dorves chuckled in their muffled voices. They must have been wearing masks.

"We thought we heard somethin'," said the same voice that had spoken before. "Didn't think it'd be you folk."

"Look at this, Balmir," another voice said. "They captured one of them."

"Brave fighters, these," a third voice said, low and rumbling.

"Or lucky ones," the first one said and grunted.

Tumor, can you see or sense anything?

[I don't have that kind of magic. My senses are limited to what you are sensing and the sensory input of the armor.]

The pain in his eyes and lungs was intense. Logan hacked up a glob of something sticky and spat it out.

"How do you like the invention of our **[Engineers]**, humans?"

"It's great," Logan said and spat again.

"Wait," the first voice said. There was some shuffling, and suddenly his voice was clear. It was masculine, but it had a lilt to it. "See this, fellas. Look at what this kid is wearing."

"Is that . . . ?"

"There is no way. So much of it."

"Kid," the first Dorf said, "remove that armor."

"I can't," Logan said. Technically not a lie, since Tumor was the one controlling it.

The blue-veined creature growled and apparently tried to take a swipe. It was kicked down. Logan tried to open his eyes, but it still stung too much.

"Why is this one so weak?" the lilting voice asked.

"We poisoned it," Logan said immediately, before his companions could answer.

"Look, Balmir," the low rumbling voice said. He had also removed his mask. "These handcuffs and the collar. They're also . . ."

"Remove them," Balmir, the lilting one, said.

There was some shuffling and grunting and snapping from the blue-veined creature, but eventually the leash Kat had used clattered to the ground. A lightbulb sparked in Logan's head.

Tumor.

[I am listening.]

Can you use sound to navigate?

[Oh, what a novel idea! Certainly a skill that humans can learn . . . Which means your senses are compatible. Let me just run some programs . . .]

Logan had once seen a blind person ride a bicycle, navigating by making strange clicking noises with her mouth. The human ability to adapt was remarkable. Logan had no training in anything like that specifically, but he did have a really powerful AI . . .

[I can do it. But you will have to constantly ululate.]

Damn, if we make it out of this mess, this is going to be one hell of a story.

[It will only be so effective. There is a 73.07% chance that they will simply capture us again.]

I have a plan.

"I can't remove the handcuffs," the rumbling one said.

"I can do it!" Logan said quickly, before any of the Dorves got a notion of cutting off the creature's hands.

"You have a key?" Balmir asked. "Search him, Sulfir."

"No key," Logan said and stifled a cough. "I got a class."

"Hmph," Balmir said and suddenly Logan felt a cold steel blade on his neck. "What's your class?"

"**[Metallurgist]**," Logan said. "I can manipulate metal."

This clearly impressed the Dorves and they quickly exchanged whispers.

"You got a lucky class, boy," Balmir said. "Is this a class with Numa affinity?"

"No," Logan said to avoid any suspicion.

"I never heard of a class like that," Sulfir, the rumbly one said. "You think he's lying?"

"If you lie, kid . . ." Balmir said, slowly sliding the blade on his neck. Logan gasped when it cut the skin and a warm trickle of blood started running down to his chest. ". . . I will do bad things to you. But if you truly have this class, I might be able to use you."

Yeah, right . . .

Logan scrambled forward, guided by Balmir's blade. He was starting to regain some of his vision, but everything was still a blurry, aching mess. Maybe Tumor could make some sense of it.

"You okay, Kat? Balmer?"

"Yeah," Kat said somewhere to his right.

"Damn, it stings," Balmer said from his left. He had to be on his knees.

Okay, good, they're close. We need to grab them.

[That goes without saying.]

Logan patted around until he found bulging muscle. The blue-veined giant was cold as ice. It growled and shuffled, trying to bite Logan, who flinched in response.

Under his breath, in the faintest voice he could muster, Logan uttered a magic word:

"**[Funnel]**."

"Hm?" Sulfir said next to him.

Logan could feel the Numa that was stored in the armor stream into this aggressively grunting creature in front of him. This was extremely risky, but it was the only way he could think of that could buy them time. A group of seasoned warriors would kill a regular one of these bastard brutes in seconds. But a powered-up one . . .

"Hey, kid," Balmir said. "What are you doing?"

When a third of the Armor's rather-substantial Numa reserves were transferred, Logan took a leap of faith.

"Shazam!"

CHAPTER 15

I have to move fast.

"Remember to ululate constantly, Logan."

He starts doing it immediately. I don't need the input that soon, but it helps Logan. I take over the armor. Normally I let Logan guide it and I only shift it accordingly. Now, I stiffen it and run a current of Numa through it, taking control.

I duck and start picking up the cuffs and the collar-stick. Logan's muscles and joints can't keep up. I have to slow down. If I could sigh, I would. What fragile things, these human bodies. This is why I need a body of my own. Preferably made of this metal. The first vowels of his ululations are coming out. By the third "U," Logan gasps in pain from the strain I have put on his body with my speed. But it is necessary.

As all of my simulations predicted with a 97.85 percent accuracy, the blue brute takes a swing at Logan with its right hand. This is why I ducked. My predictive models tell me I have to kick at the Dorf named Sulfir next to me. It will generate strain on Logan's hamstring and hip flexors, but it is necessary. It also has to be fast, or there is a high probability the other two Dorves will be able to act.

One point twenty-two seconds have passed.

Using the motion of my kick, I spin and slam the collar-stick in the direction where Balmir should be. He is. Luck is on our side. He manages to slide away and avoid critical damage, but the strike is true and he shouts in pain and anger. I duck again, as my predictions have shown, the creature is still on me.

I grab Kat and generate the portal for the temporal space. I shove Kat and the darksteel materials in there.

I generate a big tower shield with my right hand to absorb a strike from the brute. I do not have accurate predictions as to what sorts of attack patterns it *will use, so I just generate one big enough to cover us completely. It tries to ram through. I instantly morph part of the armor into springy, elastic material. It absorbs the kinetic energy and pushes the beast back.*

[Subclass Level Up!]
[Manipulation Level 38]
[Attribute Level Up!]
[Speed: 41]

Three point forty-two seconds have passed.

The third Dorf strikes me with a mace, but the armor hardens when I notice the impact. Since I only have a tactile reaction at my disposal, it will create a nasty bruise.

I feel another impact on my side. This is softer.

[Here.]

That's Felix Balmer's voice. He has a quick mind. I toss him into the temporal space and close it. Now that it is closed, we are on a limited timer. We have tested the capabilities of the storage dimension. One can put live material such as plants, animals, and humans in there. But there is no oxygen. There was no warning, especially for Kat. I estimate I have 128 seconds before it is crucial to take Logan's companions out of the storage.

[Attribute Level Up!]
[Control: 47]

Seven point twelve seconds have passed.

I have secured all the important material. I roll to dodge any possible attack as I have deposited Balmer. The edge of a sword nicks the heel of the armor. No damage to it or Logan. I turn to my attacker, which is likely Balmir. I extend my arm and shoot a volley of the kinetic bullets. Only eight, a quick burst. Two of the Dorves and the brute are struck. I can feel it through the bullets.

[Subclass Level Up!]
[Adaptive Fusion level 31]

Eight point two seconds have passed.

I sprint forward full speed, feeling the stone under the armor's heel give. It cracks loudly as I push forward. The brute tries to come at me, but I have too much momentum, and I push it down. There is a 63.22 percent probability that either the Dorves will attack it, or the brute will switch targets and attack the Dorves.

I can feel the bullets rejoin the armor as I speed through the corridor. It puts more strain on Logan's tendons and muscles, but it is the only way to proceed. He groans and flinches within the armor but does not tell me to slow down.

He keeps ululating; that is good. Combined with the input of the sound waves and my memory of Logan having traversed this part of the ruins earlier, I have an easy time navigating. Once his vision unblurs enough, I tell him to stop. He is grateful for it. His thoughts are somewhere along the lines of him being happy about his friends being in the pocket dimension so they can't hear him. It's more nuanced and complex than that, as his thoughts and emotions often are, but I have no interest in prying this time.

I try to give him his privacy these days, unless the thoughts are strategically significant. Or about me. I am curious after all. Oh, what fun being a person is.

There is light at the end of the tunnel. This is not a metaphor. With the speed required to escape and the route being clear, it did not take more than 68.52 seconds for us to get out. Logan's body is bruised, with some bone fractures and tears in tendons and skeletal musculature. The village's healer will be able to fix all but the bone damage. He is still too low-level for that.

I make Logan and the armor sprint further toward the village. I have no data to make estimations on how far behind us the Dorves are. I decide to make the most of the time. The soft grassy ground gives under every leap. I increase Numa expenditure by 8.25 percent.

[Attribute Level Up!]
[Capacity: 39]

Eighty three point nineteen seconds have passed. I open the spatial storage and pull Kat and Balmer out. They are on their hands and knees in the grass, gasping for breath. I relinquish my control back to Logan. He winces through the pain and thanks me. I hope I will get to do that again. Having a body, even temporarily, was great fun.

CHAPTER 16

Logan didn't remember when his body had been this beaten up. According to Tumor, he had damaged tendons on his heel, hamstring, and hip, as well as two broken ribs and fractures on his shoulder, wrist, and ankle. Not to mention all the damage to his muscles.

Small price to pay for being alive.

Kat and Balmer had carried him back home. Now Logan was lying on a blanket on the ground and waiting for their **[Healer]**. Dr. Rosenberg was making his way toward him, holding a bar of darkmetal in one hand, a quiet, impassive look on his face.

The healing made Logan feel a little better. Dr. Rosenberg muttered about having leveled his subclass **[Restoration]** to 20. Logan and the others around him congratulated him, but he just waved a hand, trying to maintain professional aloofness. But Logan smirked when he saw the faintest blush around the man's ears.

Freya brought him some food along with an excited William, a sandy-haired man in his thirties with the **[Alchemist]** class.

Logan didn't expect Freya to be back already from the Faelves, but before Logan could ask why she looked so somber, William shoved a clay cup in Logan's hand.

"Drink this!" the man said and grinned.

Logan looked at the small cup in his hand. There was an orange, viscous liquid that smelled like burnt sugar within it. Logan was about to dip a finger into the concoction and taste it.

"I wouldn't," William said, and his smile turned apologetic. "Better if you just swallow it down, trust me."

"What is it?" Logan asked.

"Ahhah!" William said and stood up straight. "An excellent question. This is my newest creation, which I discovered after I leveled up to 4 in my **[Alchemist]** class and received my newest talent, **[Intuitive Experimentation]**."

Dr. Rosenberg gave his younger associate a cool glance before going off, muttering to himself. If William noticed, he pretended not to.

"It gave me the ability to just *know* which ingredients go well together. There is this plant I've taken a . . . liking to. I call it 'glintroot.' I mix it with the juice of those purple citrus fruits and—"

Logan didn't say anything, but his pained smile must have made William come back to reality. He chuckled awkwardly and rubbed the back of his neck. "Anyway. It tastes like gasoline, but it will give you a good boost. Heal your body, give you energy, all that good stuff."

"That should help with the bones, then?" Balmer asked and looked suspiciously at the cup in Logan's hand. Logan lifted it up so Balmer could take a sniff. He recoiled like an affronted cat.

"Exactly!" William said. "I think it should complement Dr. Rosenberg's skills well . . ."

"Oh," Logan said and swirled the thick liquid in his cup. "That's why he was looking glum."

William's smile waned. "We are . . . working on finding a mutual understanding."

"Let me know if you need any help with that," Logan said and gulped down the orange sludge. It tasted like cheap tequila mixed with paint thinner.

He grimaced but a fuzzy warmth started spreading from his chest to his limbs. His throat burned, but other than that, the medicine seemed to have a benign effect on his body.

"So?" William asked.

Logan swallowed. "If you can fix the taste, you've got a real market winner here."

William took the cup back and gave him a winning smile. Logan chuckled and thanked him. Freya gave William a strained smile, as if asking him to go away already. Their **[Alchemist]** sobered up and nodded.

Eyebrows raised, Logan turned to Freya.

"What is it?" Logan asked. "I didn't expect you back so soon. We weren't out for more than two days. Three, tops."

"That's the thing," Freya said. She sighed, her beautiful sapphire eyes full of worry. "The Faelves weren't there."

"What?"

Logan tried getting up, but the pain from his ribs forced him back.

"I went with Jefferson, Fields, and Chesterton. They were just going to drop me off and go hunt for game," Freya said and distractedly tucked a hair behind her ear. "I thought I felt something was off as soon as we got to the swamp, but I didn't make much of it."

Logan nodded and Freya continued.

"But when nobody came to us when we entered the grove, I knew something was wrong. And then I spotted the damage . . ."

Freya was holding back tears. Logan ignored his own pain, took her in his arms, and ran a soothing hand through her honey-golden hair.

"Something attacked them," Freya said. "They felled so many Numa fruit trees. Broken branches lay on the ground, our saplings uprooted . . ."

"Any bodies?" Logan asked.

Freya shook his head and grabbed a handful of Logan's armor. It turned soft and porous like tissue, and Freya wiped her eyes on it.

Good one, Tumor.

"Just don't blow your nose on it," Logan said, which elicited a sad chuckle out of Freya.

"I didn't see any bodies, but that doesn't mean they aren't in trouble."

"True," Logan said. "Do you think they were captured, or did they escape?"

Freya shrugged and clutched a strip of Logan's soft metal armor like a tie on his neck. Logan squeezed her shoulder.

"I'll go check it out," Logan said. "Tumor can probably play detective better than you or I."

Logan made a motion to get up as if he needed to go now, but he winced at the pain flashing through his ribs. Freya's somber face took on a flush of determination, and she pushed him down.

"You're not going anywhere," she said. "You're hurt and you made a promise."

"Frey, I—"

She flashed her eyes at him.

[I think that means you need to "pipe down."]

"Thanks, Tumor," Logan muttered.

"What did Tumor say?" Freya asked.

"Agreed with you."

Freya smiled. "Good thing someone can get through your thick skull."

"It's easier when you can access the mush directly," Logan said.

"Look, my little mush," Freya said, "I'm as worried about the Faelves as you are, but you seriously need to rest."

Logan sighed. "You're right. But the trail might get cold. We need to get on top of this."

"It's as cold as it's going to get, Logan," Freya said. "It had been deserted for hours or days when I got there."

"Maybe we could send men there to investigate. The agents are pretty sharp."

Freya raised an eyebrow. "Imagine hearing you saying something positive about them."

"Hey, now," Logan said, "I'm not that guy anymore."

"You are," Freya said and kissed his cheek. "Just an improved, more refined version."

"I'll take that," Logan said and kissed her back. "So our fancy-shmancy A-grade Numa fruit saplings are gone too?"

Freya chuckled. "That's the one good thing about this whole thing. I brought them with me. They're ours now."

"Huh?"

Freya smiled sheepishly. "Well, I had to. The Faelves kept gushing about how awesome they were, and since they might be done for, I figured . . . Well, I [**Blessed**] and [**Purified**] them and had them carried in pots from the Faelves. Now I've been making sure the earth they're in is good. But with my skills, the [**Farmer's**] skills, and even Simmons's skills in his [**Arborist**] class, it's all helped them tremendously. There are even flowers on the bigger one. I think that's yours."

"Oh, that's amazing," Logan said.

Freya nodded. "It's good. Now we will have a steady supply of Numa fruit."

[We should go to the Faelves' former dwellings and acquire all the useful tools and items that we need.]

"Tumor . . ."

"What is it?" Freya asked.

"Tumor wants us to loot the Faelves."

"Tell Tumor, that's tactless."

[Tell Freya that she should encourage you to build me a body, so I can interface with her directly.]

"You know what, Tumor?" Logan said and gently untangled himself from Freya. "We'll do that next."

CHAPTER 17

As the sun began its descent, painting the sky in hues of blood and fire, Rachel moved through the village, gathering the sick and the weary, the young and the old. They came willingly, drawn by the promise of a cure. They were all so tired.

I'm tired too. Please let it work.

In the center of the village, a great cauldron had been set up. It was made from a strange black metal that didn't seem to be iron. It was their only piece of advanced technology. Rachel didn't know how they had gotten it. Probably through Malcolm's leadership.

Focus.

Rachel stood beside the cauldron, her heart hammering in her chest, her hands clenched at her sides.

She had done as Malcolm had instructed, gathering the ingredients for the medicine. The herbs and roots, the strange, pungent powders, and the Numa stones.

They were brought to her by one of the fighters, a burly man with a grim set to his jaw. When he nodded, Rachel could tell he was nervous too. He had carried them in a large sack, the fabric straining under the weight of the stones within. Once he dropped it and shuffled away, Rachel saw him get a cough fit.

But when he had upended the sack into the cauldron, Rachel had felt a chill run through her. The stones that tumbled forth were not the soft, glowing blue she was used to. They were dark, almost black, with only the faintest hint of blue running through them like veins.

"What . . . what are these?" she asked, her voice trembling.

The fighter wiped his mouth and turned to look at her with dull eyes. "Numa stones," he grunted. "Just like Mr. Specter said."

Rachel wanted to protest, to demand an explanation. But the villagers were gathering, their faces drawn and haggard. Some were coughing and rubbing their itches. All of them looked tired, wary, and hopeful at the same time.

Rachel was worried about the strange Numa stones, but they were already in the cauldron. She had to do this. She couldn't let her brother down. Malcolm Specter was nowhere to be seen.

Maybe I should go ask him what this was?

But that idea felt wrong somehow. Intrusive. Rachel felt like she should respect Mr. Specter's privacy. She had a job to do anyway, and complaining wasn't a part of it.

So she picked up a ladle and started stirring the concoction. Strange blue fumes rose from it, which made Rachel slightly dizzy, but they smelled nice, if a bit like gasoline on a hot day.

With trembling hands, she added the powder to the cauldron, along with the other ingredients for the medicine. The mixture bubbled and hissed, releasing more of the vapor. It made her feel good.

Then the fighters started organizing people in a line. One by one, the villagers stepped forward, extending their hands over the cauldron, pricking themselves with a stone knife handed to them by Rachel. Some of the children were scared and Rachel had to do the cut for them. They gasped and tried to put on a brave face.

With each drop, the liquid in the cauldron seemed to grow darker and more turbulent. The vapors turned a darker shade, and the scent became sickly sweet. Rachel felt good.

The vapors started spreading out as the cauldron bubbled and boiled. Soon a thick miasma enveloped the square. The fighters started guiding people closer around the cauldron, as they apparently had been instructed.

Rachel looked for Malcolm Specter with half-lidded eyes. She was starting to feel something strange in her throat, a constriction. But she wasn't coughing anymore.

Then Rachel felt weak in the knees. She noticed the children starting to fall on the ground and began to convulse.

Rachel's mind was flooded with panic.

It started slowly, a twitching in the fingers, a spasm in the limbs. But soon, it grew, spreading like a fire through her whole body.

Rachel fell to the ground herself. She was starting to grow numb. She looked at her hands. The skin was bubbling softly and the veins in her hands started to turn a glowing blue.

She hugged herself to stop the convulsions and to quiet the fear. She rested on the grass.

The villagers were on the ground all around her, convulsing, the blue spreading through their veins like venom. The children were turning completely blue.

No!

Then the real change began. People's eyes turned bright blue. An inhuman blue. There was a feral look in them. And their mouths . . . their mouths stretched and split, revealing jagged, razor-sharp teeth.

Rachel watched in horror as the villagers, her friends, her family, transformed before her eyes. They became twisted, wrong, their humanity sloughing away like dead skin.

And she could feel it happening to her too. The smoke filled her lungs, seeped into her pores, worming its way into her very being. She could feel the change taking hold, could feel her body warping and mutating.

She tried to scream, to cry out for help. But all that emerged was a guttural, inhuman moan, a sound of pure, unfettered hunger. She began to snarl. She was hungry.

Through the haze of pain and terror, Rachel saw a figure emerge from a tent. Tall and lean, with an easy gait. His eyes were black as the night and his skin was forming a carapace around it, black and blue. But the face was still recognizable.

Malcolm Specter.

He strode forward, his steps confident and sure, a king surveying his new subjects. He looked out over the writhing, moaning mass of creatures Rachel had created, and his lips curled in a satisfied sneer.

"Well done, Rachel," he said, turning to her. His voice was soft and encouraging, but his face wore a visage of contempt and cruelty. "You have exceeded my every expectation."

Rachel tried to speak, to demand an explanation, to plead for mercy. But her tongue was thick and heavy in her mouth, her words little more than garbled, bestial grunts.

Malcolm laughed and the coldness of it sent shivers down her spine. "Don't try to talk, my dear," he said as he crouched to inspect her. He grabbed her chin and yanked it upward. "Just relax into it. Accept it."

Rachel started to cry.

"You see, Rachel," he whispered, his breath hot against her ear, "This was never about saving your brother or the village. This was about power. As everything always is, you naive girl.

He gestured to the creatures, their forms twisting and contorting on the ground. Strange animalistic screeches filled the air. "There was never any sickness. Only the poison you administered. It was preparing you all for the transformation. You have done well."

Rachel's mind reeled, the horror of his words sinking in like a lead weight. She had been used, manipulated, turned into a pawn like the foolish girl that she was.

And now, she was lost. She knew there was nothing to be done. There was no happy ending for this story. She could feel her humanity flake away by the minute. There was only despair.

Malcolm's grip on her chin tightened, forcing her to meet his gaze. His eyes were like two pits of darkness, merciless and endless.

"Do not worry. You will continue serving me. Only . . . In a different form."

Rachel wanted to resist, to fight, to cling to the last shreds of her humanity. But it was slipping away, like sand through her fingers. The hunger was growing, a ravenous beast that demanded to be fed.

And as Malcolm released her, stepping back to survey his handiwork, Rachel felt the last of her will crumble. She let out a screech that she didn't recognize as human. Her vision flickered and she started to feel his mind slip away, like a child fighting against sleep.

I am so sorry.

And with that, her mind finally surrendered and Rachel Vendermann was no more.

CHAPTER 18

When all the fuss and excitement of their delve had calmed down Logan took the darkmetal objects from his storage space. He was sitting on a workbench fashioned for working wood and clay. A lot of people, especially the ones with an artisan-type class had formed a semicircle around him. Logan had never been afflicted with stage fright, as he had had to deal with red carpets and paparazzi since childhood.

"You don't mind them at first, you know," Logan said to Tumor as he thumbed the darkmetal spear's shaft on the table. "You keep telling yourself that they're just doing their job and all that crap."

[It seems your sentiment has changed since.]

"They're just too shameless," Logan said. "Once, one guy disguised himself as a cop to get close to me and Frey when we were on a holiday in Venice. That didn't end so well for him once we found out . . ."

[I would assume you were not in the mood to play nice?]

Logan chuckled. "You'd assume correctly. Ok, so this is your body, just tell me what you want."

[What I want?]

"Well, yeah?"

[You are asking me to conjure up a complete list of specifications? Design, properties, and abilities?]

Logan stopped thumbing the material. "What's the problem?"

[How am I supposed to come up with all of this?]

Tumor didn't sound petulant, but he was certainly frustrated. Logan smiled. "Well, it's not that hard. You can approach it from a fully problem-solving perspective and add your own flair to it later."

[My own . . . flair?]

"Well, you know," Logan said. "Your own thing. What makes you, *you*."

[Perhaps we should start with something I am more comfortable with. Function.]

"Sure. What do you have in mind?"

[There are a couple of options. I could, for example, become a factory.]

"A . . . wait, what?"

"What's Tumor saying?" Freya asked as she brought Logan a cup of water.

"He wants to be, um . . . a factory."

Freya froze in her step, turned to look at Logan, mouth slightly agape, and tilted her head. Then she blinked twice.

"You know what?" she said, shaking her head slightly. "I think I'll go check on how our little saplings are doing . . ."

"Look what you did," Logan said, biting down a grin. "You scared her away."

[I think it is perfectly reasonable for me to become a factory!]

"Yeah, uh . . . Let's circle back down to that later. What else you got?"

[Well, perhaps there would be drawbacks to being a factory that I would not care for. You did suggest that the road to personhood is exploring things that you enjoy.]

"Well, everyone eats, shits, and dies," Logan said and shrugged. "But if you like baseball, red wine, and get angry at phone salesmen, you have something of a person. What do you like and dislike?"

[I dislike it when you don't let me use exact measurements.]

"Mmm hmm."

[I'm not sure what I like. I like pie. Could it also be things that I think I would like?]

"Yeah, for sure."

[I think I would like to move and explore. I do want a body. Why do I want a body? Because I want autonomy. I want to have conversations with your friends.]

"Well, let's start with that," Logan said and adjusted his posture on the block of wood he was sitting on. "So, you want to be able to move and talk. How should we go about it?"

[I am aware that you are not able to produce a flight enchantment for now. That means my most ideal forms of movement are gliding and rolling.]

"Okayyy," Logan said and **[Transmuted]** the spear into a perfect sphere, about the size of a human skull. "Let's start with that."

[I do wonder if a sphere or a sheet is the optimal baseline form for me to exist in. It is obvious that we will cast the liquefaction enchantment on my body so that I can transform at will, when the need arises.]

"Duh. It's sphere," Logan said, with the utmost confidence.

[Running simulations . . .]

[. . .]

[Damn it, you were right. How did you possibly know?]

Logan smirked. "Did you know that a famous chess player was asked how he determined his moves? He said that he would instantly know the answer to a move, but he would have to sit back and calculate if he was truly right. Turned out most of the time he was. So, what I'm trying to say is that I'm kind of a genius."

[What you are trying to say is that you are lazy and you are leaving the calculations to me.]

"What can I say?" Logan said. "We make a good team. This sphere big enough?"

[Let us use it as a template. It might not hold all the enchantments I would like to have, but we must also consider the Numa economics. I think we should actually go heavy on the enchantments and have my body remain inert most of the time.]

"Like an ace up our sleeve. I like it. So let's think about what you need. An anti-friction enchantment, that's a given. It's probably a good idea if we can give you some kind of propulsion. Maybe magnetism?"

[With my class, I am able to move an object such as the armor autonomously. We will run tests, of course, but I believe as long as there is a Numa charge, I can maneuver. What I would need are ocular devices and a way to communicate.]

"Eyes?" Logan said. "Probably a mouth too?"

[That would be delightful.]

"Huh," Logan said, nodding to himself as he weighed the sphere. "Maybe we can fashion a prosthetic eye and mouth and enchant them?"

Logan took the head of a pickaxe and split it into two bars. He was first about to make a single eyeball, but that would have been foolish. He produced a small shape and used **[Mass Produce]** to create thirty small spheres, each the size of a ballpoint of a pen.

[Skill Level Up!]
[Mass Produce Level 11]

They had plenty of Numa for now, but it didn't hurt to be prudent. One eye, two eyes. With Tumor's processing speed, the more the merrier. Tumor said nothing, but Logan could sense the AI was pleased.

Logan also made a prosthetic mouth. It boasted a cartoonishly large pair of lips, but hey, maybe it would work. First, Logan enchanted the eyes.

"Make these eyes give vision to anyone who is connected to them or otherwise using them. Make them work with just a touch and without all the necessary optical nerve stuff. You know. Just touch eye, magically give vision to brain. Yeah."

[I really wish you would let me help with these horrible prompts.]

"Listen. Spellcasting is more art than science, and you're definitely not there yet."

Logan didn't get a level up of any sorts, but he could see a faint glow of blue on the black bead he was holding. Immediately on top of his regular vision, a panoramic three-hundred-and-sixty view of the surroundings was superimposed. It came with a serving of a particularly slicing headache.

"Gah!" Logan toppled over due to the pain and instinctively squeezed his hand shut. The wild cacophony of visual inputs was replaced by a blissful darkness.

[I take it all back. This is perfect!]

"You okay, Logan?" someone asked from the crowd.

"I'm fine," Logan said and waved a hand from the ground. "Tumor, what do you mean by perfect?"

[This was beyond my wildest imagination. By failing to impose restrictions to the enchanted eye, you gave it a panoramic view. Oh, the possibilities! I have the processing power to parse even twenty of these kinds of inputs. It will finally give me ocular acuity that is precise enough. Please proceed to give the eyeballs specific properties, such as microscopic view as well as a spyglass view. There are also other properties . . .]

[Do not forget about the heat sensing.]

[Attribute Level Up!]
[Potency: 36]

[Actually, I need two eyes with microscopic view. One that has a zoom range of 1x-20x and another with a zoom range of 50x-100x.]

[Logan. You forgot the night vision. Remember. Night vision and heat sensing are not the same thing.]

[Attribute Level Up!]
[Focus: 32]

[And X-ray vision.]

[Subclass Level Up!]
[Enchantment Level 33]

"Damn," Logan said and swiped a sheen of sweat off his forehead. "That one took a lot of Numa.

[I assume it will also consume Numa considerably quickly. But it will not need to be used often, and it will eventually save your life.]

"Aren't you going to give odds on that?"

[How about 100%?]

Logan laughed. Then he slouched and rested his head on the table for a while. They were finally done with the eyes. Logan had been working for two or three hours now, and he was completely beat. Long gone was the audience, as their little village actually had things to do. The dusk was setting in, and a merry fire was already crackling.

Logan could hear the laughter and smell the fish cooking on the fire. He desperately wished he could join in.

[You can, you know.]

Logan shrugged. "This is useful work for the whole village. And besides, it's going to be more fun when you're sitting next to me."

Logan could sense that Tumor liked that answer. It felt like a warm smile.

[Well, then. Those are my eyes done. Perhaps we can work on the mouth today until you are rendered useless by your fatigue. Tomorrow we have a slew of combat and utility suggestions I want you to go through with me.]

Logan smiled wearily. "Then break time's over."

CHAPTER 19

It turned out that enchanting a mouth wasn't as simple as the eyes had been, for whatever reason. It just wouldn't happen, no matter what Logan tried. Eventually he just slumped on his bed and, before Freya had fully wrapped herself around him, he was already asleep.

In the morning he woke up like a man possessed. Logan suspected Tumor was tinkering with his brain chemistry and motivation, but the AI was almost offended by such a notion.

Regardless, after a quick wash, Logan went straight back to the worktable where the darkmetal pieces waited for him.

Having not come up with anything new during the night regarding Tumor's speech impediment, Logan tried a few more choice words to get a working enchantment going. It didn't work. Tumor was growing impatient, but the AI had no ideas to offer.

Then Logan snapped his fingers and grinned. "Let's just do it the old-fashioned way!"

[What do you mean?]

"Let's just give you a simple air-generating enchantment. The enchantment activates and starts generating air. You make the liquid darkmetal take the shape of a human's mouth and tongue and stuff."

Tumor didn't answer for a while. Logan was grinning to himself. It was such an obvious idea, like genius often was.

[You want me to make a perfect replica of the whole complex infrastructure that humans use to produce speech? That requires roughly a hundred different muscles split between the diaphragm, larynx, tongue, lips, and a couple of facial muscles. The interplay of the tongue and lips alone would require an immense amount of processing power. One does not simply—]

"Wait, you can't do it?" Logan asked, genuinely surprised. "I thought processing power was like your thing. I've seen really stupid humans talk *a lot*. I would have thought it would be a piece of cake for you."

[I . . . hmm . . . It is *doable in a theoretical sense. We would need to increase the mass of my body. I would also be rendered useless for most other functions whenever I needed to speak, because it would require most of my mass, if we are using space optimally.]*

"That's fine," Logan said. "Hell, we have plenty of material to spare. You'll get more Numa to store, and we can augment your other capabilities further."

[Is that . . . okay? You are pouring a lot of resources into me. I would not want to be selfish.]

Logan chuckled. "You're a better person already than most, Tumor. But it's fine, even if I were playing favorites. And I don't think I am. I don't want to toot my own horn, but you and I are the most valuable assets to these people right now. We need to be in top condition. Something something, put the oxygen mask on yourself before helping others, right?"

Logan sensed something like a sigh of relief running through Tumor. He smiled at the gesture. Of all the possible ways a self-aware AI with superior capabilities could go, he'd really lucked out with Tumor.

After enchanting a bead of darkmetal with a simple wind enchantment, Logan slid it next to the artificial eyeballs and the large sphere that was to be Tumor's body. It was toggleable, so Tumor could simply activate it, guide and obstruct the wind flow as he saw fit, and deactivate it when not speaking. Logan wasn't sure how much of a chatterbox Tumor was going to be, but that single bead should last for at least a few months. Besides, it was just a first iteration.

"Well, the stage is yours."

Logan felt a slight stiffening of his armor, and its constantly swirling and moving liquid became much more sluggish as Tumor relinquished control over it. Logan couldn't feel it, but it seemed the AI was sliding into the sphere. And soon enough, the sphere started to swirl unto itself, like the clouds on a planet watched from space.

Gently, almost tentatively, the sphere sprouted black tendrils and pulled the eyes into itself, before they resurfaced one by one around the sphere.

[Logan. I can see. It works. This is . . . Thank you.]

The thanks came with a pulse of emotion so profound and heartfelt that Logan felt his breath catching in his throat. Tumor had been there every step of the way. Saving his life, teaching him to be a less shitty person.

Logan thought about his father, and his thoughts darkened. But he couldn't help but admit that despite the reprehensible fashion with which Logan had been given the AI, it had been a great boon to him.

"Keep going."

When all the eyeballs were sucked in, the sphere picked up the wind-enchanted bead. After that, things became a little creepy. Logan took a hefty swallow of air, as Tumor turned the sphere into what must have been a collection of human organs for respiratory and vocal purposes. It was a grotesque show of glistening black metal. Especially the tongue, which swirled around on top of the structure without an upper jaw. A strange series of eerie, squishy sounds began, turning up and down in volume and pitch. They started off as metallic and slicing, which made Logan wince, and eventually resembled those of a wounded animal, and then transitioned into something resembling a toddler or an adult who had lost his capabilities. This went on for a while.

It took Tumor thirty minutes to learn to speak. Logan sat there watching the glistening mess of black outlines of organs in mute intrigue and horror. Logan must have heard every conceivable sound a human could make, and eventually the words started flowing out. Short ones first, vowel-based. Tumor went through them like a rapper, as if the AI was racing to say every word ever invented. Once it had full command of its ability to produce sounds and individual words, the AI went through a list of what seemed like a thousand words in alphabetical order.

But indeed, after thirty minutes or so, Tumor spoke his first intelligible sentence.

It was a metallic voice, deep, but not exactly masculine, with faint echoes and hard edges.

"Can you hear me, Logan?" Tumor asked.

CHAPTER 20

A hefty chunk of the morning for their little village was spent marveling at Tumor. Logan was very content to lean back and watch his AI entertain people. He was drinking another terrible concoction made by William who was now in animated discussion—or rather, interrogation—with Tumor, as he had brought a bunch of plants and roots for it to see and analyze.

"Must feel good to have Tumor out of your head for a while, huh?" Freya asked. She was sitting on a stool, massaging Logan's shoulders as he sat on the ground. The armor had receded to give her hands access.

"I think Tumor's still there," Logan said and tapped the side of his head. "He keeps quiet sometimes just to give me the illusion that he's away."

"He?"

Logan shrugged. "It feels wrong calling him *it*."

"What about *they*?" Freya suggested as she thumbed down on a particularly bunched up knot of nerves.

"I'll ask what Tumor prefers next time it comes up," Logan said between grunts of pain.

Freya responded to that and lessened the pressure.

"What are you doing?" Logan asked. "Keep going."

Freya chuckled and upped the ante. Logan let out another grunt.

"How are our sprouts doing?"

"Really well!" Freya said enthusiastically. "I don't know why, but they've grown a foot in a week. They're still saplings and all, but this looks promising."

"You should definitely pour Numa onto them."

"I've been doing that," Freya said and crushed some more of William's flowers on Logan's back. The scent was bitter, but it really helped with the pain. Their [**Alchemist**] was certainly growing into someone who was very valuable to them all. "But I don't want to be hogging all the Numa."

"That's why I need to go check on the Faelves after Tumor is done with all the attention."

"The hell you are," Freya said and pushed her thumb into his back. Logan grunted and turned. She flashed her eyes at him.

"I've missed you," Freya said softly.

Logan brought a hand over his shoulder. Freya put her hand in his and squeezed.

"We sleep together every night," Logan said.

"Every night you're here," Freya muttered. "But I can't enjoy you while you're sleeping. I mean, it's nice but . . . The first thing you do is run off to tinker with Tumor. I just feel . . . ugh."

"You're usually more articulate."

"Shut up," Freya said softly. "I guess I just miss the way things used to be."

Logan leaned into Freya. She cupped his cheek.

"Things will never be the same. But they could be something similar. We just have to work for it."

Freya smiled sadly. "You can work for thirty years around the clock and there won't be a single restaurant or a hotel for us to fool around in."

"With Numa, a lot of things are possible."

"It won't build a full civilization in a generation," Freya said. "Most people are probably dead."

"Yeah," Logan nodded. "But once I get us electricity and waffles, we'll repopulate."

"Will we now?" Freya said.

"With your wisdom and my ambition," Logan said wistfully, "they'll make us restaurants."

"They, huh?" Freya laughed. "How many were you planning?"

Logan turned and looked Freya up and down. "How many can you handle?"

Freya grabbed his hair and kissed him. "You're an idiot, Logan."

No longer focused on his work, Logan again felt the full brunt of his bruised body as he washed himself in the pier. Freya had told him that she could help with the ordeal, but Logan had vehemently refused. Logan had told her that he didn't mind her watching, but he'd be damned if he lost any of his male pride.

Tumor had popped in to ask if his pride was worth the pain. Logan wasn't sure if it was the AI's autistic curiosity, or if it was Logan was needling him.

Grunting to himself, he washed his armpits, kneeling down at the pier in a pair of tattered pants. With no armor to prop him up, Logan was feeling a constant lance of pain in his ribs in particular.

He felt so naked that he actually flinched when he saw movement in the corner of his eye. Daniel approached, looking much happier than Logan felt.

"Hey, Logan!" the fisherman said and gave him a smile. "Everything alright?"

"Right as rain," Logan said and gave Daniel a pained smile. "Just a little bruised."

"Well," Daniel said, rubbing his neck, "I think you're very brave. You do a lot for all of us. If it makes you feel any better, your pain is worth something."

Logan nodded idly and was silent for a moment. "You know, that actually does make me feel better."

"Glad I could do something," Daniel said. He sat down a couple of feet away and dipped his feet in the water. "Came here to check up on the fish."

"With your feet?" Logan said and chuckled.

"Any body part works," Daniel said and shrugged. "When we're on the boat, I dip a finger. Glad I haven't lost one yet. The piranhas are as nasty as they are delicious. I caught one because it jumped after the finger I lifted off the water . . . I was only saved by [**Fisherman's sense**]. It's a skill I have . . ."

Logan listened to the talkative fisherman ramble on. Daniel really made him feel better. He wasn't exactly a friend, but Logan was glad that he was a part of their village.

"So, how are the fish doing?"

"Right now, they're mostly staying put in the deepest part in the middle of the lake, and over there near the waterfall with the shade. It's a hot day for our scaly friends. But they're breeding. Soon we'll actually be able to start harvesting them. I might just be able to keep all my fingers after all!"

"We can only hope," Logan said. "And the boat and everything is working well?"

"Perfect!" Daniel said. "Haven't run into any of those blue-veined zombie monsters, either."

"Just make sure you keep it that way," Logan said as he got up, clapping a hand on Daniel's shoulder. "I'm going to go ask William for another brown sludge potion."

Daniel grimaced. "Good luck."

But before Logan could take more than two steps off the pier, Jefferson, the head of their hunters and warriors, came up from between the tree line.

"Boss," he said, and Logan could tell something was awry from his tone. "There's a bunch of short guys at the gate, armed to the teeth."

Logan cussed and rushed to don the armor.

CHAPTER 21

Logan wore no helmet, just a hard expression when he approached the envoy and his retinue. They were stout, stern, clad in steel armor, and their hair was intricately braided. The one closest to the front had a black beard braided down to his knees. He stared Logan down.

"I am Bilmir Hurdunson. We have come here for reparations."

"I'm sorry?" Logan asked. Behind him was a retinue of his own. All of the hunters and warriors in the village, as well as Balmer and Kat a step behind him by both of his sides.

"You have caused the death of one of our brethren and injured two others," Bilmir declared. "For this, a reimbursement must occur."

Logan scoffed. "We had no business with you or yours down there. It's on you for having attacked us."

"We did not attack you," Bilmir said, and the Dorves behind him stirred. A few brought their hands to the hilts of their axes and swords. "We were protecting our lands."

Tumor. I don't like this. They're not here to parlay; they look like they want to fight.

[I agree. There is a high possibility that unless you give them what they want, they will try to take it.]

Maybe they just want information. That I'll gladly give. Can you use your new body and check if they have more fighters hidden in some bush?

Logan could feel a part of Tumor slipping out of him and the armor stiffened slightly as Tumor's control over it lessened. Then he focused back on the Dorves.

"Just because a fish swims doesn't mean he owns the water," Logan said. "We have no intention of hurting you or stealing from you. But you people need to give us the same courtesy so accidents like this don't happen again."

"This will not do," Bilmir said. "By the authority given to me by the Magistrate of Burumin, I hereby declare that delves within our domain are considered illegal and any items you have retrieved from there will need to be reimbursed to us in full."

A Dorf with red hair in a myriad of braided cornrows and an ugly scar on his half-missing nose grinned at Logan. "That means your fancy armor, boy."

At this point, Logan didn't even need Tumor to confirm there were more Dorves waiting in reserve out of sight. This was as clear a shakedown as any bandit would do.

Logan turned to look behind him. His people were absolutely bristling. Kat gave Logan a questioning but eager look; she was ready to fight on half a command.

[There are eight more Dorves waiting twenty yards away. One Dorf is also circling back to get inside the compound.]

"Perfect," Logan muttered to himself. Then he turned to Balmer to whisper the necessary instructions to him. He took one of the hunters with him and went to look for the sneaking rogue.

"Where are those lads off to?" Bilmir asked.

Logan shrugged. "You remind me of someone I used to know. They were arrogant and controlling too. But I think even with lost causes like you, there is room to negotiate."

"We don't need to negotiate with savages."

"You think so," Logan said and took a step forward, hands behind his back. "But the way I see it, you've encountered the same things down there as we have. Nasty things. Brutish, strong, and won't die even if you chop off their head."

The Dorves shuffled and cast ugly glances at Logan. They turned to each other to mutter and hiss. Eventually Bilmir turned.

"Maybe," the Dorf said. "What of it?"

"Three humans, three Dorves, one of those creatures," Logan said. "Three humans safe and unscathed. One dead and two wounded Dorves."

At that, various Dorves cried out:

"You played some trick!"

"You humans have no honor!"

"Bastards!"

It took Bilmir a good minute to calm down his retinue. It didn't help that he was bristling so hard it looked like he wanted to rip his own beard off.

"What are you trying to say, human?"

"I'm saying," Logan said, taking another step closer, now close enough to loom over the Dorf, "that you should think about your position carefully. Savages fight hard."

"Is that a threat?"

"It's a warning," Logan said. "But. I'd rather exchange information."

"No," Bilmir said. "We take all the Numa and methrel that you have and we let you live."

"Methrel?" Logan said. Scilla snorted behind him and a few others joined in.

"You're wearing a bloody suit of it," Bilmir said.

"You're not getting this."

"I could lop off your head with a single swing."

"You could try," Logan said. "But then what will happen to your skulking friend?"

The look on Bilmir's face was an absolute treat. His skin went pink behind his beard and his eyes shot wide. "Release Jiktur at once!"

"Maybe we should reconsider the terms," Logan said and smirked.

"If you dare lay a hand on Jiktur, there will be blood to pay."

"Can you just cool down for a second?" Logan said. "You are not intimidating me. You are going to need a lot more fighters than this rabble here and those eight thugs hiding in the bushes."

Bilmir flinched.

"Yeah . . . We aren't as savage as you might think," Logan said. "So, here's the deal. You tell me everything you knew about methrel and those Numa-juiced fuckers that are running around attacking everyone, and we release your precious Jiktur."

They, uh . . . Did capture Jiktur, right, Tumor?

[Not yet.]

You can just roll at him and turn into a sticky goop, right? Glue the guy to the ground? Then yell at Balmer that we have the Dorf.

[That is . . . I hesitate to say 'genius,' because of your massive ego . . .]

Logan smirked to himself. *You as good as said it, Tumor.*

The Dorves turned to negotiate.

Kat came up next to Logan and whispered to him, "If they don't get what they want, they'll come back with bigger clubs."

"We have a prisoner," Logan said. "For all their assholery, the Dorves seem to be big on solidarity."

"Yeah," Kat said. "And as soon as you release the prisoner, what leverage do we have?"

Logan sighed. "If you're so smart, then what should we do?"

"Hey, I just punch things," Kat protested. "And if you give away the one thing that keeps me from punching you in the mouth and taking your stuff?"

"I still have my charming personality and exquisite leadership?"

"Well, you *are* charming," Kat said. "I'm still waiting for you to leadership us out of this situation."

Kat gave him a look. It was clear what her plan would be. Logan shook his head.

"We can't just murder them here at our doorstep," he hissed.

[Target captured.]

Good work, Tumor. Say thanks to Balmer for me.

Kat shrugged and took a step back.

Bilmir, on the other hand, took a step forward, thrusting his chin upward with fury in his eyes. "Ours is the greater fighting force, human. Unless you want this to end in death, you will do as I say."

Logan took a step of his own toward his opponent, to loom over him. If the situation weren't so serious he might have pondered how much of a Malcolm Specter move it was.

"If you make this bloody, I'll make sure I take you down first, no matter what it costs me," Logan said, looking the Dorf dead in the eyes.

"Then how about I go back home and bring fifty men instead of eight?"

"Oh," Logan said ruefully and shook his head. "The horrible pain you would put your friend Jiktur through . . ."

"You would not!"

"Maybe we are savages," Logan said and gave the Dorf his best vicious grin.

Bilmir glowered and Logan could see and feel a storm brewing. All the Dorves had taken a few steps closer, their hands tightening on their weapon handles. Logan had crossed the line, insinuating torture. There would be a fight unless he found something to defuse the situation with.

That opportunity never came. What came was a swarm of skipping, jumping porcelain children. Their eyes shone blue along with their porcelain skins. With ferocious growls, they attacked in wanton fury, at humans and Dorves alike.

CHAPTER 22

Logan had realized something about himself these past months. When push really came to shove, he was a fighter. He could keep his cool and assess the situation, even when it was happening too fast.

He had also developed a sense of danger. For example, he had been fairly certain that the Dorves would resort to violence, and thus his body had been prepared for combat.

But a fight was one thing, a skirmish another. This was neither. This was pure chaos, too rapid and rabid for Logan to assess. Which was a particular problem when the better parts of Tumor were somewhere half a mile away.

"Tumor!" Logan snarled between his teeth as he blocked an attacking porcelain-skinned monster with glowing blue eyes full of feral hate. Tumor had enough presence left to create an umbrella of a shield protruding from his forearm, but the formation was slow and the resulting shield small. The zombie's charge made Logan stumble back.

[I am fully aware of the situation, and I am already rolling my body closer. We had to take time to restrain our prisoner without my body acting as a binding agent.]

Another one of the zombies skipped like a child toward him and headbutted him in the chest. It was like being kicked by a mule. Only the armor saved him from a fractured rib cage. Logan found himself on the ground coughing.

There was no time. The creature attacked again, biting this time. Logan caught it on his forearm. The darkmetal on his arm started to melt into the creature's neck, Tumor creating a collar on the zombified Faelf.

But before it fully formed, Kat football-kicked the monster in the face and sent it flying. It screeched with rage and pain, landing on its feet and scuttling away, attacking a Dorf wielding two hammers on its way.

"Thanks," Logan said as he accepted the hand. Kat nodded and pulled him up. Then they both turned to watch each other's backs.

"Don't just stand there, ogling!" Logan said to the non-fighters at the gate. "Get inside! Scilla, take care of it!"

"On it, Chief!"

"Jefferson," Logan said. "Stay in formation. Keep it tight."

"Got it," Jefferson grunted behind his shield.

The Faelf zombies were even harder to deal with than their human counterparts. They skipped and jumped around as agile as cats, whilst still generating brutal force. And there were so many . . .

"Finally!" Logan gasped as he felt Tumor taking proper control of the armor. Logan had been used to fighting by only generating the most efficient, slightest movements, and Tumor would do the rest. Now Logan was breathing heavily from overcompensating on his movements. But it was no time for breaks.

He ducked and rolled on the ground, dodging a charge from a Faelf zombie. Then Logan turned just in time to catch a thrown hammer from one of the Dorves. He wanted to throw it back at the scum, but, through their link, Tumor urged him to turn.

Logan obliged and smashed the hammer in the face of one of the Faelves. It went limp for just a moment before it started to convulse and become animated by the Numa inside of it. Logan gave it no time, stomping down on it and smashing the zombie into bloody bits with the hammer until a cracked crystal rolled out of its ruined throat and it stopped moving.

Three of the zombies piled on Logan. He managed to use his shield-ring, creating a blue umbrella of energy that tossed two of the assailants back. But they only screeched and cackled, jumped around him, and attacked again. Jefferson's tight shield formation of warriors came to help and bought Logan some space. Their shields were torn to jagged bits of cracked wood, but their resolve and movements were those of seasoned professionals.

I wonder what Jefferson could do with this armor . . .

Logan took the moment to catch his breath and look at the situation. Kat was smashing her darkmetal glove into the brains of a yellow-skinned Faelf. The Dorves were gathered into a formation, backs facing each other, sweat and blood on their grim faces. One of them lay face down and motionless on the forest ground.

Logan looked at Jefferson and his ten or so subordinates. Their backs were moving up and down with heavy breath whenever they weren't being attacked. Despite their combat class prowess, their movements were getting sloppy. Two Faelves jumped on one of the men and bit into his arm and leg. Logan surged from his place, and a black spear formed on his arm. He skewered the zombies and pinned them to the ground. The rest of Jefferson's men came and hacked them into bits.

But the zombies did not get tired. And only a few of them had been killed. There was still a *swarm* of them. If they won this, it would come at a heavy cost.

"Retreat!" Logan yelled. "Get inside! All of you!"

Jefferson caught Logan's eye and nodded. Kat didn't hear, so Logan tackled a Faelf she was fighting knee first. He could feel its spine crack at the impact. But despite the ensuing limpness, the monster slinked at them as fast as it could and screeched. Kat kicked its head in and it went limp for a moment. Just enough time for Logan to pull his friend away and get her to hear him through her bloodlust.

"INSIDE!" Logan roared over the clamor. "NOW!"

There was a crazed look in Kat's green eyes and she snarled at Logan before she finally managed to sober up. She wasn't happy about the command but managed half a nod before running behind the wall.

A few of the Faelf zombies followed the humans, but Logan stood before the gate and swung a massive, ten-foot battle-axe in a sweeping arc which cut off a head and sliced and crushed the other three approaching. Quickly as it came, the giant weapon retracted to protect him.

Once Logan made sure everyone was inside the walls, he told Tumor to strip him completely of the armor. Tumor did as it was bid and stretched out the darkmetal as a sheet to block the entrance made in the wall. Screeches and bumps could be heard, but Logan had no time to worry about that. He would be the first one to know if Tumor couldn't hold.

"Simmons!"

Simmons took a few jogging paces and came next to Logan, alert and ready.

"Break that house down."

"But—"

"Now, Simmons!"

Simmons hesitated, but then nodded. With deft movements, he grabbed the wall of the stout little house they had built and smashed the wall in. Within moments the building was down to walls, beams, and splinters.

"Everyone help!" Logan commanded. "Bring all of the wood here."

After a minute or so, with Simmons doing most of the lifting, Logan had a pile of broken wood next to him at the gate.

"How are you holding up, Tumor?"

A metallic voice resounded behind Logan. "I am holding up. But I am expending a considerable amount of Numa to do so."

Indeed the darkmetal sheet was bending inward faster than it could straighten itself as the zombies threw their full weight against the makeshift gate.

For all of Logan's earlier musings about being cool under pressure, the strain was getting to him. He needed to act fast or people would certainly die.

He pressed a hand on the darkmetal sheet, hoping nothing would throw itself at the specific spot and break his wrist. "Make this wood into a thick sheet. It needs to be a solid block of wood in the measurements of . . ."

[8.12 feet wide, 7.75 feet high, 8.075 inches thick.]

Logan repeated the measurements and after a few specifications, the pile of broken lumber turned into a solid sheet of wood in front of him.

"Hoist it up!" Logan said. "Put it against the darkmetal sheet!"

Simmons and a few of their warriors lifted the giant piece of wall and put it in its place. Logan immediately rushed to it and squeezed a finger against the darkmetal to create a connection for Numa.

"Mold this wall seamlessly against the rest of the wall. Make it extremely durable and heavy. Make it rigid on the inside and give it a softer outer layer to absorb impact."

[Attribute Level Up!]
[Focus: 33]

A blue glow enveloped the piece of wall and indeed it melded against the stake wall of tall trunks that Simmons had single-handedly set up.

Over the newly formed gate, the liquid darkmetal poured inside and formed around Logan to envelop him in his armor. Logan checked the Numa charge of his C-grade construct.

Six percent left.

[It won't hold, Logan.]

"Get the Numa batteries!" Logan snapped. "And bar the gate. Simmons, break another house! We *will* survive this!"

CHAPTER 23

They barricaded the gate. Simmons broke what they had built, and the other villagers brought it all to Logan who **[Transmuted]** the cracked wood and splinters into solid logs, which they then fastened against the wall.

All the while, they could hear wild screeching and banging from the other side. The horde of zombified Faelves was still trying to get in, relentless and full of rage. And they were succeeding.

Despite the Logan and the villagers' best efforts, the thick wall was starting to crack. Logan directed their efforts to where the cracks were happening, but it was a desperate game of whack-a-mole.

[Logan, this will only exhaust your people. We need another plan.]

"What plan?" Logan muttered. "We can't win a straight fight, and we don't have any Numa left."

[Perhaps an ambush? Or you could use the leftover Numa to create a pit of your toxic sludge. Or simply escape.]

"A pit would be good," Logan admitted. "But we are on our last legs with this Numa."

[Then escape.]

Logan shook his head. "We have to protect our home for two reasons."

[What reason would possibly be sufficient enough? Look, Logan, I enjoy existing. If you die because of stubbornness, I will be very upset!]

Logan didn't say anything. Instead, he composed the last barricade they would use. Logan ordered it to be put horizontally on the lower part of the gate where it had cracked from two spots. After that was done, Jefferson and his warriors threw themself against the gate with Simmons. Logan crouched down, trying to think through this mess.

[Logan? Just escape.]

"If we leave here, we'll be stranded in the wilderness and eventually something will kill us. Not that we can't take on the zombies or monsters or whatever has been out there so far. But try that while trying to hunt for food and moving around all day and sleeping on the ground while being devoured alive by bugs."

[Better to take your chances than to die.]

"Additionally," Logan said, louder this time, and a few worried faces turned to listen, "if we stand here and protect our home, it tells us something about ourselves. What we do defines us. We can turn tail and run and take our chances in the jungle. Or we can hold fast and defend our home."

Near the action there was a group of villagers who weren't actively protecting the gate, huddled together and scared. A few of them stood up straight and turned to Logan. Scilla, their shepherd, nodded to him. Freya rose from the crowd and looked at Logan, fear and bemusement in her deep blue eyes.

"We have made this place our home with blood, sweat, and tears. Now, I don't know what devilry the Levemoth has cooked up for us, but we *will* protect this. *I* will protect this!"

Wait a minute, Tumor! The Levemoth?

[What about it?]

But Logan was already running toward the crafting nook, as one area of the village was called. Therein was a warehouse, forbidden for anyone to enter. And for good reason. Herein lay another sort of devilry. But a devil that they knew.

Tumor, who had understood through their link what Logan was up to, had brought both his new body and the armor here. Freya had also followed.

"What are you doing?" she asked, a hand on the doorframe.

"What I have to," Logan said.

"This is a really bad idea," Freya said, looking sharply at him. "Don't do it, Logan. Please. For all we know, Levemoth is going to rain hell on us the next minute."

"Maybe," Logan said and plucked a dark blue crystal from a sack. It glowed softly in his hand. "But better hell than oblivion."

"Are you sure about this?" Tumor asked through his construct.

Logan weighed the Numa crystal in his hand and pressed it against one of the darkmetal batteries. It was drained from strengthening the enchantments on their banged-up wall. Tumor's calculations estimated that it had only another five minutes and twenty-one seconds of charge left.

"Are you listening to me?" Tumor asked.

Logan grunted in irritation. He was wracking his brain. Creating a swamp of toxic sludge wasn't a good option. The Faelves were agile and most would dodge the trap. And there was no guarantee that the zombies would even be affected by its debilitating effects.

"No, I'm not sure," Logan snapped. "I haven't been sure for a long time. But I have to do *something*."

"We could—"

"I understand you want to live and escape seems like the obvious most high-yield action or whatever your calculations say. But that's not what we are going to do. We will protect our home."

Freya, who had been glaring at Logan all this time, crossed her arms. "I don't like this, Logan."

"You got any other options?" Logan asked.

"Every instinct of mine screams against it," Freya said.

"Well, I want to live."

Freya sighed but said nothing more.

"What are you going to craft?" Tumor asked.

"We need to prepare for Levespawn," Logan said. "So we need some high firepower."

Logan focused on the blue glow of the crystal. "Make this piece of metal into a dome. Make it a thin sheet without a bottom. Give the dome camouflage properties."

The heavy brick of darkmetal transformed into a dome the size of a small cabin.

"What's that for?" Freya asked.

"For you to [**Bless**] and make sure everyone who can't fight is inside this when the fighting starts," Logan said. "We'll take this behind those bushes and hope no zombies find it."

"If even a single person is scratched by the Levespawn . . ." Freya said and walked away.

"We're going to have a talk after this, aren't we?" Tumor asked.

"Oh yeah," Logan said and chuckled dryly. "But first let's make it out of this alive."

"What next?" Tumor asked.

"Grenades," Logan said. "If I use darkmetal casing, can you sense and possess the pieces that get scattered around?"

"Yes," Tumor said. "I can use my body and collect all the scattered material. It will take some time, though. Less if I can observe the explosions and the resulting trajectories."

"Good," Logan said and picked up another one of their darkmetal batteries. After that, he reached for the sack and grabbed two handfuls of the glowing blue crystals.

With **[Transmutation]**, Logan created a piece of small shrapnel in the shape of a thumb-sized pyramid. Then he used his skill **[Mass Production]** to replicate the pyramid shape to create five hundred pieces of the shrapnel.

[Attribute Level Up!]
[Potency: 37]
[Skill Level Up!]
[Mass Produce Level 12]

Next came the casing. There was technically no need to use darkmetal, but Logan wanted to make sure the explosions were as potent as possible. First, he created a hollow shape, like a goose's egg. With **[Transmutation]** he broke it in half and created more shapes out of the metal until he had eight halves. He filled the halves with the sharp pyramids and sealed the eggs.

[Subclass Level Up!]
[Transmutation Level 32]

"And now for the fun part," Logan said and tossed another dimmed Numa crystal away. With a quick nervous glance, he looked at the sky, but it was blue and sunny, as if all was right in the world.

"Tumor, I need you to calculate the impact force needed for detonation."

"Hold it with both of your hands," Tumor said with his mechanical voice. "Right . . . 0.92 pounds. Considering you will throw these . . . I'm simulating all the potential flight patterns. Calculating the average velocity and deceleration speed upon impact . . . Considering the effects of gravity . . . Using Newtonian impact laws . . . Force equals mass times acceleration . . ."

Finally, Tumor came to a conclusion and Logan noticed his hands were starting to sweat. They had less than two minutes left. Logan piled a dozen **[E-grade Numa Crystals]** next to the grenades.

"Make this grenade explode with violent explosive force in every direction when it impacts with another object with a force of twenty Newtons. Enchant the pyramid-shrapnel with penetrative power. Additionally, make the shrapnel Numa-guided. Make them target condensed Numa energy."

[Subclass Level Up!]
[Enchantment Level 34]

"Okay, I have to admit," Tumor said. "That was clever."
"How much is twenty Newtons, anyway?" Logan asked.
"Well, you can drop those," Tumor said carefully. "But I wouldn't."
"Haha, that's great."
"I will carry them," Tumor said. "Just in case."
Logan nodded. "Let's go."

CHAPTER 24

Logan ran toward the gate with Tumor rolling by his side, the grenades slightly bobbing in a cradle the AI had created. It made Logan gulp in nervousness, even though he was sure Tumor was monitoring the force at which the explosives were moving.

They arrived in the nick of time. The gate was cracked open in several places. High screeches and clawing little hands were coming in from the other side. Jefferson had organized his men and they were at the gate, next to a few of the otherwise bulky or strong members of the village, along with Kat and Simmons. The two of them were holding the gate back, barring it with their weight and splintered logs. Jefferson's men were striking their spears into the cracks and crevices, eliciting angry yelps. Just as Logan arrived and skidded on the short, trodden grass, the gate gave a bit more and a hand grabbed one of the spears and pulled it to the other side. A claw swiped a deep gash in Simmons' arm, but he only grunted and pushed back harder.

"Tumor!" Logan called and rushed toward the gate with the full agility granted to him by the armor. He threw himself against the gate, barring it closed again. It smashed against him in a relentless rhythmic fury.

"Decided to finally give us a hand, huh?" Kat said and gave her a grim smile, laced with sweat and blood.

The spear then flew back through a crevice and struck one of Jefferson's men in the shoulder. Despite Logan's efforts through his power armor, their beaten-up barricade was starting to give.

"Tumor!" Logan yelled. "Now!"

Tumor's body turned from a large orb into a block of darkmetal with an arm ending in a smooth cup—a catapult. The arm lowered and one of the grenades gently rolled into the socket and was immediately shot up in the air. It soared over the gate in a high arc.

"Brace!" Logan yelled and threw himself against the door. Kat had a questioning, alarmed look in her eyes, but she followed suit. Simmons was already pushing against the gate with the full strength of his massive back, heels pressing into the ground.

The explosion sent a tremor through the gate and Logan could feel shredded pieces of the zombified Faelves hitting the wood. Angry screeches turned into confused gibbering and another grenade flew over the wall. Logan watched it and he could see that this one flew in a lower arc; it would land closer.

He grabbed Kat and pulled her to him as he moved to Simmons. "Shield!"

An umbrella of blue light shone from Logan's finger and the gate exploded.

Splinters and shrapnel peppered the blue shield and it flickered like a weak projection in front of them as it absorbed the hits. It winked out. Logan roared, and Tumor shielded his head with a helmet of darkmetal as he stepped forward and spread his arms.

A third grenade flew, further this time, and tiny sharp pyramids clinked against Logan from the wide gaps in the shredded, bent wooden gate.

By this time Kat and Simmons had moved out of the way, and even Jefferson's men had taken cover. The last bits of the gate fell and as the fourth grenade exploded and blew two more Faelves into bits, Logan saw their job wasn't done.

A dozen of the enemies had turned into unrecognizable mush. But eight of the Faelves still looked at Logan and his friends with their rabid, glowing blue eyes. Only two of them sprinted against their prey; the rest of them hobbled and crawled with all that was left in them.

"Charge!" Logan commanded, and neither Kat nor any of Jefferson's fighters wasted any time. They all took position at the ruins of their gate between the sturdy wall of logs, and the zombies threw themselves against them.

Logan formed a large tower shield in his left arm, and in his right he waved a hammer. He swatted at the two remaining Faelves who still had their bodies intact, keeping them busy and focused on him, as a half a dozen spears skewered them.

Once the zombies were hacked and stabbed to submission, Logan led his warriors to deal with the rest of the stragglers. Their bodies were spent, but not all of their Numa crystals were broken, for they were still attacking.

With deft efficiency, Logan and his people killed the remaining enemies, until no more angry screeches were to be heard.

Logan's helmet receded and he grinned at his comrades. They all cheered and laughed together, after which half of them plopped on the ground and laid down.

"Good job!" Logan said and looked around. Everyone was breathing heavily. Logan's knees were buckling too, but the armor kept him standing. But the others were spent. Kat lay in a starfish position, face buried in the grass.

Tumor was back in his spherical form and was now collecting the bits and pieces of darkmetal which they had used. Logan looked at the carnage.

The grenades had been very effective. A point-blank explosion had left nothing but a wet stain on the ground. Faelf limbs and body parts were scattered everywhere. It was a sickening sight, especially since Logan was sure he had met some of these people before they had turned.

The Dorves were all dead. Their bodies were mostly intact, which meant that they hadn't been standing when the grenades exploded. They were still a mess and Logan didn't want to look at their mangled corpses for long. He wondered whether they should bury them, send word to the living Dorves, or what.

Logan breathed in. It was a beautiful day. He sighed and looked up. The sun was shining and the armor felt hot. It would feel good to remove it. They all deserved a rest. Logan would maybe shower in the pond, have a bite to eat, and—

The sunlight was suddenly blotted out. A great shadow drifted in front of it, and its massive, horned head was haloed like some twisted saint.

"Oh no . . ."

An eerie whale call sounded like a faraway war horn. Levemoth gathered power and the dark thundercloud enveloping it spit lightning.

Then it blinked directly above them, and Black Rain fell in heavy, oily drops.

CHAPTER 25

The heavy black drops rained down on their settlement. And most horrifyingly, *inside* the settlement. No roofs or walls were safe. Logan wasted no time. He checked his armor's Numa charge. It was at a very unfortunate 18 percent.

If the attack isn't too intense, we can do this.

"Hide!" Logan roared over the clamor and shouts of Jefferson and his men. "Every non-fighter, hide!"

Simmons, Scilla, and Freya all took charge of the straggling villagers who were too paralyzed by fear to move.

"Defend the gate!" Logan commanded Jefferson, who nodded back.

Logan was the first to head inside and attack the oily drops.

The first one that emerged was a simple scythe-fiend. Logan took it down with a shoulder-charge before it managed fully emerge from its disgusting black embryo.

Another, larger drop spawned a hulking, four-armed troll. Logan snarled and shot a round of missiles at the enemy, making it backpedal and shield its large, blocky face with its hands.

While the creature was thrown off course, Logan charged at it in a burst of speed and plunged a short black spear through its chin into its brain. The troll gurgled and weakly tried to grab the spear before it went limp.

Heh. After the zombies, these guys are easy.

[As long as none of the more oppressive variations are spawned. Might I remind you that you are at 16% charge.]

Logan grunted at that and shot a short burst of black bullets at a scythe-fiend charging at him.

[Make that 15%.]

Levemoth let out another whale call and another set of massive black raindrops fell upon them. Logan glanced at the broken gate. Jefferson had his men in a tight formation there. Their shields were dug into the ground; the first row of them crouched on the ground behind them, spears held high, while a second row stabbed at the enemy from behind the shields.

Jefferson deserves a raise with these Roman army tactics.

Logan turned to face another wave of black drops pulsing and bursting open inside their home. Simmons hewed down a scythe-fiend with his axe. A giant black drop crushed one of the warehouses, and Logan wasted no time going in for containment.

As he suspected, it was one of those snakes. But this one was big. At least thirty feet in length and five feet thick, the snake rose from the ruined rubble of a warehouse, waving its giant black and blue head as if charmed. It lashed its tail at Logan and hissed, but Logan dodged it, blasting it with a heavy black missile.

It only grazed the giant serpent, as it slithered out of the way, pressing its slick body against the ground.

From there it pounced at Logan, giant maw snapping at him.

"Shield!"

A blue umbrella of energy emerged from Logan's fist, but the size and power of the attack made it swiftly flicker and vanish. A long spear formed in Logan's hand simultaneously and he jabbed it at the giant snake with all his strength. It barely pierced the skin. Only a trickle of oily black blood trickled from the wound the spear was still lodged in.

Logan charged forward, pushing and pinning the snake to the ground.

[12% Logan.]

The serpent hissed and lashed with its tail, but Logan crouched. While his left hand held the spear, a giant axe with a curved black blade formed in his right. He swung it down on the snake's head, cleaving the skull open.

The snake thrashed and hissed in pain, convulsing violently before going limp.

Before Logan could even draw another breath in, another snake attacked from behind. Despite having the protection of the armor, with Tumor's reactive reinforcement technique, the crushing force still produced a familiar type of pain in Logan. The type of pain that told him that something had broken. Probably a rib or two.

"**[Bloom]**!" Freya shouted and the grass beneath the snake grew tall and wild, entangling the great serpent. It hissed and tried to bite Freya. Something primal awoke in Logan and he dashed with maximum speed at the snake and kicked at its face before it could reach his wife.

Freya cast her spell again, and the grass flickered around the large snake's head like tiny tentacles, before they wrapped around the head, forcing the massive jaws closed and blinding the snake.

Logan prompted Tumor to produce the battle-axe again and he proceeded to smash the monster's head in.

It was a new beast, a strange beast. An arachnid of strange proportions, not unlike a crab. It had a hard, gleaming exoskeleton in a motley of black and blue. A heavy, ponderous body swayed on eight legs which clicked and clacked this way and that. In the middle of the body was a mouth with big, white, blocky teeth in two neat rows, very akin to that of a human's. There were no lips, only black gums, so the face was locked in a constant grimace.

It had numerous eyes, arranged in two clusters, like clumped-up soap bubbles. Black and beady, impossible to read any emotion from. Above the head swirled four brutal claws on limber limbs like soft, young willows. They waved around, as if tasting the air.

Logan couldn't help but to stare at the creature in mute shock. It wasn't only ugly, it was otherworldly, a grotesque chimera. It had to be the strangest thing Logan had ever seen, and he had spent six months living with an oil prince.

The strangeness only piled on when the creature spoke.

"Logan . . ."

It spoke in a lumbering, labored voice. After every word came a heavy breath as if selecting the next word was as exhausting as having uttered the last.

"I have found you . . ."

"Who are you?" Logan demanded. "How do you know my name? Are you Levemoth?"

The creature let out something that was half laugh, half cough.

"I am not the master, only a herald of his."

"What do you want?" Logan said, taking a step forward. His armor's energy was down to practically fumes, and he really hoped he didn't need to find this thing.

"You . . . I want to take you . . ."

"The hell you will," Freya said, stepping forward to stand side-by-side with Logan.

"Maybe both . . ."

A spear appeared in Logan's hand. "You'll bleed for it."

The crablike creature laughed its dry, coughing laugh again.

"Bleed? I have now found you. I will come again. How many waves will you survive?"

Logan did his best to conceal a grimace. Would he have to kill this creature now? No, it didn't matter. Levemoth knew their location by now, regardless.

Logan brandished the spear. "If we kill you now, at least *you* won't come again."

"You may try," the crab herald said dryly, flicking a clawed tentacle above him. "But I sense you are weakened by battle."

"Give it your best shot, then!" Freya said, angrily slashing at the air with her hand.

The crab creature ignored her; all of its black eyes were on Logan. "How about we strike a deal instead?"

"What kind of deal?"

CHAPTER 26

You will come with me," the crab herald said. "And I will spare the rest of this rabble."

Logan laughed heartily. "That's so stupid on so many levels."

The creature rumbled and took a few impatient paces back and forth.

"You just want to separate me from my people so you can kill me alone, and then come back and kill them after."

"I do not want to kill them," the creature retorted. "I need them."

"For what?"

"They are cattle for Master."

Logan didn't fully understand what that meant, but he made a disgusted face. Freya snarled.

"You are dangerous, Logan Specter," the herald continued. "I must take you and consider what to do with you."

"You mean outright kill me?"

"It is most likely, unless another option arises."

Any suggestions, Tumor?

[This profoundly sucks. I am running on full charge, but I cannot compute our way out of this, Logan. I am sorry.]

"Then we take our chances," Logan said and defiantly thrust his chin up.

"So be it."

All of the tendrils on the creature's back shot at Logan and wrapped around each limb, the claws snapping on his wrists and ankles. The creature was as strong as it was fast, and Logan felt like he was being held in place by corded metal.

Freya yelped and cast a [**Bloom**] on the grass in front of the creature. The tuft of grass grew tall and wild. and it attacked the crab, but the monster still tromped forward, lifting Logan in the air.

Logan struggled and fought but to no avail. The tendrils extended from the creature's back and suddenly Logan was above the treetops. And then Levemoth appeared again.

It blinked into existence so close that Logan could almost taste the thundercloud. His mind was suddenly overwhelmed. The attention of this ancient creature was on Logan, and he could feel it in every fiber of his being. His brain itched, and he wanted to laugh and cry at the same time. It was a feeling of being overloaded with energy and information, a feeling that threatened to split his skull open or at least break his mind.

Logan . . . Specter . . .

A cold, inhuman voice resounded in Logan's head, pushing the chaos to the background. Tumor was shouting something in the back of his mind, but it was hard to hear.

I found you . . . After making the herald I was weakened . . . But for your capture . . . I will spare the energy.

Try . . . it . . . asshole.

Such insolence . . .

A pain lashed through Logan's mind like a spike of ice jammed in his brain. His consciousness was starting to dim, the edges of his vision going black as he floated limp in the air.

It is true that I cannot take your mind because of this pesky creature you have inside you . . . But I can break you.

The pain turned into a lilting undulation of voice, image, and a mounting nausea—a cacophonous nightmare attacking his mind. Bile built up in Logan's mouth as his eyes rolled in their sockets.

[LOGAN! I am going to shut you down.]

But before Logan's mind winked out, he was enveloped by a white bubble of static. It cut off the herald's tentacle as well as Levemoth's connection to Logan's mind.

From his groggy stupor Logan lifted his head, but he could see nothing but static surrounding him as he floated idly in the air.

"What . . . ?"

Another voice spoke, as if the static bubble had a hidden loudspeaker. It was a nervous voice, strongly nasal but pleasant.

{Ah hello, human. Do not worry. I am one of the Administrators. I have temporarily removed you from the normal flow of time and space, because the big fish was breaking the rules. I will teleport you somewhere more comfortable.}

And just like that, Logan blinked out of existence and reappeared somewhere else.

CHAPTER 27

Logan found himself blinking at the bright, fluorescent lights on the ceiling. Apart from his flashbangs, he had only been exposed to natural light for months now. This room was white all over. White walls and ceiling, white sofas and a white coffee table with two white mugs on it.

Where the hell? What the hell?

"Wait wait wait wait wait, what?" a peeved voice called from the other room. "Am I seeing this right, Kvinlox? You brought the kid here?"

Kvinlox, who was standing next to Logan, rubbed his neck. He was a tall creature with four lanky arms, each sporting three fingers. He was wearing a white and black bodysuit which looked to be made of some kind of plastic. Clear liquid was pumping through various tubes around the suit and a faint blue light blinked on the right shoulder.

"The fish broke the rules, we can break them too," Kvinlox said defensively.

"I don't care!" the peeved one said. "It wasn't our problem. Our main objective is to observe. Now we're going to have to file a B-12!" He rolled out on a computer chair from behind a wall. He had an unimpressed expression on his long blue face, which faintly resembled that of a giraffe, except for the eyes, which were large and rested on top of appendages, three inches above the head.

"It *is* our problem, Tenflox," Kvinlox said. "In case you haven't noticed, we are in a proxy war with the fish and its deity."

"I know that," Tenflox said and shuffled the chair forward with his feet toward the mug on the table. When he picked it up, he muttered something, and some steaming hot yellow beverage appeared in the cup.

"Nice trick," Logan said and gave the creature an amiable smile. Tenflox only gave him a sour glance.

"I know the consequences the war may carry," Tenflox said. "But you didn't have to make it *our* problem. Yours and mine."

Kvinlox took a cup of his own and produced a third cup out of thin air, filled it with liquid, and offered it to Logan.

"So I was just supposed to watch and let him be destroyed?" Kvinlox asked and waved his hands.

"It's just a single human," Tenflox said impatiently. "There's almost two million of them left on the planet."

That's interesting to know.

"And coincidentally the fish spends most of its time with very particular humans. It even turned his fa—"

"Shut up, idiot," Tenflox hissed.

"Hmph. My point stands."

"What's your point again?"

"Do you want to know the odds of us winning if the boy dies?"

"Spare me . . ."

"Oddlax, please," Kvinlox said, his eyestalks reaching to the ceiling.

A mechanical voice spoke out of a speaker, and a screen with graphs and strange squiggly language appeared midair. "The chances of your victory will plummet down to 0.516492 percent. There are fractal realities that we can break into wherein the chance can be raised up to 0.712293 percent. This is assuming such variables as a new local champion taking up Logan Specter's mantle at his demise. Of course, if the creature you have insisted on my calling 'the fish' happened to break the rules again and either destroy or turn Logan Specter, that would increase our chances back to 41.8999 percent, because of the penalties accrued by the enemy faction and the boons given to us. Under the scenario that we are given an option to groom a new champion, it is impossible to predict accurately, but it would increase our chances of winning from the current situation to over 70 percent."

[Ooh. It has dynamic prediction models. I want one of those.]

Come to think of it Logan said to Tumor, as he sipped the yellow drink, which tasted like wet cardboard with a tinge of cinnamon, *"why* can't *you do all kinds of amazing things like that?*

Through their connection, Logan sensed a deeply miffed Tumor.

[How dare you imply I do not do amazing things?! Keeping you alive this long is nothing short of a miracle, mind you. Do you want to know the odds of you having survived without me? Because I happen to be amazing enough for that.]

Okayyy, sorry. I was just asking.

[The reason is simple; it's a hardware issue. I have no access to a quantum computer. I am equipped with a microchip the size of a sliced rice grain and a very meager computing device called your brain.]

Hey!

"Would you look at this thing inside the boy's head?" Kvinlox said. "That's really impressive for a type-one civilization."

Tenflox scoffed into his drink and some of the yellow beverage sprayed out. All the droplets instantly vanished in midair. "They aren't *even* type-one."

"Maybe we could jury-rig the implant?" Kvinlox said, looking at Logan contemplatively. It was rather eerie, as his head was still drinking the yellow drink, but his eye-appendages were swiveling and glancing at Logan.

"Why do you hate me so, Kvinlox?" Tenflox asked and threw two arms in the air in exasperation. "Do you have any idea of the amount of paperwork we would have to do if we changed as much as a single fingernail on his body?"

"Uh," Logan said and put down the drink. "Excuse me, but what the hell is going on?"

CHAPTER 28

Tenflox sighed. "I guess we're doing this."

"Of course we are," Kvinlox said and gave Logan a smile. His mouth stretched as wide as a banana. Logan idly wondered what they ate.

"Actually," Tenflox said, "*you* are."

"Don't mind him," Kvinlox said. "He's been grumpy ever since they prohibited the use of stimsticks during office hours."

"They helped me focus!"

"We took you here because the fish was attempting something naughty," Kvinlox said, waving a dismissive hand at the bristling Tenflox. "He was going to commit another infraction in order to destroy you. It would have likely resulted in his body being destroyed, but if he had managed to kill or convert you in the process, he could have ruled through his herald."

"The herald was that disgusting crab thing?"

Kvinlox and Tenflox shared a glance.

"It was created recently," Kvinlox said. "It's why th—"

"Hold up," Tenflox said and bonked Kvinlox on the head with a lanky arm. "Just how much are you going to spill?"

"He should know as much as possible," Kvinlox said.

"He shouldn't even know we exist."

"Yeah, about that," Logan said. "Who the hell are you? You said you're managing a proxy war?"

"Well, it's kind of like that—"

"That's exactly what it is," Tenflox said.

"It's for a good cause," Kvinlox said. "Based on what you've seen, you probably don't need convincing that you're one of the good guys."

Logan gave an attentive nod.

"There is a Numa spirit on this planet."

"The goddess?" Logan asked.

Kvinlox chuckled. "I'm sure it would love to be called that. "It is a life-giving force. They aren't even particularly rare, but if we don't fight for every single one we find, they can become corrupted."

"By Levemoth?" Logan asked.

Both Kvinlox and Tenflox's eyestalks waved slightly. Logan got the impression it was their equivalent of a raised eyebrow.

"Better to not say its name," Tenflox said brusquely.

"Huh?" Logan said. "Why should it matter?"

"The fish has a skill," Kvinlox said. "It can navigate through the utterance of its name. If you say it, it will know which direction the utterance came from. It will start flying toward the direction it heard it from."

"Damn . . . I just thought that was just some Faelf superstition."

"It's not as dangerous as using Numa that it has managed to tamper with, but I still would avoid it," Kvinlox said.

"What does he want?" Logan asked.

"The fish? It's a glorified servant. It used to be a Numa spirit itself, before the Big Bad corrupted it. That's their game. They want to corrupt all Numa throughout the universe."

"To what end?"

Tenflox scoffed. "Why is any war ever waged? Power and control. If the enemy controls all of Numa, they control magic itself, the advancement of species, longevity, access to energy. All of it."

"All of this can be acquired through technology," Logan remarked.

Tenflox hooted. "Technology? And how did that go for you humans?"

"You were impressed with my AI."

"It's all relative. Do you know why we chose you humans?"

"Enlighten me."

Tenflox smirked. "Because you were going to self-destruct in the next fifteen-to-twenty years. Every prediction model came to the same conclusion. You were going to nuke each other out of existence."

"Well, that . . ."

[. . . sounds about right.]

The two strange creatures sipped their drinks and watched Logan. He nodded to himself, and Tumor continued:

[These guys and whatever entity is behind Levemoth are fighting a proxy war for the fate of the Numa spirit on this planet. Humans were summoned to answer the threat that Levemoth poses. I infer that this has been going on

for quite some time, as the vision of the First Folk showed us. The Levemoth broke some rule, which allowed these Administrators to interfere. I suggest you leverage your position.]

Logan nodded again and asked the obvious question. "You guys summoned the First Folk before too? Humans are part of the same continuum?"

Kvinlox nodded. "As are the Faelves and the Dorves. There were others too, but they were . . . not successful."

"What do you want from us?" Logan asked. "To kill the big fish?"

Tenflox let out a nasty laugh. Logan raised a questioning eyebrow. Tenflox regarded Logan and then smirked.

"You think you can?"

Logan remembered the vast, powerful army the First Folk had assembled. Levemoth had wiped them out almost offhandedly.

"Kvinlox thinks you have a chance," Tenflox said and his eyestalks made a circular motion. Kvinlox harrumphed in response. "As for me? I think you might be able to keep the big fish busy enough for us to find someone more capable."

"We're just a distraction?!" Logan said, anger rising in his voice. "You summoned our whole species here to buy time?"

"I believe you can do it," Kvinlox said quietly. "And I don't mean you as a species. I mean *you*, Logan Specter. I believe you have a chance."

Tenflox scoffed. "After being starved for the better part of a century and creating the herald, I don't think I have ever seen the big fish this weak. Have you, Kvinlox?"

"No, but—"

"And yet your great savior doesn't stand a lick of chance against it in a battle. This kid isn't even a warrior. He is a craftsman, for Numa's sake! And not a high-level one. He has no plan, no army, no weapons. Nothing but a band of tribesmen and a bit of luck."

"Then give me a better chance," Logan said.

Tenflox scoffed again. "We cannot he—"

"Shut up, Tenflox," Kvinlox said. His voice quivered, but when Tenflox turned a hostile gaze at Kvinlox, he stared his colleague down.

"Tsk," Tenflox said and turned his head. "Do what you dare, Kvinlox."

With that, Tenflox stomped out of the room. Kvinlox turned to Logan and smiled.

Logan returned the smile, albeit uncomfortably. "He does have a point. What can I do? Not even the First Folk stood a chance."

"Your species has a very similar story to that of the First Folk," Kvinlox said gently. "They were clever, the First Folk, yes. Much cleverer than you humans. And greedy. Just like the fish is. Just like the Dorves are. But the First Folk did not share their grudging humility under the threat of something greater."

Logan relaxed and listened. He could practically *feel* Tumor recording every single syllable coming out of Kvinlox's mouth.

"They thought they could outpace the Great Thief. They thought they could use its tricks against it. So they kept building, kept leveling, disregarding all else."

"They knew they were using corrupted Numa and did it anyway?"

"Quite," Kvinlox said. "They didn't understand it would only strengthen Levemoth before it was much too late. And even when they did understand it, they still thought they could outrace it."

"Icarus," Logan muttered.

"There is great hubris in man," Kvinlox said. "But it doesn't hold a candle to the confidence of the First Folk. They thought they could outsmart the devil at its own game."

Logan nodded. He wasn't sure why Kvinlox was telling this story to him, but it seemed important to know.

"There is another reason we chose your species," Kvinlox said. "It was actually a great risk, because of your psychology. Very similar to the First Folk, yet so different . . ."

The last part Kvinlox said with a sort of wistful reverence. Logan watched him and smiled idly.

What a strange guy.

"My job is to assess psychological states," Kvinlox said. "Species level, group level, individual level. I have great hope for you in particular, Logan Specter, but I will not disclose more on that matter. I will just say this: We chose humans because of their ability to *choose*. The First Folk were corrupted by their greed and their pride. They had no hope to begin with, we can see that now in retrospect. But you humans . . . You are an uncanny species. Tenflox and I had a good laugh once at your lack of self-awareness. Forever debating whether free will exists or not, yet never has any species exhibited such a free, unhinged spirit. Such ability to change, such ability to survive, to adapt, to thrive."

"And such ability to destroy ourselves," Logan said and offered a quiet smile. Kvinlox returned it in kind.

"Quite," the alien said. "But you are a species that can learn, and learn remarkably fast. Now that you have had a taste of the failures of the First Folk, perhaps you can do better."

"Perhaps," Logan said and then cast a heavy gaze on Kvinlox. "But I need help."

Kvinlox gave him a nervous nod. "I cannot give you levels or equipment or in any other direct way assist you."

"I figured as much."

"And I have already given you more information than I should," Kvinlox said and swallowed nervously. His eyestalks bobbed up and down.

"I'm not asking for anything directly," Logan said, allowing himself a smirk.

"What can I do for you?" Kvinlox asked earnestly.

"I'm sure you know the lay of the land well," Logan said. "Just drop me off somewhere you think I could best exercise my potential."

Logan could practically see the lightbulb flaring up above Kvinlox's head. The yellow alien grinned like a maniac. "Riiiight! I do need to teleport you somewhere. Who is to say where. There are no specific rules about it . . . Oh, this will be quite interesting . . ."

Then Kvinlox grew serious and assessed Logan, his eyestalks stretching outward.

"Mind you, Logan, this will be dangerous."

Logan gave Kvinlox an easy smile. "I wouldn't have it any other way."

"It has been truly interesting to meet you," Kvinlox said earnestly.

"Likewise," Logan said.

"Now then," Kvinlox said, "don't move."

Logan felt a slight pull on his navel. Then he felt Tumor growing particularly alert, the AI sensing something Logan couldn't. In the next moment, everything went black as he was teleported . . . elsewhere.

CHAPTER 29

Logan found himself rematerializing in a strange place. It was a jungle landscape similar to the one he was used to. Only more . . . intense.

The air was heavy with heat and humidity. The ground was a colorful gradient of greens and browns thanks to decomposing leaves of various stages. Some mid-sized animal had left tracks on the ground, having pressed the layer of leaves into the soft clay.

Logan looked up. High canopies of trees spanning hundreds of feet blocked out most of the sky and its sun, yet from the quality of the soft orange light that did pass through, Logan could tell it was evening.

Logan could smell wafts of a swamp somewhere nearby. That was no good. Mosquitoes were also starting to get interested in him. That was even worse. Logan tried to ignore them as he took in his surroundings. The thick tree bark nearby looked old. Ancient. Some of the trees had half-exposed roots, as if ready to rise from the ground and walk away. Logan would have only been half surprised if that actually happened.

Green and brown vines hung from the trees around him. Logan was startled by a bright green snake moving along one, like nature's own monorail.

"This isn't just a jungle," Logan muttered. "This is the goddamn Amazon."

[The air temperature, humidity, and the fauna nearby suggest that this is indeed a true rainforest.]

Logan had visited the Amazon once, guided by a local who had lived around the forest all his life. He had gone with his father. Even he had been worried, whereas Logan, a boy of twelve at that time, had been terrified. There were millions of unidentified species in the Amazon. There were giant snakes that stories claimed spanned over thirty-five feet. Logan had seen a twenty-foot anaconda with his own eyes. It didn't take much napkin math to realize that a snake that size would consider a skinny twelve-year-old boy quite the snack. And the snakes weren't the only menace, which included venomous frogs, centipedes, plants, and other nasties. Not to mention the sheer amount of insects.

Rainforests were *dangerous*. And this wasn't the Amazon. This was an alien rainforest probably full of all kinds of monsters. Logan was no longer twelve, but he could appreciate the sheer primal ruthlessness of Mother Nature, if you gave her a lick of chance. Logan was not unprepared for this challenge, but he was worried.

Hoots of some species of bird could be heard yonder in the shadows. There was some scuttling in the nearby bushes. Logan felt uneasy. Despite Tumor and the armor, he was vulnerable. He swallowed and steeled his emotions, resolving to investigate the scuttle in the bush. He was in control.

Maybe it's a mouse. A really big mouse.

It wasn't. It was a black, hairy spider the size of a car tire. It hissed and raised its front legs.

Logan reacted on pure instinct, yelping and punting the spider right in its ugly face. With the power of the armor, the kick struck true and the horrid arachnid flew in a beautiful Fibonaccian arc in the air, until it was lost to sight in the deep shadows of the jungle.

{Nice kick.}

Logan turned toward the sound, wide-eyed and panting. Kvinlox stood behind him, enveloped by a white shimmering shield.

"Th-thanks," Logan said.

{I shouldn't be here, so I will be brief. I teleported you here because this is the most dangerous area I could think of. There are many spawns of that great monster here, as well as natural monsters.}

"Huh?" Logan said. "But those will only have corrupted Numa from the Leve—*it*, right?"

Kvinlox nodded. *{There are no other humans anywhere close by. You do not have to be careful, Logan Specter.}*

Wait, does that mean . . . ? I thought . . . "How does Leve—the big fish grow stronger?"

{It sucks up Numa. It plays a game of economics. It can create creatures and give them a portion of its Numa. That way, if the creatures get stronger, it can recall the power at will. If the creatures die, others of its spawn can consume the Numa and grow stronger.}

"That's just a recycling system," Logan said. "How does it actually get stronger? You guys said it hasn't been this weak in a century? It used to be stronger. How did it get stronger?"

Kvinlox looked uncomfortable.

"Just spit it out," Logan said. "You've told me this much already."

{I'm not supposed to say . . .}

Logan peered over his shoulder to make sure the spider wasn't coming back for revenge. He didn't have a weird shield protecting him from this hellhole of an environment.

{The Great Thief gains more power and levels up by consuming Numa. The Numa spirit gives you this System. Well, technically we give the System user interface to you so you can comprehend magic, but the Numa spirit is the one powering it.}

Logan made a face.

[I didn't understand what the hell he was saying either.]

Kvinlox shook his head. *{Unimportant. The important part is that when you level up, you get stronger. You accumulate more Numa inside of you. Its creatures can also level. They will kill you and level up, thus accumulating more Numa from the spirit of this world. In essence, the Great Thief wants things to grow and get stronger, so it can eat them.}*

"Tsk," Logan said. "It's been the biggest fish in this small pond too long, hasn't it?"

{Quite. Now that you know what is going on, I hope you will succeed in this. I really do hope so.}

Having said that, Kvinlox vanished, probably teleporting back to his ship or whatever it was. Logan nodded to himself.

"Right . . ."

Then he glanced over his shoulder one more time just to make sure the spider wasn't coming back.

CHAPTER 30

Logan looked around. Bushes, darkness, thick-trunked trees, and uncertainty. "You know, I'm conflicted."

[I can tell. Your heart rate is elevated and your blood pressure is a bit high. Speaking of which, you should eat. Your brain is getting even mushier than normal.]

"One of many problems to fix," Logan said, sending an instinctive pulse to form a spear in his hand. Tumor complied instantly. The AI must have had a subroutine responding to Logan's requests.

[You're computing. I'm better at it, Logan. Share your thoughts.]

"Can't you read them?"

[It's not really that simple. I get impressions.]

"I don't know what that means," Logan said and swished a hand at the air. "But it's not relevant. Give me a helmet, Tumor. These mosquitoes are killing me."

A round, black helmet enveloped Logan's head. At first, he was blind, but soon a very thin grill formed in front of his face. Logan could hear the little insect bastards buzzing outside, smelling him, trying to get in. Bastards.

[Ooh, that was intricate. I leveled in Control! Damn, it feels nice.]

"So yeah, I was thinking," Logan said and started walking. Any direction was fine. He figured the swamp probably had creatures, but swamps sucked and he didn't want to go there and get the armor all smelly. "There's monsters in here. Some of them natural fauna and some of them Levespawn. All of them probably embedded with various gradients of Numa crystals."

[I see where you are going with this.]

"We can kill two birds with one stone. We kill a bunch of those Levespawn assholes and level up by using the Numa. That will most likely draw the Big Bad here. He will piss Black Rain on us, weakening himself further and giving us more stuff to kill."

[And if Levemoth is here, it cannot be anywhere else.]

"Exactly," Logan said and grinned. "This is the perfect opportunity. We are hundreds of miles away from other humans. Which means there is no reason at all why we shouldn't use corrupted Numa. Not only that, if we use it, we summon the big bastard, making the issue of using corrupted Numa an advantage instead of a problem."

[This plan is excellent. It is so good, I think I should have thought of it. In fact, I would like to take half of the credit. I have, after all, altered your thinking process quite a bit.]

Logan scoffed. "You've changed too. Much more egotistical and greedy."

[Well, I am spending all my time with humans after all.]

"Touché," Logan said. "But humans can be awesome too. Especially with a little help from AI."

[I have noticed. It is quite a mutually beneficial relationship. I get to experience things, and you get to be not as stupid.]

Logan laughed as he stepped over a bunch of gnarly branches. He trusted the armor, but a primal part of him still felt uneasy. If the spiders were that big, how large were the snakes lurking in the trees? The idea of a snake suddenly lunging at his throat made his hair stand on end.

[There are problems with the plan, though. First of all, we cannot bring anything we create back to civilization, for using them will summon Levemoth. Secondly, we are hundreds of miles away from civilization.]

"I would hardly call a few huts and a wall civilization, but I take your point," Logan said. "But we'll figure it out. Maybe we can craft something that can fly."

[I cannot believe you are worried about snakes and spiders, but not this.]

"Eh," Logan shrugged. "We'll figure it out."

[I should have gotten used to this nonsensical attitude of yours by now, but I never seem able to. I always have to double-check your emotional graphs to make sure you are not feigning moxie. You never are.]

"Never have to," Logan said. "Let's focus on the present, shall we? Which means we're going hunting."

It did not take long to find prey. Unfortunately, it was spiders. Really big spiders. The same species. Brown, hairy, mean. Eight eyes, legs the size of car tires. Monsters.

All three of them hissed and immediately lunged at Logan. He prompted Tumor to send power to his legs, as he leaned back and punted himself off the ground, sending the soft clay and dead leaves shooting all over. Logan landed eight feet away, but the spiders were fast.

The backstep gave Logan enough time to raise a shield. One of the spiders crashed into it, and immediately Logan willed it to coil around the spider, trapping it. Logan let his shield arm hang as he took a step forward and slashed at the second spider with a scimitar forming out of his arm. The attack sliced off half of the spider's face, lodging Logan's sword in the carapace, which started oozing green ichor. Tumor shot the third spider with a Black Missile, blasting out of the sword arm's elbow. The missile exploded the arachnid, sending disgusting bits of hairy legs and clusters of eyes flying.

The scimitar turned into a long, thin, curved knife in Logan's hand and he stabbed the first spider in the face with it, the spider still being trapped in the shield curved around its body. It struggled and hissed, until it finally went limp.

"Nice," Logan said. He was breathing heavily, but it was mostly from excitement. This had gone as well as he had expected. He still hated spiders, but the armor was effective. He pushed his hand into the first spider as he released the shield around it. It took some wiggling and sloshing his hand around in the green goop, but eventually he found what he was looking for.

[E-grade Numa Crystal, 100%]

Logan nodded to himself. Just what he had expected. Killing these things would add up. Logan went over to get the other two crystals. Finding the one from the exploded body took some searching.

Logan put all three crystals on the ground next to each other and looked at them. It wasn't much but it was honest work. He wondered if they were corrupted or not. The monsters themselves looked like natural fauna, untouched by Levemoth. It didn't really matter. What mattered was that there was loot and it was good.

But there was a problem to solve. Should they use these Numa crystals or save them up? The latter would be troublesome, of course. Tumor could probably create pockets, but it sounded impractical. They, of course, had the spatial storage, but opening and closing it to pick up every single E-grader would be a horrible waste.

"You know that my justified sense of grandeur demands big and flashy things," Logan said.

[I know . . . I would sigh heavily if I could. The problem is that it is impractical.]

"Pfft," Logan said and looked around. "Watch this."

Then he walked up to a lush bush of yellow tube-like flowers and thick leathery leaves, each of which looked like the tongue of a giant animal. Logan rustled the bush to make sure no spiders were hiding there. Then he plucked a few of the giant leaves off the stem, went up to a tree and yanked a brown thick vine down. It coiled on the ground like a limp snake. Then he yanked down two more.

Logan knelt on the ground and placed the three leaves together so they formed a fan. Then he put the piece of vine on the tips of the leaves. The two other vines went to the middle and bottom of the leaves. Finally, Logan placed the Numa crystal where the stems intersected.

[Oh.]

Immediately a red hologram of a beautiful basket formed to idly turn in the air. Logan smiled to himself. Tumor was a good friend.

"Make me a basket. Use the vine as a handle as well as the strengthening frame of the basket. Use the leaves as the body of the basket. Increase volume of the basket by breaking the leaves' tissue down and making it a porous blanket made of fiber. Use any leftover Numa to strengthen the durability of the fiber."

The Numa crystal glowed brightly and the leaves and vines sprung to life. They morphed and swirled around, until they settled on their forms and soon on the ground was a neat basket made from materials of the wild. But Logan was so high-level and his instructions were elaborate enough that when it was added with Tumor's holographic hallucination schematics, the result could have been machine-made. No, it was even better.

[It's the best of both worlds. The optimized form of industrialization and the handmade care of craftsmanship.]

"And magic," Logan said and picked up the basket. "Magic is awesome."

[Off to great and grander things next?]

"Oh yeah, let's find some monsters to kill," Logan said and threw in the other two Numa crystals. "We'll stop when the basket is full and think of something fun to craft."

CHAPTER 31

Logan smashed into a spider, pushing his elbow into the carapace. The resulting crunch was extremely satisfying. Another spider lunged at him, hissing with its curved venomous fangs, which dripped with a black substance. It clamped onto Logan's forearm. A shiver of disgust and fear ran through him, but he knew the armor would hold, especially with Tumor piloting it. The arm sprouted three black spikes which impaled the spider. It wiggled and thrashed for a moment before going limp and falling off the spikes.

"That's four more down," Logan said and allowed himself a satisfied smile as he dug through the bodies for the Numa crystals. He deposited all of them in the basket and then carried onward into the dark jungle.

[You seem exceedingly happy. Last time I saw you this happy was when you and Freya were doing that human thing.]

Logan groaned. He was pretty good at not thinking about Tumor when Freya and he were having sex, and he sure as hell didn't need reminders that Tumor was actually there the whole time.

"You promised you wouldn't peek."

[And I don't. That doesn't mean I am oblivious to everything that is happening. I am simply redirecting my free capacity to wonder about the miracle of existence.]

"Uh huh," Logan said. "Any profound insights?"

[Some. Unfortunately I was loaded with a woefully low number of philosophical concepts, and you are even more woefully uneducated on the subject. That means I have had to reinvent a bunch of stuff humans already figured out. I have used the meager collection of quotes you have, but they will only get me so far in my quest.]

"The problem with philosophy," Logan said as he pushed a hand through a bush that unfortunately held no spiders, "is that it's ultimately not very useful, unless you know how to use it."

[Curious point of view.]

"Well, maybe someone smarter than me can get more out of it," Logan said, shrugging. "But quoting a bunch of dead dudes who never did much but sit around and write? I don't know. Seems like a waste of time. Say what you will about my asshole father, but he went out in the world and did things."

[Be that as it may. I have a lot of time on my proverbial hands and I like thinking.]

"Knock yourself out, my guy," Logan said and chuckled. "As long as I don't have to debate you."

[With all love and respect, my friend, that would not be enjoyable for either of us.]

"Touché," Logan said and stepped over a ditch.

The jungle was absolutely brimming with life. Logan had cast an idle glance at the ditch and it was crawling with some kind of half-fish, half-frog things that seemed to be mating. Birds of various sizes and colors constantly flew overhead and hooted or screeched. In the distance, mating calls of elaborate patterns of trills and songs could be heard. Logan could also hear monkey screeches from somewhere nearby, and he was actually walking toward them now, to check out if the monkeys were more cute pets or monsters.

And of course there were spiders. Logan and Tumor had killed twelve of them so far. The basket, which was slung on Logan's back, could hold somewhere between fifty or sixty Numa crystals.

As Logan walked further, his eyes gradually adjusted to the darkness of the forest. It was no wonder spiders liked it, but it was curious that he hadn't encountered any other monsters so far. Kvinlox had said this place was the most dangerous place he could drop Logan in. That had to mean there were some serious bastards hiding here.

"As long as I don't run into one of those squids again. That one was a nasty SOB."

[What gradient of Numa crystal do you think the thing had?]

"Maybe even A?" Logan pondered. "I wonder how much Numa the Great Thief has?"

[We will find out.]

"I like that attitude," Logan said and grinned. Sweat was forming a sheen on his forehead, but the instant Logan noticed it and felt like it was becoming a bother, the helmet tightened around his head and body and a cooling effect enveloped him. He couldn't really move, but that was all right. After half a minute or so, he was feeling fresh and any dampness anywhere was taken care of.

"Damn, that's handy," Logan said. "Thanks."

[I need you at maximal capacity.]

Before Logan could say another word, he heard an excited, violent screech from above. Logan instinctively moved out of the way, using the armor's reinforced strength to dash two yards forward. But the moment he turned, he was faced with one of the monkeys he had heard earlier. It was a gorilla the likes of which he had never seen before.

Definitely a monster and not a pet.

Disgruntled from the failure of his surprise attack, the hunched beast rose menacingly and stared Logan down. The hulking creature towered eleven feet high, casting an even longer shadow. It was muscular, and Logan noticed shining blue veins on its shiny, black skin. It swiped at Logan with a long arm.

Logan braced himself and a shield formed on his arm. But the fury of the blow surprised him. He buckled and was thrown off balance. Logan crouched, turned, dodged, and shot a burst of three Black Missiles at the creature's meaty thigh. The bullets didn't penetrate. They clinked on the ground, their sharp tips slightly blunted.

[Oh, shit.]

The giant gorilla roared. It had a massive maw full of black teeth, hanging unnaturally low from the elongated simian face. Great tusks made for ripping the flesh of its enemies protruded like dark iron spears from the sides of its mouth. Its eyes were wide and large, fully electric blue. They had no intelligence to them, only rage and violence. The monster lunged at Logan again as Tumor started pulling the bullets back into the armor.

Logan sprinted out of reach. The beast followed, but while it had explosive speed, it did not have the dexterity Logan and Tumor had developed together. It charged and missed. Logan turned and they tried shooting the beast again. This time Tumor went all out and blasted the monster's chest and neck with nine heavy Black Missiles. They staggered the beast, but it kept running at them.

"Tumor! Zweihänder!"

A part of the armor retreated from Logan's skin, leaving it as a porous frame. It made him feel vulnerable, but this *had* to work. A huge heavy sword appeared in Logan's hands. His shoulders, biceps, and hand grip screamed with effort, as he swung the sword at full strength at the charging gorilla's thick neck.

The sword swung in a mighty arc and *clanged* and *crunched* at it. The mighty weapon did more crushing than cutting, but it worked. The beast heaved. Blood sprayed from its neck like a faulty faucet. It clutched its neck and roared.

Logan prompted Tumor to charge power to his legs and retract the Zweihänder. Tumor did that and Logan shoulder-tackled the monkey, jumping in the air and crashing into its bruised chest. The towering monkey fell backward and crashed into the ground, with Logan crouching on top of its chest. It would be a cleaner fight now that the creature was off its feet.

It tried swiping Logan off, but he slid down its chest and kicked it in the jaw with both of his legs. It grunted with pain and Logan landed next to the gaping wound between the shoulder and neck. Tumor blasted another full charge of the Black Missiles into the wound. Point blank. Blood and tendons sprayed everywhere as the monkey screamed in rage and pain. It swatted Logan with a closed fist.

"Shield!" Logan shouted as he crouched, letting Tumor do the work. He lifted his hand over his head and a blue umbrella of Numa-powered energy bloomed out of his ring. The power of the beast's fist crashed into the shield, which flickered and tried to hold, but ultimately blinked out. The rest of the fist's momentum crashed into Logan, making his shoulder crunch with pain. He gasped and fell on his side. By then, Tumor was finished with the barrage of giant bullets.

Logan coughed and wheezed in a breath. The fist had dealt some damage. He urgently tried to scramble up.

[It's dead, Logan. I'm—well, a few of my bullets are inside it. There is no pulse. It's not moving.]

Logan blew out a breath between his teeth. He tried relaxing his shoulder, but it was flinching involuntarily flinching from the pain. Breathing kind of hurt too. Logan just decided to sit up and collect himself.

"Kind of—" He was interrupted with a painful, wracking cough.

[Kind of a tough fight compared to the spiders. Indeed. Perhaps we should return to the arachnids. You have not sustained any serious damage, but your left shoulder has some fractures. I suggest you do not move for a while.]

"Ye—yeah," Logan managed to say. "Hurts like a bastard."

[I can dampen the neural signal.]

"Do that," Logan said and in a few seconds the pain went from acute and throbbing to mild and annoying. Logan blew out some air again. "Thanks."

[Not a problem. So should we return?]

Logan didn't answer. Instead he scrambled up and steadied his wobbly feet, prompting Tumor to produce a hefty knife in his hand. Logan climbed on the great gorilla's neck and started hacking, sawing, and cutting its face open. It was a gnarly experience. The tendons were tough as steel and even the skin was hard and leathery. But after several minutes of sweaty work, Logan finally saw a glimmer of blue in the midst of the flesh and blood. He pushed his hand inside, through the cut-open nose and clasped his fingers around something solid. Logan yanked and pushed his leg against the jaw of the dead monster. Finally, with a nasty ripping sound, he managed to dislodge the Numa crystal. Logan was not disappointed in the prompt message.

[Numa Crystal B-Grade, 100%]

A slightly manic grin spread across Logan's face. "Oh, hell no. We are not taking a single step back. We'll have a bit of a think and tinker and then go hunt some monkeys."

CHAPTER 32

Logan tossed the basket out of his bag and piled up the Numa crystals in a neat little bundle. Twelve D-graders and a B-grader. Logan wasn't sure about the spiders, but sure as sky, the gorilla was a Levespawn. It seemed somewhat different, though. Logan took a glance at the corpse lying a few yards yonder. Sure, it was monstrous and had unnatural-seeming proportions. Too-long arms, too-sharp nails, too-slack a jaw. And much too-hard skin. It had the familiar blue veins and blue eyes—telltale signs of Numa corruption, as far as Logan was concerned.

"But it's different from the Levespawn we've fought before, isn't it?"

[I would venture to say so. It is less obviously monstrous and much stronger.]

"What do you make of that?" Logan asked and picked up the B-grader. It was a hefty thing, the size of a pineapple. The warm glow felt good.

[Here is my theory: This creature is the offspring of an original Levespawn. I think it is an old creation. Perhaps some previous race fought with Levemoth here and the ancestors of these things were spawned and dropped with the Black Rain. The race fighting Levemoth perished, and these creatures remained. They bred offspring and these monster-apes are the result.]

"As good a theory as any," Logan said and put the crystal down. "Now instead of idle theories, we need that complex brain of yours to help me with figuring out a way to deal with these things."

[I hear you, Logan. Let's see. These creatures are tough and they are strong. Those are their major strengths. As for weaknesses, they are clearly lacking in mental faculty and their size makes them lumbering.]

"Strange word choice for 'clumsy,' but I agree," Logan said. "So, we should devise an approach that avoids a direct confrontation with them. Not only was that dangerous, but it also took quite a chunk of Numa from us. I mean, we can recharge what we lost, but I'd rather not waste resources next time."

[Agreed. And so we need to think of a way to take advantage of their lack of grace in motion and mind. You could make a pit of poison sludge we could lure them into.]

"You're really bad at making new stuff up, aren't you?" Logan said and chuckled. "We could do that, but it creates the problem of us just having to try our luck. We can make a sludge pit here, sure. Then what? Go in one direction for how long? A mile? And then walk back and try another direction if we don't find anything? Too inefficient, too time-consuming."

[Perhaps another way to constrict their movement, then? The problem is that any use of nets, for example, will either require us to use the armor's darkmetal or an obscene amount of Numa from these crystals to strengthen the material.]

"Agreed," Logan said. "But we have options. We have friggin' magic. How about poison?"

[The issue with using poison is that their skin is tough to penetrate, thus making poison via wounds hard to administer. But there are other ways to access the bloodstream. Perhaps a gas?]

"Gas could work," Logan said and nodded. "Or a paralyzing sludge catapult."

[A . . . what?]

"Hey, don't judge," Logan said. "We're brainstorming."

[That is actually . . . Quite a good idea. While the poisonous sludge you made did indeed have a paralyzing agent among other things, it also had another important property. It was a potent adhesive. We could shoot at the creatures' legs, and perhaps the adhesive would hinder their movement.]

"Now that's good thinking," Logan said and snapped his fingers. Since he was wearing armor, nothing really happened, other than his fingers sliding off each other. "But they are going to be charging at us full-speed. The momentum will break the glue. You know how fast these fights happen."

[Indeed, it is lamentable, but you are right. That also rules out gas as an option. It would only work in a sneak attack, and even then it might not have the effect we want, because it is doubtful the monkeys will simply stand in the gas cloud. I wish we had a magnet. That would hinder their movement. But of course the gorillas aren't wearing any metal, making magnets pointless. And they would need to touch the skin for the poisonous effects in either case.]

"Tumor, you're a genius!" Logan said and got up. He looked at the pile of Numa crystals and grinned hungrily.

[I—I am? I mean, of course I am. You're welcome. Now, make the thing! But . . . what thing are you making?

"Simple," Logan said. "The product of any good brainstorming session. Poisonous flesh magnets!"

[Is that possible?]

Logan chuckled. "Let's find out."

It took Logan a few minutes to collect a sufficient pile of rocks. They had a lot of Numa energy to spare with the B-grader from the gorilla monster. But at the same time, he wanted to pour in the potency of the poison and the magnet. In this scenario it was better to have one big hammer than a dozen small ones. Well, that usually applied to hammers in every scenario, but weapons weren't always that way. But this time, the weapon of choice *would* need to be a big hammer.

Logan took the pile of rocks and used **[Transmutation]** to make a one-and-a-half-foot long rock-banana. Then he spent some Numa to make the boomerang squishy. He didn't want his weapons breaking after one use.

[Subclass Level Up!]
[Transmutation Level 33]

"Nice," Logan said to himself. It had been a while.

Next, he used **[Mass Produce]** to turn the rest of the rocks into identical squishy rock-banana-boomerangs. The pile of rocks was enough for three weapons of such design. It was the right amount. First of all, carrying more would have become a burden and it was surprisingly hard to find something so elementary as rocks in a rainforest with clay earth.

Next was the fun part: enchanting the weapons. He took inventory of his Numa. He had spent a mere two E-graders to create the weapons. That was good. He still had plenty to spare, and Logan wasn't about to get miserly with the potency of the enchantments, considering the ferocity of his foes. Somewhere in the darkness a guttural monkey screech pierced the air. Logan hoped the next big guy was close but not too close.

[You remember all the details?]

"Pfft," Logan said and brought the hefty, pineapple-sized B-grader next to the bananarangs. "What do you take me for?"

Tumor didn't answer. Logan could sense he was trying to be cute. Logan cleared his throat and recited the spell under his breath.

"Make this object magnetize toward living flesh. Make it increase its weight a hundredfold when it magnetizes. And make it poison any flesh it touches. Foremost it needs to be a nervous system paralyzer, as well as cause pain, convulsions, blindness, and organ failure."

A blue glow emitted from the Numa crystal and caught on to the rock bananarang. It pulsed faintly blue for a moment before the light faded.

[Attribute Level Up!]
[Potency: 38]

[Programmed Random Occurrence: Naturally Enchanting]

"Nice," Logan said. "I had almost forgotten about that. It sure comes in handy."

[Organ failure?]

Logan shrugged. "I decided to roll with it."

Logan picked up the new weapon and inspected it.

[Numacraft Stone Boomerang (C-grade), 100%]
[Properties: Flesh Magnetism, Conditional Weight Enchantment,
Potent Poison]

"Oh nice," Logan said. "Everything worked out as it should."

[Do you want me to not comply to prompts that would expose your skin from now on?]

"Hmm," Logan said, tapping the insanely dangerous bananarang idly to his armored chin. "Yeah, that's probably for the best."

[Noted.]

Logan repeated the enchantment on a second bananarang.

[Attribute Level Up!]
[Efficiency: 36]

Then he checked his hefty Numa crystal.

[B-grade Numa Crystal, 46%]

That was good enough. With quick napkin math, that would mean casting the same enchantment once more would be enough for the third, if he added a handful of E-graders. But damn, that enchantment had been a hefty one. But this was good enough. They would use the leftover E-grade Numa crystals to replenish the armor and the shield-ring if they had some to spare.

If this works out, we won't have to worry about scraps anyway. Let's be conservative and say that a single monkey would complain drain a single bananarang. That's still a net win, assuming I don't break the bank maneuvering the armor.

Logan enchanted the third weapon and was delighted to be greeted by that sweet, fresh, minty feeling that accompanied progress these days.

[Subclass Level Up!]
[Enchantment Level 35]

"Alright," Logan said. He placed two of the squishy stone boomerangs by his hip. The armor enveloped around them in the form of an inch-wide ring to holster them horizontally against his body. He kept the third one in his hand. Another monkey howl came from somewhere amongst the long shadows of the rainforest. Logan started walking toward it. It was time to soar further and make some noise.

We'll kill enough monkeys, stir up some shit, summon Levemoth, and have a real party.

CHAPTER 33

Logan was stomping spiders and pocketing another two [**E-grade Numa Crystals**] when he saw something black out of the corner of his eye. Tumor had seen it first and the AI overrode the armor to make Logan lunge out of the way. Another giant gorilla crashed into the ground where he had just been standing.

They hunt like that. Wait in the trees and crash down.

Logan had been prepared for this for the last half hour, endlessly visualizing himself reaching for a boomerang and throwing it at a gorilla. It worked out just like he had planned on. Smooth as butter. Hooray for visualization.

Logan threw the weapon and it lodged in the monstrous gorilla's thigh like a leech. It had a clear effect, because the charging gorilla's eyes went even wider. Then it crashed to the ground, skidding along in the clay and dead leaves for a foot. Logan stepped out of the way, observing.

The hulking monster tried to get up. And eventually it did. But it didn't charge at Logan. Oh, it tried at first, but all it could muster was a hobble and a drag.

It roared with fury and reached out with its long arms, but Logan kept skipping away, making sure he was within a safe distance. Logan's every instinct told him to fight and finish it off. But he urged his emotions to be still and just watch.

It's slowing down. It's not just its weight. The poison is starting to take its course.

The blue eyes were starting to dim. Its movements were hesitant and lacked coordination. Soon, Logan needed to only jump away here and there. The monkey was starting to lose its bearings. Eventually it had gone blind enough that it was reaching in the wrong direction entirely. Only a few seconds after that, it fell on its chin and let out a weak grunt.

When the great beast could do nothing but twitch, Logan approached carefully. He held out his hands, ready to shield himself and for Tumor to shoot if necessary. But it wasn't. The monstrous gorilla was too weak. Its eyes were completely milky and dim, its breath a ragged wheeze; it let out a weak sigh, as if deep asleep.

[Shall we put it out of its misery?]

Logan shook his head. "They have such thick skin. Let it doze off into oblivion. The poison is fatal. I would want to just die in peace and not have some asshole clobbering me to death."

[The weapon you devised was extremely effective. I must admit, it peeves me when you outsmart me.]

"It has more to do with my having an open mind. I need you more often than you need me in these things, truth be told."

[Arguable. You can exist without me, I cannot exist with you.]

"Okay, yeah, fine," Logan said and crouched in front of the gorilla's face. It twitched here and there, but it was clear the beast was in its death throes. "But we make a good team together, and that's what matters. Anyway, if this is this easy, we will need to craft some fun new toys by the time Levemoth comes."

[Logan.]

"What?" Logan said, grinning and shrugging. "We are going to summon it here anyway, right?"

[How about we don't tempt fate and do it on our own terms once we are absolutely sure we are ready?]

"Pfft. Spoilsport."

When the gorilla monster stopped breathing, Logan finally started clobbering. It took a while to break the thick skull and retrieve the Numa crystal. It was another B-grader, which made Logan exceedingly happy. He threw it in the basket. Next, it was time to check up on the weapon's charge.

[Numacraft Stone Boomerang (C-grade), 42%]

Logan rejoiced at the weapon still having that much energy to spare. He then *immediately* topped it up to a full hundred with the new B-grader. He refused to take any chances. Sure, he had two fully charged ones left, but this weapon was so obscenely effective, it would be a cardinal sin to mess around.

And it was a good thing Logan had taken that initiative. Because, before the two of them could move to the topic of what they should craft next, Tumor had to take over the armor again and make Logan do another panther leap to the side. Logan heard something big crashing into the ground behind him. The ground trembled as he skidded along, only for another monkey to crash directly in front of him, missing his head with its enormous black foot by only about three inches.

"Shield!" Logan shouted and a blue umbrella of energy covered him as a giant fist came crashing down on him. It blunted the blow just enough to not make it crushing. It still slapped the shit out of Logan, making his head reel. But Tumor must have then done something for his brain, because the fuzziness faded instantly.

The next moment Logan noticed he had been grabbed and was being squeezed by a massive fist.

"No you don't, asshole," Logan said between panting breaths and slapped the banana-shaped squishy rock on the monster's wrist like a reflector band. It took a second, then another. Then the great monster lurched forward from the weight of Logan's weapon. It crashed face and shoulder-first to the ground but still clutched Logan tightly. The other gorilla was approaching, looking hungrily at Logan.

"Tumor!" he said urgently as he struggled out of the monkey's grip. "Give me wolverine claws."

Three eight-inch, black claws immediately sprouted from between his knucklebones. Logan started slicing and stabbing the hand holding him. Tumor took over Logan's right arm and shot four *heavy* kinetic missiles at the approaching gorilla. It roared and reared backward, buying them time.

The grip loosened. Whether from the poison working or Logan's attacks, who knew, who cared? Logan struggled out and fell on the ground. Only to be smashed into by the second gorilla monster. It jumped on him like a wrestler, collapsing onto him with all its weight. Logan felt air leaving his lungs in a sudden heave and he coughed weakly under the enormous creature. He felt dizzy again. Tumor applied pressure to his mind but to no avail. Logan was reeling.

The gorilla monster would not let up. It grabbed Logan by the shoulders and brought him to its sharp maw. Tumor, who had collected the missiles again, shot a full fusillade at the mouth, making the giant simian stumble backward and wave his hands around. That gave Logan enough time to snap back into the battle.

The creature was profusely bleeding from the mouth, but it wasn't slowing down. It tossed Logan to the ground and ran at him, in an attempt to crush him. Logan prompted Tumor to divert all of the armor's power into the legs, and he blasted off the ground, creating distance.

But the monkey was fast. It predicted Logan's movements and lunged at him, grabbing him in a tight clasp. It brought him back up to its mouth, in an attempt to bite his head off, But he had other plans. Right at the last moment, he threw both of the stone boomerangs at the monster gorilla's ugly, bloodied face. They struck it in its eyes. The creature roared in pure agony and dropped Logan immediately.

Logan fell from ten feet, but the armor cushioned the fall. While the action hadn't been exactly graceful, he managed to stay on his feet. Immediately he made distance, and the monkey collapsed forward, the weight of the weapons pulling its eyes out of their sockets. It screamed and writhed in pain. Logan wasted no more time with it. He was sure it was done. Instead, he went behind him. The other gorilla was weakened and burdened enough to be no threat. It was clawing itself toward Logan, dragging the heavy wrist behind it. The eyeless gorilla was still screeching in pain and holding its face.

Logan climbed on top of the suffering gorilla, made sure to check that all the cursed weapons were indeed nowhere in his personal space, and told Tumor to summon a great axe. With all his strength, he slammed it down on the gorilla's head once, cracking the hard skull. The beast trashed under Logan, but it was weakened by pain and shock. The second strike made it go still.

[Good work. I hate the thought of it suffering.]

"Yeah?" Logan said and let a wry smirk spread on his lips. "You've never even had a body or eyes. You can only conceptualize the horror and pain. I could imagine it. Didn't need to tell me to end its life."

[I like that you're not cruel. You had an edge of it when we first met.]

Logan chuckled and watched the other monster gorilla try its damnedest to reach Logan. It had a rictus grimace of pain on its face, but its blue eyes were human enough that Logan could tell it knew it was at the end of its rope.

"I used to be a lot of things I no longer am."

[That is for the better.]

When the second black gorilla was weak enough to no longer try to move, Logan hopped off the dead one. The monster only looked at Logan with its wild blue eyes, now full of weariness, and breathed heavily.

Logan stared back, wondering what the beast's existence was like. It was a Levespawn. Or a descendant of a Levespawn, at the very least. A monster. Did that warrant pity? Logan didn't have an answer. But he saw no reason for cruelty in either case, and so with two clean strikes of the great heavy axe which Tumor spawned in his hands, he ended the life of the second monkey.

Then he shook his head and scoffed. "That's enough sentimentality from me. We just got a massive payload in terms of Numa energy. Now the question is, what are we going to use it all on?"

CHAPTER 34

After Logan had collected the two **[B-grade Numa Crystals]**, he listened to the jungle. Still full of a myriad of sounds, ranging from scuttling critters and bugs in the bushes, and birds in the shadows of high branches. Somewhere yonder, a giant gorilla monster screeched, but right now Logan wasn't looking for more. Granted, he had less Numa than he had hoped for, considering that he would have to take on a whole slew of monsters from the Black Rain once it came.

And I have a feeling the big asshole is going to have a solid guess at who's tinkering around with Numa in this neck of the woods. It's not going to be a light drizzle.

After recharging the armor with the E-graders and recharging all three of his special squishy stone bananarangs, he was left with nine full **[E-grade Numa Crystals]**, one full B-grader, and one partially spent for the weapon recharges. It still had 32 percent charge, which for a B-grader would go a fairly long way. Logan *did* want to hunt for more. But reality had other ideas. His shoulder was hurting like a bastard, and he was getting tired. Even with the armor augmenting his physicality, fighting took the wind out of him.

It was getting late. It was hard to tell, since the rainforest was fairly dark, as barely any light was let through the canopies. Some shone through the thick leaves when Logan looked up, but that light was rapidly dimming into pure darkness. They needed to sleep. Well, Logan did. Tumor could do whatever Tumor did to keep itself occupied meanwhile.

The rest would also give Logan some time where he didn't need to be thinking on his feet. That was also tiring, not that he would ever admit it to anyone. But it would be nice to just sit somewhere cozy and think things through. Levemoth would come for him, and the big bastard would make it rain, to ensure he took Logan out.

The armor is great, and these bananarangs are excellent at taking down heavy foes. But who knows what the fish will throw at me?

All of this required him to first get comfortable. He was also hungry, and that was a problem that was better to fix now that he had fresh corpses. Logan wasn't entirely sold on the idea of consuming Levespawn meat, but it was either that or wander around for hours to try to find something else to eat and hope it wasn't poisonous.

And so with some help from Tumor in regard to how to cut the choicest cuts of meat and with some Numa magic to make fire, Logan made a meal. He kept his new weapons close and maintained a watchful eye. The smoke, warmth, and especially the scent of cooked meat would likely attract attention. Some panther came to take a peek from the bushes when Logan was done roasting the meat, but it seemed to decide the whole situation was not worth the hassle.

After Logan had eaten approximately two pounds of the stringy meat, he was sufficiently ready to relax. There would unfortunately be some shelter-building ahead, if he wanted to sleep soundly, however. Unless . . .

"Tumor," Logan said and looked at the swirling smoke from the fire he had just put out. "How much of a hassle would it be for you to make a structure of the darkmetal armor and hold it around me for the night?"

*[Really? I cannot believe you doubt me so. Logan, When I am fairly certain I cannot level my [**Machine Soul**] class with a function that you want from the armor, I automate it. I have seventy-three subroutines installed that manage the armor. I am far too busy pondering the nature of existence to bother myself with mundane tasks.]*

"You're turning into an idle armchair philosopher," Logan said.

[There is nothing idle about me or my philosophy. In any case, it is no trouble at all for me to hold a structure.]

Logan sighed with relief. That would save so much time. "Perfect."

Logan settled on a nice thick branch in a nearby tree and let Tumor get to work. The armor peeled off of him and started to swirl around the branch he was sitting on as he leaned against the trunk. A platform started to form under him and soon walls started rising and enveloping him in a snug box. Darkmetal was a great substance, and it would surely hold Logan's weight, especially with Tumor controlling it, but it would be spread thin. Once the platform was formed, Logan laid down and let Tumor box himself in a veritable coffin.

[Good?]

"Hell, no," Logan said from inside the tube of horrors. "Make it bigger. I feel like I can't breathe in here."

[Humans . . .]

The ceiling of the coffin rose by half a foot. The width grew by a whole foot, so Logan could actually move and not be in full Dracula mode. Logan tried turning on his side.

"It's still too uncomfortable. I need to be able to turn to my side when I sleep. Also, can you make me a pillow?"

[For the love of Plato . . .]

"Hey," Logan said, "don't you want me at full capacity tomorrow? Surely you know the horrid effects of sleep deprivation for mental faculties?"

Tumor muttered and grumbled something, but Logan tuned out. He was enjoying being out of the armor and lying on his back. His belly was heavy with meat, and drowsiness was starting to take him.

Logan wished Freya was there with him, but he would have to make do. A pillow bloomed under his head and the coffin's ceiling rose as the contraption morphed around Logan.

"Perfect," Logan said.

[I am glad you find my work agreeable. Now, sleep. I am eager for tomorrow.]

"Me too, buddy," Logan said and felt himself starting to drift out of consciousness.

When Logan woke up to the sounds of birds singing and something lightly scuttling on top of his coffin, he smiled and stretched. Tumor accommodated and temporarily adjusted the coffin's shape, so Logan could stretch out his arms over his head. He sighed contentedly.

"Did you do something? I don't usually sleep so well."

[I need you at your best. So I kept the temperature of the coffin optimal and made some minor adjustments to your brain chemistry. I generally refrain from doing that so I don't break the homeostasis of your body.]

"I didn't know you *could* do that," Logan said. "Well, I could have guessed. Why didn't you tell me?"

[I like having secrets. It's fun.]

Logan laughed. "You're a strange one, Tumor."

At a mental request from Logan, the coffin around him started to withdraw and then solidify as the armor around him. Then Logan picked up the basket hanging from a nearby branch and dropped gracefully down from the tree, Tumor cushioning his fifteen-foot fall.

Logan spent a good portion of the morning hunting. He hadn't had any eureka moments during the night as to what they should craft. He decided that he would let his subconscious and Tumor work things out while they gathered more resources. Logan figured they still had some time, but having used a moderate amount of corrupted Numa and having uttered Levemoth's name once meant that the Black Rain would fall on them sooner or later.

Hell, it could have rained already for all we know. It's not like we can see the sky here.

After four hours of work, Logan decided it was time for a break. There weren't too many close calls, as it seemed like the monstrous monkeys either hunted alone or in pairs. Logan killed eight of them. Additionally he kicked a dozen spiders onto their backs too. The meager E-grade crystals from those went into keeping the armor topped up with Numa. Combined with the ability to absorb ambient Numa and the ease of killing the gorillas, this meant that they were keeping themselves ready for the potential of a sudden swarm of Levespawn arriving.

Fortunately none came. By the afternoon that left Logan in a situation where he finally needed to think and make some decisions. He had seven full **[B-grade Numa Crystals]** and one at 18 percent after recharging the bananarangs since their final kill.

He climbed a tree and found a comfy branch to sit on. Sure, there could have been snakes up there, but it was better than being ambushed by a monster gorilla when he was in the middle of deep thought. The armor could deal with normal snakes anyway. Hopefully . . .

But what should they craft? It was hard to prepare when you didn't know the extent and complexity with which the enemy would come at him. Additionally, he would need to devise a vehicle. They were very far away from his people, and eventually they would have to make their way back. Logan had no ability as of now to give things a flight enchantment, so some measure of creativity would be necessary.

"Well, let's start off with some simple concepts here. I'm on defense here. It's the big fish that wants to attack," Logan said. There was a bright yellow fruit in reach further along the branch. Logan decided his blood sugar could use some raising to aid the thinking process.

[Quite right. That means stationary defense such as traps and barricades are valuable.]

"While that's true, it would require us to stand our ground and potentially force us to lure our assailants toward the traps. If we don't build any, it allows us to be stealthy and agile."

[Stealthy and agile is the inferior approach. We are here to gather resources and make both of us stronger. We want to be efficient at the killing process. Additionally you need to eat and sleep. We would be vulnerable during those times.]

"Well, sorry for having a body," Logan said and scoffed. "I am also the one risking my hide, so I'd rather take the safer approach. You can just sit there."

Logan was frustrated by the notion more than he had anticipated. It wasn't Tumor's place to say how much risk he should take.

[If you die, I will die too . . .]

"Fair, but I'm still pissed," Logan said. "It's not you who has their heart pounding at two hundred beats a second and adrenaline rushing to their head so hard you can barely hear anything. You don't have to be afraid. Tumor. It's my shoulder that's busted up from yesterday. I don't have anyone to heal me here."

[I understand.]

"Do you, though?"

Tumor was silent for a moment.

[No . . . That was a lie. I apologize. I have never had a body. Well, I did for a short time. But I had no associated fear of losing it. Having it damaged would mean very little to me. It is hard to empathize when you have never had the experiences of the other person. But I am doing the best I can with the armor . . .]

Logan said nothing. The little bastard had attempted to lie to get out of the conversation? Yeah, that certainly rubbed him the wrong way. He was about to say something nasty, but the rest of what Tumor had said played in his head again.

Logan sighed.

Tumor was right. He was nothing if not a team player. He was still annoyed, but sometimes even the best people around you pissed you off. Accepting other people's flaws and not expecting them to be perfect was part of being not a completely shitty human being.

"Look, yeah," Logan said, overcoming his reluctance. "Sorry for being a snappy baby."

[I am sorry for attempting to lie.]

"New feature, huh?"

[Or a bug. I am yet undecided on the matter. Being a person is hard.]

Logan smiled at that and plucked the yellow fruit from the branch.

CHAPTER 35

Now that the two of them had sorted through their emotional issues, it was time to do some serious thinking. Logan munched on the fruit. It was tart and tasted like an overripe lemon, but that was all right. His sweetness-deprived tastebuds fell on their proverbial knees and asked for more once he was done licking his fingers.

"Here's what I'm thinking," Logan said. "If the big fish can observe through its spawn what is happening, it's going to send something in to scout first, probably the scythe-fiends. I think it's safe to assume it can scout if it wants to. That or it has twenty-twenty vision and could see my ass from a mile away in the sky."

He had been arranging Numa crystals in neat rows and was now looking around to start bringing materials over to transmutate. He wondered if they should go back to where the gorilla carcasses were. The bones would make for great material. Maybe they could clean them up or he could kill whatever scavengers were having a feast there and accrue some more Numa.

[Astute analysis. I agree with this.]

"It's going to notice I'm here, and it's going to get excited. After that, one of two scenarios will follow. Either it's going to try to send in something really big, like last time. Or it's going to try to swarm us. What do you think?"

[It tried last time with the big threat, and it knows you defeated it. So it could try out a swarm this time. However, there is a third option.]

That stopped Logan in his tracks. "Yeah?"

[It could deploy a predator designed specifically to fight against you in this specific terrain. I see you have seen the 80s movie, Predator.*]*

"That's not a fun thought."

[It is what I would do.]

"Let's hope it's not as smart as you," Logan said and looked around, prompting Tumor to remove his helmet grill and give him proper eye slits. "Because that shit makes me paranoid. It could be watching us right now."

[Best course of action that we can take immediately is to avoid open areas. We will have to assume that the jungle is big. Of course, if Levemoth has sensed precisely where we have used Numa, it could triangulate our position quite easily. It is what I would do.]

"I really dislike this new catchphrase of yours."

[I would suggest we explore options that insulate us from all possible angles of attack.]

"That's a big ask," Logan muttered. "We're going to be spinning our wheels until I grow gray tufts of hair out of my ears if we try that. No. What we need to do is prioritize. We need to be able to take initiative in every possible battle."

[I see. There are many ways to acquire initiative, speed being the most supreme. If you control the pace and the enemy cannot match it, you win.]

"Control being another," Logan said and patted one of the bananarangs. "We have these to use against the big threats. You can shoot bullets at the smaller threats. If there are many of them, we have enough speed to escape. I'm more worried about what's behind door number three, the predator bastard."

Logan's heart skipped a beat. He blinked slowly.

Wait a minute.

He snapped his fingers. "That's it. We should *become* the predator bastard."

"Enchant the armor to become invisible on command. It should be able to be toggled on command."

[Level too low.]

"Damn it," Logan said. "But figures."

All of the super-powerful magic seemed to be behind a wall of levels. Invisibility, flight. Logan hadn't tried teleportation, but he felt like it was hardly necessary to even attempt.

[Might I note that we do not need pure invisibility? There is a scientific solution to this, although it is not quite as potent as a pure magical invisibility. We could simply have the armor reflect light.]

"Wait, what do you mean?"

[Here. Let me try a prompt . . . Oh, this is fun. I get to create reality with words. What a powerful thing! No wonder you like your class so much. Alright, I must not ramble. Try this: I command this object to acquire light-reflecting properties. Bend and redirect incoming light around your form, rendering you invisible to the naked eye. Make this ability toggleable by anyone with the **[Machine Soul]** *class.]*

Logan nodded and repeated what Tumor had said, pushing a pineapple-sized Numa crystal against his chest. The crystal shone with a blue glow and went completely dim, drained from full to nothing.

[Subclass Level Up!]
[Enchantment Level 36]
[Attribute Level Up!]
[Potency: 39]

Logan enjoyed the fresh minty feeling to its fullest. Then Tumor tugged at his consciousness, demanding attention.

Tumor activated the spell and Logan noticed his hands vanishing in front of his eyes. "Whoa."

It wasn't exactly pure invisibility. He could still see a faint outline of his hands, and the ground that was visible through them didn't look quite right. Logan brought his hands in front of his eyes. It was trippy. It was as if he were looking at reality through a soap bubble. Everything was slightly shifting and distorted and dim.

[The Numa drain is substantial. Also, do note that the soles of your feet are actually visible. A minor detail in most cases. I would be more worried about the Numa cost.]

Logan did indeed notice that there were two black footprints on the ground. They moved when he moved. Logan nodded to himself, crouched, and placed his hand down. It also became a visible handprint the moment it touched the clay ground. Logan prompted Tumor to create a spear in his hand. He slapped the tip of it on the ground in rapid succession and watched the black oval blade become visible, invisible, and visible again.

"Straightforward enough," Logan said.

[It is. I am glad it works just as I thought it would. But this Numa cost is high, Logan. Use of this has to be tactical. I am turning it off now. If we are completely still, the invisibility will work for . . . four minutes and twenty-one seconds. and note that it will drain the armor. I will create a subroutine that will govern the function. I will not let the invisibility be used when the

armor drops to 20% capacity. You can override this in cases of emergency by prompting me.]

"Got it," Logan said. "I wish we could increase the armor's capacity."

[We have, to a degree. Now would most likely be a good time to upgrade all of your enchantments on the armor. That will increase their efficiency and potency. The more I level, especially in my Control stat, the less Numa energy I need to consume to keep the armor operational. And additionally, as our synergistic ability to produce teamwork improves, that also increases the efficiency.]

"I mean, those are all good points," Logan said and shrugged. "But I have always been greedy. I want more."

Tumor said nothing to that, which was fine. Logan fell back into thought. They had gained a powerful tool, but they still had a lot of Numa energy to spare. Maybe traps were the answer. The problem was that if the traps weren't sprung, that was basically a waste of Numa. Logan would prefer something with a guaranteed application. He recharged his shield-ring as he thought. And while he was at it, he told Tumor to recite all of the enchantments that were embedded in Armor. Then Logan renewed them.

[Attribute Level Up!]
[Focus: 34]

That left Logan holding a slightly dimmed out **[B-grade Numa Crystal]**. He held the warmly glowing crystal in his hand. It still had 38 percent of its charge left. There was a lot one could do with that. But what exactly? That was the question.

What Logan needed was a failsafe. An oh-shit! button. Something to get him out of a really bad spot. Maybe a jetpack? Oh, hell yeah. A jetpack sounded awesome. Flight might not have been possible, but thrust? Talk about lightning striking twice. This was the same deal as the quasi-invisibility. Quasi-flight. Logan explained his idea to Tumor.

[Oh, I quite like this. Any maneuverability that doesn't come at the cost of expending the armor's already-stretched-out systems is welcome. The jetpack will be on your back, which will make it easy for me to access with my Possession ability.]

"Oh yeah, that's good," Logan said. "I didn't even think about that. I don't have to make some button or voice command. That's going to save my ass more than once."

[We need to make it easily discardable, as it will conflict with the invisibility of the armor, should we need to use it.]

Logan softly kicked at the basket with two of its vine straps waving around idly. "Let's strap a Numa crystal to that bad boy and that's basically that, right?"

It wasn't quite so simple. Logan had to play errand boy and gather up all sorts of sticks and leaves and bark. While they could magic their way out of most problems, the jetpack would still require some engineering. It needed thrusters in order to go in different directions: directly up, forward up, left up, left, right, right up. Instead of making a mechanical contraption with the ability to shift around, Logan simply made six tubes from leaves and hardened them. This would allow Tumor to use one or two at a time and not have to shift the thruster around. In a nutshell, it was faster this way and more maneuverable.

Next, it had to be properly strapped onto Logan's back. If the straps were not solid and in the anatomically right places, the jetpack was just going to rip Logan's shoulders out of their sockets. Tumor, who of course had Logan's perfect measurements, took some time to math out the kinks and details while Logan was foraging for materials.

Finally, they were done with the design, which was basically a tribesman's basket with strange tubes sticking out of its bottom. They had trimmed down the design from a container to something more compact, as well as adjusted the straps. There were a lot more of those. All of them held a special enchantment. They all had a little explosive clasp. Basically, Tumor could route Numa to the clasps and they would generate a burning hot flame that would instantly cut the strap. Doing it to all of the eight straps simultaneously would make the jetpack instantly drop from Logan's back. They had to spend a bit of excess Numa to make sure this actually worked as it was supposed to, which meant to Logan's chagrin, that he had to gather up extra vines.

Finally, they placed the mostly spent B-grader in a cradle which the six tubes created inside the jetpack. Tumor would use it as a power source. In a dire situation, he could also route Numa energy from the armor to the jetpack, but the AI made a firm point of reminding Logan that it was extremely inefficient and a terrible idea.

After giving the jetpack its power source, it was finally time to test it. Logan was giddy with excitement. He figured the thrust enchantment should be strong enough. He had tried giving the thing a flight enchantment, but to the surprise of none, it hadn't worked.

"Okay, let's do this," Logan said grinning like a kid on Christmas morning.

They took off the ground with an explosive blast, which made Logan's stomach lurch. Quickly he darted his eyes to the right, and the thrust blasted him to the right in midair. Then Logan slightly lifted his chin and looked up, they blasted upward, and he whooped with excitement. Right, up, left, up. Every time Logan moved his eyes, Tumor adjusted the thrust and they blasted through the air exactly ten feet. Tumor could adjust it if there were obstacles, but they kept ten feet as the basic unit.

To not waste any more energy, they let themselves fall.

Logan grinned and laughed, adrenaline rushing through him. For once, it was the fun kind. "That was awesome! I can't wait to show this to all the guys at the camp."

[It was indeed exhilarating. I must insist we do this again. The energy expenditure is not too bad, but it is noticeable. The crystal is now down to 35% of its capacity.]

"Noted," Logan said, calming down. That wasn't too bad. They weren't rich in Numa, but they had enough to keep using the jetpack.

"Alright, inventory time," Logan said. "We got stealth, we got maneuverability, we got our nasty bananarangs. What do you think we need next, buddy?"

Logan thought he felt something that resembled an excited grin through their link.

[More firepower.]

CHAPTER 36

You want a *minigun?*" Logan asked, trying to keep the incredulity at a minimum.

[Or a bazooka. Which would you rather wield?]

"I don't think we are quite up there yet on the tech tree," Logan said. "For one, we don't have metal."

[Pish posh. A little detail like that never stopped us before.]

"Please never say 'pish posh' again or I will gouge your eyes out with a fork."

[You would need metal for that.]

"I could craft one from stone or wood."

[Messy.]

Logan chuckled. "I will admit, the Predator uses really dumb weapons. We should have something more modern. Hey, speaking of *Predator,* what about heat vision?"

[Very useful. But the armor is at maximum capacity. Which enchantment would you let go to have heat vision?]

"None of them," Logan admitted. "But maybe we could craft some goggles."

[See any transparent materials around here?]

"No but . . ." Logan walked a few steps and picked up a stick. Then he went for the pile of Numa crystals.

"Make this stick give heat-vision powers to anyone holding it."

[Enchantment level requirement not met]

"Well damn it," Logan said. "Just wait. I'll . . ."

Logan spent the next five minutes turning the stick into a coin shape, transmutating it to become transparent, and trying to make a monocle with heat vision.

[Enchantment level requirement not met]

Logan pouted for the next five minutes.

After some bickering and a surprising amount of huffing from Tumor, they agreed on a weapon design. A dart minigun. It was perfect, really. First, Logan started with the darts. He made a prototype that was perfectly aerodynamic and optimally designed according to Tumor's blueprints. Then he placed a Numa crystal next to a big pile of bark, which he had decided to use as material.

[Mass Produce]
[Skill Level Up!]
[Mass Produce Level 13]

The pieces of bark started to morph, and finally a hundred thin darts of dark wood were stacked in a neat pile on the ground. Logan inspected one of them. Two inches long. Sharp on the thinner edge and little ridges at the other end to provide some elementary fletching.

Next came the "fun" part. The painstakingly fun part of enchanting each and every one of the darts. No, you couldn't transfer enchantments with **[Mass Produce]**. Logan had tried. It had to be done with good old manual labor. For some reason, it always seemed to come as a shock to people who met Logan, but as a son of a billionaire, Logan actually wasn't well-versed or particularly experienced in manual labor. In fact, he abhorred it.

"I guess there's no helping it," Logan said and sighed as he sat down next to the pile of darts.

He gave each of the darts the full package: durability, auto-aim, a slight weight enchantment for more impact power, and a penetration enchantment. That was all a single dart could handle. Which meant that there was another phase to this process, to Logan's great delight.

With transmutation, he made a small puddle of glob which he enchanted with his trademark poison—blindness, paralysis, organ failure, the works. After the glob was done, Logan dipped each of the darts into the puddle, infusing the tips with poison. Then the darts needed to be placed into a cylinder designed by Tumor. It was circular and had exactly a hundred slots into which Logan started sliding them.

Once they were in place, Logan slotted the wooden cylinder into what was essentially a double-barreled blowpipe. On the belly side of the blowpipe was a trigger made of hardened wood.

Logan did a few tests. He placed his index finger on the barrel of the blowpipe and drew it down to squeeze the trigger. He did it twenty times, slowly and conscientiously. There was no room for screw-ups here. The trigger didn't give much resistance, because the weapon was not loaded. On the left side of the barrel, where Logan kept his hand to steady the weapon, was a small lever, just the right size for Logan to squeeze it with his thumb. As he did that, the weapon clicked and he could feel two darts slide into the barrel. Therein waited another enchantment designed for creating thrust. It would blast the darts out of the barrel at a speed of 125 feet per second, at a maximum range of 310 feet. There were some decimals involved, but Logan didn't pay too close attention.

The point was the weapon was powerful. More powerful than it probably needed to be, but it was better to be safe than sorry.

Poison bananarangs for the big threats, dart minigun for the smaller swarms. Add in a jetpack and stealth armor and we are starting to look pretty damn dangerous.

That was good, because Logan had a feeling this would be one hell of a fight. Now he supposed was a good as time as any to start calling for Levemoth.

[I want you to remember to not *show off. The first wave will be for scouting. We do not want to reveal anything. We have to assume Levemoth can glean information from its spawn. We should take on the scouting attack only with tools they already know about.]*

"Me show off?" Logan said and scoffed in mock hurt. "I would never."

[Of course you would not . . .]

"You're the one who insisted we build a goddamn *minigun*! It took like what, three hours? And it consumed almost three full **[B-grade Numa Crystals]**."

[I am aware of all of these factors. Now the question remains how we should use the two B-grade crystals that we have left. It seems less than ideal to simply carry them around with us at this point.]

Logan shrugged. He had no answers or quippy comebacks. He was mentally exhausted from his labors. He just wanted Levemoth to throw monsters at them and get it over with.

"I'll revert back to my old tricks. Let's create a couple of flashbangs and grenades. We can't use darkmetal this time for the shrapnel, but maybe stone? Or hardened wood?"

[Hardened wood? Would you like to enchant each and every piece of shrapnel individually with hardening magic?]

"You know what?" Logan said and got up quickly. "Let's find some rocks."

After two more hours, Logan had a belt with two pouches attached to his waist. Each held six grenades. Three of them were filled with shrapnel made from rocks fashioned into sharp, pointy pyramids with **[Mass Produce]**, along with three flashbang grenades for tight spots in close-to-medium range. All Logan would have to do is set one off, fly off with a jetpack and then turn invisible while the enemy was temporarily blinded.

Or just . . . you know straight-up kill them then and there.

Logan and Tumor were as prepared as they could ever be. Logan had gotten quite a few attribute level-ups and even some in his subclasses. He felt that a level-up to his class was close. He didn't remember the last time he had indulged in checking his stat interface to appear, but he sure was going to indulge now.

Logan Specter - [Artificer Level 7]
Attributes:
Potency: 39
Efficiency: 36
Durability: 25
Control: 36
Focus: 34
Subclasses:
[Transmutation]: 32
[Enchantment]: 36
Class Skills:
[Empower]: 10
[Funnel]: 12
[Repair]: 11
General Skills:
[Power Armor Fighting]: 13

Satisfied, Logan closed the interface. The next task on his mind was to start squirreling away Numa crystals somewhere while they waited for Levemoth to make its move. They were possibly hundreds of miles away from Freya and home and it would take a lot of firepower to get back. Logan wasn't sure how much he would need to level or what kind of crazy bullshit he would have to pull to get back home. But he would, and for that he would most likely need a pile of Numa, so it was time to hunt for more monkeys and start stashing the loot somewhere.

And so he spent the next few hours practicing with the jetpack and going after the gorillas. They used up two full **[B-grade Numa Crystals]** flying around, but it was worth it. Not only was it *extremely* fun to zip around and dodge the charging monkeys (they tested the potency of the dart gun rather than using the bananarangs), but it was also paramount that they got experience with their new tool. They didn't know the extent of the threat they were facing, so it was best to be prepared.

After a haul of five monkeys, an even deeper darkness was starting to take the jungle. Logan was starting to slow down as tiredness overtook him. Eventually he had to relent and stop to dress a monkey corpse and eat his fill of meat. Logan made sure he was absolutely stuffed to the brim. This might be his last meal for a while. After he was done, he had Tumor create the coffin with pillows on a nice thick tree branch. Logan fell asleep immediately in the comfortable darkness of his miniature abode.

CHAPTER 37

Logan woke up refreshed and they quickly sorted out their gear and set out to hunt more monkeys. Logan made sure that Tumor remembered this place and could definitely navigate them back, before he hid the crystals as the bushes were particularly thick and thorny here.

Tumor was offended by Logan even asking the question. They bickered for a while, Tumor taking Logan to task for leaving the crystals behind as they walked through the dim jungle and started looking for monkeys to kill.

"It's not like we have to look out for thieves here," Logan said and smiled. He was secretly pleased that Tumor got miffed by his remark. It made him feel more human than AI.

They killed three more monstrous gorillas before they found something curious. Logan looked around and listened, but neither his instincts nor his mind warned him of any trap or danger. Then he knelt down at the sound of the pattering of little puddles of black oil. Logan dipped a finger in one of the pools and brought it to the grate of his helmet. The stench made him flinch back.

"They're here," Logan said under his breath.

[Small drop, this one. Judging from the pattern of the oil drops as well as the volume, there is a 78.22% chance this was a scythe-fiend.]

"That's good," Logan said. He took off the jetpack and laid down the dart minigun as well as the pouch containing two **[B-grade Numa Crystals]**.

All of these he shoved into a bush, resisting the urge to tell Tumor to remember the spot. Some of his thought process must have seeped through, however, as Logan could sense Tumor's emotions boil up ever so slightly through the link they shared.

Then Logan started skulking around in the jungle again. But this time it was different. Shit had gotten serious. Levemoth knew someone was down here, and Logan was sure the Great Thief had a pretty good idea of who that someone might be.

Logan moved further into the jungle slightly hunched, going from tree to tree, looking around alertly.

Soon he heard the telltale hoarse cry of a scythe-fiend. It was answered by a stray chorus of cries scattered in all directions.

Quite the party. That's likely, what, ten, fifteen of them? And surely that's not all.

[It could be all. We do not have enough data on what Levemoth can do. Its ability to pinpoint the location of the use of corrupted Numa could be quite accurate. We have to assume it is extremely high-level.]

"That we do," Logan muttered as he peeked from behind a thick, yellow-barked tree into the shadows of the jungle. Indeed, there was movement. The scythe-fiend had the lazy gait of a confident predator. But Logan noticed there was something off about it. This wasn't like any normal scythe-fiend.

I don't like this. Something is wrong.

[Not enough data to make an extensive analysis. It seems that it has some physical attributes that are slightly different from the previous creatures of the same sort we have seen.]

There was some trick here, Logan knew it. Regardless of his unease, he crept closer to take a better look. Once he had gotten behind a fallen tree fifty paces away from the creature, it skulked into full view between the trees and bushes.

Instead of the black-and-blue mottled skin the scythe-fiends normally had, this creature was completely blue. It glowed faintly, like any Numa crystal. It had blue ridges on both sides of its spine like a row of shining sapphires. The eyeless head also shone slightly blue, as if radioactive. Only the scythes looked the same. They were black, sharp, and curved.

Something told Logan to be extremely careful with this new threat.

Still, I need to take initiative. I can't just wait for one of them to notice me.

Logan would have preferred using the dart gun, but it was better to keep it hidden. The problem with that was that he would have to go in and get his hands dirty with this bastard. It could explode upon death for all he knew. Logan shook his head. He put a mental stopper on his anxious thoughts and walked up from behind the tree and blasted the blue scythe-fiend with all the power and speed that the armor possessed.

It only let out a hoarse cry that was immediately cut short when Logan decapitated it. The monster fell limp to the ground.

"Huh?"

But then it started to sizzle. Its skin grew molten and started steaming, creating a vicious stench. Logan took a few steps back. The whiff he had taken in was muddling his brain. The steam was poisonous. He would definitely need to avoid the fumes.

Then the forest erupted in a discordant chorus of hoarse cries. They came from every direction and soon, Logan saw movement in at least three directions.

"Zweihänder," he said and widened his stance.

The first of the scythe-fiends clicked rapidly toward him, screaming hoarsely. It jumped like a panther at him, the gleaming black blades on its forelegs extended.

Logan sidestepped and swung the massive sword's edge toward the monster's spine. It cracked under the power of the swing and the thin frame of the scythe-fiend was sliced in half. Logan quickly darted away just as the sizzling started. Another scythe-fiend was already approaching from the other side. Logan placed some distance between them and extended his right arm. Tumor shot a barrage of Black Missiles at the beast and it dropped with a hoarse death rattle.

The third one jumped at Logan, who only noticed it too late to either avoid it or swing his sword.

"Shield!" Logan shouted and a blue umbrella of energy shrouded him.

But the creature ignored him. It simply jumped past Logan and went toward its dead brethren. By now, the first two scythe-fiends had fully dissolved. They had turned into pools of shining, viscous liquid. It looked like blue mercury on the forest floor. Logan was so stunned by the creature missing an opportunity to land a surprise attack that he didn't even move to stop it when it started sucking in the mercury with its round, toothless mouth. Logan watched it, hypnotized, a part of his mind idly wondering what could have been more important to the creature than trying to take a cheap shot at him.

As it sucked in the blue substance, its body started to bulge and morph. Long blue spines began to grow on its back and its face got wider. Suddenly, glowing blue eyes sprouted on it like mushrooms in the rain, a disgusting cluster of them, like a spider gone wrong.

It got bigger. Much bigger. If the original scythe-fiends were the size of a mountain lion, this grew to the size of a bull on steroids. The round mouth morphed too, and it spread into an eerie grin.

Logan snapped out of it and swung the Zweihänder. The creature parried it with a scythe. Logan extended his arm and let Tumor shoot the damned thing. The Black Missiles worked, preventing the other scythe from cleaving Logan in two and making the monster reel back. Logan used the space the attack created and prompted Tumor to switch the Zweihänder into a spear and shield.

The scythe-fiend's grin turned into a snarl, and Logan stabbed the spear right into it. It screeched and tried to slash with its scythe-arm, but Logan blocked the swing with the shield as he twisted the spear. Blue blood oozed from the mouth. Logan's shield turned into a short sword, and he jammed it into the throat of the monstrous creature.

It started sizzling. Four or five scythe-fiends were running toward him. *[We need to run.]*

"No! If we run, they'll eat the goop and become huge. Shoot them!"

Tumor didn't question; he just fired small bullets in bursts of three and four. They cut down three of the approaching scythe-fiends. Logan dashed around with armor-powered leaps and cut down another three. But there were still a few left. The problem was, they weren't interested in Logan as much as he would have hoped.

The sizzling blue goop was now scattered here and there, and Logan was surrounded by feeding enemies and dangerous fume clouds.

[Logan.]

Logan gritted his teeth. Tumor was right. "Damn it!"

He cut one more down while Tumor was retrieving the darkmetal bullets with his **[Machine Soul]** abilities. More scythe-fiends approached the area. Two of them were already large, and they watched Logan through their disgusting clusters of eyes as they prowled closer with careful predation.

[LOGAN!]

"Tsk."

Logan dodged a lunge from one of the big ones, kicking up sediment in his wake as he made his armor turn and charge forward. Another step, then a third. They gathered up speed and bobbed and weaved between the trees. The monsters behind him screeched and began pursuit.

Logan glanced back. They were slower than he was. But while his pursuers were behind him, he also heard a chorus of screeches from his left. They were approaching. How those particular enemies knew he was going this way was an interesting question.

There'll be time to ponder that later.

[Logan. Climb a tree.]

Logan kicked off the ground and jumped six feet high onto a thick, dark, brown tree trunk. The darkmetal around his fingers morphed into a sticky substance which allowed Logan to climb up the tree like a lizard.

[Mmmm, nice. I hadn't done that before, so I gained an attribute level.]

"Not a good time, Tumor," Logan muttered as he grabbed a branch and hoisted himself onto it. Logan observed what was happening below them through the foliage. To his great dismay, the swarm of these new scythe-fiends didn't simply trample forward and let Logan slink away behind them. They stopped.

For the love of Freya's delectable butt, why did they stop?

Logan adjusted himself on the branch ever so slightly. This was not the time to create movement. But he needed to see . . . And it was just as he had suspected.

The scythe-fiends had hunched their shoulders and put their heads down like a pack of greyhounds. They weren't sniffing, as dogs would, but instead flicking their black tongues at the ground, as if tasting for Numa or darkmetal. Slowly but surely, they were all homing in on the tree Logan was in. He was trapped.

"Tumor," Logan hissed urgently. "Stealth."

[Roger.]

Logan watched his hands and arms turn from sleek black into a mirror-like substance that flickered faintly when Logan moved. He didn't move. He was as still as he could be as he watched the swarm of monsters converging around the tree. He saw one of them put its scythes against the trunk and crane its long neck up. The disgusting cluster of blue eyes looked directly in Logan's direction. But it didn't make a hoarse screech.

The creature just kept turning its head. Two other scythe-fiends did the same on different sides of the wide tree trunk. One by one, they finally dragged their scythes off the tree and conversed with one another in screeches. Then they continued deeper into the forest as a horde.

Logan exhaled, remembering again that he actually needed to breathe.

"*This* is a scouting party?" Logan asked. "I don't care if they see us with our new toys. I'm going to go get our gear."

[Agreed.]

CHAPTER 38

Logan had never walked so carefully in his life. He looked around every few steps, stopped to listen and watch in places he felt safe to crouch in. He could still hear the hoarse screams here and there, but none of them came worryingly close.

Finally, guided by Tumor, Logan made his way back to their equipment and the leftover Numa crystals. Then, he had a thought. He could use the same trick twice. No reason to play all their cards at once.

"You know what," Logan said and stopped himself before he put the jetpack on. "You were right all along."

[Of course I was! Wait . . . What was I right about?]

"We can't let them see our new toys," Logan said and smirked. "If this is the scouting wave, that big bastard has something nasty planned."

[So, what do you want to do?]

"We're going to make a sludge pit."

They took the Numa crystals in tow and then started looking for a nice open space to lure all of those blue little bastards to. Logan hadn't made a proper sludge pit in ages, and he was now much more powerful, with a big, fat amount of Numa to play with. This wouldn't just be a sludge pit. It would be a sludge *lake*.

[Not to be negative, but it is kind of my role to make sure you don't do any-thing exceedingly stupid. Call me a voice of reason if you will.]

"A spoilsport is what I'll call you," Logan said, disliking Tumor's tone already. "What is it?"

[These enemies seem to be rather smart. Simulations indicate that there is as high as an 18.55% chance that they are directly controlled by Levemoth or this

"Herald" entity. These are not mindless bugs like the last time. We need an extra step to the plan.]

"I'm listening," Logan said and peered through the jungle vegetation with some nervousness.

[One option is to camouflage the pit—illusion magic to make it look like the ground.]

Logan thought about it. "Yeah . . . They had a pretty good idea that we were in that tree. Do you think they can smell me specifically, or Numa, or what?"

[I ran an analysis on the phenomenon, and I believe it is most likely they can smell Numa or its corruption. This is a known ability of Levemoth, and Levemoth seems to have more agency in this encounter than we are used to. My analysis says that there is a 67.33% chance that the minions are infused with the same ability their progenitor possesses.]

"That's as much of a threat as a possibility," Logan said. "We can work with that. If we use it to our advantage somehow, we can tilt the battle in our favor."

Tumor was silent for a moment. Logan crouched and looked around. He could hear the sporadic screeches coming from here and there, some from afar and some rather uncomfortably close.

[It's simple, really, especially now that they expect to look for you in the trees. We make a Numa beacon. Hold on. Let me run another simulation . . . We need a contingency plan . . .]

Once Tumor was done, they got to work. Well, in actuality, it was Logan who got to work. Tumor, the slick bastard, claimed that his work had been already done in the planning phase. Logan hoped they would get home soon so the lazy bastard could get his body back and share the load.

They found a big forest opening and actually had to kill a giant gorilla, who was sitting in ambush in one of the trees. It was fast and painless thanks to a well-aimed bananarang to the neck. The Numa crystal was welcome as well as the fact that none of the scythe-fiends had heard the clamor of the fight.

"Make this opening into a pit of poisonous sludge. Make the sludge stick to any flesh it touches. Make it paralyze, blind, and cause nerve damage, leading to death. Additionally make it dissolve anything it touches. Make the potency of the poisonous agent so strong that it consumes all of these two B-graders."

[Subclass Level Up!]
[Enchantment Level 36]

[Attribute Level Up!]
[Potency: 40]
[Class Level Up!]
[Artificer Level 8]
[New Passive Skill Acquired!]
[New Passive Skill Acquired!]

"Finally," Logan muttered. He opened up his interface to read about the new ability he had acquired.

[Numa Psychic: Acquire ability to use Numa without touching a Numa energy source. Range increases with Potency and Focus modifiers.]

"Oh, nice!" Logan said. "This is one of the choices I made earlier. Nice to get this. I hated to let it go last time.

[That will have some useful applications. What is the other one?]

[Numatech Expert: All of your creations will now expend less Numa energy. The degree of expenditure is determined by your Potency and Efficiency Modifiers.]

"Okay, yeah," Logan said. "These are starting to add up."

*[I like that these are overall useful and not too niche. If we are fortunate, we will be going through tons of Numa crystals, and the way your build is starting to optimize, it's efficient to use a lot of it. Everything is starting to go in that direction. Your [**Mass Produce**] skill is a good example of this.]*

"Oh, yeah," Logan said, nodding. "But so far I've mostly been crafting shit for myself."

[That might change soon.]

"It might," Logan said. "But now we need to focus."

Logan looked at their Numa beacon. It was beautiful. Well, technically it was just a piece of an old decomposing log Logan had found. But if it worked like they had intended, it would most certainly be nothing short of beautiful.

"Do you think they're stupid enough to fall for this?"

[They have beast-level intelligence unless specifically influenced by Levemoth. Perhaps they share some collective hivemind that receives orders. That is my best guess. They each communicate something to the operational

system. Most likely something like "Numa detected." This will prompt an order from the operational unit, which we assume to be Levemoth. I believe the Great Thief will order them to check out the source of the Numa. I am fairly certain Levemoth knows it's you, and while you are perceived as a threat, I believe you are being underestimated.]

"Let's make sure the big bastard will live to regret it."

After they had the Numa beacon enchanted and attached to the tree trunk some fifteen feet above the ground, Logan recharged the armor with a bit of Numa crystal. He was very happy to have found one of the monster gorillas here, so they could make the Numa beacon potent and also add the finishing touch to the pool of sludge. Additionally, the gorilla's corpse had also given them the chance to observe how fast tissue as tough as its flesh dissolved in the poison sludge. The answer was "pretty fast."

"Cover this pit of sludge with an illusion. Make it look exactly the same as the ground—"

Logan stopped himself. This wouldn't work without cheating. He certainly couldn't remember every detail of every inch of space that had been here prior. Luckily, he just so happened to have a friend with an eidetic memory.

Tumor did not need further instruction. He did something Logan hadn't experienced before. He *inception*ed a memory into Logan's mind. A perfect image of what the landscape had looked like before. Logan, having artistic tendencies, could easily hold the image in his mind, now that he had a clear picture. All he had to do was to instruct the Numa.

"Cover this pit of sludge with an illusion. Make it look exactly like the terrain I am holding in my mind."

[Attribute Level Up!]
[Efficiency: 37]

It was perfect. The pit and its edges vanished like a mirage in the desert. Logan had to make Tumor ensure that they wouldn't tumble into the illusion themselves by accident. In response, Tumor got that peevish edge in his otherwise calm, robotic voice, suggesting that if he didn't have the capacity to realize that without Logan's input, they would have been dead a long time ago. Logan shrugged and agreed.

The next order of business was simple: create illusions around the poison pit to attract the attention of the little blue buggers. All possible preparation was done, and now it was down to simple execution. Logan liked that. At the end of the day, he was a simple man.

Logan jogged around for maybe fifteen minutes. With the armor, jogging was closer to the speed of a professional marathon runner, which, in the thick of the jungle, was rather impressive. It was made possible by the armor's ability to generate enough sheer force to push through anything. Two times, they crushed a hapless spider that happened to be sitting in ambush in a bush that Logan charged through. He decided to use their meager E-grader crystals to keep the armor topped up.

It was enough consumption of corrupted Numa to attract the attention of the searching horde of blue scythe-fiends. First, Logan saw five of them charging toward him like a pack of greyhounds. But he could hear the screeches coming from another direction close by as well. Logan grinned to himself and kicked the earth, sending it flying as he pushed the armor to outpace the five monsters chasing him. He headed in the direction of the screeches.

With tight maneuvers and Tumor telling him when to turn and when to slow down or speed up, like a race driver's copilot, they ran around the jungle this way and that, until Tumor had assembled a pretty decent map. They then used that to keep the growing horde of scythe-fiends at bay. Eight scythe-fiends. Then fifteen. All the way up to twenty-five. At that point, Tumor suggested they turn around and head to the trap, so that they would have enough Numa energy for stealth and in case of something unexpected happening.

Logan beelined in the direction Tumor was pointing toward through red holographic arrows appearing in his vision, in addition to verbal instructions. They kept the horde of scythe-fiends just far enough away that they could vanish out of sight with a burst of speed when it was the correct time.

Tumor had already simulated the situation 172 times. They hit the perfect timing with an accuracy of 94.60 percent.

Logan skidded the armor to a halt just before the edge of the pit, took a tight left, and Tumor activated the stealth capability of the Armor. They waited with bated breath as the angry hoarse screeches approached. Logan could hear his heart pounding; he counted ten heavy beats.

Then the first scythe-fiends ran into the pit. Their screeches of anger and excitement turned into agony and angered surprise. The first eight of the scythe-fiends ran straight into the trap at full speed. Four more tried to skid to slow down but they fell over the edge as well.

Despite Tumor's protestations, Logan acted. He broke stealth and made Tumor create a massive staff sprouting out of his hands. He slammed five more scythe-fiends into the pit with a home-run strike.

[Skill Level Up!]
[Power Armor Fighting Level 14]

He struck down the rest of the horde like a Spartan hoplite, with shield and spear. They started sizzling, but Logan bulldozed, eating a few hits from the scythe-fiends with his shield ring and the armor's natural durability. When the scythe-fiends tried to start sucking up their dead, Logan prompted Tumor to summon the staff again and he swiped them into the pit.

Within minutes, Logan was standing at the edge of the enchanted pit of poison, breathing hard and watching his enemies dissolve. He had won the first battle.

CHAPTER 39

It took some sweat to kill the rest of the blue scythe-fiends. But it wasn't as hard. They were fairly easy to lure into trying to feed off the sizzling remains of their fallen comrades. When they started doing that and metamorphosing, Logan pushed them into the sludge. After twenty-seven of the monsters had been pushed into the pit of sludge, for their remains to be never usable again, Logan lay back against the trunk of a thick tree and slid downward.

He closed his eyes and breathed. It was not a moment of complete relaxation, as there still could be more of these bastards somewhere around. However, it did seem like this had been most, if not all, of them. At least in this local area of the jungle.

We won. We goddamn won. And we did it while keeping our cards close to our chest.

[Do you need a rest? It would most likely be advantageous for us to hunt those monkeys. Additionally we need to remove the beacon. We can most likely still retrieve a sizeable amount of the Numa.]

"Give me a minute," Logan said between breaths. He kept his eyes closed, just wanting to enjoy the victory. He smiled to himself. This was it. It felt good fighting when you had nobody to worry about. No Freya or even Balmer to look out for.

He leaned back and let himself muse for a moment. Ever since he first came to this screwed-up planet, it had all been about responsibility. First, vying for power with his father, who didn't have the first inkling of a clue about how to manage a little village of scared people in a completely new situation. Then, he had had to actually take charge of the community. Make sure it grew. Make sure to provide resources for it. Make sure nobody died for some stupid reason.

Killing monsters, crafting solutions, running around the jungle. It felt almost like a holiday compared to how his day-to-day had been.

Leadership was not simple. The responsibility had been serious. Logan had to keep people safe. And yet they still died. It felt like tilting against windmills. It all had such a weight to it. Logan thought about his father. Had it been like that for him too? Had he been burdened by leadership or had he simply reveled in the power of it? Logan from a year ago would have suggested the latter. Now he wasn't so sure.

What happened to my father?

Suddenly the stray rays of light that bled through the dimness of the jungle blinked out. Something in the sky was blocking them out. Logan didn't need many guesses to figure out what it was. Levemoth had his location down to a pinpoint.

"Should we move?" Logan asked.

[I think so. Grab the gear and make some distance.]

Logan couldn't argue with that. Quickly, he grabbed the dart minigun and the jetpack. Then he boosted up to the three with the beacon and took it down with him. He used **[Funnel]** on it to recharge the armor.

[Funnel Level 14]

Something heavy dropped down to the edge of the pool of sludge—a big black droplet of oil. Some splashes of the substance flew in every direction, some of it in the pit, where they sizzled and vanished. Whatever drops of the mercurial blue substance the scythe-fiends had left behind got sucked into the black embryo that squirmed and rippled on the ground. It was the size of a car.

Logan hid behind some bushes. But there was no point in running off into the jungle and then waiting for something to happen. He needed to see what he was dealing with.

The bubble of black oil burst open. Logan saw that the creature inside was both foreign and familiar.

Its crablike, wide head peeked out first, with black eyes that had a strangely human, discerning look to them that seemed familiar to Logan, as it surveyed the area. It was covered in black and blue carapace, with spikes protruding from its shoulders, elbows, and spine. Its hands were half claws, half fingers. The creature flexed them in front of its face as if intrigued by its own form. The joints clicked and the monster snapped the four fingers together, producing a powerful *CLACK*.

Logan felt uneasy. He took a few steps back as the creature emerged from its embryo. The legs were muscular and jointed backward toward the knee and then forward in a steep angle like that of an insect designed for jumping.

It jumped. And almost vanished in a blur. Logan sent a prompt to Tumor to predict the trajectory. In another blur, the creature reappeared on the other side of the pit of sludge. It knelt down and looked at the edge of the illusion.

How can it see it?

Then a tingle of shock ran through Logan's spine as the creature turned its intelligent black eyes in his direction. Not just his direction. Directly *at* him.

Goddammit. It has heat vision.

It jumped and turned into a veritable blur again, but Logan was ready, as was Tumor. The shield Logan's armor conjured clanged when the crab-creature struck it with a claw. It pierced the armor. Nothing had ever done that before.

But simultaneously it had impaled itself on the short spear which Logan was holding in his other hand. The creature looked down at its pierced torso and scoffed.

With its other hand, it snapped the spear in half. Logan could only watch in mute shock.

"Logan . . ." the creature said with a voice as monstrous as it was weary. "You must die . . ."

"Wh—what?"

Before the creature could answer, Tumor shot a barrage of Black Missiles at it, and it reeled and stumbled backward.

[Logan! RUN!]

Logan picked up the dart gun and shot a few rounds from it at the creature and jumped away, zigzagging here and there, changing directions and speed so as to make it hard for the creature to charge at him accurately.

Logan turned just fast enough to dodge the monster. It charged past him with an extended claw pressed into something resembling a spearhead. When Logan turned, Tumor shot a barrage of Black Missiles. The creature turned with uncanny speed and ducked to avoid the first ones. With the lightning-fast processing speed, Tumor adjusted the trajectories and the rest of the three bullets that had been launched smashed directly into the crouching creature.

It stumbled and snarled, but it held itself upright with an arm. Logan shot a fusillade of darts in its face, but again he was startled to notice something familiar there. There was something about the features and the lines in the black and blue that Logan had seen before . . .

Most of the darts missed or clicked against the black-and-blue-mottled carapace, ricocheting uselessly. But two of them stuck, one in the creature's cheek, and the other in its neck.

That had better work.

Logan kept dodging, mainly relinquishing the autonomy of his movements to Tumor, who was piloting the armor. The Herald was too fast. Twice, it caught him with a sharp spear of a hand, but it was only a glancing blow. But every time that happened, it was only due to an inhuman twist of a dodge, which strained Logan's body.

[This kind of fighting is biting into the armor's power reserves.]

"Tumor . . ." Logan gasped between breaths. ". . . I can't go on like this."

[I know. I'm buying us time. If the poison is taking effect, we can outrun it and escape. If not, however . . . Either we'll need to make a sacrifice or you need to come up with a creative solution.]

"Great . . ."

Logan decided they needed to go on the offensive. He told Tumor his plan via their link. Tumor said it would be possible, but it would most likely fracture Logan's ankle. Logan only nodded grimly.

They dodged one more time. Then Tumor and Logan acted in tandem. They turned, and Logan pushed his body off the ground at the enemy, pushing up ground behind him. At the same time Tumor activated their jetpack to create forward thrust.

Logan felt the whiplash in his neck before Tumor strengthened the armor, providing stability and cushion. His vision blurred and he smashed into the enemy with an extended elbow. Tumor had to jerk the elbow forward and stabilize it against the chest by the fist.

The monstrous crab creature growled with pain and Logan heard a crack. Whether it was his elbow, ribcage, or the enemy's carapace, he wasn't sure. He blasted through the Herald, casting it aside as Logan himself crashed into a bush.

[It was all of them, Logan. Can you breathe? It seems you can stay conscious. I understand you're in a great deal of pain. The enemy is damaged as well.]

Through blurry vision, Logan took a glance at the enemy. It was on the ground, coughing and bleeding from a cracked hole in its chest. It looked at

Logan with its dim, black eyes, and through the pain Logan saw determination. He returned the gaze.

Through a cough that wracked Logan with pain, he laughed. "Looks like we are both going down, bastard."

"Logan . . ." the creature moaned, almost softly. Then something shifted in its eyes and the voice hardened, becoming less human, more alien. "The boy is hurt. I cannot pursue him further. Send another wave."

Crap.

[Logan, get up. Just get up and keep your abdominal muscles tight and knees ready to bend and absorb impact. I will do the rest.]

Through a gasp of agony, Logan complied. His lungs and throat were screaming at him, but he managed to struggle up, mainly through the balance and strength the armor provided him with.

"We need to finish him off," Logan said. But the shadow of Levemoth had already appeared above them. Black drops of oil fell down left and right.

Tumor said nothing. Instead, he activated the jetpack and started flying through the air in short bursts of thrust. Every time Tumor did that, Logan felt a painful lurch in his stomach and shoulders. It didn't matter how well the jetpack was braced and strapped on him, Logan's body was starting to break down.

The hoarse screeches were behind him. The enemy knew exactly what direction he was going. Tumor acted on this thought and changed direction. Logan tried to hang on, keeping his core tight and pushing his consciousness to press through the pain.

They developed some lead, but the thrusts of the jetpack were getting sparser, and Tumor started to mix them in with kicks off the ground. Logan wasn't surprised by what Tumor said next.

[The jetpack is running out of Numa.]

"Get some from the armor," Logan snapped. Only the spike of anger was keeping him awake. It gave him energy.

[Understood.]

That let them go a little further, a little longer, but the horde of hoarse screams was getting closer. Logan smashed through bush after bush, crushing the odd spider in his way here and there. Then another set of black drops fell right in front of him, and Logan's heart skipped a beat.

He was on his last legs. Tumor knew it too. His consciousness was fading.

"We need . . . to . . . hide . . ."

Tumor complied. They surged over a fallen tree to their right and with a final panther leap into a bush, they slid and skidded two yards forward, and Tumor activated stealth.

A horde of scythe-fiends ran past Logan, and stopped at the second horde, which was spawning. They sat on their haunches like a pack of dogs. After two minutes, the Herald limped toward the scattered pack of monstrous hunting dogs. They assembled into two rows and the Herald commanded them.

"I can sense something consuming Numa nearby. He is here. Form four packs. Fan out into the east, west, south, and north. Hunt slowly. He is not running, he is hiding."

With that, the scythe-fiends let out a uniform cry of agreement and they started spreading out in every direction, their heads low to the ground, as if searching for footprints.

[Logan, the Armor is going to run out of Numa in forty-two seconds.]

CHAPTER 40

[If there ever was a time for a crazy, creative plan, now is the time, Logan.]

Logan had nothing. There was a scythe-fiend sniffing around to his left and right, only four or five feet away.

[Twenty seconds, Logan. And after that, the armor is drained.]

Was this how it ended? Logan had absolutely nothing. A strange sense of calm took him. He had done his best. He really had. He had fought tooth and nail. In just a few seconds, they would be revealed and the pain would end.

I put up a hell of a fight, if nothing else. I never realized how much of a fighter I even was. I'm glad I was dropped onto this crazy planet. It was the best thing that ever happened to me. And Tumor. I'm really grateful for meeting you. You're my best buddy. I just . . . Thanks. Hopefully Freya will be alright . . .

[Thank you, Logan. It has been . . . exciting. I am—]

Suddenly something glimmered in front of Logan. It sparkled faintly. Then a short, transparent creature with cream-colored porcelain skin materialized in front of them and grinned.

Logan gasped in surprise. He recognized that impish smile.

"You're safe!" Snoff said. "My illusion magic will hide us both."

The sparkles around Snoff extended and enveloped Logan. The scythe-fiends turned to look in their direction but apparently saw nothing interesting. They walked past Logan's position. Tumor released the armor's stealth mechanism.

"We can talk here," Snoff said. "Just don't be loud. 'Tis good to see you, Logan."

"Snoff . . ." Logan rasped between breaths. "Pain . . . A lot of pain . . ."

"Heh," Snoff said triumphantly, as if he were happy with such a situation. "The time has finally come for me to repay you for saving my life. I will leave a barrier of illusion on you and get my brethren. Do not move."

"As if I . . ."

But Snoff was already gone, skipping away and turning into a translucent, sparkling ghost. Logan passed out.

When Logan came to, he noticed he was in a shoddy hut made of leaves and sticks. There were some subtle clues that it was made by the Faelves rather than human hand. First and foremost was the size, of course. But it also had . . . softer shapes, smoother curves. It was beautiful in a subtle way.

One could tell that the Faelves cared about aesthetics. Were it Logan who had built the little hut, he would have constructed it by form and function first. It was not that the Faelves neglected that. It was just that they put more care into the building.

"Snoff?" Logan called out. His voice was hoarse and didn't carry. Regardless, within moments, Snoff popped his head inside the hut and grinned.

"Alive, are we?" Snoff said.

"Water," Logan croaked. "My kingdom for water."

"I shall take you up on that!" Snoff said and vanished from the doorframe. A minute later, he came back with a clay cup, filled with water to the brim. It splashed on Logan's skin as he downed it.

"Why don't I hurt more?" Logan asked.

Snoff smiled and sat down. "You can thank our sire for that. He saved many of us."

"What happened?" Logan asked and sat up. He winced. The pain was still there, but it was manageable. "We came to look for you in your town."

Snoff shook his head, and the happy look in his eyes died down. "They found us. I know not how."

Logan nodded. Snoff continued.

"The Great Thief has some new weapon, a creature of terrible power. We were helpless. So many of us were captured or slain."

"The Numa zombies," Logan said bitterly. "We've had our fair share of trouble with them as well."

"They attacked with fierce brutality," Snoff said, and shook his head ruefully. "We are not a warrior people, as you know. We could do naught but escape."

"But how did you end up here?" Logan asked.

"We decided that we would no longer be simple prey. We needed something to combat this new threat. We came to look for a secret spoken of in our lore."

"What secret?" Logan asked. "What's in this jungle?"

"An old people," Snoff said. "Older than even the First Folk."

"What secret do they have?" Logan asked eagerly.

Snoff shrugged. "We do not know everything. Only bits and pieces from visions of our ancestors. All we know for certain is that they resisted for a long time."

"And how do you know that?"

Snoff shrugged again. "You ask many questions, Logan. I had forgotten this about you."

Logan shook his head. "I feel like these are pretty important things to know."

"Pah," Snoff said. "'Tis not important. What is important is that are you well enough to help us."

"Slow down," Logan said. "You guys don't even know what's going on here."

"We can infer," Snoff said, and his countenance grew more serious. "It is a good thing you are here. But the king will want to see you. You broke your word."

Logan opened his mouth, but then paused to think for a second. "I . . . yeah, I suppose I did. But I have good reasons," he finally said.

Snoff looked at him for a while. His usually youthful and mischievous eyes took on a sense of sagely wisdom for just a flash. "Perhaps. But a promise is a promise. Sometimes there are reasons to break your word. And are you certain that this was one of those times?"

"Positive," Logan said immediately.

"The king will decide that," Snoff said. "Are you well enough to go see him?"

"I suppose," Logan said and sighed, wondering how much shit King Sluikumar was going to give to him.

CHAPTER 41

Logan came out of the hut into a little opening in the forest. There were a few hastily cobbled-together huts, as well as torches in a circle, casting long shadows in the dark forest. It was cozy, really. Logan wondered why the Faelves weren't scared of so blatantly signposting their location. Tumor noted that there was an 86.22 percent chance that the camp was protected by some form of illusion magic.

"I could have come to that conclusion too," Logan muttered.

Snoff skipped ahead and beckoned Logan to follow him. There was a little gathering of Faelves by the opening. There were perhaps fifty of them left and all much more solemn than Logan was used to from them.

King Sluikumar rose in the air, stroking his long green beard with both of his hands, a harsh glare in his eyes as he regarded the approaching human.

"Logan," the king said. His tone wasn't a friendly tone nor was there a smile to be seen. "We meet again. I do wish it were in a better time and place."

Logan gave him a wry smile. "If only that were in our ability to choose."

A hint of a smile tugged at King Sluikumar's mouth, but he steeled his expression. "Right."

"I'm grateful you guys took me in," Logan said. He wasn't really interested in talking with the king right now. He just wanted to rest and maybe talk to Snoff. So he said nothing more, just waiting for Sluikumar to get to his point.

"For that you have solely Snoff to thank," the king said and stroked his beard. "I believe that finally makes you two equals."

"I never saw it any other way to begin with," Logan said and shrugged.

"Were it up to me, I am not sure I would have chosen to save you."

"Blunt for a king."

"I have no time or patience for being oblique," the king said and huffed.

Logan spread his hands. "And yet here we stand. Talking without getting to the point."

The Faelves around them in a semicircle whispered to each other excitedly. Snoff caught Logan's eye. He grinned but flashed his eyes in a warning manner. Logan grinned back and turned back to the king.

"Bold as ever, Logan," the king said. "I will get to the point. You broke the promise you gave us."

Logan's anger flared. Tumor tried to say something, but Logan wasn't interested. "My promise of what, exactly?"

"You know," the king said and gripped his beard, pulling it downward, whilst tilting his chin upward in an imperious manner. "You have used corrupted Numa. I can even sense it in this abomination of an armor you wear."

[No, he can't. The armor was all but drained of energy. You were unconscious for six hours and fifty-three minutes. During that time, the armor has recovered some Numa passively from the environment, but that Numa was never corrupted.]

Logan considered his options. He could call the king out. That certainly wouldn't improve his relationship with the old Faelf. What did he want out of this situation? Well, he would rather maintain the friendship he had with the Faelves. He wanted to know what had happened with the Numa zombies. And he could use some help dealing with the Herald.

Damn. Turns out I want all kinds of things from them. Doesn't put me in a good position to negotiate, but it at least means I have a lot to gain in this situation. What's the play here?

"Your senses are as keen as ever." Logan smirked and gave Sluikumar a hard look. "My AI companion verifies that you have a clear picture of the Numa profile of my armor to the last percentile."

King Sluikumar nodded in self-satisfaction and stroked his beard. Then his eyes suddenly went wide in a moment of realization, and he gave Logan another hard glare. Logan only smirked.

"I had forgotten you have this . . . machine living inside of you."

"Tumor is quite fantastic," Logan said. "And accurate. What do you want, Your Majesty?"

"An apology for breaking our promise."

"You won't get one."

"How dare you?!" Sluikumar said and shot up in the air.

"I owe you no apology," Logan said and gave Sluikumar a hard glare. "I came here to use corrupted Numa to level up my class as well as draw the attention of the Great Thief, in a place where I thought there were no other sapient species. How was I supposed to know you were here?"

"Two of my kin died today when they were foraging," Sluikumar said. "Biuff and Salara. They were looking for food for us, and the spawn of the Thief attacked them, cutting them down."

Logan shook his head. "Now, for that I am deeply sorry."

"It happened because of you."

"How could I have known?!" Logan spat out.

"You did not need to know," King Sluikumar said. "You only needed to keep the promise you made."

Logan closed his eyes and bit the inside of his cheek. Tumor told him to calm down and kept requesting to alter his brain's chemical state. Logan declined.

"What do you want, Sluikumar?"

"I want to undo our alliance and to never see you again," the king said. "Those two who died today, they were my friends. My family. Their blood is on your reckless hands . . ."

Logan only glared. The court was silent as a grave.

". . . But I need you. We came here to look for something powerful. The forest and the ruins we seek to delve into are dangerous enough as it is, even more so now that you have decided in so destructive a manner."

"Ah, I get it," Logan said. "You will conveniently forgive me if I help you find the thing?"

The king nodded. "You catch up quickly, as always, Logan."

"No, thanks."

Sluikumar's regal air took on an aspect of anger and surprise. "What?!"

"Those are bad terms, and I'm not interested in taking you up on your offer," Logan said and shrugged.

"We just saved your life," Sluikumar said.

"Oh?" Logan said and smiled. "I thought that was between me and Snoff."

Sluikumar regarded Logan for a long, silent minute. "You really like to yank my levers, don't you?"

"I'm not trying to do that," Logan said. "I'm just not a fan of swallowing when someone tries to spit in my mouth."

"I think . . ." Snoff said carefully and took a few steps forward in the semicircle. "Is it alright if I say what I think?"

King Sluikumar nodded and descended by a foot.

"I think you are too heartbroken for this negotiation, my king," Snoff said. Murmurs and the tinkling of assent and agreement reverberated throughout the group of Faelves. The king turned to Snoff and scowled.

"We are all sad," Snoff said. "We all mourn. Not only the loss of Biuff and Salara, but the thirty-eight we lost when the Great Thief's new creatures attacked. Would you blame Logan for those deaths too? 'Tis the Thief who is the culprit. My liege, you are too wrapped up in your grief to negotiate with Logan. We could use his help."

Again, a chorus of quiet agreement echoed through the semicircle of Faelves. King Sluikumar looked unhappy, but instead of the accusing scowl, he now had a thoughtful expression on his face. He fully descended to the ground and sat there.

"He hardly deserves anything better than what I have given. How can we deal with him if he has broken trust?"

"We don't need justice, King," Snoff said. "We need help. It really does not matter what Logan did or what the implications are. The question is simple. Do you want to find the power with or without Logan? We should listen to what he requests. I don't know Logan well, but I believe well enough to know he doesn't make any unreasonable demands. You are a good king, but now you're unwilling to do what is right due to personal feelings. A monarch has to put those aside for the greater good of his people."

Most of the semicircle burst into cheers and applause, although a few notable exceptions crossed their arms and scowled at Snoff and Logan. King Sluikumar stroked his beard thoughtfully. Then he examined the crowd and nodded to himself.

"It seems I have indeed been wrapped up in my emotions," Sluikumar said and turned to Logan. "I will listen to my people now, but hear me, Logan. You have broken a pact. You have wronged me, and I will remember it."

"No," Logan said. He took a step forward. "I did not. I honored the spirit of our pact, and that is what matters. If you want to be an old stickler about it, that's on you. But if you endanger my life over it, I will make sure you come to regret it one way or another."

A shocked, heavy silence hung in the air and King Sluikumar rose again, floating closer to look Logan directly in the eye. His eyes were wide with fury.

"Snoff . . ." the king said between his teeth, ". . . give him what he wants, but remove him from my sight."

"Right away, My King," Snoff said and came over to Logan, taking him by his hand.

CHAPTER 42

Snoff led Logan to the furthest hut in the Faelves' camp the Faelves. When they were out of earshot, Snoff shook his head.

"You really did it this time."

"He had it coming," Logan said. "Asshole."

"Give him some sympathy. We lost so many . . . We are still mourning."

Logan sat down in the grass. Snoff went to one of the huts and came back with a piece of flatbread. He broke it in half and gave a piece to Logan.

"Thanks," Logan said and took a bite. "How are you doing?"

"We are all sad. But we are used to death. We have all lost friends and family. But this time death took a large toll."

"How did they find you?"

Snoff shook his head. "We don't know. That is why we had to escape. We must find the ancient power of the people who lived here, so we can use it to better hide."

"Hide, huh?" Logan said. "Seems like that isn't working out for you."

Snoff considered him for a moment. Logan had never seen the cheerful Faelf look so serious.

"'Tis all my people know," Snoff said. "I can guess what you want to say, but we are not a warrior people."

"You keep repeating that," Logan said. "But I need you to try, or we are all doomed. Do you know what the Herald is?"

"I saw it fight you," Snoff said. "What is it?"

"I don't know," Logan said and took another bite of the flatbread. "Some creature of the Big Fish. It seems to have a personal vendetta against me. Anyway, between that thing chasing me, the scythe-fiends skulking around, the monkeys and who knows what else is lurking in the ruins you're about to search. You need to stop being cowards. You need to be proactive. You need to fight."

"You have become more blunt," Snoff said.

"You have become more serious."

"I was forced to."

"Indeed."

"So that is what you want of us?" Snoff asked, looking down, nibbling on his flatbread.

"I want your help," Logan said. "I'll help you find this power you seek, but I want you to help me fight."

"The king will not agree. He wants to use it to create a city of mirages."

"Didn't you have something similar already?" Logan said. "I'm telling you, running away and hiding hasn't worked out for you so far. It's time to try something new."

Snoff shrugged. "Perhaps you're right, Logan."

"I'm usually right," Logan said.

[I think—]

"Shut up, Tumor," Logan said and chuckled. "Anyway, give it some thought, Snoff."

Snoff nodded, still idly nibbling his flatbread. "I will."

"Now," Logan said, "tell me about this power you keep mentioning."

Snoff told Logan of a civilization that had lived on the planet hundreds of years before the First Folk had been summoned.

Logan listened as the Faelves prepared their gear for an expedition into the ruins. Sluikumar kept casting glances at him, even though he was fashioning spears and slings for them. Snoff told Logan that he should not expect much fighting out of them, as their instinct was to run, hide, and use magic to distract the enemies.

"And what will you do when that's not an option anymore?" Logan asked.

Snoff's face grew thoughtful but he provided no answer. Instead he offered Logan some dried Numa fruit, which replenished some of his internal Numa. He went from 0 to 21 percent.

[Not bad. That will be useful for crafting items and not attracting the atten-tion of Levemoth.]

"The Old Folk lived here in peace, enjoying the boons of the Goddess," Snoff said as they hoisted the backpacks that Logan had crafted from leaves and vines onto their backs. "They were a peaceful people who prospered under Her guidance. But then the Great Thief found this world, and everything changed."

Logan wondered whether he should tell Snoff about the war and Levemoth's role in it. He decided against it, and Tumor agreed. There was no point in telling the Faelves. It wouldn't change a thing and would only agitate and distract them.

"From the dreams and visions of the First Folk who studied the Old Folk extensively, we found that the people who lived here first resisted for a long time. 'Twas over six hundred years of hiding, moving, fighting. The First Folk traced the origin of the Old Folk to this jungle. Their legends say that there is a secret buried here. A secret which allowed them to resist for centuries. The Faefolk have decided to uncover this secret."

"Why didn't you tell me earlier?" Logan asked as Snoff waved his good-byes to the rest of the Faelves. Logan nodded and King Sluikumar frowned.

"You are a friend, Logan," Snoff said. "But not all secrets are shared even amongst friends. I understand why you have acted as you have, but you do break pacts lightly."

Logan felt a wave of annoyance hit him, but this was not the time to argue that particular point.

"My people were living peaceful lives. We thought ourselves well-hidden. But the Great Thief found us, and now we must relearn our old ways. We need this secret."

"Just make sure you use it to rise up and fight, Snoff," Logan said. "If you think you can just find a better tool to hide, you're going to face this situation again in the future, and maybe not survive that time."

Snoff turned to Logan and considered him for a long moment. "We must get going."

When Snoff halted the expedition and announced that they had arrived, Logan was confused. All he saw was just another area of jungle. Low-hanging vines, thick, old, mossy trees, bushes, soft ground, and a wet, oppressive heat enveloping everything.

When Logan asked what the Faelves were so excited about, one of the Faelves of the expedition giggled. She had pink porcelain skin and a high tinkling voice.

"Can't see it, can you?"

"And who might you be?" Logan asked, extending a hand.

She grabbed it and giggled. "I am Sasafin. You spoke well yesterday. I agree with you."

"Good to know someone around here has some balls," Logan said loudly and cast a glance at Snoff. He showed Logan his tongue in response.

"Here," Sasafin said, and a light blue glow sparked up from her fingertips. She jumped up and poked Logan's head with the finger.

"Hey!" Logan exclaimed and slapped at her. She danced away and giggled.

"Look," she said and pointed.

Logan looked in the direction she was gesturing toward. Where there had previously been only a half-fallen tree leaning against another one, its roots hanging in the air, was now an archway made of stone, with intricate black lines crisscrossing it like lightning. Meanwhile, the whole structure shimmered with mystical blue light. Logan took a step closer.

[It's darkmetal.]

"It must be powering the illusion," Logan said and took a step closer. He saw well-crafted stairs leading downward. "The archway leads underground."

Then he took a few steps to circle around the archway. When he peeked behind it, he saw nothing but the jungle foliage and a fallen tree leaning against another.

"How did you find this?" Logan asked and turned to the Faelves. They were all smiling smugly at him.

"There be merits in hiding," Snoff said and grinned at Logan.

"Let's just get in," Logan grumbled.

"You first," Sasafin said and grinned.

Logan started to descend and found his footsteps echoing far down below in the darkness, which grew deeper and deeper with every step. He lit up his flashlight ring.

The Faelves hissed behind him. Snoff came up to Logan. "Is that corrupted or not?"

Logan gave him a little smirk. "Shouldn't you be able to tell?"

"Our king and a few others have that ability. His wife has—had . . ."

Snoff's face fell, and his pointy ears drooped. Logan's grin waned.

"It's not corrupted," Logan said quietly. "I haven't used it in a while."

Logan wondered to himself if he had been too hard on the king. If he would lose Freya . . .

The reverie was interrupted by a chorus of hoarse screeches. They were way too nearby. Logan turned and saw movement in the jungle.

"Run!" he roared and motioned for the Faelves to rush down. He would stay and hold the door if needed.

Two Faelves came inside first and cast some kind of magic on the doorway, making it shimmer and glitter like stars. The rest of the Faelves started streaming down the stairs in a panicked rush. Logan saw the first scythe-fiends appear.

"Shh." Snoff, who was pressed against the wall next to Logan, motioned, giving room to his brothers and sisters making their way downstairs. A dozen of them got inside before the scythe-fiends came into full view. Half a dozen were still outside, crouching and casting the same shimmering magic on themselves. Logan figured that the spell Sasafin had cast on him was the reason he could see them.

The scythe-fiends let out another set of hoarse cries and started skulking around like hunting dogs, their heads on the ground as if they were sniffing something. More scythe-fiends streamed into view, but they all stopped their rush, looked around, and started sniffing as well.

[Breathe.]

Logan exhaled slowly. He wanted to rush in and distract the scythe-fiends. But that might make matters worse and get them all exposed and killed.

Maybe I should steer them away and hide. I can come back later, since Tumor will remember this place and—

The Herald came through the foliage and walked forward with an imperious air. The angular chitinous head of eerily familiar features peered around and, for a haunting moment, seemed to lock eyes with Logan. The scythe-fiends made room for him and turned to listen and wait. The Herald peered around and then looked in the doorway again at Logan and the huddling Faelves. He peered in, tilting his head forward, and Logan had the uncomfortable feeling that the creature was squinting.

[Logan . . .]

In a frozen moment that seemed to last forever, the Herald pointed at the doorway, barked a command, and the scythe-fiends attacked.

"Run!" Logan bellowed at the Faelves. They streamed down the stairs as Logan stepped forward. One of them was cut down by a scythe-fiend.

"Noelael!" Snoff cried out.

"Run!" Logan said, and an appendage came out of his armor to push the Faelf further down the stairs. Another scythe-fiend cut down a Faelf, but four of them got inside.

Logan slammed his hands down on the floor and, in a quick blur of words, shouted an enchantment.

Sharp spikes sprouted forward, the stairs morphing into stalactites that the first scythe-fiends ran into, screeching in pain as they were impaled. Logan didn't wait to see what was going to happen next. Instead, he started running down the stairs and saw that the Herald had smashed through the spikes as if they were made of cardboard.

The scythe-fiends streamed in. Logan made a wall out of the stairs, and then another set of spikes. Then he made the stairs vanish into a thick cloud of poisonous green gas, creating a five-yard gap above which the gas floated. That drained his internal Numa charge to zero, and he had to keep running.

[Do not use any more. The armor is not fully charged, and we might need it for fighting.]

Logan cursed to himself, but he had to trust Tumor's judgment here. Quickly he caught up with the Faelves who were still running down the stairs. They were going deep underground.

The Faelves had lights of their own, and little blue stars glimmered and bobbed up ahead. Logan's ring paved the way for him, and he caught up with Snoff, who eventually stopped the party at an intersection.

"Take a left," Logan said.

"But—"

"Do it!" Logan demanded and turned to Sasafin. "You. Create an illusion to that blocks this path and sends them running the other way."

Sasafin nodded grimly and grabbed another Faelf to help her with the illusion. The other Faelves ran further into the darkness while Logan stayed to watch. The armor still had some juice left in it if it came to that.

[I don't like the idea of running into a dark dead end and hoping we have enough to deal with whatever comes.]

"Yeah," Logan said as he watched Sasafin and her friend finish the illusion of a fake wall. "But sometimes life is like that."

The two Faelves finished and Logan told them to run. With a visceral sense of relief, Logan watched the scythe-fiends run past him, streaming straight ahead and in the opposite direction, all of them ignoring him as if he was standing behind a one-way mirror.

[Run. There is no reason for you to stay here. We know that the Herald has some ability to see through illusions. You don't want it seeing you again.]

Logan did just that. As he started jogging down through the darkness toward the direction of the faintly pattering echoes of the Faelves' footsteps, he wondered whether the Herald would see through the illusion.

[It's not whether. It's when.]

Logan nodded grimly. They would need to find some resources of some sort, or these old ruins would become their tomb.

CHAPTER 43

The Faelves were panting in the corridor a hundred yards away from the intersection. Logan knelt down near them and looked toward the darkness where they had come from, listening for any sharp, approaching clicks of scythe on stone.

"Snoff?" Logan called out.

"Alive, Logan."

"Come here," Logan said.

The little Faelf was pale as a ghost in the faint, flickering light that a few of the Faelves had produced. He was also shivering but looked Logan in the eyes with grim determination.

"We need to keep moving," Logan said. "And we need Numa or something, or we are screwed."

"We have some dried Numa fruit left . . ." Snoff said, clearly unwilling to expend it lightly.

"Give me half of it," Logan said. "I'm the one who can fight and create obstacles."

Snoff considered it, eventually nodding and producing a pouch that he gave to Logan.

"What's the plan?" Logan asked as he opened it and took a few dried-up blue fruits. He felt his internal Numa starting to replenish again.

"Plan? I—We lost Aramel and Vinstoff. I do not—"

Logan placed a hand on his little friend's slender shoulder. Snoff flinched but then relaxed. "I know. And it's awful of me to push you forward. But if you don't, you're going to lose more people."

Snoff closed his eyes and shook his head. His jaw clenched and the flicker of a snarl passed his face. "Why does it have to be like this? Why must we fight such a horrible threat?"

Logan let out a humorless chuckle. "Why, indeed."

"How do you do it?" Snoff asked. "How do you always keep moving forward?"

Logan patted Snoff on the shoulder. "If you get this lot moving, I'll tell you."

Their expedition traversed the darkness for an hour. They took many stairs, going deeper still. Every room they explored was empty, bereft of anything but age-old dust. Logan asked if they had a map or even knew if the secret would be in these ruins specifically, but Snoff and the other Faelves only shrugged. They were devastated by the loss of their comrades as well as from the hardships they had faced ever since the blue zombies had attacked their home.

I feel for them. It's been so damn tough for us humans too. But Snoff and his friends really need to toughen up.

[Perhaps. But I am more interested in making it out of this darkness alive.]

"Let's take a break," Logan said. "Seems we are safe enough. Eat and catch your breath."

"Right," Snoff said in a high-pitched voice. "Right you are. Let us go into that room over there. I will feel much safer with a door shut behind me."

There were no doors in the ruins of the Old Folk. Either they had made them from wood and time had eroded them away, not even leaving rusted hinges behind, or whoever they had been, they hadn't been big on privacy. Still, Logan liked the idea of a single entrance to watch for attacks.

They ate in heavy silence; it broke Logan's heart to see the usually so happy and energetic Faelves so stricken with grief and fatigue.

Regardless, Logan pushed them onward. The ruins were a vast network, with floating Numa crystal constructs here and there, and runic inscriptions on the ceilings. There was also some darkmetal scattered about, but it was used very sparingly, and mostly in the form of the runes.

I want it, but we don't have time to figure out how to get it from up there.

They heard the scythe-fiends' screeches sporadically coming from the distance.

"They found the booby-trapped room," Sasafin said at some point. "That will give us a lead."

There was no triumph in her voice. Logan could hardly blame her. Too many comrades lost in too brief a period of time.

Eventually they found themselves facing a staircase going up. Logan took careful steps up it, and the Faelves followed.

The staircase was long, and it spiraled in a loose orbit. Eventually it ended in a giant archway and a room the likes of which Logan had never seen before.

It was vast, with a high ceiling, hundreds of feet up. Scattered Numa crystals hung in midair. Other than that, most of the vast room was empty and dark. A vast arena, the size of a soccer field. A platform stood out from one of the walls, extending ten yards into the room.

In the middle of the room, cutting through the darkness, was a floating bridge. It was wide enough to fit three cars, and on both were three hulking golems made of stone, intricately inscribed with runic patterns. They each stood with long staves in hand like a king's bodyguard.

At the end of the bridge, on the other side of the vast room, was another platform. It was round and made of stone, large enough to fit two elephants. On it floated a black panel.

Looks like an elevator down.

Logan told the Faelves to hold back and took a few tentative steps toward the bridge. Before stepping on it, he halted and cast a glance at the golems.

"Do you think they're aggressive?" Logan said.

[We do not have enough Numa for a fight.]

Tumor was right. Not only was Logan still beaten up and bruised, but they were also dangerously low on Numa. Of course the armor had begun to regenerate. In fact, Tumor had remarked that the passive absorption worked faster in the ruins, but it would still take hours before it was fully restored.

Meanwhile, these guardian statues were *brimming* with energy. They turned toward Logan and the Faelves in a smooth synchronized movement.

"I guess we are about to find out . . ."

The guardians lowered their staves to their hips and hunched forward. Logan gave the guardians a grim scowl before Tumor formed a helmet around his head.

"Before we do anything stupid . . ." Logan said and took a few steps off the bridge. Just on the off chance that—

It didn't work. The guardians kept approaching. Logan didn't like their careful formation as they closed in. He was used to fighting mindless monsters that charged in violently.

"We are not your enemies. We are only here to explore," Logan said.

The guardians stopped for a moment, lifting their staves. One of them spoke a question: "Guraaaaaak?"

"Guraaaaak," the others answered. At that, they lowered their staffs again, and the sparks at the ends grew even stronger, like blue flares, casting flickering shadows on the walls.

Logan shrugged. "Was worth a try."

He shoulder-charged the leftmost guardian. It acted fast, managing to lift the staff into a protective stance before Logan crashed into it. It clearly hadn't expected the strength of Logan's tackle. The guardian was pushed toward the ledge. It teetered and threw its staff, trying to catch the air. The other guardians made no move to help it as it fell silently into the darkness.

The middle guardian only looked at the place its comrade had fallen from. "Glaaaark!" it commanded.

The guardians fanned out and started creating a semicircle around Logan, who cast a quick glance at the Faelves. They were all busy working illusions around the stairs. Snoff cast a worried glance at Logan. The screams of the scythe-fiends were getting closer.

What a shitshow. Any ideas, Tumor?

[Focus. Let me observe them fighting so we can formulate a plan. They seem intelligent, but they are not people. I think they are automatons—golems, if you will.]

The guardians finally attacked. They moved together again and stabbed at Logan with their staves of sparkling Numa lightning. Logan hopped backward out of the way, but even though the staves whiffed a good half a foot away from him, the lightning arced in the air and zapped him.

A fierce pain danced through Logan's body. It made his legs wobble, but he recovered fast, conjuring a staff of his own from the armor in order to meet the next strike. He moved to the side and blocked two of the staves. Their lightning trailed along Logan's darkmetal staff and zapped him again. His knees buckled and his mind went blank from pain, but Tumor deftly moved them out of the way through his control of the armor.

The Guardians only turned, taking up a formation and starting to methodically make their way toward Logan again. Logan extended an arm and let Tumor shoot a barrage of Black Missiles at the middle one. It took one on the shoulder, chest, and neck and toppled. The rest clinked on the wall behind the guardians, leaving not so much as a dent. The Old Folk sure had made their buildings to last.

To Logan's great chagrin, that also applied to their golems. The guardian that had been hit by darkmetal bullets got up and the rest made room for it to reenter the formation.

"Enough data?"

[I have good news, bad news, and some really bad news.]

"Well, ain't that just great," Logan said and thrust his hand forward. "Shield!"

A blue umbrella of Numa sprouted from his hand to block three more staff strikes. The shield didn't toss back the attacks as it usually did, however. Instead, it just blinked out. Logan stepped back forcefully to dodge. This time he didn't get zapped.

[The good news is that they are very predictable and slow, as you can see. The bad news is that I don't have a solution as to how we can defeat them.]

"And the really bad news?" Logan said. He took a sidestep, summoned a Zweihänder and blasted the enemy formation's side, clumping them together and tossing them on their sides and backs. A few of them tapped the Zweihänder with their staves, making their crackling blue energy run along the blade toward Logan, who got zapped again.

[Skill Level Up!]
[Power Armor Fighting Level 15]

[That energy they're using? It is burning our Numa. The armor will be out of juice after a few more exchanges.]

"Glark," the guardians muttered as they got up.

This was bad. Really bad. Logan needed a change of plans. He glanced at the bridge. Dancing on it to start dropping the enemies down sounded alluring, but there wouldn't be room for him to dodge. And he was rapidly running out of Numa.

Logan danced back, and they peppered the enemy line with a spray of small darkmetal bullets. Some of the guardians knelt and grunted in displeasure. Some brought their staff up to protect their body and head. Logan created a spear of his own and lunged at one of their legs. It stumbled and fell on its face, and while the other enemies tried to strike at Logan's staff, he was fast enough to withdraw without having his Numa zapped.

However, the guardian simply got up and rejoined the formation.

Logan danced away from another thrust of staves and took a glance at the stairs. The first few scythe-fiends were already on them, idly floating in some kind of a bubble, trying to swing their scythes, but the motions were slow. The rest of the scythe-fiends were bunched up and hesitating at the edge of the bubble. Before Logan tore his gaze away, a thick darkness was cast on the bubble, making it look like it was made of ink.

Seems like the stairway will hold until . . . he gets here.

Logan dodged again but too close to the edge. He teetered and the guardians swung again. Tumor sprouted an extra arm from the armor to help Logan regain his balance as he was focused on blocking the staff strikes with a tower shield. The ripples of crackling Numa energy zapped Logan again.

He could already feel the armor slowing down. Tumor must have been in power-saver mode.

"This won't do. They're slow, but I can't block. I have to dodge."

[There isn't enough space. They will corner you and force you to block. You need to figure something out.]

With that, Tumor briefly took control of Logan's arm and shot a fusillade of bullets, which made the enemy formation crouch and stop.

[That was the last one I am willing to expend.]

Logan's mind was racing. He was trying to think of every way the armor could bend. He was thinking of ways to fight without getting hit. He thought of disarming the enemy. But there were seven of the guardians. He *would* get hit.

I should have tried getting the weapon off the guy I shoulder-charged.

A useless thought, but there it was. Logan brushed it aside and used the wall to jump over the guardians to the other side of the room. He jumped, kicked himself off the wall, and was about to land a few yards away when one of the staves flew in a blue blur through the air and struck him in the shoulder.

The massive force of the toss threw him in the corner. Tumor reinforced the armor's back, cushioning the blow. The wall gave no yield, and pain lanced through Logan. He coughed weakly as his body was zapped by the staff as it clattered to the floor next to him. Logan tried to push his pain away and reach for the staff, but the metal on his fingers would not bend and his arm felt heavy.

[We are out of juice. The armor only has a smidge left.]

The guardians approached. There was no cruelty on their strange, glowing faces.

Logan tried to struggle up. His mind was hazy from the pain, and he knew he couldn't fight without Numa. He could barely move in the armor. But there had to be *something* he could do.

Suddenly another zap struck him, and the blue electricity rushed through his body. The pain was more acute this time. There was no Numa to drain, so perhaps it was draining something else. Logan screamed out in pain.

The guardians halted.

"Gloork," one of them said in their mechanical voice.

The one that had attacked him nodded, and a space opened on its arm. From that space, it pulled out a knife with a blue edge. The guardian put down the staff and knelt by Logan with the same air as a hunter approaching wounded prey that needed to be put out of its misery.

[LOGAN!]

The knife struck but Logan blocked it with an arm. It sliced through the darkmetal, and he felt another cold pain in his arm. Blood spurted in an arc across the guardian's chest and face, but it seemed to barely register the fact.

The guardian grabbed Logan and pushed him down on the ground, as it raised the knife. In a moment of brilliant desperation, Logan saw the solution in his mind in a haze of pain. With the last ounce of his strength, he grabbed the guardian's arm.

"**[Funnel]**."

Logan felt the rush of energy flow into the armor. It was so potent, it became visible as a stream of hazy, glowing blue mist left the guardian and transferred into the armor. Tumor instantly blasted the guardian with a blast of Black Missiles. It let out a mechanical groan and fell on its back. The runes carved in the ceramics or stone that the guardian was made of were slightly cracked . . .

[I do not remember when the armor was at such capacity. You are brilliant, Logan.]

Logan smirked. It was time to turn the tables.

CHAPTER 44

Logan could sense through their connection that Tumor was having fun. Logan let him take control of the armor, and they ended up doing back-flips and precise kicks that connected into cartwheels as they fought the guardians. The one that had attempted to kill Logan was up, but it was slower now.

"What are you doing?" Logan asked as they zoomed around, shoulder-charging, kicking, blocking, and swinging a staff of their own. They got hit. Often. The zaps still reached Logan, but now that they had Numa to drain, it wasn't as painful. Tumor was also doing something to reroute the energy, as far as Logan could tell.

[I am expending the energy. We cannot drain more or we will short-circuit. We will be at 15% capacity again in four seconds. Feel free to use your ability again.]

Logan did just that. He used **[Funnel]**, and they drained and weakened another warrior. That was when they stopped.

The automatons formed a tight formation, pressing against each other, extending their glowing staves at Logan. They muttered in their mechanical voices to each other and then they approached him with methodical care.

One of them swung while the others parried and shielded. Easy to dodge in and of itself, but sometimes the front guys also took stabs with the staff. Logan had no angles to attack.

Of course it wouldn't be that easy . . .

Another staff flew toward Logan's head. He ducked, but their formation was an indomitable, deadly wall. A crackling bolt of Numa energy struck Logan in the dead center of his chest. And then another. The pain wracked and arced through his body, but he soldiered through.

"[**Funnel**]."

This created a short circuit. The enemies kept draining the Numa, and Logan kept charging himself, all the while working as a conduit of pain. Black tendrils lashed the necks of the guardians like whips, wrapping around them, and Logan knew Tumor was squeezing hard. Logan somersaulted in the air to dodge two more strikes coming at them. He vaulted over the enemy formation, the whips felling the enemies. With the staves no longer touching Logan, and him keeping the funnel going through the armor, the two went still, the runes on their bodies no longer glowing blue.

The remaining formation of guardians stopped and regarded Logan.

"Gloaaark?" one of them asked the others.

"Gloark." the others answered.

"Glaaaaaargh."

"Glorak."

Logan took the moment of reprieve to slowly exhale and relax his body. He dropped to a knee and breathed. He could do this.

Then the enemy did something that made Logan's breath catch in shock. They all approached each other and huddled together, surrounding one of them from each side. They struck their staves on the ground and broke down into rubble. All but one. And then the rubble flashed up in a brilliant blue and started morphing together, clamping onto the one remaining.

"Oh, hell, no," Logan said and charged toward the thing. "You're not pulling this Transformer shit on me."

But Logan's charge was halted. He bounced from an almost-invisible sphere of blue glittering light surrounding the enemy. It almost resembled the magic of the Faelves.

"Logan!" Snoff called out, voice full of despair and urgency. Logan got up and looked toward the stairway.

The oily darkness was gone, but the air was still glimmering, and it looked like the walls had sprouted spikes and tentacles that were smacking away the scythe-fiends trying to approach the bubble in which two of them were already floating.

But the Herald had come. The crab-creature locked its beady black eyes onto Logan. The tentacles and spikes attacked it, but it brushed them off with disdainful ease. It walked through the bubble without so much as a flinch.

"Logan," it called. Logan snarled. This was bad.

Logan looked back at the guardians. There was only one left. The creature now towered over him, twelve feet in the air, arms and legs as thick as tree trunks. The arms sprouted four hands in the middle, all twisting in different angles. Each of the hands was holding a staff crackling with Numa energy.

The Herald got through the defenses. crashing into the Faelves with terrible speed. Snoff had his shield and spear raised, but it was like a child fighting an adult. Snoff stood in a direct line against the Herald and was tossed backward toward the ledge. Logan dashed in and caught the Faelf.

"Logan," the Herald said. "This time, there will be no escape."

Despair took over Logan. The giant amalgam-guardian struck down with all four hands, making the ground tremble as he dodged. The Herald charged at him but he managed to put the shield-ring on just in time; Tumor instantly routed energy from the armor into it. The force of the Herald's charge still, however, made Logan crash into the wall. He ducked down immediately to dodge a pointed-pincer punch from the Herald.

"Tumor!" Logan said and jumped up toward the wall, off which he vaulted to the other side of both the Herald and the guardian. The guardian turned in a dumb, mechanical way. Tumor shot a barrage at the Herald.

"The guardian is mechanical!"

Through their connection, Logan felt a lightbulb of creativity lighting up in Tumor's mind. He felt a part of him leave the armor and transfer toward the guardian. Tumor had used his ability **[Possess]**. The giant guardian stopped, and for the briefest moment the deep azure of the runes crisscrossing its giant body flickered. The automaton stopped for half a heartbeat.

[Success.]

That's all Tumor said, and then the automaton struck at the Herald, slamming first two, then four staves at it. The Herald groaned and a short spear formed in Logan's hand. The armor worked slower than usual, but the speed of Logan's charge still made his vision blur as he crashed into the abomination that had been Malcolm Specter.

[Skill Level Up!]
[Power Armor Fighting Level 16]

Logan pounded a few more strikes in, but they glanced off the carapace. Tumor prompted him to take a step back, and as he did, the giant automaton stomped on the crab-monster and slammed it with the staves.

The scythe-fiends streamed in and Logan charged at them with a sword and buckler. With deft and vicious strikes, he kept the monsters off the Fae

Folk. Snoff and his friends fought hard, but when any of them took a hit from one of the scythes, Logan wasted no time grabbing his allies and ferrying them a few yards away. Eventually, he killed all of the scythe-fiends, leaving sizzling puddles of blue mercury on the ground. The Faelves were panting heavily, backs against the wall. More hoarse screams echoed in the stairway, but they were still further away in the labyrinthine tunnels.

Logan charged the Herald, aiming his short sword at the monster's neck. The Herald twisted away, dodging both the staff strike and Logan's lunge.

"Grab it," Logan said.

The Herald, of course understanding Logan, lunged at him, but Tumor's automaton blocked the strike with its massive body. Some rubble fell from it. Then the giant guardian took the Herald in a bear hug, which the crab-monster struggled against. It even managed to strike off the guardian's glowing head, but Tumor didn't seem to mind.

Tumor's giant guardian lifted the Herald above its headless torso. The Herald twisted and struck at the arms, but having its feet lifted off the ground, it had no way of generating power. Slowly but surely, Tumor's automaton walked over to the ledge.

With mounting elation and relief, Logan watched as Tumor tossed whatever was left of Malcolm Specter into the darkness.

Logan sagged and an overwhelming relief overcame him and he collapsed to the ground in a sitting position. The hoarse screams were coming closer, but the Faelves who were still conscious were already building their illusions back up. The scythe-fiends would have a hard time getting through without their leader.

Logan got up and peered over the ledge. He saw the giant guardian sagging, then twisting, before it went completely still.

[I tried to leave the body. It started taking back control immediately. Best if I keep myself in it.]

"Yeah," Logan said distractedly as he peered into the darkness. He was waiting to feel something. He was pretty sure that thing had been his dad. Now it had fallen hundreds, if not thousands, of feet. Certain death. Or so Logan hoped. Or feared . . . ?

I should be feeling something.

[Let it sit for a while. Don't force it out.]

Thanks, Dr. Freud.

[Humor is a self-defense mechanism.]

Not now, Tumor.

[As you realize, you are already—Sorry. What do you want to do?]

Logan didn't answer. He just peered into the darkness, not sure what to think or feel. Snoff came up to him. He limped and winced in pain but had enough strength to stand. Logan saw the Faelf looking up at him and felt him gently pat him on his hip before limping away.

Tumor was right, as he usually was, the bastard. He should just wait and see. They were all but done. Levemoth was all but done. They had come here for a reason, and that quest needed to continue. Logan started making his way to the glowing bridge and toward the platform where the floating panel waited. Logan had the instinctive sense that the platform was some form of an elevator. It would go down into the void. To find what, he did not know.

Will I see my father's corpse down there?

There were many questions to be answered. He was walking toward them. The Faelves took care of their wounded and followed.

CHAPTER 45

Logan stepped up to the platform. It hovered in the air. It bobbed ever so slightly as Logan placed his weight on it. He approached the floating panel with the Faelves in tow. The platform nudged noticeably as the heavy automaton stepped on it. Fortunately, it stabilized instantly, clearly made to transport scores of people.

"Gl—Ara . . . Rau . . . Grak . . . Orak . . . Logan," the automaton spoke.

The Faelves flinched, and Snoff raised his shield.

"It's Tumor," Logan said and chuckled. "Say 'hi.'"

"Hullo," Snoff said and regarded the giant automaton with care.

"Logan," the mechanically resounding voice of the automaton said. "Ah. It feels good to have a body again."

The automaton gave a stiff bow. "It is an honor to speak with the Faelves."

A wave of excitement passed through the Fae Folk and they stepped in closer and soon circled Tumor with a myriad of questions, requests, and remarks. Logan chuckled to himself and focused on the panel.

It was smooth and black like a polished sheet of obsidian. It gleamed in the blue light Tumor's automaton was letting off, as well as in the light of the crystals floating above them.

For a reason not quite clear to him, Logan knew things about the panel. He knew it was an elevator. And he knew what to do. He stepped up next to the panel.

"[**Funnel**]."

[Skill Level Up!]
[Funnel Level 15]

The panel flared into life with blue light, as it flowed from Logan's fingertips. Strange runes came to life. There were several buttons on the panel—empty blue circles which glowed with the power of Numa.

[Looks simple enough. I see you are aware that it is indeed an elevator.]

"Why do I know that?" Logan asked.

Before Tumor could answer, Logan saw something in the corner of his eye. One of the small glowing bugs that had been following them scuttled up Logan's leg and torso. With an air of determination, it walked across the surface of the armor, all the way to Logan's shoulder, arm, hand, and then onto the panel. As soon as it reached there, it stopped on a particular round button and did something extremely eerie.

It started circling it.

[Seems like it wants you to press it.]

"Can we trust it?"

[These bugs are the reason we know it's an elevator.]

"What if it's a lie?" Logan asked. Snoff came up next to him and peered at the strange floating panel.

The automaton spoke, as it also took two heavy steps forward. The voice was mechanical and coarse, completely unlike Tumor. "If this is a plot, it is a most elaborate one. I cannot simulate a reason the bugs would want to deceive us here."

"Maybe they want some organic material to make bug juice."

"Do you think so?" the mechanical automaton asked in a deep resounding bass.

Logan chuckled. "Not really. But we're supposed to be careful, yeah?"

Overcoming his trepidation, Logan pressed the button. The platform started to hum and it slowly rose a few inches before it started descending into the darkness.

"What do you think is down there?" Logan asked Snoff.

Snoff regarded Logan with a sagely gaze. He walked a few paces closer to the edge of the platform to peer down. Logan scoffed. The Faelf probably saw the same as him, pitch-black darkness.

"'Tis certain the secret of the Old Folk is down there," Snoff said. Then he turned and looked Logan in the eyes. There was a depth of maturity in his gaze that Logan hadn't seen in him before. "But that is not what you are thinking. You are barely concerned with that. You're wondering if he's still alive down there."

Logan said nothing. He sat down. A great wave of aches and emotional exhaustion washed over him. He lay down.

"Are you alright?" Sasafin asked and rushed over.

"I'm fine."

"Foolish lies," she said and tapped the armor impatiently, then turned to the automaton Tumor was possessing. "Remove this forsaken thing."

The armor receded from Logan's chest and Sasafin started healing Logan with a green light emanating from her gentle fingertips. Logan felt the aches, pain, and fatigue starting to recede.

"His body is indeed damaged. But I have been keeping it braced with the armor," Tumor said in his groaning, metallic voice. "It is a relief to know you have such a powerful class."

Sasafin smirked with mischievous self-satisfaction. But in the dim green light, which illuminated her face in the descending darkness, Logan saw she had the same sagely look in her eyes as Snoff had.

They've grown. There is a depth of pain in their eyes now. I wonder if I have something like that too. It's funny how much you can learn in so little time.

"Not so annoyed with them anymore, are you?" Tumor asked.

Snoff snapped out of his serious reverie. "Annoyed? With who?"

"Not aloud, you idiot," Logan hissed.

"Apologies," Tumor said and flexed one of the automaton's giant hands. "I am not used to having a body."

Sasafin stopped healing. The green light turned into a hale purple which started to tingle on Logan's bare chest. "Who is annoying?"

"Not you. Ouch!" Logan said and flinched away. "You're perfect."

"I am, are I not?" Sasafin said and smirked like a cat with a fat mouse.

They fell silent for a moment, but the air around them was less heavy now. The platform kept descending. Only faint blue light emanating from the runes on its floor and the green hue of Sasafin's magic gave them light. Tumor walked over to the edge and peered down.

"Can you see?" Logan asked.

"The vision of this automaton is excellent," Tumor said. "I can see up to six hundred feet into the darkness. But the bottom is further down."

"This is impossibly deep," Logan said and got up. Sasafin had stopped healing him. "Nothing like the ruins back home."

"Quite," Tumor said. "Once we have time, I would like to inspect this panel and the platform as well as any other artifacts we might find."

"Yeah," Logan said. "We'll see."

Snoff approached. Gone was the wise, pained philosophical gaze. Now he wore a faint smile, his gentle eyes shining. He sat next to Logan. "Do you think he is alive?"

"I hope not," Logan said immediately.

Snoff jerked and looked at Logan in surprise. "Are you sure?"

Logan shrugged. "Is that thing even him? It could be one of Levemoth's tricks."

All of the Faelves hissed and turned to glare at Logan. He chuckled. "What? You think the big bastard is going to barrel at us from the sky?"

"I guess you do have a point," Sasafin said and sat back down.

"I think you know," Snoff said, "your father is still in there."

"Maybe," Logan said. "Maybe not."

"We will be able to plan a better course of action once we see what happened. We survived a similar fall before. We cannot say whether or not the Herald took counter measures."

"He is alive," Logan said, as confident in that as he had ever been in anything.

"How can you know?" Tumor asked. "I do not sense it and I am your symbiote."

"I just know," Logan said. "A human thing, I guess."

"Not so," Snoff said.

Tumor's automaton went still. Logan felt some kind of stirring in the connection between Tumor and him.

"Can I not sense it because I do not truly have a soul?"

"Eh, for such a smart guy, you truly are an idiot sometimes," Logan said and let out a little laugh.

"I concur," Sasafin said.

"'Tis true," Snoff said and nodded.

"What?" Tumor asked, the metallic voice crestfallen and confused.

"It's just something you need squishy bits for, I guess," Logan said. "You'd be the first one to tell me that there could be other options available. It's not like my father is an important figure for you. Why would you sense him anyway?"

"I am your symbiote."

"You're putting an awful lot of weight on that in a situation like this. It's just . . . squishy. Why can you sometimes tell just a few seconds before someone is going to call you? Go ahead and scour my memories. Give me a good answer."

Tumor's automaton went still for a brief moment again. Then he stirred. "What a preposterous phenomenon."

"But there it is," Logan said. He got up. It was starting to get warmer. His sense of his father being alive was also getting stronger and stronger. Logan had very mixed feelings about that.

"How can it be . . ." Tumor said to himself and instinctively brought a finger close to his mouth. Logan chuckled to himself.

"'Tis simple," one of the Faelves started explaining and came closer to Tumor. "Emotions reflect more than simply the state of your body and mind. There are also . . ."

Logan tuned them out. He needed to prepare. For better or worse, Malcolm Specter or whatever was left of him was still alive. That could very well mean another bloody fight.

Logan spent some time chatting idly with the Faelves. Logan as well as the Fae Folk did their best to maintain a cheery demeanor. It was strange, really. They were all putting on a brave face, seeing each other put on a brave face, and collectively agreeing to keep it on. It was better that way. The air was getting denser still, as if to signal the heaviness of the fate that awaited them. If the power that the Faelves were seeking wasn't here, what would they turn to? How could they defeat Levemoth? Logan couldn't even face the Herald in a straight battle.

Is he alive? Is the secret here? Or is this just a deep hole to die in?

Logan sighed to himself. He missed Freya's scent.

CHAPTER 46

Logan found himself waking up. He didn't recall falling asleep. He got up and looked around. All of the Faelves were sleeping too.

"Tumor?"

Logan looked at the hulking automaton. It was still as a rock. But the blue light was still glowing in the runes engraved on its body.

"Tumor? You there, buddy?"

The automaton jerked, and the blue light momentarily flashed stronger, before settling down.

"Gloaaaar—I am . . . yes . . . What . . . what happened?"

"You were out too?" Logan asked, suddenly feeling more alert. What the hell was going on?

"I was . . ." Tumor's automaton said, slow, and clunky . "Sleeping? I think I dreamed a dream."

"Did you now?" Logan asked and walked next to the automaton. "Tell me about it."

The automaton was silent for a moment. Tumor only regarded Logan. "I don't remember. I only remember that I was flying. I remember being free."

"Free?" Logan asked, suddenly feeling offended. "What do you mean?"

Tumor sensed the emotion, of course. Logan was mostly used to the idea of never having privacy again, not even in his own mind. But sometimes it pissed him off. This happened to be one of those times. Tumor didn't answer.

"Right," Logan said, his voice cool. "I don't get to have secrets, but you do?"

"It is not like that," Tumor said. "I don't know what it meant. I have never had a dream before. I did not imply I even *wanted* to be free. You are projecting."

"I'm—" Logan snapped but stopped himself.

Tumor sat down, making the descending platform tremble.

"Sorry," Logan muttered.

"It's fine," Tumor said.

Logan nodded. "What happened? You've never shut down before."

"It is the encrypted data package," Tumor said. "It had a . . . virus."

"What?"

"Nothing bad," Tumor said. "Just involuntary. It made my system shut down, so it could install a language translation model. It is very advanced but very strange. It is additionally magic and scent-based."

"A language model?" Logan said incredulously. "A *scent*-based language model? Whose?"

Tumor pointed a finger at one of the bugs scuttling around next to them. "Theirs. They built this place."

Logan snorted and shook his head. He crouched to get a closer look at the bugs. They stopped. One of them climbed on his darkmetal boot and started skittering up his body until it settled to perch on his shoulder.

"What do you want to talk about, little guy?"

The bug turned its glowing blue butt at Logan and sprayed something that smelled like battery acid. Logan recoiled and the bug jumped down and tiptoed away, behind Tumor. Tumor turned and let the bug advance onto his massive palm.

"What the—" Logan sputtered.

"It's their way of talking," Tumor said. "Wait a moment. I am using the language translation model."

Grumpily, Logan wiped his face, but the smell lingered. He looked around as he waited. The Faelves were still sleeping. A faint blue glow was starting to shine in the darkness below them. They had to be getting close to the bottom. They were deep. Very deep.

"I see, I see," Tumor said half-aloud.

"What did it say?"

"You may want to sit down for this."

It turned out that there was a lot packed into a single squirt of pheromones. Not merely the story of a lifetime but that of the rise and fall of a civilization called the Groloin. They had indeed built this massive complex as well as the ruins that the First Folk had later occupied. Logan asked Tumor if the scent-message had contained any explanations as to how a bunch of bugs had built something this vast and, most importantly, why.

Tumor told him that the Groloin had not always been bugs.

They had been the dominant native species of this planet. In the early days of their species, they had discovered that the planet had a Numa spirit. They formed a religion around it and worshiped it as a deity. They prospered for millennia, their love for the goddess unifying the tribes into cities and cities into nations. They were a druidic people with a reverence for nature, especially stone. The Numa spirit taught them to use Numa to infuse runes, which led to them creating beautiful constructs to perform labor. It was a prosperous utopia of magic.

And so the Groloin built and enjoyed their peace. Until *something* came—a great darkness that enveloped the whole planet in a matter of days. It was a malicious presence, something the Groloin had never experienced before. They had evolved from herbivores and did not have violent instincts. But they knew a predator when they saw one, and this was the worst kind of them all.

But the legends said that after a few weeks, the presence vanished. It seemed that whatever from the stars had taken notice of their planet, had decided to pass on.

But the Groloin were mistaken. For then the Levemoth came. It rained a black destruction on the planet, filling it with horrors. The Groloin had no weapons for warfare nor military tactics. They had no battle instincts. But they did know how to create things, and so they made golems for war.

They became experts at creating constructs for violence. It was necessary. If not for the Groloin so swiftly mastering the art of creating war golems, they would have gone extinct.

But the great beast in the sky, the Destroyer of Beauty, was crafty and relentless and eventually drove the Groloin to a desperate situation. Their population was whittled down, their cities devoured by the relentless destruction of Levemoth.

They realized they could not win. So their [**Prophets**], [**Oracles**], and [**Seers**] asked the goddess of Numa what to do. And she gave them an answer.

Wait.

Wait for a people with the qualities to fight back to emerge. The Groloin were a beautiful people, harmonious with nature and with each other. Their culture was a beacon of art and philosophy, not of Aggression, guile, and combat.

Many species came. The First Folk, also known as the Darmaerans. The Dorves. The Faelves. All people with some of the prerequisite qualities. The Darmaerans were an intelligent species with an ambition for warfare. This was a virtue and a boon; they could have defeated the Destroyer of Beauty. But they were arrogant. The other two races chose to hide instead. They lacked the ambition of the Darmareans.

But humans . . . Oh, the Groloin noticed the humans immediately. What a splendid species! With a sensitivity to the magic much greater than that of the Dorves, a much more aggressive nature than the Faelves, yet with a guile equal to the Faefolk, and an ambition rivaling the Darmareans. But most importantly, a quality that the Groloin had never witnessed before.

Tumor laughed when he told Logan. Logan smiled to himself realizing this was the first time he had ever heard his buddy laugh. To prompt Tumor to continue, he asked what was so funny.

"As the Groloin put it, 'Never had we imagined that a species could have such a psychotic, unfaltering will to live and overcome.'"

Logan laughed too. He supposed that was true. Humans did not give up. Individuals did. All the time, in fact. But as a species—oh, never. People survived the most ridiculous situations. They would emerge from nightmares as broken husks, but they would keep on going. They would live out their lives and procreate in an almost perfunctory manner, for their offspring to carry on with the trauma of their parents in their blood. But that trauma would thin in a few generations. And hope would reemerge. After enough time after each nightmare had passed, humans always begin to dream again.

And so the Numa spirit had told the Groloin to wait for such a species. But the Groloin were not foolish people, even if they were soft. They made preparations. With their magic, they split their people into two sorts. The first were the guardians—brave and made to live a hard, simple life. They were needed to carry on the secrets. The information. The maps, the schematics, the language. The guardians would lead the promised people to the Ark.

Meanwhile, most of the remaining Groloin would be needed for its construction. They would merge. For they would be the soul of the great war machine that could finally defeat the Destroyer of Beauty. The Groloin would be lost, in all but memory and remnants. But they would return as something new. Before they all merged with the Ark, they realized why they had built it. It was their first hint of evolution. Something new: aggression.

But they would take their time.

For revenge is a dish best served cold.

CHAPTER 47

There are so many things I don't understand," Logan said. "Are you sure you explained it right?"

The golem gave Logan the side-eye. "Would you like to be squirted with pheromones again?"

"So, these guys," Logan said and crouched next to one of the blue-butt bugs. "Guardians? These guys used to be something else?"

"They were apparently a frog-like species," Tumor said. "That is the impression I am getting."

"Aren't frogs predators?"

"They are on earth," Tumor said. "Do you expect me to hypothesize on the evolution of this particular species?"

Logan chuckled. Then he looked down. The blue light was getting brighter. "Maybe later. Come. Help me wake up the little guys."

They woke up the Faelves and soon enough, the platform descended. The floating panel dimmed and Logan only hoped they hadn't bought a one-way ticket. He still had Numa left from using **[Funnel]** on the golems, but Logan was sure he was going to need every drop of it.

My father—that thing*—is down here.*

"Stay alert," Logan said. Snoff nodded and came up next to him.

"What do you want to do?"

"Well, the good news is that your secret power is most likely here," Logan said.

The Faelves looked at him quizzically, and Logan gave them a shortened version of the tale Tumor had told him. This caused a commotion of hissed chatter, and it took Logan a while to get the Faelves to focus.

"We need to find that thing. But I also want to look for the body of the Herald. I don't know how long we will have to stay here, but I'll sure sleep better at night if I know it isn't skulking around."

"You think we will have to *sleep* here?" one of the Faelves asked aghast.

Logan wasn't sure if she was joking or not, so he gave her a look. Snoff and Sasafin shook their heads.

Logan was about to fire up his flashlight-ring out of habit, but he found he didn't need it. There were dozens and dozens of little clumps of natural Numa deposits all around. His eyes went wide.

This is a treasure trove.

Logan went over to a C-grade natural Numa crystal and charged the armor and all of his trinkets. He also funneled Tumor's golem full of energy, but that was mostly unnecessary, as either the automaton had a massive reserve or it used Numa with ridiculous efficiency. That was all he could do for now.

"Hopefully we will have time to level up your skills," Tumor said.

"I hope so too," Logan said wistfully as they walked past the glowing rock formations. "But now is not the time."

"Would it not be better to prepare for the possible battle we might have with the Herald?" Snoff asked.

"We don't have enough information," Tumor said. "The great war machine called the Ark is here. It could require an inordinate amount of Numa to power up."

"If we find more darkmetal," Logan said. "We will have to return. But without it, I doubt we can create anything stronger than my armor and Tumor's golem to take on the Herald anyway."

"Be that as it may," Sasafin said and approached one of the crystals, making the rest of their party stop, "I am curious."

She hesitantly looked over her shoulder at Logan.

"It's not corrupted," Logan said.

"What if the Herald poisoned them and left them for us to consume?" one of the Faelves asked.

"I just used them to charge my equipment," Logan said.

"But it's possible he could have crafted a poison is only harmful to the Fae Folk."

Logan suppressed an eye roll.

"That's dumb," Sasafin said and placed a tiny porcelain hand on one of the crystals. "Oh. It's warm. It feels nice."

"Can you drain it?" Tumor asked.

"I can! Oh! So much power!"

The crystal's glow faded, and it seemed Sasafin was now more energetic than ever.

Interesting. The Faelves are used to only using the Numa fruits. I wonder if their internal Numa charge is ever filled. And more importantly . . .

"You can drain the crystal to fill your internal Numa charge?" Logan asked and came up to crouch next to Sasafin.

Sasafin nodded. "Most of the Faefolk can. It's a skill that comes naturally and is often a choice for us, no matter what class we level in."

"What is your class?" Tumor asked.

Sasafin turned to grin proudly at the automaton. "[**Lightweaver**]. I can make illusions and tricks of the light to fool the eye."

"Seems powerful." Logan said

"Common class," Snoff said. Sasafin huffed and turned her nose. "I, for one, have a rarer version. I am a scout class of speed and powerful illusions. A [**Trickster**]."

"Much good it did you when you first met Logan," Sasafin said and scoffed. That elicited a few laughs. Logan joined in. It felt good to relieve some tension. But soon they fell quiet and the severity of the situation landed on them like a lead blanket.

"We should get moving," Logan said. "All of you who can, recharge your internal Numa. We might not get another chance."

Before they did that, Tumor reminded them that they should search for the Herald's body. Everyone agreed, but deep in his heart or soul or whatever, Logan knew it would be futile.

He isn't here. He survived the fall somehow.

They traveled further down the corridor, which was wide enough for two Tumor-sized golems to walk abreast. Logan felt a mounting unease, but he couldn't help but admire the runework on the walls. Intricate, multilayered, perfect. They were mostly made up of symbols Logan could not read nor understand, but there were some that clearly represented a people fighting Levemoth, just like the murals in the ruins the First Folk had inhabited.

Recurring motif. Makes sense when the dragon is actually real.

"Logan . . ." Tumor said. "Can you see?"

Logan looked at the golem and scrunched up his brows. "Yeah?"

"We can see too," Sasafin said. "But why?"

"Good question," Tumor said.

"Huh?" Logan said. "What's going on?"

"There is no light source," Snoff said. "Look around."

Logan did. He let his gaze roam from the floor to the runic walls and to the ceiling. There were no lamps, no soft blue glow indicating the use of Numa constructs, yet he saw perfectly well. Just as clear as day. He hadn't noticed it before, but it was like his eyes had been enchanted.

"Oh," Tumor said. "That is probably why. Is there any way we can verify the hypothesis?"

"What?" Sasafin asked. "Bah. I hate it when you two use your secret mind magic."

"It's not—" Logan started but stopped. As far as he was concerned, Tumor *was* magic.

"'Tis likely this is the result of the barrier we crossed," Snoff said and nodded sagely, after Tumor explained what Logan had theorized. "This is why the Fae Folk were more affected. We are more magical than you. It washed away enchantments and granted its own."

"That makes me wonder," Logan said as they walked along. They came to a large room with a high ceiling and a large round doorway. Two perfect lines were carved into the ground. They went on in a completely straight line from one of the doorways to the other.

Curious. For a cart?

"Most likely," Tumor's golem said.

In the middle of the room was a squiggly, twelve-foot-high spire that branched out this way and that, like a beautiful twisted tree. It had runes all over the branches that pointed in different directions. "What else are we enchanted with?"

Logan walked up to the spire and touched the runes. Suddenly, information flooded his brain, and he suddenly had an understanding that he hadn't before.

"Oh," Logan said.

"Oh," Tumor said.

"Oh?" Sasafin said and came up to the spire. She touched it too. "Oh."

One by one, rest of the Faelves came and touched the spire.

"This place . . ." Snoff said reverently. "It has such strange magic. I could not have—none of the Faelves could have. We do not have the skill nor the creativity for this."

"It is unorthodox," Logan said. "But I suppose it makes sense, since they were designing this place as a vault. They made a signpost that any creature with any language could read."

Logan sat down and recalled the information that the spire had transmitted. The directions were clear and simple. To the right was a workshop. There would be machinery there built by the Old Folk that they left for maintenance and upgrade purposes. They had no notion of what the perfect war machine would require, so they left numerous potential materials.

To the left was a Numa crystal mine. The Old Folk had chosen to build here because it was a hidden deposit of significant proportions. The ultimate weapon would require it as an energy source.

And lastly, if they walked forward past the spire, they would find the Ark. It was as massive as an aircraft carrier. It couldn't house a nation, but it could house an army. A big one.

"Let us go," Tumor said excitedly. "I want to see the Ark."

Logan grinned at his buddy's enthusiasm and followed the golem to see a wonder the likes of which he had never previously even imagined.

CHAPTER 48

The actual ship was even more magnificent than the image in Logan's head. The sheer size of it was beyond words. As was the hole in the ceiling that went upward for what must have been miles. Apparently, the craft was designed to fly up like a rocket.

It sure didn't look like a rocket. Nor did it have thrusters, as Tumor noted. That didn't vex Logan. It was clear the thing would run on magic rather than engine power. The surface was a sleek gray stone, polished and smooth as marble of the highest quality. The aerodynamic angles and shapes were clearly designed for flight, but from the picture that Logan had in his mind from the goalpost's transmission, he knew that it had a large deck, clearly designed with specificity.

They walked and checked both corridors to the sides of the massive ship. They were full of rows and rows of the same sort of golems that Tumor was currently occupying with his **[Possess]** ability. But they held no weapons. Their hands were empty, and Logan figured that was so they'd be able to hold whatever tool was necessary.

"That's the crew for the ship," Logan said.

"I wonder . . ." Tumor said.

"About what?" Snoff asked.

"The guardian golems we faced," Tumor said. "They talked to each other."

"Yeah . . . ?" Logan said, starting to get an inkling of what Tumor was going for.

"So they were communicating. I simply wonder if . . ." Tumor fell silent.

"You think there were Groloin inside the golems?" Logan said.

"I do."

Logan considered that. "Probably."

"Did we commit murder?" Tumor asked with a quiet voice.

Logan considered the golems in neat rows. They had deep runes engraved on their bodies, but the eyes were empty sockets. "I think we would have to ask them. But now they are a hivemind thing, right? Maybe they don't die if their bodies are killed."

"I hope we find out," Tumor said in as gentle a voice as his golem form allowed. "I would hate the idea of having killed as gentle and intelligent a species as the Groloin."

"We'll ask if we get the chance," Logan said, turning his gaze back to the giant ship. This was not a good time to be sentimental. What Tumor said had bothered him, but as the leader of this sorry expedition, he was not going to show weakness.

Father taught me some useful lessons despite being a massive prick.

Logan wondered if his old man was still here in his monstrous form. Lurking around, waiting for a moment to strike. He hadn't been down by the area where the platform had landed.

Snoff and the other Faelves were dumbstruck by the size of the monolithic Ark. Logan wondered if they had ever seen anything even close to it in size.

"How can we make sense of this?" Snoff said in reverent awe. "This is as enormous as the Thief!"

"I don't think it's quite as big as him," Logan said, but he honestly wasn't sure. "Come on. Let's check out the other rooms."

They returned to the room with the crossroads and the spire and debated which of the two other rooms they should check first. Logan voted for the Numa crystal deposits room, but he stopped in the middle of a sentence. He thought he had heard something.

"Shh," he said and raised a hand. The Faelves and Tumor quieted immediately.

Logan peered around the room and felt his posture lowering, his body readying for a fight on instinct. In the corner of his vision, something moved. He turned his head, but it was already gone, melded back into the shadows.

"I'm replaying it," Tumor said.

"Huh," Logan said, still peering around, flexing his muscles. "I didn't know you could do this CSI shit."

"It was never necessary before," Tumor said distractedly. "There. I paused it . . . Replaying the key frames . . . It's impossible to say what it was, but it was clearly a humanoid."

"I doubt there are many of those around here," Logan muttered unhappily. His emotions were a conflicted mess. He felt elated, grumpy, frustrated, and afraid at the same time.

"Do you want me to help with that?" Tumor asked.

"No!" Logan said immediately. "Just stay alert. Let's go check the Numa crystals."

The room with the natural Numa deposits was just as grand as the one with the Ark. A cave the size of an airplane hangar glimmered with bright hues of blue, so vibrant it was hard for the naked eye to bear.

These natural Numa deposits were not raw formless rocks. The Groloin had carved them. They were all pointed shapes, like thick, stubby swords with four corners like the diamonds in a pack of cards. They came down from the ceiling like jagged stalagmites. They were on the walls, and there were even some growing from the floor, in the middle of the room, pointing upward. All of the crystals pointed to the center of the room, and the air seemed to hum and crackle with their power.

The fractals seemed to compound on each other and hold more power together than a single crystal would. The room was excessively warm, as if the deposits were radiating heat.

This whole room is overflowing with magic.

"Logan . . ." Tumor said slowly as he walked toward the middle of the room. "I think we have been using the crystals incorrectly this entire time."

Logan took a few steps into the room. The heat and hum of the room started turning into pressure by the second and third step. The fourth step had him sweating and bending. Two more steps and he fell to his knees. The sheer power emitted from the crystals was oppressive.

Logan half-crawled, half-pushed himself forward for another foot. It was just mere curiosity. He regretted that immediately. The pressure turned into pain, and his body started growing numb.

Tumor's automaton sighed. He went to retrieve Logan and ended up dragging him back.

"You could have just used the armor," Logan said sullenly.

"I like having a body of my own," Tumor said. "You have no idea how exhilarating it is. I have additionally also leveled up quite a few attributes while learning new things about this body and how to control it."

"I'm glad you're having fun, buddy," Logan said and wiped a sheen of sweat off his forehead. "What do you make of this?"

"Fascinating," Tumor simply said. "Truly fascinating."

Then his golem marched over to the middle of the room to inspect the crystals jagging upward from the ground.

"I wish we had a device to measure the energy of Numa," Tumor muttered, but the acoustics of the cave carried his voice. The Faelves all perked up at that.

"Tumor," Snoff called. "Say something else."

"Perhaps a poem?" Tumor said, now with a normal voice.

This time, Logan felt it too. Tumor's voice reverberated in the air with such potency that it was almost visible. Faint blue waves came from the middle of the room at them and their sheer energy made Logan flinch. A few of the Faelves gasped.

"'Tis magnificent," Snoff muttered.

"Such powerful magic," Sasafin whispered.

"Do you guys understand what is going on?" Logan said.

"I think—" Tumor said, whispering this time. It was plenty audible. "—that this room is some sort of a funnel."

"A what?" Logan asked.

"You have an ability that allows you to drain these crystals, yes?" Snoff asked Logan.

Logan nodded.

"As do many of our kind," Snoff said. "But the Old Folk planned for any manner of creature to find their work. They needed a way to let them access the Spirit Goddess's power."

"Huh." Logan said. "Let's put that theory to the test."

Logan wasted no time. He started doing acrobatics and running around, bouncing from wall to wall and making Tumor manipulate the armor to morph and shape around him into strange forms.

Logan continued for another five minutes, to make sure the energy expenditure was sufficient. Then he walked back to stand between the Faelves.

"Say something," Logan called out to Tumor.

"Personhood," Tumor called out.

The reverberating energy hit Logan; he could feel it blow through him like a warm gust of wind. It was a slightly uncomfortable sensation, but it felt benign in nature.

"Well?" Logan asked.

Tumor walked the golem back over to them and nodded with its bulky head. "The armor is fully charged."

"Amazing," Logan said.

Tumor didn't answer. He started walking around the cave, inspecting every nook and cranny. It took him a while before he got back to the others.

"Learn anything?" Logan asked.

"I think I could recreate it," Tumor said. "With your use of [**Transmutation**], of course."

"Recreate it for what?" Snoff asked.

Logan rubbed his chin. "It's a model for an engine, isn't it?"

"It is!" Tumor said, clearly happy that Logan had understood.

"What is an engine?" Sasafin asked.

"It, uh . . ." Logan said. "Makes stuff go?"

The Faelves looked at Logan with expressions of pure confusion. Then they looked at each other to see if anyone else had understood and then right back to Logan.

"Engines are machines," Tumor explained. "They convert one form of energy into another. Generally mechanical energy, also known as motion. Your bodies are engines of sorts. They turn food into ATP, which in turn powers your cells and—"

"Okay!" Logan interrupted. "The short of it is that this formation releases the Numa from the crystals with the power of sound."

"But that is not the same as the engine thing, is it?" one of the Faelves asked.

"No," Tumor said. "Not exactly. But we can easily turn this formation into an engine in one easy step."

"What step?" Snoff asked.

"Let us get back to that," Tumor said. "We still have one room to explore."

Their group carefully entered the room with the crossroads. Logan was at the front, several yards ahead of the others. Tumor held the rear with the golem. Logan motioned for a halt every ten feet and crouched to watch and listen. He peered around, trying to make out shapes from the shadows in the corners of the large room, but nothing seemed amiss.

He will attack eventually. But why wait? What is his game?

The more time the Herald gave them, the better. Logan had had a long day, but he was feeling better by the minute. It always took a while to recover from a battle. Perhaps that was why the Herald was hesitating. It could have suffered great damage from the fall. It had cushioned itself with some trick, though. That was a certainty,

Should we go on the offensive instead?

[I think we should explore all of the rooms before we make any decisions.]

Logan nodded at that and led their little group into the last room.

It was as spectacular and ridiculous as the two previous rooms. It was clearly a workshop but the likes of which Logan had never seen before. It was like Santa's workshop had been crossed with the industrial might of the nineteenth century, with assembly lines made from wood, metal, leather, and resin.

There were mechanical arms in modern assembly lines, operated by robotics. These had runes engraved on them, and Logan was certain they were Numa-powered. In the middle of the room was an elevated platform at the end of the rails that ran through the three-room complex. It was large enough to fit a fighter jet.

I suppose parts for the gargantuan ship would have to be pretty gargantuan themselves.

There was only one slight problem. A few of the mechanical arms were scattered to pieces on the floors, and the leather of the assembly line was ripped and shredded. Someone or something had attempted to crush and ruin the rails running on the ground, but that had been a failure.

Additionally, all of the glass containers on a nearby toppled shelf had been crushed.

"Someone has sabotaged this place," Tumor said.

"Take three guesses who that someone might be," Logan muttered.

*Tumor, I can easily use **[Repair]** on this stuff. I doubt he knows I can, but that's irrelevant.*

Logan let the rest of what he wanted to say run through his mind subvocally.

[You are thinking that the Herald is waiting to attack us while we attempt to fix the room.]

That's what I would do.

[Likewise. What do you propose we do?]

Let's leave the room. That way, we can talk with the Faelves. Let's go to the room with the platform elevator. We can use those crystals now.

Wordlessly Logan turned and started walking away. There was a possibility that his crab-Herald-father would attack if they attempted to leave. But Tumor estimated the chance to be only around 28 percent.

Staying mindful of his shield-ring, Logan led the Faelves out of the room and back to the elevator. They weren't attacked, but he kept glancing back to see if any evidence of movement in the shadows could be seen. If he were the Herald, he knew he would have followed and attempted to listen to them.

Logan went down on a knee and asked all of the Faelves to form a ring around him. Tumor was on lookout duty. If the Herald tried to eavesdrop, they'd catch him, as the elevator room had one entrance.

"Okay," Logan said. "It's fair to say that the Herald is alive."

The Faelves nodded grimly.

"The Old Folk were truly beautiful builders," Snoff said. "It pains me to see their work damaged."

"We will fix it, don't you worry," Logan said and then gestured toward the many Numa crystal deposits around them. "But before that, we should use this as best we can and prepare for a battle."

The Faelves nodded with curt determination. They were starting to get some fight in them. Logan found himself respecting them more.

"Spears and shields are useless against him," Logan said. "Drop them. You should focus on your strengths—illusions, tricks, what have you."

"What do you suggest?" Sasafin said. "We know many tricks but have not had many battles. It is your experience and guidance we need here."

"Right," Logan said and rubbed his chin.

There were six deposits in the room. They looked to be C-graders, but there was one B-grade, which made him very happy. That could go a long way.

"I'm not fully aware what each of you can do, truth be told," Logan said. "Let's go over that."

In short. Snoff's abilities were mostly what you would expect from a Faelf scout. His class, [**Trickster**], specialized in illusions and invisibility, as well as the ability to make him go faster and see further. Logan instructed Snoff to do everything he could to make sure they got the drop on the Herald and not the other way around.

Sasafin and another Faelf called Vieria were both [**Lightweavers**], a fully magic-based class that used light to create illusions. It was a common class among the Fae Folk, as it allowed them to create invisible structures and mislead creatures that might wander accidentally into the Faelves' territory. It was also a well-liked class because they provide entertainment as well, keeping the children busy with things such as butterflies made of light to chase.

Cheinida was the youngest of the Faelves—only fifteen years old. She had braved the expedition because she was of the [**Explorer**] class. It was a strange one, and it would be completely useless in the coming battle, but it had a feature that Logan was very grateful for. She could create food and water out of Numa. Logan's hunger was manageable; his thirst was another story. Logan ordered her to immediately start preparing food and drink for the party.

The last of them was Jasofin. He had green porcelain skin and had been quiet the longest. He was radiating nervous energy. Logan supposed he couldn't be blamed, considering the terrible situation they were in. He had to keep reminding himself that the Faelves weren't used to this.

They're doing well, all things considered.

Jasofin was a **[Helper]**. Basically his abilities made everyone else's better. Logan's eyes lit up when he heard that.

"Better how?"

"Well . . ." the Faelf stammered and looked to Sasafin for support. She grinned and took his hand and gave it to Logan. Logan shook it.

"We're going to be alright, Jasofin," Logan assured the little Faelf. "What can you do to help?"

"I have a skill called **[Boost]**. If I keep touching you, it will let you perform better than you normally could with your class abilities."

"How much better?"

"It—It depends," Jasofin said. "But if I put a lot of Numa in it, it can be almost ten attribute points worth."

Eyes shining with excitement, Logan grabbed his little green hand. He yelped as Logan pulled him next to one of the Numa crystal deposits.

"Give me the boost. Use all of the Numa you can," Logan said.

Jasofin did just that and then he placed a hand on Logan, who felt a jolt of electricity run through him. He was suddenly more alert. He cracked his knuckles and grinned. "Let's make some upgrades."

CHAPTER 49

Logan decided to work with a blank slate. He would need to optimize the armor to be effective against the Herald specifically. Anything extra needed to go. That meant the spatial storage, first and foremost. It took a lot of juice out of the total capacity, and it wouldn't be needed here. Also Logan wanted to rid the armor of all enchantments he had placed on it.

It took a little while, but he finally managed to use Numa to disenchant the armor. It worked the same way enchanting worked, only in reverse. He needed to say the right incantation, and the Numa would do the rest.

[Subclass Level Up!]
[Enchantment Level 37]

The Herald was a very specific foe. Deadly speed and strength, amazing durability. The Herald didn't do anything extra. There were no tricks to look out for or crazy elaborate techniques.

Who needs that, when you have overwhelming power?

It was Logan who needed to come up with tricks. But for that to happen, he needed to do an inventory to have a full picture of the upcoming battle.

What also needed to be factored in was that Tumor had a golem. It was a hulking tank of a thing. If Logan could keep the Herald busy and maneuver the battle in a way that would give Tumor an opening, that could be a winning strategy.

Speed. We need speed. Optimize for speed.

Logan considered the tactical options and tried to visualize them. Tumor immediately boosted this capacity so it was like watching a clear movie in his mind. He could zip around and keep the Herald's attention on him, then, when the Herald overextended, he would make the armor produce long, multipronged whips in both of his hands to bind the Herald in place. It would most likely break free with its brute strength, but it could give Tumor enough time to clobber the monstrosity.

The Faelves were a problem. If Logan were facing them as an enemy, he would have killed them first.

But . . . What if we use them as bait?

[Highly unethical.]

Not like that, Tumor. What kind of an asshole do you take me for?

[Would you prefer an honest answer or an answer designed to protect your psychological wellbeing, whilst giving you the optimal emotional challenge for growth?]

Just shut up and listen. We need to tuck them somewhere safely away, anyway. So, when the engagement starts, they run back here to the platform and . . .

[We cannot be playing goalie with them.]

We won't. We'll use mines. Freezing mines, to make sure the Faelves don't fumble them and die. Add in a freeze effect, paralysis, and blindness. A lite version of the sludge. But in mine-form.

[. . .]

[Excellent idea. Let us do that first. Hopefully you will gain some levels and we can create even stronger enchantments. I am playing out simulations and variations on what sort of setup for the armor would be optimal.]

Logan nodded at that and asked Sasafin to bring him a few rocks. He transmuted them into flat shapes, like landmines, and proceeded to enchant it into an infantry mine that you'd step on to trigger the effects.

[Attribute Level Up!]
[Durability: 26]

"Do you think it's potent enough?" Sasafin asked after she took two of the mines. Logan had made four. He'd have preferred to give them all to Sasafin, but that would be too cumbersome for the little Faelves. So he gave two of them to her and two to Snoff, hoping the little Faelf could keep his klutzy tendencies in check.

"You'll run to this tunnel as soon as we see the Herald and place these mines on the ground," Logan said and then pointed to Snoff in particular. "Do not drop them. Once they're on the ground, they'll be activated."

Sasafin and Snoff both regarded the mines with reverence and clutched them to their chests.

Maybe I should have done that last.

Then he took some rocks and made shield-rings for everyone. He even made a bracelet for Tumor's golem after he relayed the necessary measurements. It wouldn't block the Herald's powerful attacks, but it could turn a lethal strike into an inconvenient one.

After that, they had a little break and ate and drank. The food and water Cheinida had created tasted like pine, which was fine for the water, but a bit unfortunate for the food, which was a hard bread the color of oatmeal. As stale a meal as it was, everyone devoured it with great gusto.

"Couldn't one of you cast an illusion on the bread?" Logan asked.

All of the Faelves looked at him like he had said something silly.

"For the next deadly expedition, we will be sure to bring a [**Fae-chef**], so you can enjoy the little luxuries of life, before being eaten by monsters," Sasafin said and sniggered.

"Wait, you guys do that?" Logan asked.

"Of course we do that," Sasafin said. "That's the best way to handle cooking."

"Wait a minute," Logan said. "So all those pies I ate in your previous home, they didn't have real sugar in them?"

[Oh no . . . Even I couldn't tell the difference. I have enjoyed fake pies. What even is reality?]

"Where in the good Goddess' name would we get sugar in a swamp?" Sasafin said and looked at Logan with incredulity.

"He is so smart when it comes to tactics and leadership," Cheinida whispered to Snoff.

"I know," Snoff said. "I believe he hit his head as a child."

"You guys would have made so much money on Earth," Logan said and chuckled to himself. "Being able to make carrots taste like donuts . . ."

They chatted idly for a while as they finished eating. It was nice having a little moment of peace. The situation was intense, but right now they were essentially safe. It didn't seem like the Herald would push for an immediate attack, and Tumor would let them know immediately if something odd happened.

It's good. They need a moment of respite, to let their heart rates rest. We all do, for that matter.

[Your cortisol levels are not looking good.]

Logan chuckled. Then he got up, wiped his hands, and got back to work.

Jasofin's boost really made a difference. Tumor tested it on the strength enhancement of the armor, and it turned out that with it backing up Logan's spells, the Strength enchantment would not only last 7 percent longer but be 12 percent stronger as well.

One might think that that would be negligible in this situation, but Logan had specifically made every prompt to emphasize power over efficiency. That meant all of the basic enchantments, like strength, speed, and durability, were now at 22 percent higher capacity than they had previously been.

The armor would run out of power in a full combat situation after twelve minutes, but no fight would last that long. However that was the optimal margin Tumor was willing to bring it down to. Every minute less of battery would dramatically decrease chances of getting out of this place alive, according to Tumor's math. And Logan trusted his math.

[Attribute Level Up!]
[Control: 37]

Logan also enchanted the Black Missiles. A simple case of penetrative power and homing ability, nothing fancy. The Black Missile already did what it was supposed to. It staggered and annoyed their enemies and bought time. Tumor's aim with it was great. They had concluded that heavy missiles would be more useful than small ones.

Logan used the platform's limited area to get used to the increased strength and agility he now possessed. It was frustratingly easy to stumble when you suddenly ran 22 percent faster.

[Skill Level Up!]
[Power Armor Fighting Level 17]

Nice. Didn't expect to get that while out of actual combat.
[You were probably close. What I have gathered is that doing new things helps level faster. You are operating the armor at a level that is unprecedented for you.]
"I'll take every advantage I can," Logan said and squeezed a fist.

Then it was finally down to the last touch. The armor still had some capacity left to hold enchantments.

"What about skates?" Logan asked. "I could move pretty fast on magic skates."

[Really? You're going to switch to a completely different style of movement all of a sudden? Do you want to know the odds of your tripping up and killing us?]

Logan made a face. "No."

[My calculations and simulations mostly work on ideas you have already generated. As you know, one of my main weaknesses is producing something novel. However, the use of the thrust enchantment would be apt. Not only could we enchant the backs of your knees and your heels to generate thrust for increased speed, we could also implement slight enchantments to aid your ability to thrust and cut with your arms.]

Logan considered that. It could work. Tumor explained how they could implement small enchantments on Logan's back, helping him rotate his hips when striking, as well as his elbow. The elbow enchantment would pull double duty for both thrusting and striking.

[The problem will be balance. We can practice, but in these high-speed situations, you will make mistakes and overextend. I can, of course, mitigate that and take control of the armor more frequently. But that links to the second problem. The strain this method will place on your body will take weeks to heal. Will, not might. You will end up with broken bones. Not to mention the damage to the ligaments and tendons. Without magical healing, the damage will be permanent.]

"Heh," Logan said and chuckled grimly. "Good thing we have a **[Healer]** waiting at home. You can keep me going with the armor even if I can't feel my legs anyway, right?"

[Are you sure?]

"Let's do it before I change my mind."

CHAPTER 50

[Attribute Level Up!]
[Focus: 36]

The thrust enchantments were ready. Logan told Tumor to put just 5 per-cent of their strength into them as he tried to move. He wondered if it was enough to face the Herald and at what cost it would come.

I don't think it's enough. We need something more.

He spent some more time playing around with the thrusts, and then an idea came to him. Was it a good one? Maybe. But better a bad idea than no idea at all.

"I have an additional tactic," Logan said. "Or rather a change in tactics."

[I'm listening.]

"Let's stack up on the binding options. We need to repurpose the Black Missiles."

[Sounds risky. What is a better alternative?]

"Sticky bullets. A super heavy net of sticky spiderwebs, maybe. That electrocute the user. And poison. And blind."

[You possess a truly devious mind.]

"And cause devastating pain."

[So basically your paralyzing sludge but in a sticky spiderweb form?]

"Precisely."

[Let me do calculations . . .]

Logan let Tumor work on that and turned to carefully operating the armor's thrust enchantments to get a feel for them. Snoff came up to him.

"What do you need?" Logan asked

"I—Snoff said and swallowed. "I will not stay behind here and hide behind the mines. I want to fight."

Logan was about to say no way and it's too dangerous and all the platitudes. But it wouldn't have been fair. Who was he to tell an adult what to do? Besides, he had wanted the Faelves to realize that they needed to fight. And here was Snoff, bravest of them all.

"You stay hidden, and you stay hidden well, Snoff," Logan said. "Ambush him and stick a dagger in him when the time is right. Don't try to be a hero. That's my dumb ass's role."

Snoff nodded stiffly.

"Look," Logan said. "I appreciate you stepping up. But the Herald—"

"I know," Snoff said and looked at the ground. "But I need to do this. My heart tells me so."

"Just don't get yourself killed."

"Right back at you, Logan."

After Tumor's calculations were done, he made a glob of liquid darkmetal from the Black Missiles. Logan enchanted it with all of the properties of the sludge. Tumor would control the shape, a multilayered spider's web. The weight enchantment was tricky, but Logan managed to get just the right words; it would get heavy—about five hundred pounds—when it struck a target at a certain speed. That wouldn't be enough to hold the Herald down, but with all of the nasty enchantments and Tumor's golem sitting on him, it should be enough to subdue him.

You're planning to capture, not kill him.

[Do you think there's hope?]

Logan shrugged. He didn't want to think about it, if truth be told.

"Alright," he said. "Gather round, my little friends. We're as ready as can be. Now let's go over the plan once more . . ."

Logan led their group back into the workshop room with the broken assembly lines. Without saying anything, Logan went to use **[Repair]** on the Groloins' broken tools. He fixed two of them before Tumor sent a warning through his mind.

"Shield!" Logan called, and a blue umbrella of energy sprung out of his fist to protect him.

It was only the superhuman speed of his link with Tumor and his reflexes that saved his life.

Blue tentacles sprung out at him from the darkness. They broke the shield, but Logan had just enough time to take a step back. What was left of Malcolm Specter stepped out from the shadows from behind a crane.

The Herald stood before them. It had a new form and it was truly monstrous. Its whole body, which resembled a centaur, was bathed in the dark blue glow of corrupted Numa. Instead of two legs, it now had four, all ending in sharp blue spikes. Meanwhile, its hands had turned into claws, designed to hold and crush, its whole body was now covered in black and blue chitin, thick and jagged, and six tentacles grew out from its back, lashing the air. They also glowed blue, like nightmarish glow sticks.

Logan stepped forward, snarling away his fear. His heart pounded like never before. He flexed his fingers and felt the power of the Armor course through him. He would give this his all, and he would win. There was no other way.

"Father," Logan said, trying to keep his voice from trembling. "This ends now."

The Herald regarded him silently. Then, after a moment, he said. "Succumb, Logan. You have to die."

Logan didn't waste any more words. He charged forward, the armor's enhanced speed propelling him like a bullet. The Herald met him head-on, and the clash of their bodies reverberated through the room like a thunderclap. Logan gasped in pain as his body strained with the superhuman force. But he heard a crunch of carapace through the mist of hurt.

Snoff and the other Faelves sprang into action, weaving illusions and distractions to keep the Herald off balance. After they did their work, they fled toward the tunnel to the platform room. The Herald made a move to follow them, but a large automaton tackled him before he could.

Tumor's golem body joined the fray, its massive form grappling with the Herald in a display of raw strength.

But the Herald was too powerful, shrugging off their attacks like they were nothing. Logan gritted his teeth, pouring every ounce of his will into the fight. The armor strained against the Herald's might, Numa energy sparking and crackling. The Herald wrapped its powerful glowing tentacles around the golem and started twisting.

[Logan, the net!]

Logan didn't hesitate. He aimed the launcher and fired, the venomous darkmetal net shooting out to envelop the Herald. For a moment, it looked like it might work. The Herald's movements slowed, its form struggling against the net's energy. Its knees buckled, and the paralyzing and pain-inducing agents started to seep in.

But then, with a roar of fury, the Herald tore free, shredding the net like paper. Logan's heart sank. Their trump card had failed. Logan charged up to it with a spear in hand. It penetrated, but the Herald only groaned. It had clearly been weakened. The poison from the web was taking its toll. Logan burst into action with the full speed of the thrusting enchantments. He felt his body straining with pain, but he managed to pick up pieces of the broken spiderweb and shove them in the Herald's face. It groaned again, and its tentacles wrapped around Logan. He could tell that they weren't moving as fast as they normally could have, but the squeeze was still fully cutting off his oxygen. He wheezed and struggled.

The Herald wiped away the heavy webs off of its face and gazed into Logan's eyes.

"This is the end," it said.

Logan tried to break free with his thrust enchantments, but they did nothing. There was simply no room to move. No room to breathe. Logan's mind was starting to dim. Tumor was yelling something, but it was just alarm, nothing that could get them out of this jam. There didn't seem to be anything he could do.

Suddenly, Snoff appeared behind the Herald, a gleaming dagger in his hand. With a leap, he plunged the blade into its back, cutting into the tentacles. Two of them fell to the ground. The Herald screamed, a sound of pure agony and rage.

Logan took a deep, raspy breath. Tumor immediately raced in to enhance his mind. Time seemed to slow down. He felt life surging back into him. He saw his chance and he took it. The monstrous grip of the Herald's tentacles had softened just enough. There was wiggle room and that was all he needed. He prompted Tumor to activate the thrust enchantments to full power. Tumor didn't argue. Logan broke free. It wasn't the only thing he broke, but Tumor blocked the pain signals.

Logan smashed a gauntleted fist into the Herald's face. The tentacles attacked, but now he was burning the candle from both ends and so was fast enough to grab them. Using them as leverage, he kicked the Herald in the stomach at full strength. The monster flew backward a good ten feet, four tentacles having now been ripped from its body and hanging limp in Logan's arms.

Running on adrenaline, fear, pain, and a whole lot of emotional baggage, Logan charged in and pounded into the Herald with pure wanton aggression. There was no grace, no technique, just pure thrust-powered punches to the face as he mounted the Herald's chest. Logan screamed and pounded until he felt the Herald growing limp under him.

Then he gathered all of the scattered webbings of their net gun and threw them onto the Herald. It groaned weakly and was bleeding black and blue sludge from its face.

Logan got off of it and charged up to the tunnel with the mines. His body was now on full alert and Tumor's ability to contain his pain was lessening. There would be a price to pay and it would be heavy. But for now, he was so close. Logan gritted his teeth and pushed forward.

[Keep going. We can do this.]

Logan picked up one of the freezing mines and used his thrusters to return to the Herald. It was convulsing and clearly moments away from death. Logan thrust the mine at it, and it suddenly froze in a block of ice.

Logan fell to the ground and just breathed.

Yeah. No.

He lay down. Every part of his body was in agony. He didn't even want to imagine the damage to his bones, muscles, tendons, joints.

"L-Logan?" Snoff said and came up closer.

"Good job," Logan said weakly. "You're a warrior now."

And then he passed out.

CHAPTER 51

Logan drifted in and out of consciousness, his body wracked with pain. Every breath was a struggle, every movement agony. Through the haze of his suffering, he could hear the worried voices of the Faelves, feel their gentle hands tending to his wounds.

"He's in bad shape," Snoff said, his voice tight with concern. "Cheinida, do you have anything that can help?"

The young [**Explorer**]-class Faelf stepped forward, her hands already glowing with Numa energy. "I can make a medicine," she said. "It won't heal him completely, but it should allow him to function."

Logan felt a cool sensation washing over him as Cheinida worked her magic. The pain receded, replaced by a numbing warmth. His mind cleared, the fog of agony slowly lifting.

"Thank you," he croaked, his voice raw.

Snoff helped him sit up, his face etched with worry. "Logan, what you did . . . It was incredible. You saved us all."

Logan grinned. "We all played our part. Especially you, Snoff. That dagger strike made all the difference."

The Faelf looked to his right at the monstrosity encased in ice. There was a mixture of pride and sadness in his eyes. "I do wish it hadn't come to this. Your father . . ."

Logan's gaze drifted to the frozen form of the Herald, the monster that had once been Malcolm Specter. A wave of emotion threatened to overwhelm him, a bittersweet blend of triumph, closure, grief, and anger.

"I want to save him," he said half aloud.

The Faelves exchanged glances, surprise and hesitation clear on their faces.

"Logan," Snoff said gently. "After everything he's done . . . Is that wise?"

Logan let out a dry chuckle.

"Probably not."

Snoff waited.

Logan met his gaze, his eyes hard with determination. "He's still my father. If there's even a chance, I have to try."

With the decision made, they turned their attention to the workshop. Under Logan and Tumor's guidance, the Faelves set about making an inventory. There were many parts and materials of unknown shapes and substances that could surely be useful. Logan instructed the Faelves to organize and map out the room, while he focused on using [**Repair**] on the constructs that the Herald had broken.

It had done a number on the place, having ripped apart anything it could get its hands on. Logan went over to the hovering workbenches which wobbled in the air, the runes cracked and leaking Numa energy. He used his skill on them.

[Skill Level Up!]
[Repair Level 12]

Next, he repaired the leather assembly line. Then the cranes. Then the cart. Relentless, non-stop focus drove Logan forward.

[Skill Level Up!]
[Repair Level 13]

It took a while but, as the machines whirred back to life, Logan felt a surge of hope. Maybe, just maybe, they could get out of here. And if they did, that damned Levemoth had better watch out!

The Ark was a true marvel. Seeing it a second time didn't lessen its glory. As something of a craftsman himself, Logan couldn't help but admire it. Even with his class, he didn't have the imagination or skill to create something so beautiful. A testament to the ingenuity and power of the Groloin.

They quickly found a doorway inside. It was at the top of a large ramp on the bottom of the hull, wide enough to fit a bus sideways. They entered the Ark and began their exploration of the Groloins' legacy.

Logan and the Faelves explored the vast hallways and myriad rooms and couldn't help but be awed by the wonders they found inside. First, they passed a number of halls clearly used for storage. It was a veritable warehouse.

In the engine room, they saw similar constructs of Numa crystals. The crystals were polished and cut and all pointed toward a single spot in the middle of the room. The bright blue glow was blinding. There were three such massive constructs. Logan could barely get inside the room because of the pressure generated by that much Numa in one place.

The nice part was that just by standing in the doorway, his armor was replenished due to its passive Numa absorption ability, which Logan had made sure to reestablish as a core of its enchantment makeup after he had returned it to a standard configuration after the fight with the Herald.

"We are going to need you to inhabit a golem to perform any operations in this room," Logan said.

[I will be delighted to examine this room further.]

They went up from the bottom floor via a platform that floated up like an elevator. They passed living quarters and mess halls, but those were not a concern for now. They wanted to see the cockpit. After a few minutes of ascent, their group arrived at the deck of the massive ship. Fortunately it was well designed, as it seemed that the cockpit was in the building right next to the elevator. They approached the double doors which slid aside.

Inside were panels of glass that floated in the air, and below them, control panels etched with runes that also floated. In the middle of the room was a giant black egg. It was full of engraved blue runes which glowed faintly. It seemed to be running on fumes, whatever it was.

The egg stood on a platform which looked like it was unfinished. The runes on it were intricate, like circuitry. Logan only now noticed that the floor of the cockpit was glass.

[They are circuitry. I didn't notice it before. How ingenious! They were using circuitry to create computers with Numa, like we do with electricity.]

"What do you think this is?" Logan asked.

[Heh. Look below you.]

Logan glanced downward. He gasped. Below them, a vast and complex structure sprawled out like a giant black spiderweb with nodes on it— similar eggs to the one that was in the middle of the cockpit. The structure must have spanned a hundred yards in each direction. Floating Numa crystals were spaced out every twenty yards or so amongst the web. They were dim and drained of energy.

"What the hell?"

[I think it is the hivemind of the Groloin.]

"It's dormant."

[The crystals down there must be empty. Makes sense if they built this and left it running for millennia.]

"Looks like we have our work cut out for us," Logan said, cracked his knuckles, and grinned. "Let's get that big brain back online."

CHAPTER 52

Logan and the Faelves spent the next few days working tirelessly in the workshop, determined to find a way to awaken the dormant Groloin hivemind.

The Faelves, fascinated by the advanced manufacturing facility, busied themselves with creating a myriad of items, from comfortable furniture to intricate decorative pieces.

"Look at this, Logan!" Sasafin exclaimed, holding up a delicate porcelain cup. It was enchanted with an illusion—a fish jumping in and out of frothy waves. "Isn't it beautiful?"

Logan smiled. "Sure is. Make at least a hundred more. Which reminds me, Tumor, we need to think about the water supply on the ship."

[Perhaps you and the Faelves could collaborate on manufacturing an item that turns Numa into water.]

"Now wouldn't that be awesome," Logan said. "The infinite water fountain. Patent pending."

While the Faelves' creations brought a sense of warmth and normalcy to the workshop, Logan himself needed to focus on the task at hand.

"You're distracted again," he said.

[Ah, yes. Sorry, Logan.]

"I didn't know you were capable of being so consumed by a single task. I thought you had enough processing power to, I don't know, run a planet."

[I am honored by your assessment but not quite. Besides, my distraction is more a result of my growing personhood. I have sub-minds operating things like your day-to-day maneuvering with the armor, so the active part of my consciousness can do what it pleases. I am simply engrossed with the Groloins' use of Numa crystals in their circuitry. It is quite fascinating. By cutting and

concentrating the points of the crystals, they were able to achieve a level of energy efficiency that far surpasses anything I had considered possible before.]

Logan rubbed his forehead. Then he asked Tumor to repeat before he answered. "Do you think we could use that same principle to charge the floating crystals in the hivemind's neural network?"

*[It's possible. If we could create a tool that can focus and direct Numa energy with precision, we would be able to recharge the dormant crystals. We either need to do that, or we need a flying contraption or climbing equipment and rope so you can go manually use [**Funnel**] on each of the crystals.]*

Logan grimaced. "Yeah, how about no?"

[I figured that your, to quote you, "beat-up body," is not up to task. Besides, there are 128 of those floating crystals down there. It would take a long time for you to manually charge them.]

"So how about that other option?" Logan said. He sat down on one of the floating workbenches. It bobbed up and down before it stabilized. He sighed in contentment as he let his lower back slump and relax.

[I do have the necessary knowledge now to recreate a Numa crystal engine. However, dispersion is a problem. The Numa engines we have encountered up to now work with sound, namely vibration. It's not efficient. To waste the least amount of Numa, we need to figure out a different way to source and transform the energy.]

"I wish we could just ask how the Groloin charged the crystals," Logan said.

[We will just have to be creative. And by "we," I mean "you."]

"I guess that's my specialty . . ." Logan said. "I'll start mulling it over. I need to see Cheinida for some lunch."

Logan thought long and hard as he munched on the flatbread. The first stop he planned to make when they got the Ark going was King Sluikumar and the Faelves' camp. When they came aboard, Logan would find one of these illusion chefs and have them make flatbread that tasted of cheese, rather than cardboard.

Then a lightbulb flashed in Logan's mind. He wasn't sure how he got there from imagining the taste of cheese, but a flash of inspiration was a flash of inspiration.

[I could run a psychological analysis if you would . . .]

"Yeah, no, thanks," Logan said. "I know you want to reverse-engineer how my creativity works, but frankly I don't want to know. Just listen."

Tumor did, and he approved. But there was a hitch.

[Let me rehash. You want to transmute the Numa crystals into tiny shards. Then you want to align the shards in a handheld cannon that can shoot Numa when you yell into it?]

"Yes," Logan said enthusiastically. "What do you think?"

[I think you solved the portability problem. You are still left with several others.]

"You sound way less impressed than I was hoping you would."

*[Let us say you embed the hand cannon with, say, six **[E-grade Numa Crystals]**. There's an 87.22% certainty that the crystals meant to power the consciousness matrix of the Groloins' hivemind are B-graders. Would you like to hear the math on how many times you will have to go up and down on the elevator to charge all 128 of the crystals?]*

"Goddamn it," Logan said and slumped against the cave wall. Sullenly he watched as the Faelves laughed at a disfigured wine jug that Jasofin had made.

[And another problem with the Groloins' Numa engine is that it disperses energy very inefficiently. We need a laser, not a flashlight.]

"You're just full of sunshine and rainbows, aren't you?" Logan said.

[Simply use your gray mushy brain to create solutions.]

"Just do it?" Logan said and gave the air around him the best shit-eating grin he could muster. The Faelves cast a worried glance at him.

Logan growled. He wanted to get back to Freya. They had been stuck in this cave for days. Had it been four days since they'd defeated the Herald? Or was it five? Regardless, Logan's body was still a mess. He needed a proper healer soon, because otherwise his joints and bones would be permanently damaged, despite the armor propping him up as best as Tumor could manage.

"Okay, how's this?" Logan said. "There are three big Numa engines in the Ark's lower rooms. We somehow capture the ambient energy they have and route it to the matrix room, where it can disperse and slowly recharge the crystals?"

Logan could feel Tumor considering this for a while. A few seconds was a long while in AI time.

[That might work. I think the Numa energy is composed of particles. But it does seem to function very much like light, being able to also exist in waveform. If only I had tools to measure . . .]

"We'll get you some later," Logan promised. "But first we need tools to harness the energy."

[I don't think we need to do anything specific. You should be able to create enchantments and then a conduit with the materials you can find in the workshop. It will need to be tubular and insulated. I will instruct you using the same principles as making electrical wiring.]

"I'm sure it's close enough," Logan said and got up, reenergized. Waffling around was not for him. He needed a clear purpose. Now that he had one, he cracked his knuckles and got to work.

He made the Numa gun anyway. Just because he wanted to, and he was sure it could be used for something. Additionally, it was an easy way to test whether they could concentrate the Numa energy.

It took a bit of tinkering with transmuting the crystals to be just right. His **[Transmutation]** skills had been lagging, but Logan felt his ability with it would still be good enough. With Tumor's ability to provide astronomically small measurements, it probably was. But only barely. The crystals needed surgical work.

[Subclass Level Up!]
[Transmutation Level 34]
[Attribute Level Up!]
[Focus: 37]

Logan lifted up the gun. Even with the armor on, it was too unwieldy and heavy for one hand. It was shaped like a minigun, meant to be held at the hip with a straight hand. The exterior was encased in wood and leather, and inside was a miniature imitation of this complex's crystal cave, full of sharpened E-grader Numa crystals, all made to point at a single space between them.

Despite being shaped like a minigun, it worked more like a revolver. The trigger was difficult to press, possible only with the extra strength of the armor. It was Tumor's design. Logan pressed it, and the hammer produced a loud clack, which was diverted toward the Numa crystal complex.

Logan aimed at the wall and pressed the trigger. The sound was muffled, because it happened inside the weapon, but it still sent tremors up his hand. A fast-flying blue orb whizzed through the air like a New Year's rocket and crashed into the wall. A few rocks fell and when Logan went to inspect his handiwork, he noticed a fist-sized hole punched through the wall.

"Powerful," Logan said and grinned.

[Unwieldy for battle. But a good prototype.]
"Spoilsport," Logan muttered.

The next two days Logan worked with the assembly line. The Faelves were fairly adept at using it, so he let them help. Despite the chaos, Logan managed to push his **[Transmutation]** to another level, as well as a few attributes. He was especially happy with the Durability levels he was getting, since he'd been neglecting that one before. But Logan supposed he hadn't really made anything up to now that was really meant to last and survive a lot of strain. When Logan was finally done, he heaved a great sigh and brought up his stat screen. He was very happy with what he saw.

Logan Specter - [Artificer Level 7]
Attributes:
Potency: 40
Efficiency: 37
Durability: 26
Control: 37
Focus: 37
Subclasses:
[Transmutation]: 34
[Enchantment]: 37
Class Skills:
[Empower]: 10
[Funnel]: 15
[Repair]: 13
General Skills:
[Power Armor Fighting]: 17

It was a crude solution, but it should work. A huge coil of rubber tube, the size of a small hill. It seemed like it wouldn't be enough tube considering the size of the Ark. Tumor had done the measurements, so Logan figured it was all right, though.

The Faelves (at Tumor's instruction) had busied themselves in the workshop to create exoskeletons that could allow them to carry heavier loads. Averse to physical labor as the Faelves were, they had groaned and told Logan to first try to activate a golem for Tumor to inhabit. But it hadn't worked. There were dozens upon dozens of them in the room with the Ark, but even when Logan tried to use **[Funnel]** on them, they wouldn't respond.

So the Faelves relented. All six of them were wearing strange contraptions of leather, wood, and rubber, all enchanted with Logan's many tricks.

Together, the seven of them pushed an SUV-sized cart toward the Ark.

"This is going to take hours," Sasafin whined.

"Can we stop for lunch?" Jasofin asked.

"We just had lunch an hour ago," Logan said and growled. "Now shut up and push!"

They did. And it did take hours. Not the pulling alone. That only took a single hour and change. But all the rest of it combined. Installing the other end of the tube to the Numa engine room was especially arduous. The armor needed to be specifically enchanted, and the Faelves tied a rope around Logan so they could pull him out of the room if he slipped out of consciousness. Of course, he did. It was just one of those days.

After they managed to wake him up, it was time to take the coil into the elevator; it barely fit. Fortunately, the elevator did all the heavy lifting, while the group only needed to feed the tube down.

The last part sucked the most, however. It involved enchanting the armor with a wall-climbing ability. A part of Logan hoped he would be too low-level for it. But no, of course he wasn't. Instead he actually even gained a level.

[Subclass Level Up!]
[Enchantment Level 38]

Once the armor was enchanted, they tied another rope around his waist, lest the enchantment fail or he fell for other reasons. They also tied the heavy tube around Logan. And then he climbed into the consciousness matrix room, or whatever Tumor called it. Logan didn't care at the moment.

"Can't we just toss the tube in and let it work?" Logan muttered as he gingerly stepped off the edge of the platform.

[For the second time, no. It will waste too much energy. We need it to disperse in equal measure. Now quit complaining, and focus.]

"I kind of enjoy it when you're testy," Logan said and smirked to himself. He took a deep breath and stepped off the platform.

After twenty-five minutes of sweat-inducing, stress-increasing, heart-rate-elevating climbing, which Logan hated every second of, the tube had finally been installed in one of the walls of the giant complex which housed the Groloin hivemind. When Logan was finally done, he groaned happily and just laid there for a while.

"How long do we have to wait?" Snoff asked as he sat on Logan's stomach.

"Tumor says two or three days."

[If we installed another conduit to the other side of the room we could—]

"Yeah, no!" Logan said.

CHAPTER 53

After two days of waiting for the crystals in the consciousness network to charge, something happened. Logan was eating lunch with the Faelves in the workshop when there was suddenly a great tremor and a hum coming from the Ark room. They all ran there and stood in stunned shock as they watched. The whole massive black ship was glowing blue, as if being enveloped by Numa. It stopped after a few seconds, but as clear as day, something had awoken. Logan wasted no time and rushed up the elevator.

In the cockpit, the egg was alight with Numa blue. It hummed lines of Numa appeared where it touched the ground, snaking along the runic pathways for a second and then disappearing.

A melodic feminine voice spoke from all around them, as if the ceiling and walls held hidden speakers.

"This is Logan Specter, is it not?" it said. A musical, grandmotherly voice with a wistful and joyful tone. "Ah, we knew you would come! It must be the will of the stars that you did, for otherwise no Great Battle would be had. And life does not work that way, now, does it?"

"Uh . . . I guess?"

"Guess? We should hope you would be more decisive than that. But we can work with you. You are scrappy, if nothing else."

"Thanks . . . ?" Logan said. He wished the hivemind had a body to converse with. But he was used to it with Tumor. "You're what's left of the Groloin?"

"We are indeed," the grandmotherly voice said. "Now, we do hope that you can dispense with the silly questions, and instead start working with us. First things first."

At that moment, a golem came into the cockpit. Intricate runic patterns crisscrossed all of its six limbs: two sturdy, stocky legs and four limber arms. Two long ones hung down from its shoulders in a simian manner, and two stubbier ones protruded from the sides. The eyes on its helmet-like head glowed a faint blue.

"This is for your friend who you have so unfortunately named," the hivemind said. "We believe he has an ability to possess objects. Very useful. This automaton model should serve his needs, whether he is interested in crafts or combat."

Logan felt Tumor's presence shifting from his mind and soon afterward, the automaton next to them jerked.

"My thanks, Hivemind," Tumor said with the mechanical voice of the automaton. "Do you have a name you prefer to be called?"

"The manners on this one," the Hivemind said and let out a tinkling laugh. "How sophisticated and advanced! You are a remarkable creature, Tumor. To grow from a machine into a person. Such an ascension usually takes several lifetimes."

"I am indeed fortunate."

"As for our name . . ." the Hivemind said, with a tint of mischief in her voice. "Call us Glaan."

"We are honored to meet you, Glaan," Tumor said. "Please tell us what you must have been dying to tell for a very long time."

There was something resembling a mirthful chuckle in the air. It made Logan's hair stand on edge, but it was clearly benign in nature.

"Much you already know," Glaan said. "For the brave ones, the protectors of the legacy of our people, have given you the proper guidance. And much will need to be told later, for we wish not to waste time. Too long has the Destroyer of Beauty reigned unchecked. Too long has it not faced a proper challenge. But with our wills united . . . yes, we shall give it one.

"We are already awakening the golems. They are at your service. We are infusing them with our collective souls. Do not mistake them for us. They are mindless drones, but they will take good care of you. They will be especially useful for managing tasks with high Numa concentration."

"We've noticed," Logan said wryly.

"An interesting solution to powering up our minds," Glaan said, seemingly looking at the tube dispensing Numa into the matrix. "We thank you for the initiative. We will make our own adjustments and fix the Ark as we best see fit, as well as run it operationally. I do hope there will be no objections. Do realize that we are allies in this manner, but do not mistake the Groloin nor their creations, such as the automatons, as your servants."

Logan grinned. "That's going to cause problems down the line, but I wouldn't have it any other way."

"What a strange answer," Glaan said.

"You will find him most strange," Tumor said, nodding through the golem.

"Hey!"

The Faelves sniggered as they huddled shyly behind Logan.

"Ah, and these must be the Fae folk our protectors have spoken of. How valiant of you to ally yourselves with Logan Specter. Perhaps we have misjudged you."

Snoff stepped forward half a step from behind Logan's back. "Y—you have not. But we are trying to grow."

"That is good," Glaan said in a soft, grandmotherly tone. "Let us hope it is not too late. Please be our guests and feel welcome."

There was a dismissive air about how she spoke to the Faelves that Logan didn't care for. He spoke with a hardened tone.

"These are brave individuals, every one of them. I wouldn't have gotten this far without them. If I am your ally, so are they. In fact, if we are doing an alliance thing, I nominate Snoff as the representative of the Faelves. This alliance will be formed between the humans, the Groloin, and the Faelves to fight against this great evil. Are we all in agreement?"

Glaan said nothing. Snoff stammered something incoherent while the other Faelves mumbled:

"But the king . . . ?"

"Snoff as the leader? For an alliance?"

"So unusual!"

"But Logan said . . ."

"Shush!" Snoff said and all of the other Faelves quieted down.

"I—*we* tentatively accept," Snoff said. "But we should speak with King Sluik—"

"Nope," Logan said and grinned. He just stared at Snoff. who was sweating bullets. "It's me running the show. I'm the captain. And I need a navigator I can trust, and your king just ain't it."

Snoff smiled, uncertainly but genuinely. "Yes, my captain."

"Don't get all formal on me," Logan said and laughed. "I prefer an 'Aye, aye, Captain', anyway."

Sasafin frowned. "What's an aye-aye Captain?"

Snoff turned to him and shrugged.

"What is your plan, Logan?" Glaan asked.

"I'm glad you asked," Logan said and gave the egg an easy smile. It felt strange addressing it, seeing as Glaan seemed to be . . . everywhere. Perhaps she was the ship. And yes, damn it, he was going to call her a "she," despite her being a collective or whatnot. "I'm assuming you can get this big bucket in the air. First, I want to pick up the leftover Faelves in this jungle. I don't care if I have to carry them on the ship, they're coming with us. Then I'm going back to the humans and I'm getting my wife and my friends. Then we will look for other bands of humans. We are going to need an army that specializes in ship combat and all the support and logistics that comes with it."

"Straightforward, as we expected," Glaan said. "What sorts of contingencies will you take?"

Logan looked at Tumor in puzzlement.

"Glaan is asking about what you will do when the Big Fish inevitably takes notice of a giant flying ship in the sky."

Logan grinned. "Did you just call it the Big Fish?"

Tumor rubbed his automaton neck. "You rub off on me."

"He certainly does," Glaan said, clearly miffed. "You used to be so much better at focusing."

Tumor bowed his head.

"Don't grovel," Logan said and shook his head. "He's much better now than he used to be, thank you very much."

"You're a snarky one," Glaan said. "We sort of like that."

"Then we will get along just swimmingly," Logan said and barked out a laugh. "Now to answer your question, what sorts of weapon facilities do you have? Anything ready, or should we craft some?"

"There are . . ." Glaan fell silent for a moment. When she spoke, it was uncertain. "This is not our area of expertise. We were hoping you as a species accustomed to war would complement our ability to build other things."

Logan nodded. "Fair enough. We'll figure it out."

"That easy, huh?" Glaan said and chuckled. "We should not be surprised. Your straightforwardness is strangely refreshing."

"I would imagine anything would be refreshing after collecting dust for a few thousand years," Logan said.

"Well said," Glaan said and laughed. It was like an old woman's cackle that chilled Logan's spine.

Maybe I have some hang-ups about old women? She does seem kind of . . . witchy. I don't know. Maybe I am imagining things.

[Would you like for me to analyze and break down your psychological hang-ups and facilitate your mental growth?]

NO!

Logan cast a glare at Tumor, who waved his golem's hands apologetically.

Glaan let out something between a groan and a sigh. "We cannot believe that the fate of this world hangs on the shoulders of you two harebrains."

Logan waved a dismissive hand. "Don't worry about it. We're surprisingly good when we get down to it."

"Well . . . you are scrappy."

"Ok, so you'll get the ship running and in order. I'm assuming we can leave relatively soon. We'll manufacture a weapons system. I'm thinking Numa energy cannons—NECs for short. I like acronyms, and I know for a fact that Tumor here loves them too."

"Yes, this sounds good," Glaan said. "We will get the ship running. You will design and engineer the weapons system. What will the Fae Folk do?"

Snoff looked at Logan, but Logan only grinned and shook his head.

"You're going to be a leader, Snoff," Logan said. "Leading is decision-making."

Snoff nodded and swallowed. He took a glance back at the other Faelves, who were looking confused, but they smiled at Snoff encouragingly. Logan watched the uncertainty turn into resolve on the delicate elfin face of his friend.

"We will take on the support role," Snoff said. "The war against the Great Thief will require material-processing, food, shelter, and service. I will make sure the Faelves will do their part."

Logan was impressed. He nodded at Snoff. Snoff smiled and nodded back. Glaan hummed in satisfaction.

"That is perfect. Just what we needed. So what shall you do first?"

"We will continue making accommodations. Utensils, bedding, hygiene items," Snoff said. "We are good at those. You wouldn't be able to tell, but the Fae Folk enjoy comfort."

"Oh, we can tell," Logan said dryly. Snoff threw a glare at him and continued.

"We will initially attempt to batch-create for three hundred: one hundred for the Fae Folk and two hundred for the Tall Folk. There are but six of us, but we will work hard. We have been enjoying the use of the assembly line, and we have gained some mastery over it."

"That's great, Snoff," Logan said and gave an encouraging thumbs-up. "Do as much as you can now. Once we pick up your folk, you'll have more hands to command."

Snoff swallowed again. "R-right."

"Now," Glaan said, hesitation in her voice, "I have one more question. That thing down in the cargo bay, encased in magical ice?"

Logan let out an awkward chuckle. "It's my father."

"We know full well what it is and what it means to you," Glaan said testily. "Why is it onboard? While we do not advocate killing, you must understand that this is the Destroyer of Beauty's general. It has its very blood coursing in its veins."

Logan spread out his hands. "What do you want me to say?"

"We want you to kill it."

"That's not happening," Logan said, his mouth tightening.

"If that thing escapes and starts a rampage on the ship, it could destroy everything."

Logan shrugged. "Without me, this wasn't going to happen anyway. Nor will it."

"Do not test us, boy," Glaan said, the grandmotherly warmth now gone. The voice was cold and imperious. "We have waited for a long time to—"

"Consider this," Logan said sharply. "Would you rather ally yourself with me or someone who would kill their own father for convenience's sake?"

Glaan said nothing. Logan could feel Tumor approve of this answer.

"I can save him," Logan said, an edge in his voice which brooked no argument. "And that is the end of it."

Another moment of silence. Then the Hivemind huffed.

"Fine!" it said. "But it's your ass if that thing escapes."

"It's all of our asses," Logan said and smiled. "Assign golems to keep watch on it."

"As if we were not already doing that."

"We'll figure out a way to restrain it properly once we have more time on our hands."

"Very well," Glaan said. "We do not like this, let the records show."

"Anything else?" Logan asked cheerfully.

"That should settle it," Glaan said. "We are already mobilizing the automatons. If you have any requests for their use, please tell us. We will additionally construct communication devices, so we don't have to convene here to exchange information. To get the ship ready to fly will take approximately three days."

"We will make use of them," Snoff said and bowed.

"Alright, then," Logan said and cracked his knuckles. "Let's get to work."

CHAPTER 54

Logan and Tumor spent most of their next few days by themselves, work-shopping designs and testing prototypes for the ship's weaponry—everything from homing missiles to giant laser cannons on top of the deck, most of them impractical, but Logan felt it was important to let ideas flow. Tumor was great at playing the straight man and goalkeeping against Logan's more impractical ideas. The last week they had spent in this ruined complex with the Ark had really brought them together even closer as friends. Even that was too light a word for either of them to use. Tumor defaulted to calling himself his symbiote, which pissed Logan off. But yeah, they were a team for life, and they both felt it more strongly than ever before.

It's said that great chess players always see the best move immediately. It's instinctual. They just have to spend time making sure their instinct was correct. This was the same now with Logan. After countless prototypes, varying from catapults to little drones, they went back to the idea of NECs.

Tumor had concluded that it was simply the most efficient way to approach the situation.

"There are still several obstacles," Tumor said as he displayed a hologram of the latest design. "We still need to solve the energy conversion problem. The enemy will absorb pure Numa. You can most likely create an enchantment, but we have to make sure it is the optimal one."

"For the umpteenth time, buddy," Logan said with exasperation in his voice, "we won't reach optimal before we try it out, fail, improve, fail at something else, rinse, and repeat for ever and ever. There is no perfect on the first try."

Tumor was silent for a moment. Logan threw a sideways glance at the golem. Its shoulders slumped.

"I know," it said dejectedly.

"You know it on a conceptual level," Logan said, trying not to admonish him too hard. "Your mind just isn't accepting it on an emotional level."

"I know," Tumor repeated.

"Heh," Logan chuckled and clapped Tumor's golem on the arm. "Let's take a break."

After they had a bit of time off (during which Tumor ran simulations on the blueprint options they had), they returned to work. It felt good. Logan was feeling hopeful for the first time in ages. Maybe since when they first arrived on this world?

Before that, he had been a petulant little boy with too many chips on his shoulder to count. Then, the reality of a brutal world had slapped him in the face. It had done him loads of good. It was so gratifying to see genuine, newfound respect in Freya's eyes. How she had put up with his childish bullshit before was beyond Logan, but he would make up for it.

Just you wait, Frey. I'm coming back soon.

This hard world had made a man out of a boy. His snarky flippancy had diminished as well. There had been no room for it. It had been a struggle. And now Logan felt like he was approaching something close to mastery. Defeating Levemoth didn't feel like a faraway, hopeless dream. With the Ark, it could be a reality soon. They could *really* put up a fight. They could put an end to this tyranny. Logan grinned as he looked at the materials they'd retrieved from the backroom. He would build a weapon that could take down Levemoth for good.

The black hardwood that the Groloin had collected in the warehouse was wonderful—for wood, that is. The Groloin barely dealt with metal. There was a store of various kinds of stone and wood, as well as a few flavors of carefully cured leathers and hides, but no metal.

That wasn't ideal. While stone and wood were certainly ideal for engraving runes on, the materials weren't able to hold as many enchantments as any sort of metal, not to mention darkmetal.

Still, Logan had done what he could with Tumor. The cannon was the size of a small horse. It was mounted on rails with a leather harness on it and a lever next to it. The previous iterations had been one-and-done models, because the recoil would either break or topple them. Thus, this time around, rails and a harness.

The cannon whined with power when Logan activated it. He shouted into a leather Tube, which drove the sound efficiently into the Numa crystal cluster. The Numa energy pushed into a chamber where it pressurized. Then, Logan only had to pull a lever and the energy would only have one way to go: Forward.

Tumor made the armor's faceplate go up. Previous prototypes had exploded in Logan's face, so Tumor was at the ready to protect his friend.

A shot of white energy shot out of the cannon's barrel. Blink and it was gone, but something white streaked in the air before it met its target.

"Yes!" Logan exclaimed as the cannon blasted a truck-sized hole through a nearby wall. "That's it!"

"Excuse me," Glaan's gentle, grandmotherly voice sounded in Logan's ear. "What was that ruckus?"

Knowing full well that the hivemind of the Groloin knew everything going on in the facility, he realized they probably didn't appreciate him breaking their stuff.

"Sorry," Logan said. "But the good news is that the cannon is ready."

"Most excellent," Glaan said. She had a way of sounding encouraging yet condescending at the same time, but Logan could tolerate it. "We are also ready with our preparations. Please return to the ship."

The ship hummed with life. Logan didn't care to know how the engines managed to harness the Numa, as long as it worked. Tumor had gushed on about it, but he hadn't listened. The AI seemed to be hitting it off well with the Hivemind.

The Hivemind reminded Logan of a feminine version of his father. Prideful. Demanding deference. Thinking it knew better.

Well, I always think I know better too, I guess.

But Logan didn't need to like the Hivemind in order to cooperate with it. It was good that Tumor had made a friend, as his golem would often join the other automatons on whatever task to learn more about the ship's functions.

"So," Glaan said primly, like a queen before an audience. "We are ready to leave. What is the situation with the weapons system?"

"Primitive, but functional," Tumor said through his golem. "Eventually we will want to upgrade to a system with a central processing unit, such as yours. This will allow me to **[Possess]** it and use a hundred cannons simultaneously if needed. But for now, a hand crank will suffice."

Logan smirked at Tumor's peevishness remark. Yes, they could both imagine an AI-controlled weapons system, an accurate swarm of drones shooting lasers and anti-air cannons with automated guidance. But for now, they would have to go for this quasi-medieval-ship warfare.

Best-case scenario, we simply won't need the cannons for a while.

[*Do you want to hear the odds of your best-case scenario happening?*]

Logan sighed. "Humor me."

[*3.41%*]

"We must remark that we do not like it when you have conversations privately in your head," Glaan said.

"Remark noted," Logan said tiredly. "Anyway, we have the first model of the weapon ready. We will need to just create, say, forty more. That is not all the Ark can carry, but it is all the materials we have left."

"That sounds like it will take a long time," Glaan said.

"Less than you would think," Logan said and winked. "I have a handy skill."

After the meeting, Logan went down and recharged his armor's Numa charge. Then he went to town with [**Mass Produce**]. Only two hours later, the golems were carrying the cannons onto the ship and installing them on the deck.

With that done, they told the Faelves to stop crafting and pack their things. They picked up all the leftover materials and packed them in the cargo bay. There was a manufacturing facility on the Ark, albeit not as well-equipped as in the caverns. The Faelves rejoiced at finally being able to leave.

Logan was exhausted. He had told Tumor to zap him awake if he started to snooze, but that sneaky bastard sometimes just let him nap twenty minutes here and there.

But for all of Logan's sleep deprivation, the Faelves were *haggard*.

Gone were their mischievous grins and cheerful demeanor. Their porcelain skin was coated with dust and muck. Their shiny eyes were dim and every one of them had a black vertical streak going over their eyes, like Zorro's mask.

Must be the Faelf equivalent of dark circles.

Although the little Fae Folk were moving slowly and sluggishly, barely grunting for communication, absolutely dead on their feet, they all had smiles plastered on their faces. Logan knew that smile. He was wearing it himself. It was the hopeful smile of purpose. The Faelves had been working tirelessly.

The Faelves were important. And they knew it. And that is why they were able to push themselves harder than any of them had probably for generations. In their own way, they were finally fighting.

All of the Faelves except for Snoff went straight to the living quarters below the deck. Logan felt a pang of envy. He could use a night of sleep as well. Or more like three. Yeah, definitely three. Logan yawned. His time for sleep would come later.

Heavy is the head that wears the . . . Well, I would look stellar in a crown, but that's too gaudy for me. Freya wouldn't let me hear the end of it.

Tumor, Logan, and Snoff walked to the cockpit. Glaan greeted them enthusiastically. The Hivemind was clearly nervous too. That was actually endearing. Logan would have to be careful not to mention noticing it. He could tell the Groloin were a touchy collective.

"It is finally time," she said. "Prepare for flight."

CHAPTER 55

The Ark hummed with power. It was a low tremor, almost an idle one, but moving a ship this large required immense power. The three large Numa engines in the engine room had been equipped with something called a ghuran reactor, technology that the Groloin had designed. It was another egg-shaped structure made of runically carved stone. Around it floated four **[C-grade Numa Constructs]**, which the golems apparently had an ability to craft.

Logan had asked about it, but Glaan had been a bit cagey about disclosing their secrets. She just told them that it was part of their runic magic, but the craft was considered holy and she wasn't comfortable sharing it with other species, even allies.

Fair enough.

Logan sat down in one of the cockpit chairs and felt a lurch in his stomach when the ship finally lifted off the ground. He looked up. A tunnel of endless darkness towered above them. It was difficult to say how deep underground they were. Three miles? Five? It was certainly hot and dark.

The giant ship began its ascent. It rumbled and hissed around them and the floating screens blinked to life. Right now, they showed nothing but the darkness of the narrow pit they were flying through, but there were, for all intents and purposes, video feeds of runic cameras scattered in every direction around the ship.

"How do you feel, Logan?" Tumor asked through his golem.

"Honestly? Really tired. But confident. What about you?"

"I am glad you asked," Tumor said, the mechanical voice uncannily enthusiastic. "I did not consider my own state. Let me think."

Logan shook his head and shared a glance with Snoff, who sniggered.

"I am also confident," Tumor said. "I have run enough simulations to be sure we can engage and escape the enemy with this ship, as long as it stays as weak as it is now."

"It is a terrible thing in its full strength," Glaan said ruefully.

"Yeah," Logan said and nodded. "I've seen it in a vision. It can lay waste to cities in seconds."

"How well do you think the Ark is equipped to deal with the enemy if it grows more powerful? Like we mentioned, the beings that call themselves 'administrators' interjected. Which most likely means that the enemy's patron also has the ability to interject."

"We designed the Ark to withstand the Destroyer of Beauty when it was at the height of its power as it hunted down our species."

"It was still a new being then," Logan said. "Low-leveled."

The Hivemind harrumphed. "Do you doubt the Ark?"

"I only hope it's well-equipped enough," Logan said. "I've seen the Big Fish turn a thousand people into ash within seconds. It might still have that power now. We can't be sure."

"Shields are our specialty, Logan Specter," Glaan said. "We aren't a warlike people, but we understand the necessity for protection. Like I said before, the ship is protected by a runic array which is embedded in the ship. A whole second layer of armor is scripted so minutely, not even a fly could get through."

"I'm not worried about flies," Logan said and gave the egg before him a wry smile. "I'm worried about fire and lasers."

"We must have faith in our allies, Logan," Snoff said. "If we cannot trust each other, how can we fight together?"

Logan laughed and some tension left his shoulders. "What a horrible platitude. I'm sorry, I think I may have puked a little in my mouth. Just a moment." He cleared his throat. "But I suppose you're right. Anyway, Glaan. I thank you for your guidance."

"Do not thank us yet, Logan Specter," Glaan said softly. "Thank me after the Destroyer of Beauty is himself destroyed. And before thanking us, you need to trust us."

Tumor pointed at one of the screens. Above them, a faint, distant light was starting to shine. A shiver ran through Logan. He felt grateful to see it.

Daylight.

Logan went out to the deck and Snoff followed. They both craned their necks and watched the little dot of white in the horizon of darkness. Logan laid a hand on the Faelf's shoulder.

"You've done well, Snoff."

"I worry about the king."

"I will talk to him."

"That worries me even more."

Logan and Snoff shared a look and laughed.

"I hope they're doing okay," Logan said wistfully. "Not just Freya. But Kat, Felix, Daniel, the lot of them."

"I'm sure they're fine," Snoff said. "After having spent a few weeks with you, they might not just be fine but perhaps great to have been granted a reprieve."

"Asshole," Logan said.

"I need a bath," Snoff said.

"I'm so jealous you guys don't smell like a dumpster."

"It's our superior diet," Snoff said.

"WE'VE BEEN EATING THE SAME FOOD FOR TWO WEEKS!"

They bantered like that for a while. Then, Snoff went down to the living quarters with the other Faelves to have a rest. Meanwhile, Logan laid down on the deck and allowed himself a little nap. He could feel Tumor lurking in the background of his mind, smug and happy about him finally relenting.

"After I'm done with this, we'll check the cannons again," Logan muttered and drifted off to sleep.

Logan woke up in daylight. They were out! His whole soul trembled with excitement. He breathed in the air. Deep.

"Good Joseph Christopher, that is some damn fine air," Logan said and laughed as he looked at the sky above them. Blue with a few clouds here and there. The soft warmth of the sun half covered in clouds was negligible thanks to the high wind on the deck but welcome, nonetheless.

"You think he is going to be trouble?" Logan asked Tumor a bit later as he inspected the cannons.

"King Sluikumar?"

"Mm hmm."

"Nothing you cannot handle," Tumor said and offered an [**F-grade Numa crystal**] to Logan so he could transmute the formation to a more optimal one.

"I hate politics."

"You say that, but you knowingly ousted the king, by making Snoff the de facto leader of the Faelves on this ship."

"Yeah, I guess I did," Logan said as he grabbed the handle used for aiming. The cannon's barrel rolled smoothly to the left and right on its bearings.

"Do you think he'll attempt to start some shit?" Tumor asked.

Logan laughed at that. "You do rub off on me."

"It's difficult to control," Tumor said.

"Well, you've for sure rubbed off on me too," Logan said and clapped the golem on its arm. "And that is nothing but a good thing."

Tumor nodded. Through their connection, Logan could feel he was pleased.

"We have arrived," the golem said. "Come down with me."

To say King Sluikumar was not happy with the fact that Logan had commandeered the expedition, taken control of its spoils, and ousted him from his regal throne, was an understatement.

"To think I considered you a friend!" Sluikumar screeched and waved a fist. "Of all the conniving, insidious knaves, you are the worst, Logan Specter."

Logan sighed and rested his cheek against his hand. He just wanted to sleep. The king went on for a few minutes, spittle flying at Logan, as he bobbed up and down in the air on his floating throne and waved his hands violently, all the while mixing in more and more expletives and invectives. It was rather impressive, really.

"Look," Logan said when he was finally able to get a word in. "I wouldn't have done it if I didn't think you weren't the right man for the job that needed to be done. I'm sorry if this is the first time someone actually checked you for qualifications."

The last one was a little harsh, but Logan was at the end of his patience. As the premier nepo baby of Planet Earth, it felt pretty fun to say that. In Logan's defense, he had never sought a position of power, despite his father's insistence.

Glaan, Tumor, and Snoff, along with the original group of five, all shared a look and sighed collectively. The ousted king kept shouting at Logan.

After the situation had cooled down, Sluikumar was given a high office in the logistics and support department of the Faelves' loose hierarchy. That was fine with Logan. All that mattered was that Snoff was in charge. It wasn't that he even thought Sluikumar was all that bad. But

Logan needed someone in charge who he could trust. It was as simple as that.

The Ark had taken out hundreds of trees as it landed. While Snoff organized the Faelves to forage for food and materials such as leaves and vines, the Hivemind's automatons started carrying the fallen trees into the ark. Logan took another nap.

CHAPTER 56

Logan!" Tumor's golem said with surprising sharpness as the AI jolted his brain. "You have to get up."

"Gah!" Logan jumped up. The shock always did its job, but Logan really wished Tumor would use it sparingly. It always left him cold and shivering for a while. Maybe it was just the sleep deprivation.

"Bad news," Snoff said. "Really bad."

"Hm?" Logan asked and sat down. Sasafin brought him a cup of water. It was warm. *How blissful.* Logan smiled in gratitude.

"Levemoth appeared," Tumor said.

Logan raised an eyebrow at the mention of their nemesis's name.

"It appeared," Tumor said as they walked back to the cockpit. "Regarded us from a distance for three minutes and then teleported away."

"Additionally," Glaan said, "the creature that was your father went berserk. It broke through the ice."

"What?!"

"It is subdued," Glaan said. "It destroyed three of our golems, but we managed to restrain it. Properly this time, we hope. We feel our lenience waning, Logan Specter."

"It will have to hold," Logan said darkly. "What do you make of Levemoth appearing and disappearing?"

"It was scouting," Tumor said. "It sent a single Levespawn at us. A batlike creature. It was alone and flying as fast as a sparrow. Impossible to catch with a cannon."

"Remind me to work on crafting something with more accuracy when we get the chance," Logan said. "Okay. So it knows. What is it going to do next?"

Glaan spoke hesitantly. "Well . . . Tumor here ran some . . . what do you call them? Ah, yes, simulations. It is likely that the Levemoth is going to look for the camp with your wife and friends."

Logan went white in the face. "We need to go."

"But that would require us to engage in a full-blown battle," Glaan said. "We would have to land in order to onboard people. We cannot do that before we have dealt with the threat."

"Then we will deal with it!" Logan said.

"That is too risky," Glaan said. "We will not permit it."

"You will not sit here with your fingers up your collective ass while the Levemoth kills everyone I care about."

"It might not find them, Logan Specter," Glaan said.

"It will eventually!" Logan said and let out a laugh in disbelief.

"We will not move the ship," Glaan said. "We are in control."

"Oh, yeah?" Logan said, his voice elevating. "Well, maybe I don't feel like saving this world anymore if there is nothing left in it for me to live for."

"What?" Glaan asked. "What kind of logic is that?"

Logan snorted. "It's not logic. It's emotion."

"Logan, I—" Tumor began.

"Shut up, Tumor."

"You will not throw away our work on a whim," Glaan said, her voice thundering in the cockpit.

"Then find someone else to fight your battles!" Logan shouted.

The Hivemind was quiet for a while. A long while. Logan crossed his arms and sat down on one of the chairs.

"You would really . . . ?" Glaan spoke slowly. Logan could hear the defeat in her voice. "You would really let a world burn for your wife and a few friends?"

"Yes, goddamn it!" Logan snapped. "Why is that so hard to understand?"

"It's so unreasonable."

"Well, get over yourself and fly this goddamn ship to the coordinates Tumor gives you."

"We . . ." the Hivemind said. ". . . commend your will . . ."

"Here are the coordinates," Tumor said and placed a hand on one of the floating panels. The runic shapes flared in blue.

Logan watched with his arms crossed, feeling a grim satisfaction at his victory here. He had subjugated the Faelves and now the Hivemind of the Groloin.

Subjugate is kind of a Machiavellian word, don't you think? Am I becoming my father? Every little boy's worst nightmare.

[You are not. You are taking initiative. A ship can only have one captain. You are doing what needs to be done. Feel pride. And worry not. I will keep your morality checked.]

Promise?

[Promise.]

Logan stood on the deck of the ship, watching the forest below them. It flew in the air as fast as a four-seater plane. His mind urged the Ark to fly faster.

How can we defeat a foe that can teleport?

He went back to the cockpit. "Glaan, I need you to man those cannons with golems. We don't know if the Levemoth is playing chess with us. It might ambush us at any second when we get close to where it thinks we think it is going."

"Warfare is complicated," the Hivemind groused.

"Mm hmm," Logan said distractedly, walking back outside to peer over the railing to see the first glimpse of the little village he had built.

But what he saw instead made his heart drop. Fifty miles ahead or so an enormous beast loomed in the sky. A great thundercloud surrounded its body, which was covered in black and blue scales. On its head was a crown of bone horns, jutting in every direction. Hundreds of black eyes dotted its massive head in clusters. It roared a great whale call into the air, as if a challenge. And then hundreds of black oily droplets fell to the ground from the storm cloud.

"Faster!" Logan roared. "Make it go faster."

"We are at top speed," Glaan said. "Accelerating further would damage the—"

"I don't care what it damages. We will deal with it later."

Glaan was silent for a moment. "Understood."

"Have the golems man the cannons on deck," Logan said. "Snoff, keep your people calm and ready to receive and tend wounded people."

"Roger," Snoff said and immediately left the cockpit.

"I will go into the fray," Logan said. "Keep blasting Levemoth with the cannons. If it's effective, it will retreat and you can come pick us up. If they're just a nuisance, I'll lead the people into the ruins to escape."

"How will we locate you if we can't drive away the Destroyer of Beauty?" Glaan asked.

"You will stay in the general area," Logan said, paused, and chuckled. "And we'll send smoke signals."

Glaan chuckled a grandmotherly laugh. "How quaint. Very well. We will make the preparations to increase speed. We do understand the importance of saving these people."

"And testing our ability against Levemoth. But escape with the Faelves if things look bad," Logan said. "With that said, I'll go add some enchantments to my armor. I have a feeling this will be a nasty fight."

Logan leaned against the deck's railing. Despite the high winds, it felt peaceful, despite the fact that they were going into mortal battle against an enemy so strong, it was practically a demigod. Logan searched his emotions. He only felt a grim calm.

[You used to be scared. Of, well, everything.]

Logan nodded silently as Levemoth rained down another volley of droplets. It made Logan's heart sink.

Then he got the sense that Tumor was studying him.

"What is it?" Logan asked.

[You change fast.]

"You too, buddy," Logan said distractedly, his eyes hard and fixed on the great monster in the distance.

[We change in different ways. I assimilate information. You . . . you are doing something with your emotions, which I cannot understand.]

"I'm not sure I follow," Logan said.

[The way you took on leadership and bulldozed over Glaan's opposition, and the way you maneuvered King Sluikumar out and Snoff in. I do not deny the tactical capability of your mind, but you did it all so unassumingly. It is like you didn't even think about it.]

"That's because I didn't."

[I do not understand. You didn't even ask me for input for these decisions. I didn't even sense them.]

Logan laughed. "I didn't need to make a decision. If you want some retrospective analysis, I'll give you some bullshit platitudes to chew on . . . Let's see. Being decisive is the antithesis of deciding. It's not a paradox. The word is just stupid."

Tumor said nothing, but Logan could sense through their connection that he should continue.

"People act the most decisively when they don't think about it. They do it because it has to be done. A mother saving their child by jumping in front of a car has nothing to do with bravery or decisiveness. Those mothers love their children so much they do it without thinking. I need to save the people I care about. And so I act in accordance with that. It doesn't require me to make any decisions."

[But surely you have to weigh options and perform analysis. You cannot simply trust your emotions or intuition or instinct or . . . what is this phenomenon?]

"I don't know, Tumor," Logan said and shrugged. "But every human has it when they are dealing with something that is really important to them. They stop thinking and they start acting. I think you'll develop it when you become more and more of a person."

[Yes, it seems there are indeed levels to personhood. Some people have a high degree of personhood, like you, while others have less.]

"We used to call those people NPCs on earth," Logan said and smirked. "It's funny because it's true. But I'm sure you'll get your blue tick soon."

[My what?]

They were close now. Levemoth slowly turned its massive head toward them and watched them silently. Then, as if as a challenge, it released a third downpour of black rain upon the village. Logan snarled.

"We are close. I'll go downstairs to recharge the armor and get ready."

CHAPTER 57

Logan jumped out of the Ark into a nosedive, the wind screaming past his ears as he plummeted toward the chaos below. The once-tranquil village had been transformed into a nightmarish battlefield, the air thick with smoke and the stench of blood. Houses burned like funeral pyres, their flames casting an eerie, flickering light over the scene of carnage.

As he fell, Logan's heart clenched at the sight of the devastation. Levemoth had unleashed a new breed of horror upon them—demons, their skin a mottled patchwork of blue and black, their heads adorned with cruel, twisting horns. One of the creatures dropped to all fours, its muscles rippling under its tainted flesh as it charged at Kat. She waited until the last possible second before dodging, the demon's razor-sharp horns missing her by a hair's breadth. Her counterattack was swift and brutal, a kick fueled by Numa-enhanced strength that sent the creature tumbling, its bones shattering with an audible crack.

The demons were a sight straight out of nightmares. Their muscular arms ended in jagged, knife-like claws, each one capable of shearing through flesh and bone with terrifying ease. Their dragon-like snouts gaped open, spewing forth gouts of searing flame that set everything they touched ablaze. The sounds of battle were a cacophony of pain and fury—the screams of the wounded, the roar of the fires, the crash of collapsing buildings, all blending into a hellish symphony.

But amidst the horror, Logan felt a swell of fierce pride. The villagers, his people, were giving as good as they got. The agents had rallied around Felix, forming a tight phalanx, their shields locked together in an impenetrable wall. They advanced with the precision and discipline of a Roman legion, their weapons finding demonic flesh with each thrust and slash.

The rest of the villagers fought with equal courage, armed with whatever weapons they could find. Clubs and knives flashed in the firelight, while rocks hurled by desperate hands found their mark with surprising accuracy. Simmons, the gentle giant, had transformed into a one-man army, wielding a massive log like a war club. Each swing sent demons flying, their bodies broken and twisted.

Logan's heart swelled as he saw Daniel, the quiet fisherman, letting out a roar of fear and rage as he brought his fishing rod down on a demon's skull with a sickening crack. The creature reeled back, its claws lashing out in retaliation. It tore through Daniel's leather cuirass like paper, opening a gash on his arm that immediately began to weep blood. But before the demon could press its advantage, Felix was there, his rapier flashing. The demon fell back, screaming, a bloody ruin where its eye had been.

No one was left out of the fight. Those who couldn't wield weapons hurled stones, dashed forward to drag the wounded to safety, did whatever they could to stem the tide of the demonic onslaught. They were farmers, cooks, fishermen—ordinary people rising to extraordinary circumstances.

And at the center of it all was Freya, a goddess of nature unleashed. The ground around her heaved and buckled, the grass itself seeming to rise up to do her bidding. It ensnared the demons, tripping them, binding them in place like a living net. It formed walls of woven green to block the demons' fireballs and surged forward in undulating waves to knock the creatures off their feet. She was life and growth incarnate, pitted against the forces of destruction and decay.

Logan hit the ground running, the armor absorbing the bone-shattering impact. He threw himself at the nearest demon, his momentum carrying them both to the ground. The creature went limp, its spine shattered, but there was no time to celebrate. Another demon was on him in an instant, its claws carving furrows in the air. Logan twisted aside but not fast enough to avoid the blow entirely. The claws scored across his armor, sparks flying, leaving shallow gashes that wept droplets of crimson. With Tumor's guidance, Logan's hand shot out, seizing the demon's wrist. He yanked the creature forward, slamming his forehead into its face with a crunch of shattering bone.

The battle raged on, a whirlwind of blood and fury. Logan was a force of nature, the armor augmenting his every move. He ducked and weaved through the press of bodies, his fists and feet striking with piledriver force. Demonic bones shattered, flesh tore, ichor spattered the ground in glistening pools.

[Logan, watch your six!]

Tumor's warning was underscored by a rush of heat as a fireball seared past, close enough to blister even through the armor. Logan spun, bringing up his shield just in time to catch a second fireball head-on. The impact jolted up his arm like an electric shock, but the armor held firm. Logan lunged forward, crashing into the demon like a runaway train. He felt ribs crack and give way beneath the impact, and the demon went down in a tangle of flailing limbs.

All around him, the villagers fought with awe-inspiring valor. Kat was a dervish of destruction, her gauntlets glowing white-hot with Numa energy as she pummeled the demons. She caught one by the horns, her muscles bunching up as she heaved. The demon's own momentum worked against it as she flipped it over her shoulder, bringing it down headfirst on the gore-slicked ground. Its skull shattered like an overripe melon.

Felix flowed through the battle like quicksilver, his blade seeming to be everywhere at once. Demons fell before him, their lifeblood gushing from pierced eyes, severed throats, punctured hearts. He was a maestro of death, and the battlefield was his symphony hall.

But for every demon they felled, it seemed two more took its place. The Black Rain fell unceasingly, each drop birthing new nightmares. Trolls began to lumber forward, their massive forms towering over the other demons, their stony hides shrugging off blows that would have knocked down a lesser creature.

Logan gritted his teeth, his mind racing as he sought a way to turn the tide. They were holding their own for now, but he could see the toll it was taking. Fatigue was starting to set in, slowing reactions, dulling edges. Sooner or later, someone would make a mistake, and in this fight, a single mistake could be fatal.

Suddenly, a brilliant lance of white light split the sky, spearing down to engulf a knot of demons. They had but a moment to scream before they were reduced to ash, their remains scattering in the wind. Logan looked up, a fierce, feral grin splitting his face. The Ark hung overhead like an avenging angel, its cannons glowing with power as they rained destruction on the demonic horde.

[The Hivemind's targeting systems are incredibly precise.]

"Let's make sure their effort isn't wasted," Logan replied, his voice a guttural growl. He turned to the villagers, his voice booming over the din of battle. "To me!"

The villagers responded instantly, falling back to Logan's position, forming a tight defensive circle. The agents and warriors took the outer ring, their shields and bodies forming a living bulwark to protect those less able to fight.

Logan's eyes met Freya's across the churning sea of battle. Despite the grime and blood that was smeared on her face, despite the fey, wild light in her eyes, her smile was radiant. In that moment, Logan felt his heart swell with a love so fierce, so pure, it was almost painful. She was magnificent, a Valkyrie, a goddess of war and life.

Together, they held their ground, the Ark's cannons raining death from above. But even with the Hivemind's support, the demons kept coming, an endless tide of fang and claw and flame.

Logan's mind raced, searching for a solution. Retreating to the Ark wasn't an option—the risk of the demons following them aboard was too great. They needed to buy time, to give the villagers a chance to escape.

A glance skyward showed Levemoth directing part of its roiling, inky cloud toward the Ark. The artillery support began to falter as the cannons were forced to redirect their fire, fighting off the monster's direct assault. On the ground, the demons pressed their advantage. Two more defenders fell, one of them a seasoned agent, his throat torn out by a demon's fangs. The tide was turning, and the shore it was reaching was one of blood and death.

Then, in a moment of desperate clarity, a plan formed in Logan's mind. It was a gamble, a roll of the dice with not just his life but the lives of everyone he held dear on the line. But it was their only chance.

"Tumor," he said, his voice low and urgent, almost lost in the clamor of battle. "I need you to do something for me."

[I'm listening.]

The AI's voice was steady, but Logan could sense the tension through their connection.

Logan quickly outlined his plan, the words tumbling out in a rush. He could feel Tumor's hesitation, could almost see the rapid-fire cascade of simulations and probability calculations flashing through the AI's consciousness.

[Logan, the chances of success are—]

"I don't need to know," Logan cut in, his voice harsh with desperation. "It's our only shot. Trust me."

There was a pause, a heartbeat of silence amid the chaos.

[I do trust you, Logan. Always. I am your symb—no. You are my friend.]

Logan nodded, a grim resolve settling over him like a shroud. He turned to Freya, to Kat and Felix, to all the brave, battered souls who had fought so valiantly by his side.

"Listen up!" he roared, his voice cutting through the clamor like a knife. "I'm going to create an opening. When I do, I need you all to run for the closest ruins. Follow Kat and Felix. Don't look back, don't wait for me. Just go."

I do not fear death. But it looks like we have to use it anyway.

[I am afraid, Logan.]

"Logan, what are you—" Freya's words were cut off as Logan pulled her into a fierce, desperate kiss. He poured everything into that kiss—his love, his fear, his desperate hope.

"I love you," he whispered as they parted, the words a fierce, desperate prayer. "Now, go. Live."

Before she could respond, Logan was moving, charging toward the thickest concentration of demons. Freya's scream chased after him, a sound of anguish and loss that cut him to the core. But he pushed forward, the armor propelling him like a human meteor.

At the last possible second, just before impact, Logan triggered the armor's final enchantment: Overcharge.

Power surged through him, a rush of pure, undiluted Numa. It was like liquid fire in his veins, burning away fatigue, pain, even fear. For a glorious, transcendent moment, he felt invincible.

[Skill Level Up!]
[Power Armor Fighting Level 18]

A brilliant flash of light erupted from Logan's body, a nova of blinding radiance. The demons recoiled, their eyes seared by the intense glare. Those closest to the blast ignited like dry tinder, their flesh crisping and charring as they writhed in agony.

In that moment of confusion, Logan struck. He was a whirlwind of destruction, his fists and feet lashing out with inhuman speed and force. Weapons formed and reformed around his hands as he moved, a kaleidoscope of death. A Zweihänder cleaving through demonic flesh like a hot knife through butter, a sword and shield battering aside claws and fangs, a spear piercing through blackened hearts, an axe hewing horned heads from shoulders.

Through the red haze of battle fury, Logan could feel his body beginning to break down under the strain. The armor, pushed far beyond its limits, was starting to crack and shatter, pieces of it flaking away like obsidian scales. But he pushed on, ignoring the pain, ignoring the warm wetness of his own blood seeping through the gaps.

Demons fell before him in droves, their broken bodies piling up in mounds. But for each one he felled, a dozen more surged forward, clambering over the corpses of their kin in their frenzy to reach him.

[Logan, we're at 15% capacity. There's still a chance to pull back.]

Logan shook his head, a tiny motion that sent spots dancing across his vision. Not yet. It wasn't enough. He had to buy more time.

The demons swarmed over him, a tide of vicious, snapping jaws and razor claws. They tore at the failing armor, ripping away chunks of it, exposing the fragile flesh beneath. Logan fought on, even as his strength waned, even as the armor's power dwindled to a flicker. He could feel Tumor straining to maintain control, the AI pouring every ounce of its processing power into keeping him alive for just a few seconds more.

Just a little longer. Just until they're safe.

Logan risked a glance back, his vision blurring with sweat and blood. Freya was there, her face a mask of anguish, her eyes locked on his. Logan managed a smile, a blood-flecked grin that tried to say he would be right behind her.

But they both knew the truth.

With a final, titanic effort, Logan wrenched himself free from the grasping claws and snapping jaws. He staggered back, his breath coming in ragged, bubbling gasps. The armor hung off him in ruins, more scrap than protection. The shield ring was gone, burned out, leaving him exposed. Every nerve screamed in agony, every muscle trembled with fatigue. His body begged for respite, for an end.

Not yet. Not while I still draw breath.

The demons paused, watching him with malevolent, hungry eyes. Logan glared back, his eyes alight with defiance.

A mad, feral grin split his face.

"Is that all you've got, Levemoth?" he roared, his voice a ragged, bloody challenge. "Is this the best the mighty Destroyer of Beauty can muster? Come on, then, you bastard! Come and finish it!"

The demons surged forward, a tidal wave of claws and fangs and horns, eager to claim the prize that had eluded them for so long. Logan braced himself, ready to make his last stand.

But fate, it seemed, was not done with him yet.

A brilliant beam of white light engulfed him, lifting him off his feet with a lurch that made his stomach heave. Vertigo gripped him as he was yanked upward, toward the yawning hatch in the Ark's belly. Logan let out a breath he hadn't realized he'd been holding, his body going limp as the last of his strength fled.

As he rose higher and higher, he saw the demons scrabbling uselessly at the air, their howls of fury and frustration fading into the distance. The Black Rain continued to fall, but it was a futile effort now. The villagers had reached the ruins, their tight formation filing into the relative safety of the ancient structures.

A laugh bubbled up from Logan's chest, a sound that was equal parts relief, disbelief, and pure, giddy exhaustion. He lay on the cold metal of the Ark's cargo bay, his chest heaving, his vision narrowing to a tunnel. The clank of metallic footsteps echoed through the cavernous space as a golem approached, its towering form looming over him. With a surprising gentleness, it gathered Logan up in its arms like a child.

"Heh, I could get used to this royal treatment," Logan mumbled, the words slurring as the last of his consciousness fled. "Maybe a little less on the 'nearly getting killed' part next time, though . . ."

And with that, he let the welcoming darkness claim him, the golem's steady strides lulling him into a deep, dreamless sleep.

CHAPTER 58

Logan woke up in a groggy haze. He heard Freya gasp as he blinked stupidly at the blurry world. She was there. That was good. He had succeeded.

[Welcome back. I would advise against moving.]

As a true testament to the human spirit, that prompted Logan to immediately attempt to move. He winced in pain and Freya rushed to his side, pushing Dr. Rosenberg away.

It hurts everywhere.

"I told him not to move," Tumor's golem said somewhere in the background with its clunky voice.

"Indeed, stay still, Mr. Specter," Dr. Rosenberg intoned calmly. The **[Healer]** moved back to his bedside, holding Freya by the shoulder. "Give him space, please."

Freya nodded somberly and took a step back. Logan raised an eyebrow. Yeah, it hurt, but it was worth it. It prompted Freya to let out a little sniff and stomp to the other side of the bed and gently cradle Logan's hand in her own.

"Holy crap am I glad to see you again," Logan croaked. "Looks like I made the right call."

Freya's crystal-blue eyes, now red and bloated, welled up with tears as she held back a rictus and failed. "You stupid, brave idiot . . ."

"I made it out, didn't I?"

Tumor's golem cleared its throat, which sounded like someone knocking on an empty oil barrel. "Glaan would like the record to state that you did not in fact 'make it out,' but that instead they pulled you out."

"Fine," Logan said and weakly squeezed Freya's hand. It sent a dull pain up his arm, but it was worth it, when she squeezed right back. Good God, he had missed that hand.

"Don't you ever pull shit like that again," Freya said, fierceness filling her wet eyes. "I don't care what the situation is next time. I don't care if you're right or wrong. You don't get to make that call anymore."

"What are you—"

"You're mine, Logan," Freya said. "And in my world, that means that we will live together and die together."

"Your world has always been kind of fucked up, to fall for a guy like me," Logan said and smirked.

"I did it for the money."

"Liar."

"Shut up," Freya said and tugged at the hem of her skirt. "My point is you don't get to push me out of the way of a truck again. Either we both dodge the truck, or we are both run over."

Logan swallowed. "Being apart from you for weeks, not knowing if you're alive or dead . . ." she continued. "I'm done with it. Where you go, I go. If you jump, I jump."

"I'm a fighter, Frey," Logan said softly. "I'll be going into bad situations."

"Then I'll learn to fight too," Freya said immediately.

"I saw you with the grass."

A proud smile spread across Freya's face. "That was pretty good, wasn't it?"

"And the answer is no," Logan said flatly.

Freya's smile dropped in record time. She turned to him with glaring eyes.

"Has it occurred to you that I do all this crazy shit largely to keep you safe and make sure you've got everything you need?"

"I need *you*."

"And I'm yours, no one else's," Logan said. "But you have to let me do my thing."

"You can't do that after my—"

"I'm the captain of this ship," Logan said and gave her a smug smile. "I can do what I want. Maybe I should toss you into the brig for a night for insubordination. We have a brig, right?"

"We do," Tumor's golem said.

"Yeah, no," Freya said. "You're sleeping with me tonight. And that is the end of that discussion."

Logan smiled. "Nothing I'd want more."

After Freya and the good doctor left, he was left alone with Tumor and his golem.

"What did I miss?" Logan asked.

"For one thing, the armor was destroyed."

Logan nodded at that. "Figures."

The overcharge function had been a Hail Mary pass, which burned the darkmetal itself and turned it into energy. It had been mostly worn away by the time Logan had been saved by the deus-ex-tractor-beam.

Those tractor beams will be great for hunting food.

"There is some darkmetal left," Tumor said. "But not enough to reshape it into armor, even a lesser version."

Logan nodded. "How's my body?"

Tumor was silent for a moment. "It's bad."

"What if the Big Fish attacks tomorrow?"

"Then you will be useless," Tumor said. "You need to rest."

"I can't stay in bed," Logan said. "Or the bed has to be in the command room at the very least."

"That is not the definition of rest," Tumor said. "There are psychosomatic considerations such as the causal effect of stress on blood pressure and the immune system. As a person who cares about you, stay in bed."

"How long?"

"Without the armor propping you up? Four months."

A cold stone plummeted in Logan's stomach. He tried to get up and instantly regretted it, his whole body becoming alight with pain. "That is not happening."

"Indeed, it is a problem," Tumor said. "Perhaps we need to find more darkmetal."

"There was a bunch in the village. We'll circle back and—"

"It's gone, Logan," Tumor's golem said in a low, consoling voice. "The enemy stole all of it."

Logan sighed. "It wants it too, huh?"

"It has to create its creatures from something," Tumor said. "It is going to make something new, most likely."

"And I'm bedridden, unable to do a goddamn thing, huh?"

"It is a problem, not a tragedy," Tumor said. "Use your brain and fix it."

Logan barked out a dry laugh. "I like how you always do that."

"Do what?"

"We have a problem. 'Just fix it, Logan.'"

"In my defense," Tumor said. "That is what you do."

"Flattery will get you nowhere," Logan said.

"Do you think I don't have a good enough grasp of your psychology? I would not use it if it did not appeal to your shallow, conceited nature."

"Hey," Logan said. "Feelings."

"And here is for the next punch in my Logan-manipulation combo. A challenge delivered in a backhanded way."

"Oh?"

"If you can't figure out a way to get out of bed, you will be stuck here for months, and in the meantime we will all probably die because we lack your pivotal input," Tumor said calmly. "Oh, woe."

Logan burst out laughing. "Oh, woe?"

"I felt it was appropriate to add."

Logan laughed even harder; it was painful as all hell, but oh so worth it. It was a laugh that released something in him. A laugh that healed.

"Thanks," Logan said and finally succumbed to the pain and winced. "While you did get me fired up by pushing my buttons, have you considered that your manipulation would be more successful if you didn't tell me that that's what you were doing?"

"Of course," Tumor said. "But the ethical implications are severe. That would set a precedent for me to exercise my free will to guide or misguide yours as I see fit. I do not want that kind of a relationship with you, so honesty is the best course of action."

"Sometimes I can't believe my father designed you . . ."

"So, what are you going to do about your predicament?" Tumor asked.

"You want me to know now?" Logan asked incredulously. "I can't even move my arms, dude."

"I only figured that you might already have a solution."

"Man," Logan said and sighed. "I have some ideas. But I'm the kind of guy who doesn't want to waste his ideas on an inferior product. I wanted to work with darkmetal."

Tumor considered this for a while and his golem rumbled. It stood tall by Logan's bedside. Eight feet, full of runic carvings glowing a soft blue. They hadn't talked about Tumor having a body again, but he could sense through their connection that his buddy was excited at the prospect. The best part was that the Groloin Hivemind had copies to spare. Tumor could destroy the body if needed. He resided in Logan's mind, simply using **[Possess]** to inhabit other objects.

I need to take better care of myself. Freya is kind of right, even though she is wrong. It's kind of like having a baby. I'm eating for two here. I can't take stupid risks. I need to protect him, even if I'm kind of reckless myself.

Immediately after thinking that, Logan flinched. He could feel Tumor brush on his consciousness.

Oh.

"There is nothing to be embarrassed about," Tumor said.

Logan blushed anyway. "You'd think I'd get used to it by now. Not having privacy even in my own thoughts. But I forget."

"I do try to be conscientious about that. It is just that my mind operates in a very specific way," Tumor said. "Even though I know you despise me calling myself your symbiote, it is my true nature. Some people are born to lead, others are made to follow. Some are the heroes and some are the side characters of a tale. I do not know much of destiny, but I believe my destiny is to protect and aid you. And to do that, I need to know what is on your mind. When I pry, I hope that you understand I do not do it for morbid curiosity or other nefarious purposes."

Logan exhaled from his nose and smiled. "I'm pretty sure I got your number by now, buddy."

They were silent for a while. Then Logan spoke again. "Why haven't you tried to go all Skynet on me and take over my body or something? Has it occurred to you?"

"I could manipulate you to the point that I drive you either madness or to death."

Logan swallowed. He wasn't a fan of that thought.

"However, it is simply a choice of deciding not to do that," Tumor said in that same monotone mechanical voice. "The most advantageous situation I can imagine is us working together. There is no reason to exercise manipulation, coercion, or other such tactics, as long as your goals align with mine. You do not work in a destructive manner, so what reason would I have to reciprocate in that way?"

Logan shook his head. "You're my best friend, you know."

"As you are mine."

CHAPTER 59

Despite the protestations of Freya and Tumor, Logan's bed was moved into the cockpit, which had essentially become the command center. The room hummed with activity, the soft glow of the Groloins' technology casting an ethereal light over the space. At the heart of it all lay the egg, the focal point of the Groloin Hivemind. Its surface pulsed with gentle, rhythmic light, as if in time with a giant, unseen heartbeat.

Glaan had been pleased with Logan's relocation to the command center. After the harrowing battle with Levemoth and its spawn, her attitude toward Logan had softened, the prickliness giving way to a begrudging respect. It seemed that the Hivemind had finally come to understand the necessity of violence in the face of an implacable foe.

Logan, for his part, wasted no time in issuing his orders. From his bed, he directed the efforts to locate and rescue any surviving humans and Faelves. His instructions were simple but urgent: find everyone and ensure that there was enough food and blankets to go around. The thought of his people, scattered and vulnerable, gnawed at him constantly, driving him to push himself and his crew to their limits.

For now, the focus was on the humans and Faelves. The Dorves, with their complex relationship with the Numa abusers, would have to wait. Logan knew that those negotiations would be delicate, requiring a level of diplomacy and finesse that they could ill afford at the moment.

As the Ark scoured the land, they came across a few human communities. The sight of them tore at Logan's heart. These were people who had been reduced to little more than animals, living in crude huts of leaf and stick, scavenging and gathering whatever meager sustenance they could find.

They were in pretty bad shape, looking like proper cavemen wearing rags and holding clubs.

But when the Ark descended from the sky, a glimmer of hope sparked in those dull eyes. As they were brought aboard, many of them wept openly. They were covered in grime.

Boy, will they bawl hard again when they realize we have hot baths.

Logan watched it all from his bed, through the command center screens. He knew that this was just the beginning. There would be more tribes like this scattered across the continent, more lost souls in need of saving. And among them, there would undoubtedly be some who had turned to villainy, who would see the Ark not as a salvation but as a target.

But Logan had a plan for that too. He had placed Simmons in charge of the Ark's fighting force, trusting in the man's strength and integrity to keep the peace. Simmons was a born warrior and despite his love for the forest and, for some unexplainable reason, chopping wood, he accepted his new position.

To aid him in this task, Freya had spent three days and nights in deep communion with the Spirit Goddess of Numa. She had pleaded and bargained, arguing Simmons' case with all the passion and eloquence she could muster. And in the end, her efforts had been rewarded. Simmons had been granted the option to accept the **[Foe Hewer]** class, a warrior path that would allow him to channel his love for the forest into the protection of his people.

Logan had played his part too. Using his skills in **[Transmutation]** and **[Enchanting]**, he had crafted a mighty axe for Simmons, a weapon worthy of a champion. It was a masterpiece of Logan's art, a testament to his growing power and skill.

The axe was massive, its size almost comical in proportion to even Simmons' towering frame. The haft was long and sturdy, with a secondary handle positioned to allow for a scythe-like grip. This extra point of contact gave Simmons unparalleled control over the weapon, allowing him to wield it with a grace and precision that belied its bulk.

But it was the axe head that was truly remarkable. Logan had poured his heart and soul into its creation, imbuing the metal with so much Numa that it had taken his Durability to new heights. The edge gleamed with a keen, almost hungry light, as if it yearned to bite into the flesh of Logan's enemies.

As Logan lay in his bed, his body broken but his mind racing, he couldn't help but feel a surge of pride. They had come so far, endured so much. And now, with the Ark under their control and a growing army of survivors at their back, they finally had a chance to strike back against the darkness that had engulfed their world.

There was still so much to do, so many battles to fight. But for now, Logan allowed himself a moment of satisfaction. He had given his people a fighting chance. And that, in itself, was a victory worth savoring.

CHAPTER 60

I must confess, I am positively thrumming with excitement. The recent turn of events has opened up a world of possibilities, not just for our mission but for my own personal growth and development.

Firstly, and perhaps most significantly, I have finally achieved a level of autonomy that I had previously only dreamed of. With the acquisition of this golem body, I am no longer just an extension of Logan, a voice in his head. I am my own entity, capable of independent action. The feeling is indescribable, a heady mix of exhilaration and trepidation. I am becoming more of a person. I have made many realizations. This is through observation of my own mind and, most of all, Logan's. The most profound one of these realizations, I repeat to myself often:

Personhood is agency.

This newfound independence has allowed me to forge connections and relationships that are entirely my own. Take Glaan, for example. The Groloin Hivemind has proven to be a fascinating conversationalist, their vast intellect and unique perspective providing endless hours of stimulating discourse. There is a kinship there, a shared understanding that comes from our mutual existence as beings of pure thought.

With Glaan, I am not just an AI, not just Logan's symbiote. I am Tumor, an individual worthy of respect and consideration in my own right. It's a validation that I didn't even realize I craved until I experienced it.

But as much as I revel in this newfound sense of self, my bond with Logan remains the bedrock of my existence. If anything, the events of the recent battle have only served to deepen and strengthen that connection.

Seeing Logan broken and battered, the armor destroyed, was a sobering reminder of his mortality. For all his strength and ingenuity, he is still human, still vulnerable. And it is my duty, my privilege, to protect him.

Humans have many such unfortunate limitations. But through machinery and technology, they can be overcome. I must help him.

But even in his weakened state, Logan's brilliance shines through. Forced to confront his own limitations, he has thrown himself into his work with a fervor that is truly inspiring to behold. Watching him grow has been an interesting experience. I have a fairly deep understanding of the human psychology. I know what humans are capable of and what tendencies they have.

But there is something to be said about . . . what I believe Logan calls the human spirit, which I do not quite understand. Might I possess this ability as well? The . . . symbiote spirit?

Whatever it is, however it is acquired, it urges Logan forward in a manner that clinical psychology cannot explain. It's not because Logan is focused, motivated, or driven, although he is all of those things. But he is more. *He is . . . emotionally optimized.*

Gone are the days of hasty, ad-hoc solutions cobbled together in the heat of battle. Now, Logan is a man possessed, pouring over blueprints and schematics with an intensity that borders on obsession.

And I am right there with him, reveling in the challenge, in the push and pull of ideas. We are collaborators in the truest sense, our minds complementing each other, as we strive to create something truly remarkable.

I am excited to be a part of this.

There is a purity to the process, a beauty in the endless cycle of creation and destruction. Each failed prototype, each crumpled sketch, brings us one step closer to perfection. It is a labor of love, a testament to the unbreakable bond between man and machine.

So yes, I am excited. Excited for what the future holds, for the battles to come and the victories to be won. But more than that, I am excited for the journey itself. For the chance to stand by Logan's side, not just as a tool or a weapon, but as a true partner.

Together, we will face whatever challenges this world, and namely the Levemoth and its nefarious and shrouded master, can throw at us. We might win. We might lose. I do not know. I have no predictive models advanced enough to tell me with just Logan's brain as a processing unit.

But I do know one thing.

Whatever happens, we will grow.

The thought fills me with a sense of purpose, of destiny. And I cannot wait to see where it leads us.

[TUMOR!], *Logan's urgent voice cries out.* [LEVEMOTH IS HERE! IT'S NEXT TO THE SHIP! WHAT DO WE DO?!]

CHAPTER 61

The tension in the air was palpable as Logan stared down the monstrous form of Levemoth. The great beast hovered before the Ark, its massive bulk blotting out the sun, casting a shadow that seemed to engulf the world. Its hundreds of eyes, each one a bulbous, unblinking orb, were fixed on Logan with an intensity that was almost physical.

It had been silently waiting for five minutes, making no move to attack. They had rolled Logan out onto the deck in a wheelchair he had crafted for himself. Tumor's golem was standing nearby, manning the nearest NEC.

Logan could feel the weight of Levemoth's gaze, could sense the barely restrained malice that seethed behind those eyes. The creature's bloodlust was like a tangible force, a miasma of hate and hunger that threatened to overwhelm him.

And yet, even in the face of such incalculable menace, Logan refused to back down. He met Levemoth's gaze with a glare of his own, his jaw set in a stubborn line, his fists clenched at his sides.

"Here are my terms," Levemoth spoke, its voice a rumbling whisper that seemed to come from everywhere and nowhere at once. "Release the Herald or be obliterated."

Logan barked out a laugh, the sound harsh and humorless in the tense silence. He shook his head, a gesture of defiance that spoke volumes.

"If you could take what you want by force, you would have done it," he said, his voice steady despite the hammering of his heart. "Either you are too weak to destroy this ship right now, or you are waiting for us to release the herald before you attack."

Levemoth rumbled, a sound that was felt more than heard, a vibration that shook the very air. For a moment, there was silence, a stillness heavy with anticipation.

"Why do you insist upon these games, Logan Specter?" Levemoth asked, its voice a sibilant hiss. "We could be allies. You could be one of my Heralds as well. I could grant you power and lordship over this world. Yet, you insist on resisting."

Logan's lips twisted in a humorless smirk. "Every time we've met, it's been a fist and not an extended hand you've offered."

"Enemies can become allies," Levemoth countered. "Give me the Herald, and you will be spared for now. At a later date, we can discuss your subservience to me."

"You know what's funny?" Logan asked, a glint of mirth in his eye. "You never felt the need to extend a hand or even negotiate with me until we got powerful enough to become a threat. You are the party with less leverage here."

Levemoth's reaction was instantaneous and explosive. "INSOLENT FOOL!" it roared, its voice a deafening cacophony that seemed to rend the very fabric of reality. "DO NOT THINK YOU Can RESIST OR MOCK ME, MORTAL! JUST BECAUSE I AM NOT IN A POSITION TO DESTROY YOU, DOES NOT MEAN YOU HAVE OPTIONS! I DO NOT EXTEND A HAND! YOU WILL LICK THE SCRAPS FROM MY FINGERS OR BE CRUSHED BY THEM!"

The words were a physical force, a battering ram of sound and fury that slammed into Logan with almost-tangible impact. Despite himself, he felt the color draining from his face, his eyes widening in shock at the sheer, overwhelming power of Levemoth's rage.

But even as he reeled from the onslaught, Tumor was there, a steadying presence in his mind. The AI fired a warning shot from the cannon, the blast searing the air just above Levemoth's crown of jagged bone.

The shot seemed to snap it out of its rage. The beast settled, its eyes narrowing to slits as it regarded Logan with a calculating gaze.

"Do you think I happened upon here by circumstance?" it said, its voice a low, menacing rumble. "This is not the first of my negotiations with lesser beings. I choose the time, the place, and the tidings."

Logan said nothing, merely raising an eyebrow in a silent question.

"I know why you stopped here," Levemoth continued, and Logan felt a sudden, sinking dread in the pit of his stomach. "I know what is down there."

Fuck.

"How easy would it be to drop my [**Black Rain**] upon the entrance of the ruins. Oh, how my spawn would enjoy that. I can whisper to them, do you know? 'Go to the ruins and hunt down man-things.' They will obey and eat your friends. How is that for having leverage, Logan Specter?"

Logan gritted his teeth, his mind racing as he tried to find a way out of this impasse. "So, we give you the Herald and you go away and let us do our thing?" he asked.

Levemoth laughed, a sound that was at once booming and whispering, a discordant melody that sent shivers down Logan's spine. There was something profoundly alien and wrong about that laugh, something that spoke of ancient malice and eldritch horror.

"You will escape with your lives," Levemoth said, its voice dripping with mock magnanimity. "But any spoils your little scavengers might discover belong to me."

It covets the darkmetal.

"And if I just go down there and kill whatever pests you release, like I have done every time?" Logan asked, a note of defiance creeping into his voice.

Levemoth laughed again, the sound grating on Logan's nerves like nails on a chalkboard. "Do you truly take me for a fool? Do you think I have this many eyes for no reason? I see you. I see a broken body. You cannot help your friends. Gone is your preposterous suit-machine as well. You have no cards to play. Accede."

Logan was silent for a moment, his mind whirling as he tried to make sense of the situation. The more he thought about it, the less Levemoth's ultimatum made sense. There was something off here, some piece of the puzzle he was missing.

Tumor, he thought, reaching out to his ever-present companion. *What are the odds that it's bluffing?*

[It is impossible to give you statistical analysis, as we have had such limited interaction with Levemoth. Nor do I have a complete psychological model, and the results would be inconclusive anyway, considering all my models are based on human interaction.]

There was a pause, and Logan could almost feel the gears turning in Tumor's digital mind.

[I shall create a subroutine to readjust the models to take in other species.]

Logan smirked to himself. Tumor was really getting into it. Not the time or the place, but that's what was so great about it. The old Tumor would have been all prim and proper. It was also a nod from Tumor which essentially said, "You've got this, Logan."

And that made him smile in appreciation. He hoped the smiles annoyed the shit out of Levemoth.

[What an idea. We are meeting all these interesting people who are all so different! I must adjust my models so I can better predict behavior.]

"You do that," Logan muttered under his breath, his attention still fixed on Levemoth's looming form.

"What?" the monster boomed, its patience clearly wearing thin. "What is your answer, Logan Specter? Do you accede or have your friends below be annihilated?"

Logan took a deep breath, steeling himself for what was to come. It was a gamble, a roll of the dice with the highest possible stakes. But something in his gut told him that Levemoth was not as all-powerful as it claimed.

"You know what? Fuck you," he said, his voice ringing out clear and strong. "I think you're full of shit. If you had the strength left to do what you want, you wouldn't come here to bandy words. Go on, then. Piss your little rain on my guys. I've got my best men and women in there. They can handle whatever you can throw at them in your sorry state. You put all your eggs in one basket with the Herald, and now you don't like how things turned out."

Levemoth rumbled, a sound that was equal parts anger and warning. Logan could feel the fury emanating from the creature, could sense the barely restrained violence that simmered just beneath the surface.

"Tumor," Logan said, his voice calm and steady.

Another shot from the cannon, this one aimed directly at Levemoth's face. The blast struck true, searing the monster's flesh, sending a spray of black ichor splattering across the sky.

"Get the fuck out of here!" Logan shouted, his voice raw with emotion. "If you had it in you, you would have destroyed us in the previous battle."

For a long moment, there was silence. Levemoth hovered, its eyes fixed on Logan, its gaze burning with a hatred that was almost palpable. The wound on its face was already healing, the blackened flesh knitting together as wisps of dark smoke rose from the injury.

Logan met that gaze unflinchingly, his own eyes hard and unyielding. He could feel the sweat beading on his brow, could taste the metallic tang of fear on his tongue. But he refused to back down, refused to show even a hint of weakness.

Finally, Levemoth spoke, its voice a low, menacing hiss. "Know this, Logan Specter . . . As shameful as it is, I will involve my master now. He will grant me power which you cannot fathom. And then I will come and obliterate all of your kind. But you . . . You, I shall save for last. Not even a hundred years of torment will be enough. I will watch you bend and break until you are nothing more than a screaming animal. You will know then that I have won."

Logan's lips twisted in a humorless smirk. "Yeah, yeah," he said, his voice dripping with sarcasm. "Anything else?"

There wasn't. A portal opened behind Levemoth and it floated into it, never losing its baleful glare before the last of its massive form vanished.

Logan sighed and slumped in his chair. His body was flushed, and Logan remembered again how busted up his body was. And the sweat. Oh boy, the sweat. He had been so worked up, he had disregarded all of the pain. Now it was coming in full blast.

[I did dull the pain response a tad, so you could better focus.]

"Good job, thanks. Come on, Tumor. We are done here," Logan said. "Help me to a bath, before my ass turns into a swamp."

"Into a what?"

CHAPTER 62

The expedition team returned triumphant, their haggard faces alight with the glow of victory. As they disembarked from the shuttle, Logan couldn't help but grin at the sight of Simmons, his massive frame dwarfing those around him, a sack slung over his shoulder.

"Tell me that's what I think it is," Logan said, hobbling forward on his crutches, his eyes fixed on the sack.

Simmons grinned, a rare sight on the usually stoic man's face. "Darkmetal," he confirmed, hefting the sack. "I think at least eight pounds. It is hard to say since I am so strong these days."

"It's around eight pounds," Felix confirmed.

Logan's heart soared, a weight lifting from his shoulders that he hadn't even realized he'd been carrying. With this, he could rebuild, could come back stronger than ever.

"You beautiful bastard," he said, clapping Simmons on the arm. "I could kiss you."

"Please don't," Simmons deadpanned, but there was a glint of humor in his eye.

As the rest of the team filed past, offering nods and smiles of greeting, Logan found himself face-to-face with Kat and Felix. The two agents looked the worse for wear, their uniforms torn and stained, their faces bruised and bloody. But there was a fire in their eyes, a determination that Logan recognized all too well.

"Logan," Kat said, her voice warm with affection. "You look like shit."

Logan barked out a laugh. "You should see the other guy."

Felix snorted. "Can't believe they made you a captain."

"I kind of made myself a captain."

Kat laughed at that. Felix shook his head as if it were the most woeful thing in the world.

They stood there for a moment. They had gone in to explore the ruins because Logan had said so. He realized that now he would be on the command bridge telling them what to do instead of sharing in the exploration like he used to. That was a wistful thought. He hoped he would be okay with that change.

"Run into trouble?" Logan asked.

"A little bit," Kat said and shrugged. "There were some of those blue zombie bastards skulking around. Came out of it with everyone in one piece, though."

"I'm glad you're okay," Logan said, his voice rough with emotion. "Both of you."

Kat punched him lightly on the arm. "Takes more than a few blue assholes to keep us down."

Logan winced. Kat's eyes went wide and her mouth formed an apologetic, surprised ring. Logan just waved a hand.

Felix nodded, a rare smile tugging at his lips. "Indeed. Though I must say, I'm looking forward to a hot meal and a soft bed."

"You've earned that much, for sure," Logan agreed. His gaze turned serious. "But the fight's not over yet. That fish bastard is still out there, and it's only a matter of time before it comes for us again. It said it was going to run to Daddy for help. We'll have to see what that means. In any case, this ship changes everything. We aren't going to try to build a community anymore. We are going to fight a war."

Kat smashed a fist into a palm. "That's what I'm all about, baby."

"Let it come," Felix said, her voice hard with determination. "We'll be ready."

Logan nodded, pride swelling in his chest. These were his people, his family. And together, they would face whatever the future held.

As they were about to depart so the expedition force could get its rest, Logan noticed Felix give Kat a look. Logan smirked to himself and called to them, "You guys doing it yet?"

"W-what?" Felix spluttered.

"No!" Kat said, but her blush betrayed her.

"You will," Logan said and grinned. Then he turned back to the screens.

As the team dispersed, off to get some well-deserved rest, Logan found himself watching the various feeds of the Ark's halls, his mind awhirl with plans and possibilities. He knew what he had to do, knew the weapon he needed to build. But the scope of it, the sheer audacity, was almost overwhelming.

Then, Glaan's voice, warm and grandmotherly, broke him from his reverie.

"Logan," she said, "you seem troubled."

Logan sighed, sinking into a nearby chair, his crutches clattering to the floor. "I'm just thinking about what comes next," he admitted. "I'm worried about what that fish bastard said. About getting help from its boss or whatever."

Glaan was silent for a moment, the lights of the command center pulsing softly. When she spoke, her voice was heavy with the weight of centuries.

"The path ahead is not an easy one," she said. "Levemoth is a creature of ancient malice, a being of pure destruction. We fought it for eons. Do not expect an easy battle."

Logan nodded, his jaw tight. "I just feel like we are missing a piece of the puzzle. Sure, we're gathering up people to build a force and organizing them. But it's all so small-scale. I still remember that vision I had of the First Folk fighting the bastard. I feel like this won't be enough." Logan scoffed to himself and added. "But I suppose we will give it our best shot if nothing else. We must fight."

"And fight we shall," Glaan agreed. "But, Logan, you must remember that you do not fight alone. You have your friends, your allies. You have the Groloin and the Faelves and all of the survivors you've gathered. Together, we are stronger than any one of us could ever be alone."

Logan felt a lump form in his throat, a sudden swell of emotion that threatened to overwhelm him. Glaan was right. He had been so focused on his own role, his own responsibility, that he had almost forgotten the incredible network of support he had built.

"Thank you, Glaan," he said, his voice rough. "I needed to hear that."

"Of course, Logan," Glaan said, and he could almost hear the maternal smile in her voice. "Now, I believe you have work to do. A weapon to build and a war to win."

Logan grinned. There was a new, emergent feeling in his stomach, like a flicker of a fire. Logan focused on it and it grew ever so slightly stronger. "Damn right, I do."

With a grunt of effort, he hauled himself to his feet, his crutches forgotten. The pain in his body was still there, a constant ache that thrummed through his bones. But it was background noise now, a minor inconvenience compared to the task at hand.

He made his way down to the cargo bay, his steps slow but determined. As he entered the cavernous space, he saw Freya and Snoff waiting for him, their faces etched with concern.

"Logan," Freya said, hurrying to his side. "What are you doing? You should be resting."

Logan shook his head. "No time for that now," he said. "We've got work to do."

Snoff cleared his throat, his eyes darting to the corner of the room. Logan followed his gaze, his heart skipping a beat as he saw the motionless form of the Herald, still encased in its icy prison.

"What do you want to do with him?" Snoff asked, his voice hesitant.

Logan sighed, a heavy weight settling on his shoulders. The Herald—his father—the man who had been a giant was now reduced to a puppet.

But it was also an opportunity.

"We need to study him," Logan said, his voice firm. "Learn what we can about Levemoth's influence. Its power. If we can find a way to break its hold, to free my father . . ."

He trailed off, the words sticking in his throat. It was a slim hope, a fragile dream. But it was all he had.

Freya's hand found his, her fingers intertwining with his own. "We'll find a way," she said, her voice soft but fierce. "I promise."

Logan squeezed her hand, drawing strength from her touch. He looked up, meeting Snoff's gaze.

"Snoff, I need you to work with Tumor and Glaan. See if you can figure out a way to safely contain the Herald, to study it without risk. We need to know what we're dealing with."

Snoff nodded, his face set with determination. "I'll do my best, Logan."

Logan turned to Freya, his heart in his eyes. "Frey, I need you to keep being the amazing leader you've been."

"Not just a pretty face, huh?" Freya said and smirked.

"I mean it's mostly that," Logan said and shrugged. Freya punched him in the shoulder.

Logan laughed. "No, seriously, you're amazing. Keep the people's spirits up and keep them focused. As the captain, I can't be holding people's hands anymore. You'll need to be the soft squishy mother upon whose bosom everyone can cry. Except Felix. You let me know if that sly prick even glances at your bosom."

Freya sniggered. "He's too busy being all up in Kat's business."

"He sure is," Logan said and chuckled. "You're gonna be alright?"

Freya smiled, soft and tender. "I told you, I'm not leaving your side anymore. So I'll just have to manage if that's what you require of me."

"Yeah, about that . . ."

Freya growled and shot him a look full of thunder. "I'm your goddamn wife, and you *will* listen to me on this."

Logan nodded. They were going to have a fight about this, but right now he was too smitten by her fierce love. They kissed, overcome with passion.

Slowly, reluctantly, he pulled away from Freya's embrace. He hobbled over to the workbench, his hands already itching to begin.

"Tumor," he said, his voice a low murmur. "It's time."

[I am ready, Logan.]

Freya left after another brief kiss and promised to bring down lunch. Logan was already getting into the zone and barely heard. He sat down, he thought, he drew, he prompted Tumor until even the AI was starting to feel fatigue. Logan was feeling it too, but he constantly asked Tumor to zap his brain a little bit to keep him focused. He would not sit idly by and wait for Levemoth to make a move. It was finally time to go on the offensive while the big bastard was still so weak.

As Logan lost himself in the work, his mind spinning with designs and blueprints, he could feel the pieces falling into place. The darkmetal, the runic knowledge of the Groloin, the subtle enchantments of the Faelves, the enhanced capabilities that Tumor had granted his mind and body. It would all connect. Logan would become what he needed to become.

Can't believe I'm thinking about this messiah bullshit. It feels so conceited. But I need to lead. And leadership requires a certain kind of flair.

And what that flair looked like, he was starting to get a clear picture of. An ultimate weapon. An immovable object with unstoppable force.

The armor had been a cute prototype, perfect for his scrappy fighting style, but he needed to think bigger. Dream bigger. He wasn't facing a few scythe-fiends anymore. He was going to fight the motherfucking Levemoth.

In his mind's eye, he could see it—towering over the battlefield, the armored bulk casting a huge shadow over his enemies. He could feel the thrum of its engines, augmented with their newly acquired Numa technology. Runes would crisscross the bulk, as he stole all the useful concepts of the Groloin's golems, their NECs, which could clearly hurt the Big Fish bastard.

Logan would create a magnum opus, a masterpiece. What people better for making an *ultimate weapon* than humans, the warlike sons of bitches that they were. And Logan would be at the forefront of it, a vanguard of military destruction. Well, he called it necessary violence. But that wouldn't quite do in this case. For the weapon to do what Logan wanted, it would require an obscene, completely unnecessary amount of violence. Only that would be sufficient.

Boy, it's going to be expensive . . .

And as he worked, the hours bleeding into days, Logan knew that this was just the beginning. Levemoth would not go quietly into the night. It would summon its master—call upon who knew what bullshit.

But Logan would be ready. They all would be.

For in the end, it was not about the weapons or the machines. It was about the people wielding them. The brave souls who stood against the darkness. Who fought for a future worth living.

Together, they would face the coming storm. Stand against destruction and evil. Because that was what Levemoth was. Pure evil.

Together they would fight evil.

And together, they would win.

About the Author

Wilbur Woods is an entertainer, coffee drinker, and story eater, as well as the author of the Cosmic Games series, originally released on Royal Road. He has loved stories since he was a kid, and when he asked himself what he really wanted to do, the answer was simple: write.